FINDING DAVEY

FINDING DAVEY

JONATHAN GASH

This edition first published in Great Britain in 2006 by
Allison & Busby Limited
13 Charlotte Mews
London W1T 4EJ
www.allisonandbusby.com

Copyright © 2005 by JONATHAN GASH

The moral right of the author has been asserted.

A catalogue record for this book is available from
the British Library.

10 9 8 7 6 5 4 3 2 1

ISBN 0 7490 8130 9
978-0-7490-8130-0

Printed and bound in Great Britain by
Bookmarque Ltd, Croydon, Surrey

JONATHAN GASH is the author of a number of crime novels. A qualified doctor specialising in tropical medicine, he is married with three daughters and four grandchildren. He lists his hobbies as antique collecting and his family.

Novels by Jonathan Gash:

Lovejoy novels:
The Judas Pair
Gold From Gemini
The Grail Tree
Spend Game
The Vatican Rip
Firefly Gadroon
The Sleepers of Erin
The Gondola Scam
Pearlhanger
The Tartan Ringers
Moonspender
Jade Woman
The Very Last Gambado
The Great California Game
The Lies of Fair Ladies
Paid and Loving Eyes
The Sin Within Her Smile
The Grace in Older Women
The Possessions of A Lady
The Rich and The Profane
A Rag, A Bone and A Hank of Hair
Every Last Cent
The Ten Word Game

Doctor Clare Burtonall novels:
Different Women Dancing
Prey Dancing
Die Dancing
Bone Dancing
Blood Dancing

Dedication

To Matthew John Lewis

Thanks

To Susan, for graft and more

Chapter One

The little boy's mind floated.

People were talking in faraway voices. Calm, warm. The voices droned.

* * *

"The boy's medication will require balance." A man.

"Is it safe, Doctor?" A woman.

"I've never had a failure."

"He's beautiful. How old is he?"

"Six, maybe and a half." The voice huffled. "The police will confirm it."

"*Police?*"

"Broadcasts," the doctor's voice reassured. "My clinic staff monitor local and national. They'll come on air soon. Photographs, details how we abducted him. I'll change the boy's identity into something he never was."

"You're sure?"

"Trust me. I'm the expert."

"How long?"

"Before you can take him home? Months, after careful

clinical judgement, but he'll be your child one hundred per cent."

"Will he remember anything from...before?"

"Not a thing. I guarantee. Sure, you can touch his hand."

A touch.

A woman's voice. "Hello, honey. I'm Mom."

Mom, not Mummy.

"And Pop's here, with Doctor."

"What shall I say?" A man.

"Tell him his name. He's Clint, from now on."

"Hello, Clint." The voice broke, recovered. "Can the process be shortened?"

"Medicine can't be hurried, Pop."

"I don't want him remembering things and taking off."

"He'll only have the memories I put in."

"You can really do that?"

"My clinic aims to please, Mom."

"Mom!" the woman sobbed. "I never thought! My very own child!"

The little boy slept. The voices faded.

A quiet whispering began to speak a name over and over: Clint, Clint, Clint.

For just one moment, in the very far distance, vague and blurred, was a figure. It smiled. Davey wanted to smile back because the old man belonged to him. He wore his multi-coloured paint-stained apron and held a piece of carved wood. Davey knew he was going to say *Hello what's all this* but sleep came as that whispering said Clint, Clint.

The smiling old man finally dwindled and soon was completely gone.

Chapter Two

It was the fifteenth day of horror.

Bray Charleston heard the two office girls talking.

He worked on, planing the wood. Loggo, the youngest lad in the workshop, watched in silence. Soon he would explode. Bray knew these youngsters wanted everything done yesterday, with electric bandsaws and computerised auto-routers shredding your eardrums.

"How can he keep coming in to work? I ask you!"

That was the nasal grumbling of Karen. God knows what she was like under her cosmetics. Fingernails constantly filed, mirror at the ready, never answering the phone if she could help it. Bray could hear because the BBC's music and feeble wisecracks had temporarily failed.

"Maybe work keeps his mind off his grandson." The other typist, Tracy, was much the quieter, given to coming in with bloated after-party eyes. "It's terrible."

Tracy said terr-i-buwww, true South London failing terminals.

What could they know? Bray alone felt the horror. What else could he do but come to the work he loved? News about a missing child could only be bad.

Loggo's patience finally broke. "Mr Charleston, can I do that?"

Bray straightened, aching, but he was fifty-three, it was to be expected.

"No, ta. I'm fine."

"I'd have it finished in a sec with the rotary."

Bray used to call Loggo "son", but now caught himself. The horror had begun at twenty minutes to three, two Tuesday mornings since. It was death for Bray, learning that his little grandson Davey had been stolen. In America, land of the free. From now on, all eternity would be different.

"It'd save your hands." Loggo's kindness was born of exasperation at the senior craftsman's slowness.

The girls heard the apprentice's voice, realised that they too were audible, and moved away from the window.

"Electrics don't please the wood," Bray told Loggo.

The piece was a dark walnut brown, with an oddish matt shine.

"Eh? It's only ordinary walnut, innit?"

"This isn't walnut." Bray paused to focus. Pages from old glossaries flickered through his tired mind. No, not tired, for he had no right to tiredness, would never now sleep in case news came, in case anything. "Kokko's only *called* East Indies walnut. See the untouched surface?"

Loggo squinted, cheek to the workbench. "It's no different, Mr Charleston."

"You'll see better when I've done."

Bray felt knots inside his chest. He should be speaking like this to Davey, in that last precious half-hour before daughter-in-law Shirley whisked the little lad up to bath and bed. He cleared his throat.

"Don't be misled because kokko's durable and heavy.

It's brittle as chocolate. That's why it needs such careful seasoning. Modern kiln-drying takes the heart out of wood."

"Seasoning takes too long, Mr Charleston."

"It preserves the life within." Bray went quickly on, sensing a wrong choice of words. Some lives were not preserved. "Gilson Mather's lucky to have got hold of a properly seasoned piece like this. See how the grain crisscrosses like tangled wool?"

"Yes." The lad was itching to get some electrical planers whirring, mincing the precious rare wood to shreds.

Loggo wasn't a real apprentice, of course. No such thing these days. Once, an apprentice worked seven years and learned the soul in the wood. Now? Now they sat at some computer for twelve weeks and called themselves expert. At joinery, at anything, at aviation for God's sake.

"Treating the surface properly can up the price of a kokko wood cabinet tenfold. The texture is woolly, see? An electric plane would pick up, and you'd lose half the wood. Nigerian kokko is its cousin, *Albizzia ferruginea*, a shade heavier so it picks up worse." Picking up was the master cabinet maker's dread, showing damaging plicks on a finished surface.

"Can't I give it a go?"

"No. I'm almost there."

On any normal day, Bray would have added that wood required respect. Not now, not since six-year-old Davey had been stolen in America. Respect, even that ominously fragile term "care", seemed ghastly anachronisms. He worked on. Loggo could ask and learn more if he wanted. Unfair to feel resentment against the sixteen-year-old whose life remained his own while a little fair-haired boy was…

Bray tapped his hand-plane's hull to keep the blade settled.

"Mr Charleston?"

Bray looked up. Loggo had gone. Astonishingly the workshop floor was vacated. How long had he worked on? The firm's owner Mr Winsarls was standing there. It wasn't news, Bray knew instantly, merely something to do with time, that newly superfluous commodity.

"Yes, Mr Winsarls?"

"It's gone five. Just thought I'd say."

"Thank you, Mr Winsarls."

Loggo started sweeping the joinery workshop even before Bray had hung his apron and put away his tools. In Bray's day an apprentice had to clean every common tool in the place, except for the craftsmen's specials. Bray could tell some tales, all true, about cabinet makers' implements, if anybody nowadays wanted to listen. And, new to him, if ever he himself wished to bother with anything any more. Hope was a blessing, a reverence for life intimately concerned with the future. It had gone with little Davey, at that holiday centre, in Florida.

"Goodnight, sir," he called up to Mr Winsarls as usual, his tools carefully racked, his bench ready for the morrow. He hung his leather brat on its hook, smoothed the heavy canvas apron over it and washed his face and hands. He avoided the mirror, in case he saw horror staring back.

Chapter Three

The famous theme park's name once stood for laughter, children's holiday fun. Not now. Now, it was horror grimmer than any TV news. For it was from that theme park that Davey had been stolen away, an act of unspeakable evil.

The American police had appointed Liaison Officer Jim Stazio, who had spelled out the pointlessness of hope.

Since that night call from Florida, when his son Geoff had told him, voice shaking, that Davey had vanished among the crowds, horror settled into Bray's brain. The world was now a place that allowed little grandsons to be stolen by forces so malign that the mind had to stop thinking.

And start planning.

Police were powerless (but weren't police Over There armed and omnipotent?). Officer Stazio phoned, and promised the fullest action. Theme Park Security also promised this "fullest action". Some smooth Consulate woman with a career voice promised "the fullest inquiry", a carping shift of terminology there. Diplomacy was death to hope.

That first night, Bray had decided what he must do.

He sat alone in his house until morning, hearing the avenue begin its routine noises – milkman, post girl, school bus, mothers in car pool chitchats. Bray confronted the gathering fright, fright that Davey would be...unable to come home any more. Bray couldn't face that terrible consequence.

Was there a hope?

He rummaged around his exhausted mind. He was fifty-three, a joiner, restorer of antiques, maker of classical furniture. He knew nothing of crime, had never knowingly met a criminal.

Hours later, conscious on that first morning that people had shoved things through the letterbox, knocked and gone away, he bathed and dressed, letting the mind cope with routine. His spirit though? Might spirit succeed where cleverness failed?

Later, on that first evening, he had phoned Gilson Mather and gave excuses. Bray thought and believed Davey still lived, would live for ever as long as they didn't bring the very worst news of all.

Day Two of the horror, he called his boss Mr Winsarls. Newspapers were full of it. The phone rang incessantly but Bray never answered. He went to a neighbour's house and asked Shirley's friend Christine and her husband Hal to deflect the phone calls and look after Buster, Davey's golden retriever. They were pale and silent. It had been a terrible visit. Hal's solution was that Bray's son Geoff would ring four dialling tones then wait five precise minutes before calling again. That would be the signal for Bray to pick up the receiver, sure it would be Geoff and not some ghoulish newshound. Carloads of paparazzi and cameramen lurked in the avenue, rang neighbours' doorbells wanting to use their toilets, any pretext to get in, begging teas and coffees, asking housewives to heat up fast foods for them. Hal got the police to remove photographers who climbed Bray's fence.

Christine started taking Buster over Avery Fields. She fed the dog, released Buster into Geoff's garden. Bray supposed he had still made Buster his pints of milky tea, but couldn't remember when.

Horror Day Three, the newspaper folk left the avenue never to return. Some pop star had committed a lewd act in Beverley Hills, USA. The singer's parents lived near Romford, were newsworthy, and exploited easier. Bray blanked the TV.

Three more days he waited, weighing circumstances, hearing Geoff out when he rang each night from America. Then he moved. Sluggish, feeling blindly about for purpose, he tried a dusk walk out with Buster as far as the Victorian herbarium in Avery Hill Fields beyond the rugby ground. No lurking photographers. Buster was reluctant to let Bray out of his sight, sensing woe. The golden retriever lay across the doormat in Bray's shed occasionally rousing to stare at Bray at the workbench.

Bray spent hours in his shed, doing no carving. He did not even paint the figurines he and Davey had already finished. He went over every memory of Davey's inexpert hands as the shapes on the ledges and sills had evolved and become real. Real to Bray and Davey, of course. To no one else.

To *nobody* else.

The important word seemed to be *else*. It became strangely dense. Was this how words seemed to a child?

Bray remembered with sudden clarity how Davey had laughed, quite helplessly, on first hearing the word "umbrella". Tragic that adults lost that childhood imagery. Do we lose them altogether, Bray wondered, or did they possibly still live in some vestigial mental Limbo of the mind?

Horror Day Seven, Bray arrived in Gilson Mather's workshop, with loudmouthed Karen noising off about how unfeeling old Charleston must be to come to work. Quiet Tracy tried to shut her up. Mr Winsarls and the others all went silent whenever Bray cleared his throat and spoke his gentle stuttery guidance to the younger joiners.

Bray's soul took on a new fluidity. As a cunning beast wakens, Bray made his soul start to think about the malice of the evil child thieves. They thought they'd got away with it, scotage free, taking little Davey.

On Day Eight, Bray realised they had miscalculated. They'd forgotten one person, and one other vital factor. That one person was Bray Charleston, master joiner, daydreamer, carver of wooden hobby figures. He was Davey's grampa.

And the other vital factor? Okay, Bray thought, as he stood alone in the timber yard judging a consignment of Ugandan nsambya wood. Okay, the factor didn't exist in any practical sense. It was ephemeral. Mythical, in fact.

Yet might it persist when police efforts dwindled to zero, when consuls moved on in career climbs? And even when officialdom had long since shelved the troublesome file about a little stolen boy?

The vital factor was memory.

Fairy tales had endured for centuries, hadn't they? Word for word. Didn't children's schoolyard chants live on, even as civilisations were blown away?

On the way home that same day Bray bought five notebooks, held them on his lap for the entire journey.

Heart brimming, he stared out at the darkening fields and thought, others can give in, forget or despair.

Not me.

He called at the Lumleys', collected Buster, and walked him over Avery Fields as far as the brook. Christine had fed the dog, but Bray gave him a biscuit and a pint of milky tea as usual before settling him down in his flock pit on the back porch.

Midnight in his garden he stood gazing up at the night sky, and said with a burning conviction, *I'm coming to find you, Davey. Soon, you'll look up and say, I knew you'd come, Grampa.*

Slowly he went back inside, took up the first notebook, and labelled it KV.

Chapter Four

"What's with the stolen kid?"

As usual, Tietze was loafing, feet on anybody's desk except his own. Officer Jim Stazio heaved his bulk to what soon would no longer be his chair.

Police Precinct Central O-One hummed, elevator doors crashing, occasional shouts making nobody turn, phones shrilling, officers wanting the world to leave them the fuck alone.

"You made two calls already."

"It's my job." Jim Stazio grimaced apology, then admitted, "I had to talk, tell the guy I'm *forcibly* retired. I chickened."

"Couldn't, hmmm?"

"That's right, Sam." Daily Diner did a great burger but it was hell of a bloater. Sam Tietze could eat like a hog, stayed thin as a pole. "I'm going to thin down, forty pounds."

"Staying in town after, Jim?" Sam Tietze asked, inquisitive because it would happen to him in another five years. "Stay local. Retirees don't do bad."

Somebody at the far end threw the phone and slammed

out the door. Two officers by the water cooler shrugged and followed.

"Maybe." Jim looked at his handset. "A funny guy. Grampa, back home."

"Broke down, right? Yelled we were useless fuckers, all that shit?"

"No." Jim thought over the words. "Know what he said? Calm as you like, said, *Thank you, Mr Stazio. May I ask what the chances are, if I came over?* He meant finding the boy himself. I told him zilch."

"How'd he take it?"

Jim de-capped a bottle of water, starting his slimming plan. "Like asking, *Where do I start looking?*"

"Loony tunes, Jim," Sam said. "They all say that. Learn the hard way. Needle in a haystack? I wish!"

"The guy just said thanks. But I got this feeling."

"It's retirement blues, Jim," Sam Tietze told him. "Don't drink water. Fish fuck in it."

"W.C. Fields said that."

Jim Stazio pulled out the file on abducted minors and flipped it, C for Charleston. He knew the data by heart, but read it all the same.

The third week, Geoff and Shirley came home. Bray used up seven priceless days and nights in braving routine. It was hard, but had to be done.

Bray travelled to and from work mechanically. This was every commuter's art, to journey without registering the details. Sometimes on the train he read or dozed. He recognised people, never spoke. A woman used to say "Good morning". Now Bray avoided catching her eye, and sat farther down the compartment. He was sure she'd identified him from a grainy local newspaper shot. Questions would be unwelcome. She seemed to understand, and was already checking over a typescript when he boarded.

Listening to the desultory conversations all around was the entertainment he liked – used to like, before the horror. Shirley, his son Geoffrey's wife, always argued that Bray ought to be more gregarious. She was a great one for trying to make Bray "join *in*!" Competitions, flower shows, garden parties, Shirley raised teams to win mantelpiece trophies. Invariably Bray declined. Too busy in his workshed, adapting and reinventing ancient woodworking tools, making carvings while Davey invented stories. Now, Shirley was silent, Geoffrey frantic, both tortured.

At Liverpool Street Station, going home of an evening, Bray found a seat in the third compartment. Not too crowded tonight. Formerly he would have hurried, making sure he caught the express that tore out of the capital into the countryside, and so win Davey for a little extra time. No longer.

The train filled. A whistle blew. It slowly drew out heading east.

Not seeing the cluttered streets of London's East End, Bray thought of tenses. The present tense had become the past, the continuous into past pluperfect. Shirley *had been* a great one for competitions. She *used* to get up teams. Bray *had* assumed that tomorrow would come with somebody small and laughing, bouncing on the bed to awaken him.

Davey had shown astonishing traits.

Davey usually sat in the shed and watched Grampa. They played games, drew maps, carved creatures. Davey knew the names of most tools, extraordinarily bright for six. They argued! Bray almost caught himself smiling, angrily quelled the response and stared out into rain because, correction, they *had* argued; Davey *used* to know the names of woodcarving tools. Now?

The train rocked through Romford.

Commuters read newspapers, talked of tax, work, motor cars, engaged in life's absurd deception. They trusted chronology with certainty about the coming hours, went from hour to day, season to year, exactly as laughing children crossed stepping stones daring each other to get their shoes wet, yet knowing they would safely reach home. The presumption of permanence was the human sleight-of-mind.

He had been the same, once. The woman in the seat opposite, papers on her lap, met Bray's eyes and looked away.

Bray remembered waking when the phone rang.

Geoff spoke words that failed to penetrate: lost, police, investigation. Other words came: crowds, search. Security officer this, agent that. And "sighting", like for birds.

Most terrible of all, "The search is being extended further afield." Then, terribly, "It's no good you coming, Dad. People are doing everything they can."

His heart bled for his son, his daughter-in-law. Twenty minutes to three a.m.

Bray came to, surprised to be on the train still. Or was it a different day, and he'd been home, and it had become tomorrow?

The train slowed. Normally he would nod off and be woken by the changing fiddle-de-dee, fiddle-de-daa, of the wheels on the station approach. Had he slept? He wanted proof of distress, making sure his anguish would never leave. He had no right to doze. Anything less than constant pain would be treachery to Davey.

Bray rose and stood swaying as the train drew in. He thought, with a curious satisfaction, *I'm on course.* He'd endured sixty miles and never once allowed Davey's two game words in, that only Davey and Grampa Bray knew.

"Night," somebody said as he clambered over briefcases.

"Night," Bray replied mechanically. It was the manuscript woman.

He alighted and shut the door on the fug. Conversation was forbidden him. It might be allowed back into existence tomorrow, when it conceivably might have a function. Until then, silence was his first ally. You didn't trick an ally. Tomorrow he might silently think Davey's two words, and make a start.

How, he did not know.

The village bus was four minutes late, not bad at this hour. When it came, he sat alone. He didn't see the dark fields go past, the chain of headlights linking the A12. Most passengers alighted at the village shop.

Among them, a stout woman betrayed him, as that stupid Karen had, saying to her companion as the bus doors hissed shut, "Wasn't that David's grandad, y'know, who —?"

Rage could make killers of us all. Bray struggled to control the fury he felt. Was? *Is,* you stupid cow, *is* Davey's grandad. *Present* tense, not past, you idiot bitch.

He'd driven his emotions back beyond consciousness by the Kings Head pub pond. He became an automaton. The same instinct had driven him back to work and endure the faltering expressions of commiseration everybody came out with. And ignore inane Karen's attempt to press him for details until Mr Winsarls drew her away while she went, "What? What?" Stupidity was always indignant.

He walked down the familiar lane trying to quieten his footfalls to protect more silence.

Lights were on in Geoff's and Shirley's adjoining dwelling, but his own semi-detached house was dark. Tea would be tinned vegetable soup and unbuttered bread. Odd, but Bray found he'd abruptly gone off cheese. Like meat, ham, and stews.

Television was a lesion in time. It showed some comedian drawing the Lottery, then a cops-and-robbers. He dowsed the sound and put an Albinoni piece on. Hard to look at the silent flickering screen and synchronise thoughts. He gave three knocks on the wall to show he was home, and heard a couple of thumps in reply from Geoffrey. He set about his evening rites, Buster before anything. He crossed the road to Christine Lumley's house and knocked. She was immediately there, smiling, Buster leaping for joy. Bray wondered if she watched behind the curtains.

"Hello, Bray!" She spoke with determined brightness, handing him the lead. "He's been as good as gold, haven't you, Buzzie?" And swiftly corrected herself, for Buzzie was Davey's name. "Haven't you, Buster?"

He stood there. "Thank you, Christine."

"I've left his tin and packet in your back porch, Bray." She added awkwardly, as if he'd made a lengthy apology, "No, really. He's no trouble."

He returned, unlocked the door and released Buster. "Tea. Then a walk, eh?"

His kitchen door opened into the garden. His workshed

stood there by the hedge and the tall rear fence. Buster ran expectantly about sniffing the grass, and scratched at the shed door. One paw raised, he stared at Geoffrey's house before doing a laconic patrol about the garden, stopping to listen at intervals. Bray made his tea and got Buster's dish ready. The ritual would have to be preserved until he learned otherwise.

The outside light on, he got the kettle on the go. Buster gave him a new riotous greeting outside.

"Wotcher, pal. Another hello, is it?"

Bray endured the daft leaps, grumbling he'd be covered in hairs. He threw a stick for the dog to chase before bringing Buster's bowl, a mess from a tin and some dry biscuity stuff. He never got the hang of Buster's food. The tinned stuff was repellent. Shirley laughed at Bray's fastidiousness; *used* to laugh.

This was a new ritual. Buster was Davey's dog. The two adjoining gardens were not separated, so Davey and Buster had the run of both.

Bray's sure instinct was not to mention Davey when with the dog. He walked Buster to Avery Fields, down by the river path then back past the herbarium, his plastic bag and scoop at the ready. Usually he'd speak, about work, wood, of the countryside years before. Now, he spoke to Buster but filled up, the retriever staring into Bray's face to see what was wrong. Closing his own mind, Bray kidded Buster into normality.

Almost.

For Buster would glance doubtfully from the house to Bray's shed, from there to Bray. Or, he'd listen on his walk, halt, stare again, then listlessly move on.

"Time for my grub, Buzz lad," Bray told him, and went inside.

Buster knew not to follow. Shirley's orders, dog in the kennel. Okay, it was insulated, dry, and had a thermal blanket. Bray admitted Buster to his own downstairs. Who now would care?

In another pretence, Bray checked on the answer phone. No blinking red light, no news. The phone's red light had glowed since Davey was stolen. Two weeks ago last Tuesday, at twenty minutes to three in the morning.

Which made it what time in the United States of America, land of the free?

Chapter Five

He sat at an imposing mahogany desk on which stood a sign, SILENCE! in nacre on ebony. He was Doctor, the expert, proprietor of *Rehabilitation Par Excellence, Inc.*

"You are Pop," he told his client. "Your wife is Mom, and only Mom."

Doctor had an eagle stare, and now used it on the businessman.

"Got it."

"I am Doctor. No abbreviations. The situation we have right here is that women generate convictions, and we men acquire purpose. It runs civilisation."

Pop had often thought this and reached the same conclusion. He watched the other's compelling gestures.

Doctor semaphored, to demonstrate his profundity. His clients were compliant audiences. They had to be. Statistically, women owned America's wealth. A man was simpler, honed and arrow-like. Pretty simile, no?

To Pop it was more bitter than pleasant.

Women had whole lexicons expressing every grade of fault, dubiety and expectation for men. Because of their semantic cosmology the male was redundant except as a meal ticket. The laws of good old U S of A made men mere bystanders forced to watch females compete. The women in a Reproductivity Superbowl, the spectators silent men.

And Law made man blameworthy, when a wife somehow failed in that sorority of combat, *failed* to match her own self-generated image of mother, where fecundity was the sole criterion of triumph.

Lucky, Pop thought with bitterness, that he had the money to buy the boy. His wealth would convert his wife from a mere Hey-You to Mom. And himself Pop from a Him. Why not ask straight out, now he'd come this far?

"The boy, Doctor," Pop said. "Get to the boy."

Pop saw Doctor's face cloud with annoyance, but shit, he was paying big dollar. The USA stood for private enterprise in everything, children included.

Pay, you got the goods. Doctor's crap philosophy he could do without. Doctor's enterprise had stolen the boy and brought him to the point of delivery. Cut the corny existentialist gunge, it came down to goods bought and received.

"The boy is physically fine. No need to worry."

Doctor steepled his fingers. Pop was not exactly overcome with awe. Chrissakes, he'd shovelled gelt into this clinic like it grew on those fucking Florida palms waving in the costly breeze out there.

"Mentally," Doctor intoned, "it'll take time before Clint is re-adjusted."

Pop put the biggie, the question Mom was pestering him with night and day.

"When do we get him?"

Doctor's only problem was disguising his contempt.

Being sterile – Doctor liked the Bible's "barren" better

– they had to buy. So they came to him cap in hand, wallets bulging.

He smiled reassuringly. "You have him now, Pop. You're already a complete family. Your own apartment here. You can attend the boy's psychiatric conversion at every stage."

"Those I paid for," Pop said bluntly, unmoved by Doctor's litany. "Give me a time frame."

"A few weeks. Then the domiciliary phase."

"Taking how long?"

"Five months to Clint's final phase. We call it re-entry. Clint will be your son. His mind will know no other parents, remember no other life. He'll attend a school of your choosing. That's the only true test."

Pop went for his nagging doubt. "Except for memory."

"Something troubling you, Pop? Spit it out."

"How much of his previous life will Clint really remember?"

Sadly Doctor shook his head at such lack of faith. "Clint will remember only what I let him remember. His language, of course. But American English, not English English. His past I shall delete. The process has already begun. You, Pop and Mom, will create the boy as surely as if Mom delivered him in the obstetric unit."

Pop had a gesture of his own, the aggressive pointing finger.

"Will the boy be normal?"

Doctor felt intimidated for only an instant, quickly recovering behind his shield of expertise.

"One hundred per cent."

Doctor sounded a truly dedicated professional in the service of suffering humanity, far above sordid greed as he said with dignity, "Certainly."

This client had had assurances from other experts, and

would not let go.

"Do you ever fail?"

Seriouser and seriouser! Doctor felt nothing but contempt for these rich inadequates. They made him laugh – in the privacy of his own secluded apartment, of course.

Having committed the ultimate federal crime – buying a stolen child – they wanted guarantees plastered on the label. How on earth did these people become millionaires?

"Never. Look, Pop, 350,000 children are abducted annually from legitimate marriages! My clinic is a drop in that ocean. I provide wholesome children, ready to take up a decent moral life with wealthy families. It's that simple."

"I'd have thought a girl would have been easier."

Doctor smiled at the lamebrain. "Mom asked for a boy. You paid for a boy. I get you a boy!" Sensing trouble, he went for generalities. "Girls are more facile and can be programmed into a new life right up to the age of ten. Boys are more trouble. We can tune them into a new existence before eight, maximum. A few prove recalcitrant, sure, need extra handling. But I never fail."

"There are grades?"

With dispassion Doctor appraised Pop.

The client was a man who, like himself, dealt in absolutes. The one benefit of Doctor's business was its immunity from law. (Slight correction: from litigation.) Nobody could sue him or his clinic. Wariness however always paid when some rich fatgutted oaf like this one quibbled.

Doctor composed his features into humility. Galling, to play the serf to such a man, but financial transactions must be smooth.

"Yes, Pop," he said comfortably, registering real pleasure at the other's sudden alarm. "Everything isn't always plain sailing. Every child is different."

Doctor knew he had got round the awkwardness, for now. Marvellous what fear did to these rich contemptibles.

"Case complexity is my problem, Pop, not yours. I always win in the end. And you are the beneficiary of a complete, ready-made son!"

"Thank you."

Humility now? Doctor felt his lip curl in disdain.

"The boy is hundred per cent yours for ever."

He injected a twinkle into his eyes. Nurses had loved it, during his hell year as intern.

"Ours!" Pop now spoke with wonder. "Our son!"

Doctor was disgusted to see tears fill the client's eyes. He felt his power. This was how God felt on a good day.

With an endless supply of children, he was omnipotent. He'd proved his invincibility scores of times. Nothing could stop him.

"Clint," he intoned, smiley, "is a routine case."

Chapter Six

With flashlight and walking-stick, Bray walked Buster to the fields. On summer evenings, Davey liked to people the trees with imaginary cloaked figures. Now alone in the autumn gloaming, Bray trudged the course, mentally speaking the names of Davey's imaginary footpads. He caught himself saying them aloud and thought, watch it, people will think you're barmy. He returned, washed up, and went to his shed.

The evenings were drawing in, the day's air moist after drizzle. People here in the coastal villages believed bad weather circled round Wormingwood, but Bray had his doubts about that, as had Emma.

Emma had left when Geoff was eighteen, lecturing Bray on his shortcomings, his ineffable dullness, all one morning. He "bought her out", the solicitor's phrase. Thank God she quickly married again, some building contractor. She had attended Geoffrey's wedding, making the gathering surreal in an orange dress that drained all colour from the church flowers. Emma wasn't bad. Bray's sad conviction was that many wives secretly despised husbands, thinking, What loon contracts to provide for a woman lifelong, for possibly nil return? That farewell morning made him believe that scorn was inevitably part of Emma's marital contract.

He sat in the shed, not switching the light on, not even lighting the candle Davey loved. Buster sprawled on the doormat, Geoffrey following to perch on the workbench.

"Dad?"

"'Lo, son."

Bray took Geoffrey in with a glance. Even that felt fraudulent. Every Friday, Bray had made a thing of having his weekly egg, with chips, doing a daft over-the-top performance for Davey's entertainment, rolling his eyes at every mouthful.

Tonight, Bray could tell that Geoffrey's meeting at his Fair Isle Investment Banking Trust Accounts Division had been grim. One thing on top of another.

"Still nothing, Dad."

His son was showing signs of utter defeat. Bray knew only that he himself had to be on constant guard. Unceasing vigilance. Signs of returning normality had to be watched. A single spark of normality might make the image of little Davey fade, very like sunlight faded inky scrawls on a windowsill. This was how time, that thief, stole grief. It was how time healed, as the proverb said. Well, Bray wouldn't let time get away with it, the bastard.

Tomorrow, he would go for it, risks and all.

"I saw the policewoman, the coordinator in Sidhall." Geoffrey gave Bray a second or two. "She's talked with the people in Orlando. They've got three special units…"

And so on.

Bray's stool stood among piles of shavings. He hadn't swept them up, from when he'd worked of an evening before Geoffrey and Shirley took Davey on their first

American holiday. Sweeping up, challenging Grampa to do better when Bray made jokey grumbles, was Davey's job. Would the shavings ever be swept?

At one point in his sombre monologue Geoffrey switched the shed light on in sudden exasperation. Bray knew he was being a pest, a problem his heartbroken son could do without, but pain was faith. A grampa had to keep it.

He would never let it be diluted. Pain was a stimulus, as fleas on a hedgehog stirred it from its winter hibernation.

Bray felt close to madness, sitting under the shed's one bulb quite as if he were a suspect being interrogated while his sorrowing son pedantically went over the useless prattle of some baffled policewoman.

"What, Dad?" Geoffrey asked.

He must have spoken aloud. Bray saw his son's expression change to alarm, thinking his father might be losing his mind.

Bray tried to find something quickly, and failed.

"Look. Shirley says you should come in tonight. There's no heater here."

"Right, son."

"You spend too long in your shed." Geoffrey hesitated, trying to gather frayed ends of normal life. "Want a cup of tea?"

"No, ta, son. I'll step in presently."

It must be doubly hard for Geoffrey, with the horror, with Shirley to worry about, his own job. And now his father muttering in a dark shed. Bray guessed Shirley was laying down some return-to-sanity rules.

Instinct did it, made women the more practical, far less likely to go doolally. They were emotionally stronger, able to face loss with resolution. Bray sat listening to his brave son, nodding, ignoring every syllable.

"We mustn't let each other become withdrawn, Dad. We have to keep our hopes up. The liaison officer has a number of additional leads…"

Tomorrow, though.

"Tomorrow what, Dad?" Geoff said.

"You see the liaison lady tomorrow?" Bray invented quickly. He must have spoken his thoughts.

"I went today."

Geoffrey nodded, sagacity the watchword. Just hold on, the sum would work itself out with X equalling the correct integer and all. Fond expectancy was Geoffrey all over. Even as a little boy playing football at school, three-nil down and minutes to go, Geoff's features would light up at the chance of a goal when everybody else was despondent and exchanging oh-well-next-time glances.

Emma had transmitted that particular gene of hopeful expectation to Geoff. It had done him proud, got him a grand career in the Fair Isle Banking tower block at Moorgate.

"Is work all right, Dad?"

"Work?" Bray's attention was caught, fear plucking. "Gilson Mather?"

They usually weren't so frank, him and Geoff. Talking like a soap opera, since it happened. "You went in today. Was it okay?"

"Course. I just work, son."

Had Mr Winsarls phoned Geoffrey secretly? Bray could imagine Mr Winsarls saying *Your father's increasing withdrawal…* The owner would be full of correctives: *No, hasn't said a thing about, sorry, y'know… Mr Charleston's never really been an outgoing sort of chap…talks to the drivers now and again but that's it.*

Soap operas used so many banal expressions: *We've got to talk.* And *What's going on?* quite as if speech held some remedy. Babble inanities, and everything would be solved. Life wasn't like that. Life was more like wood, in a way, the wood he and little Davey loved. And carved, preserving its life in some new and vital form.

"Shirley's counsellor will give you an appointment if you like, Dad."

Poor Geoffrey, trying to do the right thing. Bray almost felt tears. He scuffed his shoes in the shavings, stop that right now. He had things to do.

"No, ta, son. Maybe I'll go up town tomorrow." And heard himself say, "I wish I was some help. Tell me if there's anything."

Geoffrey paused. "Dad. You're not working on your wall, are you?"

"My wall?" Bray was startled. He'd reflexively sat himself down facing the shed's end wall, the closed off wall, the shuttered wall where Davey's game was hidden, words and all.

"I might, in time."

A moment's awkwardness, then Geoffrey went back across the grass to his house. Buster did not follow. Yellow glim cut a wedge into the dusk, then dowsed as the kitchen door closed. Bray looked at the workbench. Much smaller of course than his own splendidly worn bench at Gilson Mather.

Nearby was Davey's low stool, more elaborately wrought than his own three-legger. On the wall, low down to be within Davey's reach, hung a hinged double shutter that concealed his and Davey's secret world beyond.

Tomorrow needed planning. He'd never done anything like this before. Who, dear God, ever had?

Only after tomorrow would he turn the screw peg – its sides precisely filed, sanded and finished to avoid cutting the skin of Davey's hand – and open the three-ply wood panel.

Madness to simply look now, though he knew everything concealed there. Self-indulgence was the most destructive element in grief. Ever since the news came, Bray had sat here of an evening looking at the closed panel on the narrow shed wall.

He didn't know how long he'd stayed there immobile under the shed's single naked light. When he came to, his clock – wind-up, radii on an Art Deco face – showed going on for nine. Only eleven hours and thirty minutes to his interview. After that, he'd know. Maybe.

"Come on, Buzz lad."

Buster yawned extravagantly. Bray switched the shed light off and locked up.

The Containment and Rehabilitation Facility was like any other prison. They all stank of that thick male odour and boiled broccoli.

"I really want to waste my time in this heat?" Sam groused morosely when Jim Stazio said he wanted to go down to Allovan Pen and see the kid broker. "You wouldn't be going less'n you're retired."

"Not *retired* yet, you bastard. Retir*ing*."

"The city's finest might be doing you big favours."

"Meaning what?"

"Leave soon, multo pension rights. Coupla years, it'll pay less."

"I might see Menzoy."

"Menzoy knew nothing last time."

"Kid broker who worked the whole state? It's worth a try."

Menzoy was a child abductor. His trial had been a four-year saga in which appeals, technical duck-outs and evidence battles all but sprung the kid broker. He'd eventually been pinned on a technicality beyond Stazio's comprehension. Menzoy had completed almost two years.

Jim left, behind again with his paperwork. Clear desks meant promotion, which was why he'd stayed at grunt level, always thirty phone calls late from yesterday and files stacked on a chair.

Clothes sticking in the heat – AC fails when you need it – he drove north-east to the prison at Allovan. One hour, he flopped down opposite Menzoy the kid broker.

"The grille's reinforced, Aldo. What you been doing?"

"New glass and mesh, Officer Stazio."

Menzoy was thin, edgy, and kept one fingernail for flicking like he was trying to shake off something stuck to his thumb. His other nails were bitten down to the quick. He had a black eye, a high neck bandage and looked a mess.

The prisoner shrugged. "Bad day is all. They knife us in the showers. I take my washbag, a book in there."

Jim nodded. Kid pervs were on borrowed time, anybody could take them with a sharpened spoon, nobody sees anything. They rarely lasted their sentence. Menzoy was on a sixteen-twenty, give or take. Jim Stazio had been in on the arrest.

"Cut to it." He harrumphed, edged forward. He hated talking into the mike beside the grille, for Correction Authority records. "A lost kid."

Menzoy showed his palms in astonishment. "You asking me?"

"Pattern, Aldo, I want pattern. Kid in a theme park, recent. Names, addresses, what you can."

"Look, Officer Stazio. Is there a deal?"

"Don't fuck with me, Aldo. I'm hungry. I'm tired. I'm sticking to this chair. I'm out of time, want to clear one thing up, you foller?"

"Anything in it for me?"

A warder tramped to the concession grille where an old woman was waiting to put a package through. Menzoy quivered, nervously smoothed his lank hair. His fingers pressed the grille ledge as if testing putty.

"Yeh." Jim Stazio had readied lies on the drive down. "Somebody I know."

Menzoy said eagerly, "There's tell of a new lawyer in the Appeals Office, related to some cop."

State pens were stiff with hopeful rumours, all worth a fart in a storm.

"Is there, now," Jim said flatly, giving him the blank stare. Sam Tietze had advised against this tactic, saying go for the straight threat, but who had months and months?

"Is it you?" Menzoy breathed, nodding desperate encouragement, praying he might gain a yard.

"I wouldn't drive ten fucking hours to this shit-store less'n I had something."

"It's you, yeah?" Menzoy's eyes lit with hope. "You got pull in the Squawk Office?"

"All I'm saying is give me, you might get. No promises."

"Off the record, right?"

Jim Stazio sighed. Who the fuck said *Off the record* in street talk? Journalists in movies, that's who.

"Off the record, Aldo," he intoned, grave as a hanging judge.

He listened Menzoy out, asking one or two short questions when the kid broker finished.

"Not promising anything," he said finally, heaving

himself to his feet, sweat thickening his clothes. "You might hear something in a month, maybe not."

"That's it?"

"That's it. I might be back."

Stazio left, walking with his arms away from his body to get air under his armpits showing cameras he carried nothing away. Once he'd retired, he'd have to learn normal.

Chapter Seven

The few times Bray travelled at weekends, he was surprised. Plenty of room, the tea trolleys able to move, families on holiday. He chose a seat beyond earshot of children.

He was surprised the manuscript woman was on the train. He thought, She goes in on Saturdays? He avoided her. No time to talk.

Lottie Vinson read the page a second time, realising she wasn't concentrating. He was the man in the *County Gazette*, caught in grainy light like an anguished animal what, getting on for three weeks ago, was it now? His little grandson had been kidnapped in America, and never been found. A joiner for a Long Acre firm. That was her word for him, anguished. She could feel his pain across the compartment's centre aisle.

She sighed and returned to the typescript. It was dross of course. The publishing firm's young whirl-girls, all Cambridge MAs and brimful of detestation for a part-time middle-aged divorcee, had airily passed it to her with, "Make something of that, Lottie, okay?" She wondered why the anguished man was going to work on a Saturday.

Now that today had finally come he felt shaky. He needed to preserve the pose, make sure his questions came out right.

Shirley and Geoffrey had approved of the journey, but that was only Bray's deception. Dr Feering had arranged the psychiatric consultation. Shirley had begun to worry about Bray's withdrawal. She was a good caring woman. It was exactly as Bray planned, though what if the psychiatrist decided you were off your head and certifiable? Bray's grandmother had been a great one for Grasping The Nettle. This was simply Bray's first nettle.

He blanked thought out, as the train bucketed through Maryland, then he was between Platform Nine's cream-coloured pillars. Others might chatter and lug their holiday bags looking for friends. Bray went alone among strangers, to have his head tested.

"You are for Dr Newton's clinic?"

"Charleston. Bray John Charleston."

Bray wondered about the lady's nasal syllables. Was it thought "professional"? Tracy and Karen spoke that way when buyers asked about Gilson Mather's cabinets or priceless antiques to be restored.

And was the pretty receptionist eyeing him with dread, here's another lunatic for Dr Newton? Perhaps cameras were secretly concealed in the *Cyclamen repandum* depicted on the pots along the window sills, wrong shade of red.

Bray took the end seat. How come that they already had a folder named for me, when I've never been to a psychiatrist in my life? Nor many doctors. Inguinal hernia fourteen years ago, nothing since except first-time specs for eyes tired of a night.

There was one other patient. She sat brooding, making handwashing movements, wore leather gloves and was smartly dressed. What, thirty? Nervously he read a motorbike magazine.

He was called after fifteen minutes. By then he'd almost decided to leave, say this wasn't for him. His heart was banging as he entered the consultation room.

"Mr Charleston? Do sit down. I'm Dr Newton."

Bray might have been surprised by her affability but matters were too serious.

"Dr Feering explained the circumstances. I gather you want advice concerning…?"

He had it ready. "Memory."

She gazed back. Say forty, and calm. Well, knowing everything about the human mind would make you pretty tranquil.

"I think you've read my book, Mr Charleston."

"I tried." Frankness was his tactic. He wasn't here to bugger about. "All those brain cells. I skipped the arrow diagrams."

Odd, women and earrings. He'd read somewhere that females of every culture wore earrings. Dr Newton's were blue lapis lazuli studs.

Diffidence was part of his planned gambit: I'm nothing like as brainy as you, Dr Newton.

"Do you mind if I record this, Mr Charleston?"

She was reaching across her desk to a button bank when he replied, "I would rather you didn't, please."

She sat back. He wondered why she didn't have a white coat on. To suggest everything was okay, be at ease with your psychiatrist, your pal, something like that?

"Suppose a six-year-old child was abducted," he said evenly. He'd rehearsed it in his shed, Buster listening, head between paws, ears cocked. "Would he remember his home?"

"Yes. Features would persist for a considerable duration."

Duration? He grabbed at the word; it was finite, would end sooner or later.

"What things?"

The doctor paused. Bray noticed prints on the wall, some river estuary. He thought them quite good. Her inspiration?

"Childhood memory can be a form of deception, Mr Charleston. You might think you recall events from your infancy, when in fact they might never have happened. Memory can sometimes be a catalogue of imaginings. Some memories endure with remarkable tenacity."

"What decides it?"

"As many factors as events. A child's existence is in a sense an accumulation. Data comes in. The child's mind learns to classify things as worthwhile, or rubbish for discarding. If you read —"

"Yes, thank you." Bray caught himself. "All those tables in your book. Can you really count memories up?"

"Which tables in particular?"

She became guarded. His manner was too abrasive, perhaps showing he'd prepared for this malarky.

"The ones proving when students could really remember, and when they only said they could."

"Phoney tales from the cot?" she said, unexpectedly giving him a smile. "Yes, you can be certain – if there's a way of checking veracity."

"The memory itself?" It seemed weird, said outright like that.

Which turned her attention from concepts. He

suddenly saw the intensity of her concentration. He'd come to the right person.

"I'm sorry," he said, and he meant it. "I got myself ready for this. I suppose I'm scared."

She regarded him with candour. "Mr Charleston, I shall help any way I can. You don't need a psychiatrist. Unless I'm wrong, you're going to do whatever you've already decided."

"Probably." He waited for her to be angry at having nearly been tricked.

Dr Newton seemed to scan some inscape and came to a decision. She leant forward.

"Very well. Where we left off: Memory itself, as opposed to memories themselves. They are classified often quite stupidly. You're concerned with what actually can be retained?"

"Yes."

"Memory loves the extraordinary." Dr Newton kept her gaze on him. "It's psychiatrists' catchphrase. Memory eschews the dull."

"Please. I want it to have some bearing."

"Let's omit all those memory-is-a-computer analogies. Memory comes down to two sorts of events. Routine things go into what I call a mind pouch, for quick use-and-discard function. Examples? Well, you look up some bus route. A woman sees a particular blouse she likes, remembers the price and which shop it was in. That quick I'll-use-it-once memory is for ordinary events. The mind retains it just long enough then discards it."

"Disposable?" He *hated* disposable. He wanted permanent memory.

"That's it. After all, you don't need to keep mentally recycling casual phone numbers. Railway timetables. So it's use-and-ditch."

"Unimportant routine events get erased."

"Simple, isn't it?" She was trying to encourage but it came out as failed humour, making her grimace with embarrassment. "Sorry, Mr Charleston. The other's enduring memory. I call it the docked or housed memory."

"The cortex section in your book?"

She was sombre now, and donned spectacles. Bray thought, so they too rely on gestures, like us mortals.

"Well done. Persistent memory is what might help you. There are ten milliard cells in the cerebral cortex. A notable stimulus sets this kind of memory into action. It need not be sudden – a plane crash, or an explosion. It may be a joke, a mere childhood event."

Good, good. Getting somewhere. "Notable?"

"Notable to the adult or child receiving that stimulus. It has a special effect, indeed an *affect*. The stimulus enters our cortical cells, and nerve cells there are sort of set alight. A blob of cells changes its function as the memory is retained. If the blob establishes links with other activated blobs, the memory is reinforced and retained."

"The more valencies, the more chance a child will remember?"

She smiled at his use of the term.

"Literature does it. Art does it. Love does it. Sights and sounds of home do it. So we humans have a particular vocabulary. We say a particular occurrence *evokes*, or *suggests* some memory. The greater the stimulus intensity to a child, the more likely a memory persists. We adults may not even notice, but to a child some seemingly insignificant event might be dazzlingly memorable for life."

"What does it?"

"Do tell me if I go on too long. The hippocampus, a double-shaped part in the middle of the brain, gets the activation signal from the cortical cells. It 'decides'. If the stimulus isn't important, into the emptyable pouch it goes, and stays just long enough for you to find your comedy TV channel, or whatever, then is ditched for good. But the *important* events get handled differently. The hippocampus docks them, and these candidates for permanence get retained. A search instantly begins for linkages with other retainable memory-candidates. It's as if our memories nudge each other, saying 'Good heavens! I encountered that attractive person last year in this very town!' A memory becomes more permanent when it is re-nudged into activity. You want the mechanism?"

He was lost, but said, "Yes, please."

"We think a chemical called N-methyl D-aspartate's got a lot to do with it." She interwove her fingers. "Dendrites ramify from neurones, and have NMDA there. If this all coincides with some electrical prompt from its cell, then the message gets across. Calcium dithers about, encouraging the memory to endure – and reinforcement occurs. Calcium in fact might be the necessary nudge. Exercise stimulates some vital molecules. We know of one – it may actually be many types – we call brain derived nerve growth factor; BDNGF in our deplorable medical acronym. It is vital for neurone protection, and in memory's longevity."

He tried to speak. She waited. Five goes later, it came out.

"Can a permanent memory get lost?"

"I'm afraid so, Mr Charleston. The absence of reminder nudges results in loss. The memory fades. Re-nudges, if they happen to occur, keep the memory alive." She shrugged. "These are linked to related memories. Similar events, similar subjects. Kin-based memories link up and keep themselves going."

Bray said quietly, "What eliminates housed memory?"

She sighed. "Sorry to say, a person over fifty, give or take, regularly loses one per cent of the brain cells. You can slow the memory loss, though. After all, we humans are trainable. What we call 'experience' is merely the art of being really cunning in cortical cell management. Illnesses, especially circulation or malnutrition, deplete memory. So older folk must exercise. Our journals are full of nerve-growth factors and brain-derived molecular structures. All they mean is eat the right foods and stay active."

"Can doctors take memories away?"

This made her uncomfortable. "You're thinking of a child? Yes. Some drug regimes abort memories. With behavioural psychotherapy it can be done fairly quickly."

"How fast?"

"Within months. A child grows. And loss of some memories is important for our sanity. I mean sometimes." She spoke with quiet sorrow. "Just think, Mr Charleston, of all those news items, phone codes, car registration numbers you and I have seen over the years. How intolerable life would be, to keep them all rushing around in our brains! The sane mind keeps itself stable by simply deleting mental junk mail. It does this automatically, to help us cope with each new day."

Bray thought in silence, and came to with the clock having moved on. He gestured apology.

"Do some events help?"

She knew what he was asking. "A child's memories can be reinforced later, but only sometimes. They can be ablated by drugs, by psychotherapies."

"Memory can be tricked?"

"Of course." She seemed surprised he had to even ask. "Deceptions are as common as stage tricks on music halls. We all suppress memory. For instance, we hate to recall that terrible time when we got told off at school, or missed some prize on which we'd set our heart. Forgetting helps us to carry on.

"It's a benevolence. Maybe we chose the wrong person to sleep with, went for the wrong job. We can rebel, or pretend we made the right choice. We can suppress truth.

"It need not be a cataclysmic event, either. Like, a woman may simply select a terrible dress for a party and all her life remember how embarrassed she was. Or she can say to hell with it and laugh it off."

"Could she accept that it's been a good thing, when it was bad?"

"Certainly."

Dr Newton subjected him to a steady scrutiny. It unnerved him. He'd drilled himself, and now he was forced to speak first.

"I'm frightened that my grandson will be made to forget. I'm assuming," he said, uttering the lie quite well, "that he'll remember home when he's found. You see?"

"Yes." She didn't fiddle with objects on her desk like a movie psychiatrist. "Do you mean how long do you have, Mr Charleston?"

He reddened, caught out. "Yes."

"That age, a child's memories can be changed in six months. One-fifth might linger a little longer."

So twenty per cent of Davey's memories might still be there after half a year? So many *ifs*, squared, cubed.

"There's some intermediate stage?"

She smiled, a bit wintry. "You're giving me my own

book's terminology! Yes, but it has different segments. So memories —"

"Are patchy?"

"Well spotted." She let him think a moment. "Some memories have remarkable persistence. Others in a child could well fade under a new regime."

"Deliberately taught, you mean," Bray said dully.

"Of course. Transference is a feature in all of us. We change lovers. We switch adherence from one employer to another. An allegiance alters as quickly as a woman changes her name on marriage, and sometimes for the same reasons. Transference can be a survival factor to a child. Belonging to a new team, say."

"Family, Dr Newton?"

"Yes. There is no let-up for a child who joins a new family. New reinforcement is constant. His every mouthful, every stitch of clothing, is prescribed. His speech is controlled, his accent determined by those he speaks with."

"Thank you. Can I tell you what I think I've learned, Dr Newton?"

Haltingly Bray summarised her interview. Twice he returned to the problem of time passing in the mind of a child abruptly living among strangers. Patiently she went over the same ground. Bray doggedly went back to selective memory.

"Patchwork?" he questioned her. "Like a quilt?"

"A child may not understand whether they represent some actual event in his past, or something he dreamt."

"Like true or false?"

"That's so, Mr Charleston. Remember that we're speaking of a child moved into a totally new world. All his old points of reference will vanish. New lamps for old, certainly, but he won't detect which is which for absolute certain at first. It goes on normally in all of us, until old age where we can no longer detect the new. We then say we're senile."

"Patchwork," he repeated. It meant hope.

"Here's my number, Mr Charleston. Do call if I can help."

"One thing, please. Could you tell Dr Feering nothing of this, please, say I didn't show up? My son and daughter-in-law, you see."

With some surprise she agreed, then asked, "What will you do, Mr Charleston?"

"Try," Bray said. "I'll try."

Outside, he'd somehow expected gathering dusk, and here it was still broad day with London traffic chugging about.

He knew a small caff near Charing Cross. He walked there and bought tea and some tomato thing. He ought to have brought sandwiches, for London floated on a sea of cholesterol and saturated fats. He vowed to watch this in the future.

Future? Carefully he allowed in that dangerous notion. No sugar in tea from now on. No margarine, no soggy puddings. Health was vital. Correction: *will be* important, from now on. He listened to tourists arguing theatres, what was on, museums. He was exhausted by the morning's ordeal, until the counter lady asked him with concern if he was all right.

He told her yes, thank you, fine. Rising, he got himself into the onrush of pedestrians and allowed himself the thought he'd been saving until now.

They were only two words, but he thought them with deliberate clarity, the outlines mentally burnished in bright luxuriant brilliant gold. It was still only early days, so he restricted himself to initials.

He thought, KV. He'd got six months, in which a child's memory might hang on, maybe a whole year at the very outside until there was nothing of Davey left.

Hurrying, he caught the train and was at the library by four o'clock looking up local technical colleges.

Chapter Eight

Bray wanted a plus, any hint of a plus.

Next door, Geoff and Shirley had gone to bed. Occasionally through the wall Bray would hear Shirley explode, shriek insanities at Geoff, as familiar as a church litany. "Why don't you do something?" And cruelly the malicious, "Think yourself a man, lying there doing nothing when our son...?" It always ended in the shrillest denunciation of all: "You don't care!" and a terminal wail, "Get on that phone! I want us to go back and search! They're doing nothing!"

Bray had heard every combination of screamed incoherences. Shirley saw Geoff's reasoning as subversion, the words of an enemy.

How much longer could Shirley go on? Bray guessed that she might crumple in less than another week. Would psychiatry in hospital be kinder for Geoff? Geoff, Bray saw, was dying within, actually shrinking physically, walking hunched, his features grey. And how was he faring at work?

Eventually the din next door lessened. Bray turned the television on, the sound down. Buster dozed in his circular padded pit.

The programme, *Documentary Dispatches*, was familiar, its technique interviews between video shots. Violence was its theme. No interviewers were shown, voice-overs lending portentous comment. It came on at one a.m.

Bray made notes.

Tonight's programme concerned some place in the King's Road, Chelsea. Suite 107, an address at PLAZA. Men's names were spelled under their talking heads. *Executive Outcomes* was the name of one firm, *Sandline International* another. People looked respectable.

They were involved with mercenary armies, complete with tanks, mortars. The mercenaries themselves were shown, streaky night shots, tracer fire, corpses twisted in undergrowth.

If Bray understood the drift, they had fought in Angola, Sierra Leone, Papua New Guinea. They battled against rebel armies and did deals at international arms fairs in the Gulf. They even had an air force. Bray took down Capricorn Air's number, N123W, not knowing its significance.

He paid attention to the rewards *Executive Outcomes* expected, a million USA dollars a month in Sierra Leone. The sums grew. Diamond mining rights, tens of millions for mercenary wars. Companies were floated on Canadian stock exchanges, mining concessions wrested from African governments.

Bray watched the credits roll after a mocked-up trial of a company administrator. They had failed in Papua New Guinea, yet somehow fortunes had changed hands.

He switched off and tidied his scribbles, using an indexed notebook. The cover of another bore a single black question mark.

The last task was to enter Mercenary Action in his

Query notebook, and painstakingly delete it. He had considered that option. He carried the notebooks back to the shed, placed them in their new plastic case – purple, the first colour Davey had learned to name. Then he slid the case into the slot he had constructed over the shed door. He had built it the third day of horror.

He went to bed, to the ritual of reading for an hour then pretending to sleep the night through.

As Monday afternoon drew to a close Bray made sure his work was well finished by five o'clock. He told Harry Diggins, the oldest labourer, he would stay and close up. Only when he was sure everyone had called goodnights and gone did he walk to the end of the workshop. He switched on the display lights over his prize possession.

Bray truly admired the Garvan Craftsman, sometimes called the Garvan Carver. Bray actually owned this piece personally, and was certain it was created by that wonderful ancient expert. It was his personal property, bought as a relic quarter of a century previously, and painstakingly restored in the lantern hours. Now, it was of stunning excellence. It stood encased in the workshop for all to admire.

Philadelphia, in the years before their Independence, had a handful of genius furniture makers. Hercules Courtenay was one, Nicholas Bernard another. Closest to Bray's heart was the Garvan Man, called after one Mabel Brady Garvan at Yale who had a furniture collection. The unknown Craftsman from those long-ago times had made furniture of genius level. Nobody carved leaves or vines on card tables, on desks, like the Garvan Carver.

Bray had given almost a year's salary for the derelict turret-topped card table. He had restored it with love. For years it had stood in a security case on the workshop floor, as example and tribute. Mr Winsarls often showed visitors the special piece, laughingly refusing offers. "It's not ours," he told people. "It's on loan."

Mr Winsarls had pointed out to Bray that he could make a giddy sum by selling it at Sotheby's, who specialised in 1759 Philadelphia furniture. Bray always smiled and shook his head.

Now, though, he stood appraising it. It glowed, positively glowed, the lovely turrets, the wonderful carvings of vines, the slender feet each clasping a ball. He shook himself for feeling fanciful emotions, and spoke aloud.

He said softly, "Time to earn your keep, Craftsman. All right with you?"

He locked up, set the usual alarms, and caught the train. On the way, he bought the *Writers' and Artists' Yearbook*. The manuscript woman, looking tired tonight, glimpsed it and raised her eyebrows, almost as if to say something. He moved elsewhere, and read it in silence all the way home.

Chapter Nine

The boy could see strange trees, and people playing tennis in a park.

Doctor was nice. The nurses said so. One nurse told him the sea was over there. The sun never stopped shining. The nurse was nice.

This time he asked Doctor a question. Doctor was pleased that he asked a question, straight out without thinking for the words.

"Can I go and see the sea?"

"You sure can, Clint! We've got your old surfboard here! Sure!"

The nurse brightly put in, "And Clint likes football, Doctor!"

Doctor laughed. "Clint's going to be a hotshot quarter back!"

"He changes TV channels on his own now."

"Great!" Doctor exclaimed. "Now, Clint, no more accidents, right?"

"Right."

"This clinic's the best for accidents. Pop and Mom already knew that."

Alone, Clint clicked the remote control. On came a show, much laughter and clapping. He liked these shows. He didn't know any answers, because he'd had an accident.

He dozed, was woken later for medication by another nurse. For an instant he imagined he'd heard a child cry out, but he must have been wrong because here was nice. They wouldn't let anybody cry.

This nurse wasn't fat like the morning nurse. She showed him pictures of her children. The children's daddy was a pilot on a plane. The children went to school. One was in second grade, just like he'd been before his accident.

Doctor interrogated the nurse near the secluded room.

"How did he respond to the photographs?"

"I showed him Number Forty-One M and Sixty-Two N," she said quietly. "I gave him school grading information and my supposed husband's career. Clint responded as you predicted, Doctor. Acceptance plus."

"What TV does he select?"

"Comedy, cartoons."

Doctor harrumphed. "That travel programme was careless. Delete it."

"Right away, Doctor."

"Take no chances with this one."

The nurse hesitated. "Should we worry, Doctor?"

"This kid's buyer is a real operator. Know what I'm saying?"

In the room the sleeping boy didn't stir. Vapour trails crossed as blue sky darkened to indigo.

On the ceiling and the wall shadows cast by the fading sun became diverse shapes with blurred outlines. The boy's eyes opened. For a moment he glimpsed the shadows, then he dozed, his mind slipping away. Doctor and nurses were nice.

Doctor sat at his desk across from his framed diplomas, reviewing the listed staff of his Special Care Rehabilitation Unit. He had a star system – four stars for maximum reliability, down to one star. Such was his scheme of profit sharing, and so expert was he in employment pre-selection, that only three ancillary staff had ever merited only one star.

One star meant deletion, death by accident.

The first had been a medical technician, now twenty years deceased. A road accident was always the most reliable, and least investigated, means of elimination. The second had been a nurse whose man, a loutish beachblower, persuaded her to attempt to blackmail Doctor, so amateurish as to be laughable. Both had oh-so-accidentally drowned, drugged up, under the breakwaters by Old Bayonne Beach. He didn't regret the cost. Their insolence deserved an ugly death.

The third member of staff had been a secretary. Her jealousy had become intolerable and her imperious demands on him ridiculous. He regarded hysteria as forgivable. But to insist that he decline sex with willing nurses in her favour was effrontery. From a mere clerk, to the prime mover of the enterprise that put bread in her mouth? Yet, he thought with satisfaction, her shrieked ultimatum that he marry her had been a compliment. She was found dead, victim of an unsolved assault in her apartment on Congreve and Vane. Expensive again, but requisite.

None of these deaths was Doctor's fault, for the Clinic had to remain sacrosanct. Every employee received a heavy bonus for each child abducted from its parents and satisfactorily processed before being sold on with its new identity. Staff either believed, or were removed. Simple as that. And only three among so many was a superb track record.

Starkly, the truth was this: The original parents of the children he acquired didn't *deserve* them. Society needed somebody to rescue the children, and simply transfer them to decent strangers. If biological parents couldn't be bothered, then he, the Doctor, had a medical duty to pass their children to better parents.

That's all it was: duty fulfilled. Richer people, sure, who could pay well. But so?

There were fees, naturally. Had to be. He set the fees at whatever he judged they could afford. They were glad to pay.

After all, look at the product! Every child guaranteed ready-made, with all of its first memories blanked out. He felt inexpressibly moved whenever he entered up the details of a new child in his copperplate handwriting. He had created the perfect system. The fuss over the new boy had already died down.

Nothing could go wrong.

Two in the morning, Bray roused and went downstairs. Buster woke, stared, came with him while he made some cocoa. He sat in his armchair. The dog lay on the rug to listen.

"See, Buster," he explained, "people who steal a child don't do it just once. They steal one child after another. It's money."

Buster's ears moved, but he was already into a doze.

"They're rich enough to bribe anybody." He tried the cocoa but it scalded, too hot. "Like police." He never got the hang of cocoa.

"Two questions, Buzzie. Can I trust that Officer Stazio?

Or is he really one of them, keeping an eye on this sad Limey grampa?"

Buster gave a trial snore. Bray didn't mind. The past weeks had been hard. He wanted eyes and ears, anybody's, to test his suggestions. Even pretence would do.

"I can trust nobody, Buzzie," he said. "I shall tell Geoffrey and Shirley nothing. I'm not trying to do my son's job, or take anybody's place. God knows I'm nothing special. But Geoff's up to his neck, everything falling apart, Shirley broken."

Buster fell sound asleep.

"I'm only the grandfather, no more, no less. So it's down to me. I must remember. Trust might be a trick."

He tried the cocoa. Stone cold. He told Buster goodnight and went back to bed and stared at the blackness.

Chapter Ten

"Departments are closed," the porter said.

Bray was buffeted by milling youngsters. The technical college hall seemed wide as a football field. The pupils – all "students" nowadays – were attired in various team strips. Everybody seemed to be shouting.

Bray kept his anger down. Normally he would have accepted the porter's rejection and gone. Now, he had resolve.

"Somebody in computer technology, please."

"They've all left."

"Where's the dean's office?" Bray looked at him.

Agitation finally stirred the man. "Got an appointment?"

Bray saw a sign, *Office of the Dean*, and walked. Down the corridor the hubbub diminished. Carpets began, administrators awarding themselves status symbols. Doors were darker here, but still modern shoddy. The corridor ended at stairs.

He climbed to the floor above, got help from two giggling girls, their arms full of folders.

"Computers? Next floor. Mr Walsingham's still in."

One rolled her eyes at some unknowable joke.

"Thank you, miss."

That set them off again. He heard their laughter all the way to the next level. It was quiet except for a radio. The doors here were plastic veneer monstrosities pinned to warping pine. He felt disgusted. Who on earth?

A door marked with Walsingham's name stood ajar. He knocked. A man was on the phone. Bray could see the reflection.

"Look, Gordon," the speaker was expostulating, swinging in his chair. "I *know* it's class ratios. We'd be deluged in a week."

An academic row? Bray hesitated.

"It isn't a question of delegation, Gordon," Walsingham went on with bitterness. "It's teaching time."

Confidential. Bray moved down the corridor to wait. Somebody was tapping a keyboard. Courageously he peered in. A scruffy girl sat at a console, chuckling, smoking a cigarette, utterly absorbed.

Bray was shocked to see a couple on her screen making love. Both were naked, something jerky and Cubist about them. The screen's periphery was rimmed with symbols. The girl heard him and tapped a key. The screen blanked.

She docked her cigarette, squeezing it slickly.

"You stupid cunt! I thought you were my dad." She snarled with such savagery Bray recoiled.

"I'm sorry to startle you, miss," Bray stammered.

"What the fuck you creeping about for? Piss off!"

She looked unwashed, unbelievably unkempt, her shoes caked with mud, her jeans tatty. He wondered why a pupil would still be working, the college closing.

"I'm for Mr Walsingham," he apologised. "A computer course."

She sneered. "They don't start for three months. Dad's rowing with that fucking Registration pansy."

Angrily the girl swivelled back, clacked the keys and produced a scene of a blonde performing fellatio on a naked male in what appeared to be a church nave.

"How do you make it show pictures?" And, as she turned to stare, "I'd like to learn."

"You a dirty old fucker or what?"

He pondered the words. She was manipulating the crudest images he'd ever seen, yet she suspected him? Of what, exactly?

"I must learn to use a computer. I can pay."

She lit a cigarette, looking quickly round. The room was larger than Bray had realised. Sixteen consoles stood on benches, a blackboard and white screens occupied the end. For a class?

"What sort you got?"

"Computer? I haven't got one. I don't know what to buy."

"Jesus fucking Christ. You real or what?"

"I hoped someone might advise me."

"I'll get you one cheap. Not nicked." She sounded hopeful.

"I'm no good with electrics. I'd want it set up."

"Any fucker can plug it in. They never go wrong, except for hackers and virus wankers." A sullen interest kindled. "What you want it for?"

"I don't know. What can it do?"

"Any fucking thing." And now she really did weigh him up. He was conscious of the age gap, the gender gap, every wretched gap. Except she knew these gadgets and he didn't. "You don't know even what fucking *for*? You're loony."

Her dreadful language was exhausting him.

"If it turns out to be useless, that's my..." Bad luck? Luck mustn't come into it. "Misfortune," he ended lamely.

"You're off your fucking trolley."

"Do they stay on all the time?" Several other screens seemed to have been left on, glowing. It was wasting electricity.

"Best never to switch off."

"How far can they reach?" He explained at her puzzlement, "I heard they can write between different countries."

She laughed, shaking her matted hair. Did she ever comb it? "Jesus, you really are thick." She looked at him. "Got wad?"

"I'm afraid I don't smoke."

"Money, you prat. Pay me and I'll show you. Got a modem?"

"I don't know what that is, miss."

"Stop saying miss like that. You're doing my frigging head in. Kylee."

He'd never met anyone called Kylee before, said the name over to himself in anxious rehearsal. Her coarse language was increasingly tiresome, and her oddly thin cigarette produced a pungent yet cloying smoke. It made him feel queer.

"How do you do? I'm Mr Charleston."

"How de fucking do," she said. He coloured. "Bread. Packet for ten?" And when he looked blank, translated with exaggerated weariness, "You pay me twenty fags every ten minutes, okay?" As he tried to work out the hourly rate she said belligerently, "Dad'd cost you three times that and be fucking useless."

"I'd have to pay you money, I'm afraid. Are you old

enough to smoke?" He felt drawn in. He wished Mr Walsingham would get off the phone.

"I'm fourteen." She dared him. "Deal? Or are you going to report me?"

What could he do? Time mattered. Who could wait three months? This girl might be his only ally.

"Deal," he said. "What do cigarettes cost?"

"Where do you want to *write* to?"

"America, I think."

"Easy peasy. Who to?"

He said carefully after a protracted pause, "Everyone."

She eyed him. "What for?"

He could see his mood was infecting her. He looked at the screen. How come the young were so enthralled? He knew they played games, saw them on the second floor in Griffins and Empdale, screens bleeping, children clustered round.

"I don't know yet."

"Here, you're not one of them queer paedies, are yer?"

Her meaning struck him like a blow. His face must have changed because she raised a hand in peace. "Okay, 'kay."

"Ah, I think I should ask your father for permission before you give a stranger instruction."

Kylee spat venom. "Look, old man. I'm back with Dad for a wasted fucking weekend because Mum's getting herself shagged brainless by some burke in Marble Arch. I'm your tug-of-love child." She spoke the term in a bitter falsetto. Bray felt moved. "I do fuck all every happy weekend. See my problem?"

"I apologise."

She cackled a laugh and pointed to the screen. "You talk like them Dickens serials on telly. Listen up. We'll dig skunk as example, okay?"

"Very well."

A skunk? Many skunks? He supposed she had her reasons. She eyed him as he approached to watch. He noticed then that she had several mini bottles of nail varnish. Her computer keys bore coloured marks. Some keyboard letters were indecipherable under the colours.

"You haven't a fucking clue, have you? Skunk is cannabis, weed, hash, grass." She gave a smile like sleet. "Naughty, but it'll give you an idea."

Bray sat there ashamed. He didn't feel out of his depth at work. Wood was malleable, its living spirit within reach of a man's hands. This machinery was an impenetrable metal world where intangible electrons flew in Outer Space. Yet these unknowable machines just might help.

"Can you explain, please?"

"This is a slow old heap." She kicked the bench in anger. "The college is too pigging mean." Her manner became furtive. "Somebody owffed Dad's – offed its cards in her knickers. Sold it for illicit herbal substances." She grinned with surprising gaiety. "I'll *bet* that's what happened!"

Bray was out of his depth, understanding nothing.

"This isn't what I must buy, then?"

"One fucking candle power? Watch. I'm going to switch it off, start you from scratch, okay?"

Kylee clicked something, and it resumed its glow. "Time starts now, okay?"

He agreed. She only meant the start of her instruction fee, in cigarettes. Bray meant something different.

The computer world seemed to have no beginning and no end. His mind reeled. Kylee, young enough to be his granddaughter, cursed obscenities at his incomprehension. Twice she made him take her place, only to shove him aside to restore the screen's mad universe of signs and numbers. Stupidly he kept forgetting the punctuation, colon, comma, backslash, whatever, until she exploded, actually striking him and yelling, "You gotter say it, you senile prick! Have you no fucking sense?"

"I'm sorry," he'd said, wondering what he'd got himself into.

She calmed down after a moment. "I don't know letter. Gerrit?"

He examined the screen, where various emblems were displayed in three lines. He glanced at her, back to the screen, then at her array of coloured nail varnishes. Suddenly it became clear. If he'd had half the sense he was born with, he might have understood. Dyslexia, was it called? Yet if she couldn't read, how did she manage? Why bother with symbols, letters, numbers on a fluorescing electronic screen if they meant nothing?

"I apologise, Kylee. You're right. I'm thick."

She barked her manic laugh. "No, you're 'kay. I hear it, I do it in my head, see? You poor prats need it written down."

That had given him his first smile. She had a simple deficiency. Except, he reflected, *was* it a 'deficiency'? She'd airily said at one point, "No, Owd Un. Back five screens, yer'd gotter different picture, right?" He'd have needed pages of notes to help him remember what the hell she had made the screen do five clicks before. A brilliant child; just different. Like Davey.

Mr Walsingham entered the computer lab. He must have heard his wayward daughter spitting invective at a stranger.

"What's happening here?" he barked.

Bray rose and waited to be introduced. Kylee took not

the slightest notice, simply kept going.

"Pillocks like you buy toy computers," she said, "cos you're prats. Don't buy shit sticks like this old heap. Buy RAM to spare. My mate's daft on old shifters, but what's the fucking point? Everything's extinct in half a mo'. You'd know that, if you'd half a brain."

"Erm," Bray said finally, hesitantly offering his hand to the newcomer. "May I introduce myself? I'm Mr Charleston. I wish to register on a computer course."

Walsingham glanced from Bray to Kylee, who said, "I told him your college is fucking all use."

"Private tuition is not allowed." Walsingham shook Bray's hand perfunctorily and switched the computer off. Kylee gave an angry squeal. Her father extinguished her cigarette. "Registration is closed. Introductory courses begin in three months. Leave your name downstairs at Information."

"See?" Kylee snorted and took a backhanded swipe at her father. "Told you."

"Your daughter has been most considerate, Mr Walsingham," Bray said helplessly.

"Kylee?"

Walsingham made it a command. He brought out a bunch of keys, evidently locking-up time. Bray moved to the door as Walsingham went out for his briefcase. Bray took his chance, fumbling three notes to the girl. She pulled a comic grimace of mock terror as Walsingham reappeared.

"Sorry you've missed the boat, Mr Charleston. College procedures must be followed. Courses fill up from industry, business."

"Can you suggest somewhere?"

"I said I'd do it," Kylee put in. "Except you're a right

frigging tortoise, you." She cackled one of her laughs, already ahead of them down the stairs.

"I'm sorry about my daughter," Walsingham said quietly, locking the IT laboratory. "It's been a troubled year. I'm divorced. She tell you? She announces it like a leper rings a bell."

"My sympathy, Mr Walsingham." Bray hesitated. "She's bright. Can you recommend a private home teacher?"

Walsingham shook his head as they started after Kylee. "Don't choose from the phone book. Most teach extinct systems."

"Only, I need to learn speedily."

"Leave your name. Somebody on the staff might free up a slot."

Bray's mind screamed, *Future? There is no future unless*…painstakingly he wrote out his name and address.

"Will this do?" He read his print aloud.

Walsingham and Kylee headed for the car park. Bray caught the bus home.

The episode was painful. He'd made a fool of himself. Worse, he'd failed.

Chapter Eleven

Bray heated his supper, beans on toast, a banana, apple, potato cakes, tea. Buster was dozing listlessly after his feed, bones on Saturday and different biscuits.

Shirley was visiting a psychiatric support counsellor Dr Feering had arranged. Geoffrey was staring unseeing at football results. It was later than Bray thought.

Waiting was their sole purpose now, the phone there on the coffee table. Conversation, once incessant, had gone with Davey.

"Officer Stazio phoned, Dad. No news."

Stazio loomed in Bray's mind: stout was he, perhaps chewing tobacco, belly bulging over his belt?

Geoff cleared his throat, looking unseeing at the soccer scores scrolling on TV, colours for score draws, plain for others.

"What?" Bray asked in dread, knowing his son.

"They want some of Davey's hair."

Bray stared. "They want…?"

"DNA tests. One will do, they said. To go with the fingerprints."

That had been a harrowing time, finding books Davey

read in his story hour. Bray had thought of the modelling clay he used to teach Davey. It showed the little lad how to shape wood.

Fingerprints Bray could understand. You discovered if the child had been at this cafe, that garage. Heading where, though? North? Or south, to some quayside and across the sea? Unlikely that whoever had stolen Davey would head for the Bahamas or Antigua, they having historic connections with Great Britain and all that. Except you took DNA samples when you'd found somebody who could no longer say his name, because... To go with the fingerprints. Right.

Bray looked at his son. He was ageing at such speed. So much was on him. His complicated job, money always pressure, fractional losses that magnified to inconceivable amounts.

"Sorry I'm not much use, son."

"No, Dad, it's me." They didn't see some re-run of a dynamic goal, the crowds erupting.

"You've been great, Geoff. I feel I'm letting the side down."

"I know, Dad." Bray was appalled to see his son's cheeks glisten with tears. "I think of things. Us grumbling at Davey playing when he ought to've been at his sums."

"You were right, son."

"No, Dad. I should have..." A pause, then, "Shirley's breaking down. I don't think she'll recover."

There, it was out. Shirley's psychiatrist had given a bad report.

"Women manage better than we do, Geoff. They're more resilient. We men often can't cope. I mean, look at us. Officer Stazio probably has all sorts of leads."

"Anything Davey chewed, Officer Stazio said. Or

maybe if Davey grazed his knee, where it got bloodstained. Or a comb. He has scientists."

The sportscast ended. Geoff stirred himself. "How did your session go?"

"Oh, a woman doctor. Talked a long time."

"Have you to go again?"

"I'm to phone for another appointment." As good a lie as any.

"I won't go to our counsellor again." Geoff usually had a glass of wine of an evening. Now, nothing except a late coffee. "I'd rather be here."

Bray understood. "Dr Feering wants me to have a physical. Nothing serious. Much good, eh?" Bray said. He quickly added, "Let's keep hope up, son."

Geoffrey looked. Bray didn't usually speak in those terms. "Yes, Dad," he said. "Let's."

They went to Davey's room and found a comb, put it in a plastic freezer bag. They left all the clothes untouched.

"If it isn't enough we can ask Shirley," Geoff said. "She'd do this better."

Bray said goodnight and left. He hadn't been down to the shed since reaching home. He wanted the shed and garden to become dark. Let an urban fox come sniffing, the hedgehogs come trundling by in the pitch night.

He had bought a paperback to read in the lantern hours. Computer work to do alone, for only he and Davey knew KV. He finally whistled Buster. The dog, a creature of ritual, came astonished and grumpy. Saturday's late football was for a doze. Bray told him. "No putting it off, Buzz." Buster came trotting, looking up.

Shirley and Geoff had long since gone to bed. To lie grieving, listening for the phone that might bring Davey back.

Alone in the gloaming Bray sat on his stool, Buster twitching by the shed door. It was cold, a cutting breeze from the sea ten miles away stirring the perfumed wood shavings. Along the shed walls hung pieces of wood, all justly seasoned. He finally lit a candle, saw Buster's eyes gleam as the dog glanced about as if expecting to see a bright-haired lad appear.

Bray quite liked feeling cold. In normal times, Shirley would forever pull his leg because who on earth didn't like being warm?

Some pieces were being carved – Davey's own hands, too, showing consummate skill for a boy. Bray was proud. Geoff had never shown much aptitude in this direction. Maybe folk were right, that skill skipped a generation?

Now, he had no illusions. At first he had believed it was all some ghastly mistake, and Davey would be found on some coach among a Methodist children's group from Tampa Bay or wherever, and the nightmare would pass.

Several days into the horror, Bray had phoned the American police officer. Officer Jim Stazio.

The man had wanted proof that Bray wasn't some news reporter or pervert "getting off" on the story. Stazio had insisted on ringing Bray back at the Charlestons' home number, making sure. Bray learned afterwards that Stazio had checked with the Liaison WPC at Fenwold and the British consul, doubly testing Bray's identity.

The conversation had taken place when Geoff and Shirley were in mid-flight. Of course they had stayed in Florida, going over photographs and security camera tapes until they were advised to go, the ultimate deception. The police simply meant *Go away for Christ's sake and can't you see the obvious?*

Shirley and Geoff did the same tortured rounds of

interviews and tearful question sessions with local Fenwold's liaison police. It had ended in a fiasco.

On that call, Bray had his questions worked out to the letter for Officer Stazio. He had them written and numbered. He thought them over.

"What are the chances, Mr Stazio?"

"I gotta be frank, Mr Charleston. We got a Child Abduction Unit keeps records, provides data." Then had come that hesitation that shot Bray's hope dead. "Chances are small."

"Who would do such a thing?"

"Bray, there's weirdo, weirder and weirdest. Expect the worst, hope for some fluke. All kindsa shit flying here, political shit, police shit, commercial shit."

Bray closed his eyes in pain. Question Four couldn't be avoided. He'd rehearsed it using a midget tape recorder.

"How many do you recover, Officer Stazio?"

"Few. When you say recover, Bray, you're qualifying that before hoping too much, right? Y'understand what I'm saying?"

"Safe, then?"

"There's some natural theft out there. Child stealers sell kids to rich folk who can pay. Even now papers are full of all kindsa embryo things, old biddies with no man around, still they get themselves made pregnant in clinics. Seems unnatural to me, but they do it all the time."

"What does natural theft mean?"

"Thieving a child, buy one, to raise as their own."

Bray almost lost track, but this was important.

"Who would buy a child?"

"I dunno what kinda news you get, Bray, but here people go abroad to adopt. Romania, the Balkans, anywheres there's war, Asia. You'll have heard of Vietnam

Americans and Philippinos?"

"They just want to adopt?"

"Seems so."

Bray prompted Officer Stazio by grunts and false starts, encouraging him to speak on. The man seemed relieved to do so, prevent himself being "put on the spot" – one of his frequent phrases. Bray listened.

At the end he spoke his thanks. From novels, American police seemed to get little gratitude so, he reasoned, appreciation might stimulate Officer Stazio to more zeal. Bray replaced the receiver, and went to replay Stazio's words over and over. The day before making the call he had bought a tape deck from a pimply young electrical retailer.

Meticulously, he had labelled the miniature tape, *Officer Jim Stazio, USA*. He carried it out to the shed and placed it in a wooden sawdust box.

Since that first call he had had further conversation with Jim Stazio. Probably pointless, Bray thought, but who could tell? He had asked that Stazio avoid mentioning to Shirley and Geoff that they ever spoke, saying it might distress them. Stazio agreed.

This evening he decided against playing over his phone conversations with Officer Stazio. Not tonight. Too many decisions. Tomorrow he had so many journeys to make, so many people to wring dry of information.

Instead, he leant forward and turned the screw-bar on the far wall of the cramped little shed, and swung the right-hand leaf aside. He felt breathless, opening the door on Davey's drawings.

Chapter Twelve

The following Sunday Shirley broke. Dr Feering was called at five in the morning, the rain beating down speckling his car lights. He was kind, Geoffrey told Bray when, roused by the disturbance, he came in. Dr Feering explained that no, it wasn't "madness". Tears, moans, repetitive rocking, loss of perception, a troubled mind's defences were simply overrun.

In a way, Feering said quietly, it was her way of mimicking the trauma experienced by a missing loved one. Not too fanciful an explanation. Shirley had hung on until hope was gone. Geoff was brilliant, Bray saw, but at what cost? Everything seemed in ruins.

Christine Lumley went with Shirley to the Psychiatric Unit. The Lumleys were close friends, their Thomas being Davey's schoolfriend, car-pooled for the morning run. Christine's husband Hal stood palely by, holding Samantha the baby, saying was there anything, absolutely anything. It was turgid and distressing. House lights came on down the avenue as Geoff followed the ambulance in his motor. Bray was to stay by the phone. Nobody thought *in case* any longer. Buster lurked wanting reassurance.

Bray sat in his kitchen, stirred the teapot. Always sugar for the first cup of tea in any day, thereafter just skimmed milk. Coffee dilute and black, only one cup in mid-morning, Bray's frugality a joke at Gilson Mather. Had been a joke. Geoff had come to an understanding with Officer Stazio about phone calls. In future Bray would call once a week. Stazio was never to call back unless asked.

Under the staircase was his hellhole, where Bray kept small triumphs of the past. He left his mug of tea to cool and rummaged, Buster getting in the way testing for new scents. Five minutes, and Bray found the papers.

Bray had painted the folder purple, to please Davey. It was his colour.

The article was there, poor quality paper yellowing, the dotted photograph too vague to be any help: "*Reproduction Miniature Mock-Final Regency Corner Cabinet of William Vile at the Treasurer's House, York, England,*" Bray read aloud. "By Bray John Charleston." Geoff had laughed at the pedantic title. "I'll wait for the film, Dad!"

But laughs were for back then, not now.

Four enthusiasts had written letters to the Editor about his meticulously worded article. Bray had answered their queries, and received two letters of thanks.

"Not much of a plan," he said, but it was a start, and better than unthinkable nothing. Buster came to, saw things didn't concern him, and flopped back down.

He donned his spectacles and re-read the article. He could remember having hellish difficulty with his old Remington typewriter.

One correspondent lived Ipswich way. Bray found the address between rust-stained staples. Would he still be there, three years on? You could never tell these days, mobility, spouses wandering off.

"George Corkhill, printer," he told Buster. "That's him."

They had once conversed by phone, over a question of finishing Regency wood surfaces.

He hadn't kept Mr Corkhill's letters, so much discarded in clear-outs after Emma went.

Sunday. Would Mr Corkhill be home? Bray knew nothing about the man except he signed himself *Printer*. If he'd moved, might a printers' guild have his address? Bray started a lie, in case.

"If ever," he clearly remembered Mr Corkhill half-joking in their last conversation, "you want some private text on Regency mahogany furniture printed, Mr Charleston, come here first!" They'd had a chuckle.

Bray made his habitual porridge Lancashire style, only water and oats. He watched the clock, waiting for news of Shirley, but wanting Mr Corkhill, printer, to enter the day.

Half-past nine, Bray finished vacuuming, washed up his breakfast things and started his laundry. He would give Mr Corkhill, printer of Saxmundham, until ten. If the printer was having a lie-in, hard luck.

The difficulty with gardening, he thought as the doorbell rang, was being under the reproachful gaze of neighbours. It *was* reproach, no mistake. What family would go on holiday and lose a child?

Christine was minute, dark of hair and normally smiley. A library volunteer three mornings.

"Hello, Christine." He stood aside.

She came in a pace, no further, and stood cupping her elbows.

"They've decided to keep Shirley in. Dr Feering told

Geoff a few minutes ago. He stayed with them. Isn't he brilliant? You can visit Shirley this afternoon."

"Thanks, Christine. Sure you won't come in?" He was already moving the door, making it easy for her to decline.

"No, thanks. I'd better get back to…home."

She did the pursed lips with which women escaped giving offence, avoiding mentioning the children she managed to protect, unlike some people.

"Say ta to Hal." So many thanks.

"It's no bother." She hesitated. "If there's anything."

Gently Bray closed the door. He instantly went to the phone and dialled Mr Corkhill. It was picked up on the fourth ring. Somebody was arguing about football, mid-sentence.

"Could I please speak with Mr George Corkhill, printer?"

"Speaking." Bray recognised the voice.

The hunt was beginning. Bray felt himself shaking slightly.

"I don't know if you remember me, Mr Corkhill. Mr Charleston, joiner." He halted, giving the other a moment. "We corresponded some years ago."

"William Vile of York!" Corkhill interrupted enthusiastically. "Of course! I finished the piece, gave it to a small museum we have here. Nothing like what you'd turn out, I'm sure, but I was pleased."

"Very complimentary, Mr Corkhill."

Bray hesitated. He'd forgotten his written questions and lost direction.

"Have you entered for the competition, Mr Charleston?"

Competition? Something in a cabinet-making journal? The latest issue was still in its postal wrapper among other mail on the hall table.

"Er, no. I hope this isn't a terrible intrusion, Mr Corkhill. It's personal. Perhaps you've read in the papers?"

A silence, then Corkhill asked him to hold on while he changed phones. Something clattered, Corkhill saying to freeze the video. Youthful voices pierced Bray. He stayed impassively looking at the hall's frosted glass, going over the sentences ploddingly worked out.

"Hello? I read something in the paper, Mr Charleston. The surname…I almost rang. I hope not?"

"Afraid it was, Mr Corkhill." Bray went straight on to forestall any questions, "No news yet."

"I'm so sorry."

"Can I ask your advice?"

"Anything I can do?" The offer seemed a long time coming.

"Would you tell me about printing?"

"Printing?" The man sounded startled. "What, exactly?"

"A small book."

"Have you a word count? What computer language have you?"

Bray cleared his throat for the hard part. "It depends on what you tell me."

Corkhill went quiet with puzzlement. "How many copies? Illustrated or —?"

"It isn't written. Not a word."

Bray had the first twinges of doubt. He would have spoken more directly but for the agony of missing even the most fragile chance.

"Look," the printer said at last. "I'm at a loose end. How far are you from Saxmundham?"

Bray almost sweated in relief. Now for the *hard* hard part.

"The job might not be altogether legal, Mr Corkhill."

"I'll tell you if it's not, Mr Charleston," Corkhill answered drily.

They arranged to meet at a coastal wharf. The printer would borrow his niece's motor.

That morning Bray read his paperback on the hieroglyphics of the Internet. Could computers really do all these things, chat, explore, roam, "surf"? He lost the thread, took Buster to watch football on the park. Later he attacked the incomprehensible book for another hour.

He cooked Geoff egg and chips, and left his weary son sleeping in front of the TV sports. As Geoff dozed, Bray made an appointment at Dr Feering's surgery for the morning Well Man Clinic. He then booked a finance session at some all-hours investment office in London.

It was then, dozing after that greasy lunch, that he saw the note on the matting by the front door. For a frightening moment he had a wild vision of a ransom demand. It was nothing so hair-raising. The note was typed.

mr charlston a m8 can get u a pc with the busniss but itl
cost its clean av u wheels hav 2 b cash its a 1 of OK
I told him ur strite Kylee

Kylee, offering him a computer? It sounded decidedly rum. What if it was stolen?

Strite for straight, and m8 for mate, presumably? How to explain to Geoff why he was buying a computer from a loutish teenager? And what of her father?

He wondered whether to talk it over with Geoff, but his son would be horrified and want to know what Bray planned, thinking his father had lost his marbles.

No. He had to do it alone, get help from anywhere, anyhow.

Officer Jim Stazio talked most with Sam Tietze. His partner was still doing some crazy night school law and criminology, the course not worth a belch. And would never finish it, Jim knew. He suspected Sam had something going with the woman who ran the gas station over Benksayne. Sam argued strong points, pardons, kind of stuff Jim thought a waste of a good evening.

Nobody should get pardon.

"See, Sam," he told him. "That crazo Menzoy had a partner. We never got the two, right?"

"Aldo, he talks, he gets his throat cut in Ablutions, Jim. He fed you a load of shit and shine."

"I didn't ask what he done, Sam. I asked about others."

They'd made an arrest that morning, a lowlife receiving stolen goods looted after crowd disturbances, what Sam called a shout bout, women shrieking yelled about fascist hogs, what gave you bile hours later. They were in a diner on Coltra, five roads met there, giving town loafers a pile-up every time some drunk overshot the lights, be right there on the spot when the next happened.

"Jim," Sam sighed. "We know about others. It's them we ain't got."

"I milked him, Sam. Three names I got, two buyers and one mebbe."

"Buyers?" Sam Tietze talked cagey, looking like lock and load, not really believing a word. "You got names of kid buyers?"

Jim said, "I should be so lucky. People he says adoptions gone wrong, past felonies stopping foster-parenting, Christ knows what."

"How'd he know them?"

"Didn't say. Been knifed once, didn't want no more."

Sam chuckled. "Not all bad news, right?"

"I'm going to call them. Want to come?"

"Jim, we done that shit. How long you got before your bus pass?"

Jim thumped his feet down and waved to the counter girl. They changed every week, Aquilina the Maltese paying them half the legal hourly.

"I'll give it a miss, Jim. No hard feelings?"

"Just don't call me as alibi for that night school you pretending."

Sam beckoned more coffee and shook his head, like hadn't an officer anything better to do with his time.

The house was as elegant as anything the burbs had to offer. Jim Stazio left his marked police car in the long drive, visible from the road as intimidation, what will the neighbours think? He regained his breath before ringing the doorbell. His water supplement wasn't taking effect yet, dieting four days and still thirty pounds overweight.

A small neat woman in her fifties admitted him. Her husband was somewhere in transit, Hawaii to San Fran, home tomorrow. He said he was making enquiries.

"A few crosses on paper," he told Mrs Baines. "Nothing important."

Sam Tietze had a smoother line, which was why Jim had wanted him along. Sam had a habit of smiling at windows, sofas and maybe carpets like he knew them, hey, I got one in my apartment, that way. Homely, Jim would say if asked, Sam could look homely, things reassured a woman. Sam was a natural, Jim wasn't.

"It's about that adoption business again," Jim said. "That old thing. I'm retiring soon. Loose ends, Mrs Baines."

Her hand went to her throat. "Loose ends?"

"Nothing serious." She seemed a mite paler. "Can you just go over how you went about it again? Then I can tick the box and that'll be it."

Haltingly, she said how she and her husband had tried for adoption. "All kinds of agencies, Officer Stazio," she said earnestly. "You've simply no idea." She coloured. "There's a cut-off. My husband calls it stalling speed. A single day over age, you've no hope of adopting."

They eventually heard of a lawyer in another state, an expert in adoption. There were medical centres specialising in orphans who, once they'd recovered from accident or mental trauma, were adoptable.

You had to go through registered doctors licensed to practice.

"All above board, Officer. My husband doesn't do dishonest."

"You met the lawyer?"

"No. We had a name. I gave it to your people."

He already knew it but pressed her. It checked. "Did you take it further, Mrs Baines?"

"No. My husband worried they might be false. We tried other agencies. We got their names from state attorney people, but gave up. You can't keep on for ever."

He said there was nothing wrong with giving up, and left. Blank. The walk to the car was downhill. He felt better.

That afternoon he slogged through lists of medical centres, clinics, medical A and E units with different radii from where the kid had gone missing. Trouble was, the Charleston kid was one of many.

Long shot. Sam was right.

Still, ignore the enormous stack of pending reports and he'd nothing urgent on, so he compiled a grid map for kid abductions. Like, he thought dejectedly, nobody thought of that before. He marked them with colours to indicate time lapses.

He had a few days left.

Chapter Thirteen

Bray asked Mr Winsarls for permission to go over some past Gilson Mather sales records. The owner's jocularity covered his awkwardness.

"Mr Charleston, do exactly what you want in Gilson Mather! You've had your own keys for ten years."

"Thank you, Mr Winsarls."

He began only when Tracy and Karen had left. The last of the craftsmen called so-long, Harry Diggins shouting up that he was locking up, Mr Charleston. The place quietened. Bray started excavating sales ledgers. Three centuries of craftsmanship, after all, documents crammed in higgledy-piggledy, none computerised except for the last three years, and those uncertain. He finally found it, realised with a shock how fast time was passing. He'd guessed that a Thomas Sheraton was sold four years previously. It was nearer six.

Meticulously he copied down details. After Mr Winsarls called his goodnights, Bray picked up the phone. Mr Leonard Ireland answered fourth ring and immediately started an apology for not having read some tract but promised he'd do it soon, soon.

"No, Mr Ireland," Bray put in when he could. "I'm from Gilson Mather, furniture makers." Into the pause, a little desperate, he said, "I made your table. Turned stump feet, as Mr Sheraton's."

The long pause gave Bray a gripe. Was this a terrible mistake?

Then, "You made my table?"

"Yes." Bray felt his palms go clammy. "I'm sorry to trouble you at home, Mr Ireland." This was the hard bit. Go round the houses, a retired publisher like Ireland would probably hang up, think he was a nutter.

"I'm calling to ask advice. You," he rushed on, "being a publisher."

Ireland barked a gravelly laugh. "Don't tell me, Mr Charleston. You've written a Jane Eyre lookalike and it's brilliant?"

Bray was taken aback.

"No, Mr Ireland. I wouldn't presume. You are the only person I've ever…" But Bray hadn't ever known the man. The furniture order had come through some Charing Cross publishing house. Special delivery, and that was that. He ended lamely, "I can pay an interview fee."

"A fee? Highly original, Mr Charleston! Tell you what. Eightish, I go for a pint. You're in Spitalfields?"

They arranged to meet.

The White Hart in Drury Lane was crowded. Bray was greeted by the whiskered portly man standing among the mob by the saloon bar door.

"This is the pub where Ben Jonson and his mates met up when Shakespeare died," Mr Ireland said without preamble. "They sat over there. One actor said that Shakespeare never crossed out a single line. And Ben

Jonson cracked: *I wish he'd crossed out a thousand!*" Ireland laughed. "Rivals, see?"

"Squire Aubrey," Bray guessed. The retired publisher somehow got Bray a pint of cider. It would have taken Bray all evening to get served.

"They know me, Mr Charleston." Len Ireland lit a cigarette and smiled. "I still have the furniture you made. Sheraton. My retirement prezzie. I'd longed for a table like that for years. Reproduction; well, you made it, so you know! Other firms said it was too difficult to make by hand, but Gilson Mather said easy-peasy because they had a genius joiner of the old school."

Bray was embarrassed. "Mr Sheraton didn't actually do much himself. Left it to his workmen."

"It's still dazzling. Conical tables in fashion now, are they?"

"No. Yours is the only one I've ever done, except some restoration work for the Hesketh family in the north."

"You have the gift." Ireland eyed Bray through his spectacles. "What's this about? Checking I'm dusting it properly?"

They had to raise their voices to be heard. Bray had worked out a story on the bus. "What is a bestseller?"

"That serious? Your hour begins now, then." The old publisher had a double whisky, kept giving nods of recognition to bar regulars. "Know that actor, Michael Caine? *Zulu, Alfie*? He wrote a book. Claimed he could have made it an instant bestseller by buying a few thousand copies. Time it right, his volume would soar."

"Is it true?"

"That sales shoot you up the charts? Sure. It's fiddled all the time. Not by mates buying in selected West End bookshops. Adverts can do it, or talk-show hostesses giving you a plug. Or by sleeping around. A publishing joke, Mr Charleston, is *Lie down, you'll soon be on your feet!*" The publisher laughed.

"Who decides?"

"Trade groups listed in the reference library. I only know one writer who doesn't lose sleep the night before the *Bookseller* is published."

"What are they for?" Bray asked.

"The charts?" Ireland chuckled. "You're innocent, Mr Charleston! For track records to prove how good publishers are! Art craves attention, do anything to get mentioned by some DJ. They don't see the horrible truth."

"Which is?"

"They're wrong. Publicists, film stars, everybody assumes that attention *is* fame. Wrong! Fame is Keats, Byron, Gainsborough. Attention is a column-inch of innuendo between haemorrhoid cream adverts."

"Can it be faked?"

Ireland weighed his visitor.

"Define your question, Mr Charleston. Do you want to fake book sales? Simple! Invent a publishing category. Like, claim your book on Ancient Babylonian farming achieved most sales *in its class*! You can even invent your own literary prize! Bribery's good; I bribed judges for twenty years."

"How many?"

"Copies? As few as one thousand in a specialist category. Fifty thousand for some popular novel."

It was difficult to ask, in view of what he'd learned. "What if you don't want publicity, Mr Ireland?"

A small crowd pushed in, Ireland greeting them with the skilled repartee of the bar fly. He returned to Bray, his expression quizzical.

"You're an odd bugger – sorry. More difficult. It'd need complete deception." Bray nodded. This was more like it. "Is there a real book, or not?" Ireland kept his voice down.

"No. And maybe never."

"Yet it's got to top sales charts?"

"At least become a household name, in the United States."

Ireland whistled his admiration.

"Well, Mr Charleston, I'm not saying it's never been done. Remember the forger Thomas Walker? He nearly brought down the government, claimed Prime Minister MacDonald was a Soviet spy, 1934 I think it was. The Welsh revivalist movement came about by faked publications. Chatterton is famous, of course – it took a genius like Dr Johnson to spot him. I'm not *advising* you, but you need a text to base a falsehood on. Like the Hitler Diaries. Remember them?" He eyed Bray. "Goes to prove that you can exalt any trash."

"Thank you, Mr Ireland."

"Is that it? Look," the publisher said, for the first time showing hesitancy. "Don't let me pry, but give me a ring if you get stuck, eh?"

"I don't want to bother you unduly."

"Then bother me duly, Mr Charleston." Smiling, Len Ireland reached to shake hands. "Will I see you on TV late-nighters?"

"I hope to go unnoticed."

"Really?" Ireland was intrigued. "How soon?"

"That's the next thing I need to find out."

Bray felt the publisher's gaze all the way to the pub door. He didn't care. He was getting there, getting there.

That same night, he noticed the manuscript woman, even though it was a much later train. They almost exchanged a greeting. That was once, now no longer. Not now. Bray turned away. Talk had to be useful, which meant for only one purpose. At Kelvedon he saw her eyes on the book he was reading, *Publishing for Beginners*. He simply read on, and she returned to her endless typescript.

Chapter Fourteen

Bray had built the shed twenty years before.

When Davey had come along it became a resort and Bray installed a dust extractor. Davey's job was to switch it on. Davey had a toy toolkit of his own, graduating to a genuine miniature pin hammer, screwdriver and rulers. One of Bray's proudest moments was hearing Davey repeat, "Block plane," seeing the lad hand it up. Such brilliance!

The guiding incident was just before Davey's bedtime one evening.

Reminiscence was all very well, unless it served a cunning purpose. It could easily become a placebo of the kind grievance-hunters wanted. Bray once heard an elderly woman tell how her family – her accent was Middle European – had been dispossessed of art treasures by "enemy forces" during World War Two. She had given up her campaign to recover the wealth by letters to the United Nations. Her account shocked Bray.

What was the balance between repossession, and the temptation to hark back? Had she got it right, and he, Bray determined to hunt alone for his stolen grandson, utterly wrong?

A lone hunt could be the road to lunacy.

"Think, Bray," he said aloud in the shed. They had been his own father's constant words.

"Against the hunt," he said aloud to Buster, sprawling by the shed door where he could keep an eye on Bray. "America is huge; just look at the map, Buzz."

The United States of America was vast. He'd never been there. Time was against him. The longer Davey was gone, the more he would blend in. Bray had never seen a theme park, didn't even know what one was. His image was Blackpool funfairs and plastic cartoon monsters gambolling among fairy castles. And he didn't know where Davey was.

Ignore that strange certitude in the candle hours when he lay awake and suddenly felt that Davey was still out there.

Had he enough money for a private eye? And how to choose a good one? What if he paid someone who simply pretended and did nothing?

Another factor: fifty-three was ageing. He knew nothing. Were kidnapped children spirited abroad, or kept brainwashed in that country?

He didn't know.

There seemed to be as many police forces and security systems as there were policemen. A book from the local library, *Policing In USA*, he finished none the wiser.

A couple in the next avenue had lost a baby soon after its birth from illness. They blamed themselves. For a year they had gone to mediums, done table rapping, visited spiritualists. Neighbours funded trips to famed psychics. Nothing came of it. Maybe it was the same as Shirley was currently experiencing, unorthodox psychotherapy of folk origin? Bray didn't know.

"We've factors against us, Buster," he told the retriever. It gazed back.

For once, he lit his storm lantern. It was a small oil thing and had been Davey's passion. (Correction: *is* Davey's passion.) Angry, Bray reminded himself of those tenses. Present tense. He would find Davey. He would take those evil opponents on and win.

"What's in my favour, Buzz?"

List them: Sound of mind, not barmy. And fifty-three wasn't bad. Not as fit as he ought to be, so he must exercise from now on. Stay fit and healthy.

Other plus factors?

He was solvent. Emma had married her builder bloke, fine. Bray had investments. Geoff and Shirley needed no financial help now. Bray had made out a will in his family's favour. When his bank account grew and incurred the bank's attention, Bray simply told them to buy him some shares. The certificates went into a drawer. Dividends went into the bank account. That was it.

A couple of times he bought unit trusts, their names forgotten. He didn't have a motor. He'd bought Geoff a saloon car when Davey was born, to enable Shirley to get about. He was surprised he'd afforded it so easily. He didn't go out much, preferring to read and watch telly and take care of fair-haired Davey. In sum: Healthy, solvent, mentally fairly capable.

Skill? Joiner. This made him wince. It wasn't much, though something flickered in his mind for an instant. Hope maybe? Except *maybe* also meant *maybe not*. He thought, let it mean whatever it bloody well wanted, for KV was there behind the shed's end panel.

Bray opened the wooden leaves and stared in the lantern light at the images before him.

The words were Davey's invention. He laughed at many new words as they registered. Purple was the colour of his KV landscape. Purple was Davey's first hue. The land was peopled with armies that did nothing.

Maybe they were derived from games all children played. Who knew what they talked about in playgrounds?

He and Davey had painted the landscape on the shed's end wall, using cheap acrylics from the corner shop. Soon after, Davey began calling the land KV.

The name was an enigma. Bray searched for it, even tackling the British Library at Kings Cross. The two words really did come from Davey.

"Hats!" Davey exclaimed, four years of age.

The people of KV thereafter wore hats, all various shapes. Some were spherical, some tall and rectangular, others conical and extravagantly brimmed. Shapes defined status. Of course Davey's was the most important, for he too lived in the mythical land.

Bray carved Davey's own figure out of American maple for his fifth birthday, a four-inch shape with a tall rectangular hat surmounting an enormous brim. Davey's hat alone was purple. On the rectangle was Davey's unique inverted pyramid, ball, crown. Bray had laughed at his grandson's seriousness as the carving took shape. There was an immensely complex hierarchy of folk in Davey's imaginary land. Bray never quite got the hang of them. When Bray carved the miniatures Davey always watched each statue take shape, swinging his legs as his grandfather worked life into the wood.

"Too fat, Grampa," he'd say, or simply a condemnatory, "Wrong!"

Bray would comply. Rejects were stored in a box on a shelf. And Bray would start again, asking Davey what, how, about a figurine.

Davey knew with amazing consistency.

Bray started keeping notes of each character and pencilling in the carving techniques Davey liked. He had a hard-backed book for the data, kept on an under-shelf because Geoff objected. Davey was spending too much time whittling wood, and not enough thinking of school.

"What the hell's it for, Dad?" Geoff asked. "Davey's got schoolwork."

Bray felt helpless. "What can I do, Geoff? If Davey wants a carving done am I to say no?"

"Yes!" Shirley and Geoff had said together.

Davey must not be distracted. Play was all very well, but school meant ambition. The other was only minor value.

"You're too indulgent, Dad," Geoff decided.

"We must set a limit, Bray," Shirley insisted.

Then Davey reached six, when learning was assessed against a curriculum. But by then Davey had his own tool kit and could even carve. Nobody was prouder than Bray.

And the game began. KV had its own coins, the K, and the smaller V. One huge coin belonged only to Davey. Bray didn't say the words, for they were Davey's own.

The game, though, was real. Davey and Bray played it indoors while Geoff watched the financial news. It was always KV against Prussia. It was the only game on earth where two opposing players were on the same side against a mythical but determined opponent, and was played with a single balloon.

Bray and Davey defeated Prussia every night. Always a near thing, especially when Davey tried to score double or the fire suffered a faint back draught and the balloon strayed. Always the same victorious score, twenty-nineteen.

Counting the wooden figures on their narrow ledges in the painted landscape, Bray's vision blurred. He blotted his eyes with a sleeve, and reached the correct total of 119. Another seven carvings stood on the window ledge, ready to take their places when finished.

He studied every one. Acrylic paints were safe, no toxicity, needing only water and easily painted over should Davey change his mind. The only problem had been the tramway signalman – Davey changed it back to blue stripes on yellow the following day.

Thirty wooden figures had names.

Bray heard Geoff approach, and quickly closed the panel. He was extinguishing the lantern when Geoff opened the door. Buster rose and wagged.

"Dad?" Geoff switched on the electric light and stepped inside. "Don't you think you spend enough time in this old place?"

Geoff had been crying. Some psychiatrist had doubtless been at him.

"Maybe you're right, son," Bray said.

"The doctors think maybe Shirley's going schizoid, Dad. Things can tip people over."

They walked towards Geoff's house, the retriever scouting ahead.

"You never used to lock it up, Dad. Why now?"

"Not sure, son. Maybe a weird compensation." It was all Bray could think of to say. They said goodnight, as if they had miles to travel.

That night Bray sat up until three making sketches of the KV landscape. He checked his detailed drawings of the wooden figures, added notes as forgotten features came back.

Draw five a night, with luck he'd have them all done in

twenty-four days, say four weeks give or take. Then he could colour them, making sure each shade and hue was correct. He had to get on; urgency drove him. Unless Geoff lodged at the hospital with Shirley and left Bray free? He'd be quicker then. He'd get more paints and use better quality paper.

What, two months to transfer all Davey's figures to paper? He decided to include the seven half-completed carvings. More difficult, but the harder the task the better. Aching muscles told an athlete he was training to the limit.

No word from Kylee.

Chapter Fifteen

The wharf was crowded. The greensward was now a picnic area beside the estuary. A new funfair was thronged with children. Distantly, the church's ancient spire was now an extraordinary yellow. Paddling pools made him wince. He tried not to hear their squeals and excited shouts as he parked.

He bought a newspaper, discarded three or four sections into a waste bin, and sat in the café with a complicated sandwich and tea. Two families, three boatmen, and a uniformed attendant from the parish car park were having a meal among impatient children, their parents trying to make them eat. Bray read an article about computer hackers.

Two young Americans had seemingly hacked into the USA Pentagon computers. They had also, the report stated grimly, offended Harvard. The damage was costly. A defending lawyer claimed it was all in fun, paradoxically conferring benefit on the American military by exposing weaknesses, no hard feelings. What *was* hacking?

Bray thought of Kylee. Pornography chains were well publicised these days, computers a route for beasts who preyed on the young. Further than this Bray couldn't force himself to think. It might prove a blank, even after a life-long search. But what other option was there?

"Mr Charleston?"

The man seemed so unlikely. Ganglingly tall, there could never be another printer like him, with a shock of untidy hair, crumpled jacket and baggy trousers. Bray stumbled to his feet and they shook hands.

"Mr Corkhill? Would you have something?"

"I'll get it."

Corkhill bought three cheese rolls and tea into which he spooned sugar. Bray watched the man down the scaldingly hot tea and engulf a thick roll. In normal times he would have felt admiration for the performance.

"I'm sorry to bring you out on a Sunday."

There too he had difficulty. How easy it must be, to be female. Women would be instantly into that overlapping chat of womankind. Men spoke in alternates, you speak and I listen, then here I come, and thus we speak turn and turn about, the only way a ponderous serial exchange.

"No harm done. I've had to take my daughter and her, erm, family to my sister's." The thin man smiled. "Glad to meet you. Never thought I'd have the honour. I'm only sad it's under these circumstances."

Honour? Bray waited as Corkhill swiftly finished his food. They talked of designs remembered in the woodcraft magazines. The printer shyly confessed that he was working on a toy carousel, with metal moving parts. Carving the roundabout's horses was difficult. A wooden hippopotamus had proved strangely easy. He asked about maple variants.

"Give Rock Maple a try, but not the British variety. You'll get it from Spitalfields."

The printer gave a wry laugh. "Mr Charleston, you're speaking to one who's all thumbs!"

"Choosing your wood is half the battle. American Rock Maple – they call it Sugar Maple over there, *Acer saccharum*. It's got a fawn tinge and is stiff, so your carving tool won't wander. It works lovely, the grain close, compact."

They were silent a moment, each with a difficulty. "I'll show you the result. You won't laugh?"

"Promise." Bray's moment had arrived. "I'd do it for you, in payment."

Corkhill watched children enter, choose a table noisily and bargain with the mother for the wrong foods. She overruled them with spirit.

"Payment?"

"I need a printer."

"I do most styles, jobs, typefaces. Come and see."

"I want something to *have been* printed, Mr Corkhill." Bray let a moment go by. "I want proof that a booklet, quite small, was published months since."

"And it wasn't?"

"Correct." A balloon had floated from an infant's hand and risen to the ceiling. Bray returned it to the staring child.

"How many copies?" Corkhill seemed to be holding out his hand for a handshake. Bray pondered, then realised he was being asked for the book.

"Every book has an ISBN, isn't that so?"

The printer was obviously wondering what he'd got himself into. "The International Standard Book Number."

"And a publication date?" Bray added helplessly, "Before the story begins?"

"Yes. Who has your volume?"

"Nobody." Bray cleared a space on the Formica table, dishes to one side, condiments to the other, as if about to demonstrate. "I need one copy urgently. I need an invoice from an established printer who supplied, in the fictitious past, a number of copies. How many," Bray quickly anticipated Corkhill, "I haven't a clue."

"Invoices," the printer said doubtfully. "I can print you your book anytime. My cousin Teddy's boy's recently joined me. He's a designer..." He petered out, drummed his fingers. "Your book's no problem."

"But invoices are?"

"Correct. We'd get in serious trouble defrauding Customs and Excise. They're Value-Added-Tax."

"They come to Gilson Mather." Bray was leaning forward now, fingers linked, intent.

"There's no way round them, Mr Charleston."

"If I pay you as the customer, could you then?"

"Yes. But the full job is just as easy. One copy would cost the earth. Ten thousand copies cost virtually the same as nine thousand and the cost per copy becomes negligible."

"Then I'll set up as a printer." Bray drew out a handwritten page. "Supposing I'm a printer. Ten months back, suppose I pretend I rented the use of your workshop, say three evenings a week, weekends, I don't know. Here's my supposition in writing. If I pay you, *then* could you give me an invoice?"

"Ye-e-es. I don't see why not."

"How much would it be?"

"Will you really want my printshop, Mr Charleston?"

Bray looked at the other with astonishment. "Good heavens, no! I haven't the faintest idea how to print anything."

Corkhill passed a hand across his brow.

"Then why do you...?" He paused, gauging Bray. "Simply to prove this booklet *was* printed?"

"That's right." Bray wasn't sure he'd won the point. "It would convey the belief," he said gently, "which is all I have. I want to make it a possible."

"Am I to know the purpose, Mr Charleston?"

"The less you know the better. Every tax will be paid."

"Then why do you need an actual book?"

Bray couldn't blame the man. Authorities would come down hard if he transgressed.

"To prove there was an actual printing."

When there wasn't anything of the kind. Bray saw the conclusion reach Corkhill's eyes.

"And my invoices would prove what, exactly?"

"That in the past I rented your place and printed a book."

Corkhill nodded. He'd got it. Bray essayed a smile. It didn't work, but showed willing. "I'll quite understand if you say no."

The printer frowned. Bray's heart sank. "Would it help your, er, plan?"

"It is essential."

"Okay, Mr Charleston," Corkhill said unexpectedly with false gravity. "But if you mix my Bembo and Sans Serif fonts the deal's off. Agreed?"

Bray didn't know what those were. It seemed some quip. He said fine.

"Now," Corkhill said, businesslike. "Shall we walk, and work out details?"

"That would be..." Not fine or nice. He concluded, "Yes."

They strolled to the wharf where fishing boats were

readying for sea. They stood watching first one then another cast off.

"As soon as you give me an idea of your size, colour, format, Mr Charleston, I'll get the rent invoices off to you."

Bray's success unnerved him. He felt scared. "Send them as soon as you like, please."

"It's not a fake of a book written by someone else?"

"Of course not!"

"Sorry." Corkhill smiled. "Since you're now a master printer, you'd better drop in. At least learn where to find the light switches!"

"I suppose so." Bray could see he might fall down on details. "I'm very grateful. I'll see you don't lose by it, Mr Corkhill."

"Call me George," the printer said. "Seeing we're partners in – what's the word, Mr Charleston?"

"Crime," Bray said. Easiest word so far.

Chapter Sixteen

He woke about three and went downstairs. Television had cricket from Sri Lanka against the South Africans on the only channel he felt safe with. It avoided news. Buster gave him a bleary look and resumed snoring. The retriever now slept in Bray's small hallway in his flock pit.

Kylee's cell phone number had not replied, the several times he'd rung. Nothing.

His Internet paperback was uncommonly difficult. The previous evening, while Geoff shuttled between hospital and home, Bray had plodded through its pages of advice. Some aspects proved alarming. One such was IRC, the Internet Relay Chat, which seemed to be the equivalent of radio talk shows. Anybody with a computer seemed able to join in, though what on earth had Finland been thinking of, starting such a thing in 1988? Very worrying, for the "chat" was live.

His nerve began to fail, as the living room curtains showed the pallor of coming day. Live chat on a computer? When you don't even know anyone? He read on. Type your opinion, and your words appeared that instant on computers all round the world.

This logging business had him flummoxed.

He hadn't understood Kylee's testy explanation. How did you know that you *had* sent your message? Could the computer say, *Hey, hang on, you've sent it to the wrong country, so rub out and start again.* Kylee hadn't shown him that, in her one angry lesson that day.

There were other frighteners: computers could hand over control of your own computer to strangers. He felt sickened. Like your private belongings ransacked by a burglar. Sick.

Tiring, he found himself thinking of Kylee. Very improper, the young these days. He almost smiled. How often did older generations think that? He must watch himself. The poor girl had her own difficulties. It wasn't her fault, dyslexic, partly autistic. Nor was it her poor father's. Divorced, a problem child, trying to hold on. The thoughts hurt.

Distantly, he heard Geoff's toilet flush. Morning had broken. Bray switched off the television to start the day. Important steps had to be taken. Work at Gilson Mather had to be fitted in somehow.

The morning flew. Bray watched the clock.

"Some days are like this, Suzanne," he warned the new assistant cabinet maker. "No problems, then pandemonium."

"The pillars in your drawings look too thin in the middle."

Suzanne – to Bray a lady joiner still seemed a novelty – was nearing thirty. Buxom and energetic, she started new jobs with briskness, then lost heart. Bray corrected the angle of her mahogany. She should have been inducted more gradually. As it was, complete with glittering diploma, she had serious gaps in her knowledge. Bonny, with blind spots.

She was taking over a bureau bookcase from Old Steve, the seniormost craftsman, now hospitalised for something undiagnosed but prolonged. "The entasis is all too often exaggerated."

Suzanne had made drawings of two matching pillars. The entasis, that slight but planned convexity of columns, was meant to correct the apparent thinning that the human eye was tricked into discovering in cylindrical forms. Ancient Greeks, of course.

"Mine looks right," she argued. "We can talk it through at lunchtime."

"Have to go and see somebody."

"News?" she asked.

He said firmly, "I've asked to down the bureau bookcase from a double dome for simplicity. Mr Winsarls says no, but he agrees the candle slides would be superfluous."

"I can do it," she said, instantly heated.

"I'm sure," Bray said kindly. "But time is against us."

"Would it matter if it was a fortnight late? Your idea of candle slides was lovely."

He looked at her at such length that she reddened. His mind unclouded.

"Yes, it would matter. I want it out on time."

"Who's it for?" she asked truculently. "Somebody special?"

"Yes. A customer."

Leaving the firm exactly at twelve-thirty, Bray felt he had been unnecessarily brusque. She was only coming to terms with workshop practice. But time was all anyone had.

Fifteen minutes of quick walking and he reached the

medical unit. On the way he drew out enough money to pay in cash. He wanted no traceable records.

The reception nurse got him to fill in forms documenting past ailments. He gave an accommodation address in City Road as his residence. He had fixed it up the previous Thursday.

For almost an hour he was listened to, tapped, had radiographs, scans. His blood pressure was monitored. Embarrassments came and went. Doggedly he submitted to two different doctors. He breathed in, out, lay supine then prone. He had alarming tubes pressed into orifices he'd assumed that even doctors didn't bother with. He gave specimens of this and that. He struggled to read midget lettering. He had gusts of air blown on his open eyes. He gagged on tongue depressors, was finally released with urbane smiles of dismissal.

He felt worn out. He needed to be sure he was likely to survive long enough. How long is that? he demanded of himself, hurrying back. Well, was it two years? Longer than that, then he might have to start thinking of a substitute. Who would that be? No. His one chance of finding Davey rested on himself alone.

The afternoon went well, in joinery terms. Suzanne worked stoically, becoming pleased as the bureau bookcase measured up. Bray's idea was to give younger crafters a notion of scale against dimensions, as pieces of the carcass took their separate forms. He taught Suzanne the history of mahogany. She didn't believe him, about Dr Gibbons wanting a candle box made from oddly tough wood brought by his nautical brother from the New World as mere ballast in the 1720s. Her disbelief was arrogant, but she was young.

Failure of the young was anger's ally. He would pike on.

He continued to explain as they worked, telling her tales of the great joiner Wollaston, how the genius had actually had to fashion entirely new tools to work the strangely exotic new wood and make the candle box, thus changing all furniture in England, and thereby everywhere, for ever.

She replied tersely that she would bring in her notes from college. She meant she'd correct his wrong ideas.

Five-thirty the same day, Bray entered the investment company offices, carrying details of his assets, some pension plan he didn't understand, his savings certificates. He had a list of his shares.

The manager was a Mr Condrad, a dapper portly gent who looked as if he ought still to be in school. Bray would have placed him in some junior college, soon about to shave. The office wall was adorned with certificates.

They greeted each other with shielded warmth. Condrad said, "Coffee? Tea?"

"No, thank you," Bray answered, though he had hurried almost every pace of the way and was parched. "I don't want to keep you."

"I've read through the lists you sent. You are worth a considerable sum, Mr Charleston." Condrad gravelled out a laugh, his voice tubular and reverberant. "We usually remonstrate with clients for not putting enough by. You've been almost parsimonious."

"All I want to know is, what are these worth?" *And if there's enough to rent a printshop, then do a great deal more.* He didn't say it.

Condrad sat back, fingers steepled. "You want to sell up?"

"Certainly not. I have…family."

"Schooling?" Condrad cried eagerly. "Our comprehensive plan —"

"Please." Bray searched for a way. "I need to cope with some expenditure, how to cash things in."

"What precisely, Mr Charleston?"

"Several things. Buying the best computer available. Internet, all that. And to update it. Duration, two years minimum. Four years, possible."

Condrad scribbled. "Go on."

"Three trips to the USA, three weeks each time. Travel, hotel bills."

"Right." Condrad waited, pencil poised.

"And I might need a representative there within a year."

"How often? How long?"

"Perhaps five or six times." Bray thought. "Oh, and a new modern Scandinavian shed with windows."

That was it. Without secrecy the whole pack of cards, teetering on a single insubstantial hope, would collapse.

Condrad cast aside his pencil. Bray saw the investment man examine his folder, checking dates, figures. Eventually he straightened.

"Mr Charleston. Do you follow share movements?" Bray shook his head. "You don't follow the FTSE, Dow, Asian indexes?"

"No."

"How did you select my services? This interview has a price, though a small one." Condrad's smile was wry. "Even so, I'm among the costliest in the City."

"I heard your name on the train."

"Do you have earned income, Mr Charleston?"

"I make furniture, all my life in the trade." He pointed to his lists. "And get commission on auction sales of restored antiques."

"Mr Charleston, you're quite a wealthy man."

"Your conclusion?"

"If that expenditure is all, Mr Charleston, your assets can take it without even a blip." Condrad translated, "Ah, these USA visits…?"

Bray thought a moment. "If I wanted to begin some enterprise in the USA – employ a helper, start my own workshop – would I have enough?"

He passed Condrad a guess-list. Condrad examined the costs of tools and shipment in Bray's copperplate thick against the white.

"Easily, Mr Charleston. Ah, Lunnon Devizes could lend assistance. We have transatlantic companies engaged in various enterprises. I'd be pleased to help. And we lend at favourable rates."

Bray heard the man out. He asked a few questions, only to please Mr Condrad, then took his leave.

He had no doubt that Condrad had kept records of his assets. The amount the investment counsellor had written down ("Very approximate, Mr Charleston, of course!") startled Bray. He was well off.

Was he a bore? The thought worried him. He'd only ever gone to work, occasionally had a flutter on the Grand National and Derby. Was he dull? His main costs had been his mortgage, until he'd paid off the Church Street Building Society as, simply, a nuisance. Who'd have thought? Such graphs. Condrad had been proud of his charts.

"Your assets, Mr Charleston, can laugh at such expenditure," Condrad had said almost with regret. "Your residuals ought to be more active. Pity to let them rust like a derelict motor."

"I'll consider that, Mr Condrad."

"You have no phone number, I notice." More reprimand.

"I'll notify you if I decide to change my lifestyle."

He'd been really proud of that. It was Suzanne's term, her *lifestyle*.

Bray could laugh at the expenditure, which until an hour ago had loomed as such an obstacle. The best computer? Trips to the USA, assuming he knew where to go? The cost of hiring an agent? All now cheap at the price.

He caught the seven-thirty from Platform Nine, with time to buy a flaky roll, jam concealed in some new, possibly Continental, manner, and a dilute black coffee. Indiscriminately he bought four weighty computer magazines, vaguely hoping to learn without Kylee.

As the crowded train started to move, excitement stirred in him. Once the telephone company connected his shed to their magic machines circling up there in Outer Space, he could start, God knows how. He ate his curved bread thing, shedding greasy flakes onto his knees, and drank the coffee as soon as it was cool.

He'd had a troubling day. Enough money, presumedly dependable health. All he lacked now was a computer. Pity about autistic Kylee, but she would have been uncontrollable with her dyslexia and her queer-smelling cigarettes.

The train's wheels changed beat and roused him. Angrily he rebuked himself. Had he dozed? Self-indulgence was out. No room for it. He had no right to let Davey down like that.

The crowd was slow coming out of the booking hall. As he shuffled out with the rest somebody spoke.

"You took your fucking time!"

"I beg your...?"

Kylee swiped at him in irritation. "I been waiting here bleeding hours."

A passing woman tut-tutted in reproof. The girl glared.

"What you staring at? Stupid old cow!" She took Bray's arm. "We got your clack. Porky's got wheels."

Clack? Porky?

She shoved him through the press disgorging onto the station forecourt. A lout was sitting in a derelict truck, taxi drivers and station police arguing with him.

"My dad's here now," Kylee shouted. "Sort it out wiv him."

Bray found himself having to apologise on all sides, was bundled into the vehicle's cabin. Kylee shouted abuse, and they were off.

"You have what, Kylee?" Bray asked humbly. "I didn't quite catch…"

"Clack. You fucking deaf or what?"

"Comp – yooo – tah," the lout said, laughing, swinging the pick-up's steering wheel alarmingly. He looked about fifteen, spiky hair, studs in his nose, earlobes and what appeared to be a line of staples along his chin. He looked unbelievably frayed. "He's thick. You fucking pick 'em, Kyle."

"I see." Bray hadn't come across the term in the Internet handbook, because he had disgracefully fallen asleep on the train.

"It's clean," the lout said, doubling with laughter, interrupting himself to bawl obscenities at some saloon car.

"Tell Porky," Kylee said. The truck stopped. They looked at Bray. "Tell Porky where to."

"Directions? Ah, left, please."

"Jesus," Porky growled. "You fucking pick 'em, Kyle."

Shouting angrily at the traffic, the lad pulled out in front of an approaching bus. Bray thought, *three* successes now? He clung on as the vehicle swerved towards his village.

Chapter Seventeen

Geoff was home, his lights were on. Bray asked Porky to drive round the back.

"Here." Kylee did her glare. "You shamed of us?"

"Not at all." Bray was aching. The truck slewed every few yards, jarring his teeth. "I want it in my shed."

"Fucking shed?" Porky braked with vigour. "He's a fucking loon, Kyle."

They unloaded three boxes. Porky shinned over the garden wall and undid the bolts. Buster came playing hunting dog at them. Unbelievably he took to Kylee and Porky. The boxes occupied almost all the floor space.

"He's called Buster," Bray said. "Lives next door at my son's, really."

Porky looked around in the shed. "Where's your phone?"

"I haven't got one, I had rather hoped —"

"Fucking *rather hoped*?" Porky exploded. "Jesus fucking Christ!"

"I shall try to expedite —"

Porky was disgusted. "He fucking real or what?" He slammed out.

"I'm so sorry," Bray said, distressed. "I really have asked for a phone."

"Leave it to Porky." Kylee calmly inspected the interior. She picked up a wooden figure. "Where you get all these toys?"

"I made them." Bray tried to work out an apology for this odd girl and invented, "I thought maybe a hospital or a nursery."

Kylee said they were nice. "Whyn't you buy proper tools, with labels? Porky'll get you a new set, not nicked."

"I make my own," Bray said quickly. "But thank you."

"You make the titchies too? How?" She picked up a miniature wood plane and casually dropped it. Bray winced, replaced it with care. "Clever old sod."

"Not really. Best to have the right implement."

She gauged him. Bray could hear Porky returning across the grass. He seemed to be talking to himself. "Why you always saying sorry?"

"Am I?" he asked mildly, and measured his reply. "I'll watch myself."

"What's your name? What they call you."

"Bray."

"Got the money?" Porky entered the shed closing a cell phone.

"Of course." Bray felt satisfaction. He had quite sufficient. "Would you come inside? I'll brew up and write you a cheque."

Pleased, he led the way. They followed, Porky annoyed at everything.

"He fucking real, Kyle? I can't use paper."

"Give us money, eh? We're cheaper than anybody else, wack." The sum Kylee mentioned was less than half what the magazines had said. Bray asked if there was some mistake.

Kylee's glance warned him. "You'd okayed it, Bray, right?"

"Ah, right. I haven't that much cash on me, I'm afraid."

"You've a phone here," Porky accused.

"My son's, for business," Bray fibbed. "I've only the shed."

"They'll bring your phone. Don't unpack them boxes, right?"

"Very well," Bray said. "Shall I send the money in care of your father tomorrow, Kylee?"

Eyes rolled. "Porky'll collect it."

They left before Bray could finish making tea, but took two packets of biscuits, a loaf, three tins of beer and a battenburg. Porky was disappointed Bray had no cigarettes. Bray gave Kylee what money he carried, thanked them for their trouble, and asked Kylee if she could bring a receipt the following day. Both grinned. Buster came with Bray to wave them off. Bray heard Porky say, "Receipt? His fucking ta-very-much is doing my fucking head in."

"He's all right." Kylee waved back. "He's just thick."

He was finishing supper when Geoff rang from the psychiatric unit wanting to meet him there. Nothing desperate, but to come soon. He promised not to be long and took Buster to Hal Lumley's.

The psychiatrist, Bray suspected, deliberately dressed down as a concession. He took against Dr Torrance's practised manner. Were they ever off duty?

They listened to the vague predictions.

"I feel it would be better to move Shirley. Not far, just enough to show differences: location, staff."

Shirley, Bray thought. You use a child's first name,

talking down, assuming them imbecilic. Would he do the same to dyslexics like Kylee?

"How long for, Dr Torrance?" Geoff asked.

"Maybe only a month, maybe longer. A great deal depends on Shirley's response."

"Would it improve my wife's chances?"

"Of recovery? Very much so. I take it there hasn't been any…?"

"No, no news."

"We must be kept informed, Mr Charleston."

"I'll be in touch daily. Where will the new unit be?"

"Some twenty miles away. You know Colesden? It's quite a retreat, just enough to be interesting. May we move Shirley tomorrow?"

"I'll try to get off work to come with her."

"Charge Nurse will give you directions and names of contact staff. We have bungalows for visitors. One perk," Dr Torrance snuffled a chuckle, "the Health Service still provides!"

They said their thanks and went to wait for the senior registrar.

"Who's that girl, Dad?" Geoff suddenly asked. "Scruffy, looks off the street."

"She's a computer lass." Bray was put on the defensive. "Her father's Mr Walsingham from the technical college."

"She was hanging about the avenue for over an hour. She knocked, wanting to deliver something."

"It was by arrangement."

"Why didn't you say?"

"I forgot," Bray said lamely.

"How old is she?"

"She's fourteen."

"This is with her dad's approval?"

"Not quite." Bray shamefacedly explained how he had tried to enrol at the college. "She gave me an impromptu lesson."

"She came in a *truck*, Dad. In the avenue. And that youth looked a tearaway."

"They waited for me at the station." Might as well get it over with. "They've put the computer in the shed. It seems to need some special phone."

"Dad. This isn't anything to do with...with Davey?"

Bray looked his son straight in the eye and lied, "No." He had rehearsed this endlessly, muttered on the Tube, startling other passengers. "How on earth could it?"

"Work, is it?"

"Mr Winsarls is starting a survey," Bray invented recklessly. "I'm ashamed. Everybody uses them except me. I want to learn, before all the rare imported hardwoods are blotted up."

"Good idea, Dad."

They rose as the senior registrar approached, matter forgotten.

Chapter Eighteen

Next morning, the workshop was in uproar.

A wood shipment was in, which always threw Karen and Tracy. Karen's usual response was to hurry between craftsmen complaining that nobody had marked the timbers. With Karen, blame was always somewhere else. The quieter Tracy simply matched each pencilled guess to what she actually saw.

Bray approved of the mousier girl. Karen possibly had many excellent qualities elsewhere.

Mr Winsarls checked every cubic foot, and spent hours with monosyllabic wagon drivers signing receipts. Bray had to help. Hitherto, his role had been to joke about the number of timbershakes in each length while the hauliers bantered back that joiners couldn't tell hardwood from hardboard. No longer. They now cast sideward glances in Bray's direction, no jokes thrown. Karen had her usual tantrum, leaving Bray to accept the timber as roadsters backed and drivers shouted at the crane man.

Yet it proved the first stroke of luck. Bray was able to ask the exhausted Mr Winsarls if he could go for a break after two o'clock. The owner approved. Bray was soon in Pimlico, walking fast through crowded London heading for Victoria.

Meeting Mr Ireland in Drury Lane had given Bray the confidence to visit the publishing house.

The place was surprisingly austere. Bray had expected an enormous edifice with threatening mirrored windows. Instead he found a docile redbrick building, steps into a quiet hall with books laid out on small glass tables and bookshelves carrying unnecessarily gaudy displays.

Still, gaudy was a promise. Too late to back out now.

He gave his name to the receptionist, said his piece. "I'm an acquaintance of the young lady's father, by correspondence. I made an appointment." She gave him that eventual smile. Leonora Blaisdon would signal him up in a few minutes.

The paper was in his pocket. He had time to read it through several times before he was called. On his way to the fifth floor he encountered only women, all young and fetching. Were there no men in publishing?

"Pods," the lass who met him announced. "No separate offices, not like —"

She mentioned rival publishers, talking over her shoulder. Curved glass structures extended from floor to ceiling, looking for all the world like exterior lifts likely to plummet at any moment. Leonora entered one, flung herself behind a small desk and waved Bray to a chair.

"Ten minutes only, Mr Charleston." She signalled to others through the glass, waved at one, laughed, and swivelled to face him.

The place was crammed with books. Boxes piled against the glass partially obscured posters he vaguely recognised from Tube billboards.

"You know my father, I believe."

"Only by correspondence, I'm afraid. He lives in Lancaster."

"That's so." She gave him a winning smile. "Can't leave that crummy old barge he's forever building. You helped him with the doors."

Doors? Bray actually remembered a figurehead, but didn't argue.

"I hope I'm no trouble. I need to learn something about publishing."

"Don't tell me you've got a manuscript?"

Did all publishers live in terror of manuscripts? "Nothing like that, no." He shrugged as he'd rehearsed. His confidence grew. One lie is dicey, two lies uncertain. Tell three lies well, you're capable of anything. "I might have to do a display. International exhibition, you see, two years from now."

"Can I know who for?"

"I haven't been told yet. I'll tell you the minute I hear."

"Better not." She leant forward to confide, "Word spreads in publishing like a grass fire."

"I need an idea of, well, what a publisher of children's books actually does." He gestured with unfeigned helplessness. "This seems so modern."

She laughed. "We don't think so. We all hate these pods, like goldfish in bowls. They're why we do contracts in restaurants."

"What makes a bestseller?" he blurted.

"Sure you've not got a manuscript?" She overrode his denials. "Sales. Money coming in. Nothing else."

"Not quality?" He was honestly amazed. "Arthur Ransome —"

"Dark Ages, Mr Charleston. Sorry. Now, it's numbers. Finish."

Hesitantly he began to explain about cabinets required for his mythical display, but she was already into her world.

"Look. We sold forty thousand of a title. You know the new children's spooks? Came from USA, so popular. Fifty titles – can you imagine, fifty in one series?"

"How many's the least?" Where could he keep forty thousand books?

"Sales? Less than four thou. It's been down to fourteen hundred."

He suppressed his relief. That few he could manage.

"Do you control the price?"

She wrinkled her eyes and looked at him with mischief.

"Are you into a pricing contract, Mr Charleston?"

"Not really." He opted out, embarrassed. "Could you show me the different bits of the, er, house?"

"Glad to." She rose and marched out throwing words over her shoulder as Bray hurried after. "Pardon the shambles. This is editorial. We commission, contract in, contract out. Copy editing, subbing…"

He hoped the recorder in his jacket pocket was working well. One thing he was good at was mensuration, keeping records. Words surely couldn't be much different here. Like wood, like children?

Listening, he followed, realising now that his plan was becoming complex and might take months. Even years. He had costed two years out in his head walking through Pimlico.

"You all right, Mr Charleston?"

"Sorry," he told Leonora in the dispatch rooms. "It must be the dust." He blew his nose, gave a grin. "I wish I had words to say how grateful I am."

"Has it been of help?"

"Vital." He'd told somebody else that recently. "Vital."

She showed him out, walking him to the main entrance with its glass shelves and tables. He wished her father well. On the way back to Gilson Mather he paused to dial George Corkhill's number and say he'd take him up on his offer to visit.

That evening he bought a range of children's books from WH Smith's, ignoring a keen assistant's advice. He also bought a book about publishers and publishing, and a daunting catalogue. That is, it *might* have once seemed daunting. Once. From now on, there was only resolution.

As he boarded the train, he dropped three books. A woman helped him retrieve one that had escaped under a seat. It was the manuscript woman. She smiled and handed it over.

"You're going to be busy."

"Thanks." He sat, and during the journey made a list of the number of pictures in each of the books. By the time he reached his station, he had also made a count of the words. He was conscious of the woman giving him curious glances, but curiosity was her business, not his. He made certain he alighted without mishap.

At home, two phone men were waiting in a van outside his house. They installed a telephone line in his shed in minutes. He was almost breathless. They accepted a heavy tip, said to say hello to Porky and they'd do a split.

"You'll do a split," he repeated, driving the words in. Split what?

He made his evening meal, working out how to explain to Geoff his new influence with the telephone companies. He went for Buster, and found a curious peace walking the bouncy retriever across Avery Fields.

"No such thing as a hunch, Jim."

Jim Stazio was drowning his sorrows in Poppers, the cop refuge mostly kept for squad rankers, the grunts of the city's finest. Promotion sent you to Frankly Ranks two blocks down.

"Never had one, Sam."

His partner eyed him. "You called how many clinics? Dozen?"

"Eight. Seems like eighty." Jim hated tonic, but Vera in Crimstats swore it took pounds off. "Not a sniff. All legit. Wall to wall diplomas."

"The names Menzoy give?"

"Saw two. One's moved to New York. Called them, nothing. Agencies wanted money, more money. They all three got suspicion, called it off."

"No links?"

Jim snorted. "Losing my touch, Sam. One give me some contact at a kids' camp. I spoke to the local cops, still nothing."

Officially he was to retire the following Thursday. There would be the usual boozy talk, them good old days, then seeya-seeya out the door, headache for breakfast and nowhere to go.

"Done your fitness thing?"

"Yeah, Sam. The docs say don't become a dud spud, get a hobby."

"You still carrying out the bodies?"

Sam's crack made Jim smile. Retirement cops had a strange addiction to old cases and mementoes. The sick joke was that retiring cops got Christmas turkeys from photocopy firms, the folders they took home. Cops called it carrying out the bodies.

Jim owned up. "I've no illusions, Sam. I know I'll never

look at them. Another year, I'll say what the hell and throw them out with the garbage."

"You're still moving out of town?"

"Trailer city beyond Pleno. Not far."

"You come in some time," Sam said, the conversation wooden. Soon they'd be into promises to meet for a drink, talk over old days.

Jim cleared his throat. "Look, Sam. You staying here, right? Not still thinking of transfer to Tarpane?"

"Right here. What?"

"I might give you a call, coupla questions. Nothing much, just loose ends."

Sam was relieved. Retirement cops chased mirages. Past cases were the stuff of cop gossip. If that was all Jim wanted, Sam could chase shadows with the best of them. Christ, they'd been on an airport hassle beyond Alloa Flats an hour, they hadn't even got started, proving one mirage was good as the next.

"Glad if you do. What are partners for? I'll maybe take a ride out, see you're not laying too many old biddies out there giving yourself a heart."

They chuckled. Jim had two or three questions already lined up for Sam Tietze, but today was too early. Have to wait till he was really walking the streets and nothing to do. Make the cops work a little, no charge.

Chapter Nineteen

The next day Bray drew out the money Kylee and her friend Porky wanted. It felt bulky in his trouser pocket.

On the train, he read about computers. Like learning the names of unknowable football teams. Uncomprehending, he stared at names, names. What *were* they? Firms? Devices?

He would have to rely on Kylee, if she turned up again. Maybe she'd leave Bray to it. She'd said nothing about teaching him more of her slick expertise. He'd ask her about another instructor. The phone connection seemed so inadequate, just one simple white fixture. Could it really talk to entire continents?

One magazine had a wounding find: There seemed to be sections – what were they called, addresses, sites? – principally for missing children. It stopped his breath.

The evil people would brainwash a child to eliminate his former life. They would remake him, set out his new future like items in a playpen.

As Davey entered that new false existence, they *would be* his parents. All the assumptions families made from year to future year would be theirs to define. Those assumptions had been stolen from Geoff and Shirley.

Most horrid of all was one that almost made him cry aloud.

There was the Name. The children's Big Fun theme park. He read it with horror. Write for a catalogue, the magazine invited, listing computer sites providing music, films, book titles, CD Roms. He felt ill. As the train shot through Ilford, he disposed of the magazines into the waste bin.

"Pity," someone said. He looked up. The typescript woman was seated across the aisle. She explained, "We publish one of those."

"Those?" He felt stricken. What was she on about?

"Magazines."

"Oh." He invented quickly, "Wrong sort."

"Computers. I hate them. I find they rather take over."

"I suppose so," he said dully, and said no more.

With part of his lunch hour still to spare, he hurried to the accommodation address on Grays Inn Road and paid another two weeks in advance. He was only able to send off two advertisements before he had to get back.

The journals in which he advertised were quite proper. He had decided on women's magazines after what Leonora told him about publishing. Painstakingly Bray had rehearsed her words from his miniaturised recorder:

"Girls mostly buy books, not boys. We often say boys don't read, girls do. Between five or six to one."

And, some sentences further on, Leonora's information was: "Boys – and so men – go for exotics, creatures, systems, 'specials', we say. Think of boys as dinosaurs and gadgets, girls as ponies and winning through with the help of a slightly older boy groom." Leonora laughed at this point. "From six onwards, hearing about kissing, learning girlfriend rivalry, all that."

It seemed impossibly young to Bray. His advertisement read:

The KV Story!
Read the story of KV!
The
happiest
story
ever
told!
Suitable for ages 6 to 8.
Write to Dept KV
(Postal sales only. Not available through commercial
booksellers.)

With his heart in his mouth, he gave a price, arrived at by taking an average of nineteen children's books at Kings Cross Station. His claim, *the happiest*...he'd simply copied from the front of a magazine. It was an embarrassment. Still, booksellers must know what they were doing.

He gave the accommodation address. No author's name, of course. It was only later that he remembered he ought to have mentioned postage money, but by then it was too late. Nobody would actually, really, want to buy it after all. He was astonished that the magazine offices made him fill in a form. He paid in cash.

At home he went through Buster's greeting ritual. He was only now learning the benefit of a whole-hearted welcome from a creature who flung itself at you with unconditional love. Life should be as sane and uncomplicated.

Speedily, he walked Buster and on their return wiped its paws clean. Raining again, but Geoff's lean-to porch where Buster could loll was invaluable. Bray gave the dog its blanket, and settled down at his old typewriter. He had bought envelopes for sending replies to anyone who might answer his adverts, and laboriously typed out a formal letter of regret. It was exactly as he imagined real publishers wrote to disappointed customers:

Dear   ,

Thank you for your letter ordering a copy of "The KV Story". I sincerely regret this, but we have none left because they are all gone.

I am very sorry, and will try to remember to print a lot more next time. There are many other excellent stories printed by other publishers and I expect you will find some that are just as good.

Yours sincerely,

Mr Asquith V. Verdreeker

The name he made up. Doubtfully he read it over. Somehow the letter didn't quite ring true, though he thought it slick and commercial. Perhaps he ought to have asked Leonora? It was the best he could do. That last sentence was faulty. He rewrote it several times but it now kept coming out wooden. Would George Corkhill have a better idea? It was a headache.

His idea was simple, to run off a hundred photocopies, fill in the would-be customer's name, sign with a squiggle and post off. That would be the end of it. Of course, he had no book. As long as the myth held, he could at least get going.

Geoff had gone to see Shirley. His note said he would

stay overnight, and talk to the doctors in the morning.

At ten o'clock there was a knock at the back door. Buster did his hunting-dog game, delighted at the digression. Kylee and Porky stood there wanting payment. Bray invited them in. Porky absorbed the wad of money.

"You di'n' fucking fix it," he said with disgust.

"Fix it?" Bray asked blankly. "Fix what?"

"The fucking lurch, did you?"

Kylee took a swipe at the youth. "I told you he's thick. Why don't you listen?"

She pulled Bray and they went to the shed. "Don't take any notice. Porky'd be useless at them carvings, just like you're useless at other things."

Bray hesitated, returned to shut the back door and made it to the shed just as Porky was endeavouring to drag the door open, kicking and mouthing off. Bray produced the key.

The one light seemed thin and garish. Porky made to light a cigarette.

"I'm sorry. I don't have smoke in here. It's," Bray added seeing Kylee look, "a special place. Nothing against you nipping out for a cigarette." He explained solvents might take fire.

Porky cursed, ripped at the cardboard computer boxes, throwing the packing anywhere. Kylee started clearing the wooden carvings off the workbench but Bray quickly told her he would do that.

"One thing," he said, hoping to please. "I bought an aerial."

They halted, stared. He coloured, indicated a long box by the door.

"Aerial. It's the best they had, Morgan's in Stowmarket."

"Fucking idiot." Porky resumed. "Empty that over there."

Kylee was helpless laughing, "Nobody uses aerials, Bray, stupid old cunt."

The large cardboard cases were thrown out onto the grass. Bray felt unnerved. There seemed so many bits encased in plastic bags. Porky was impatient, shoving tools aside, hanging the cable over a fretsaw, kicking Bray's stool while he yanked the console along the surface.

"I brought the fucking tutorial," he told Kylee scornfully. "He'll need it. Don't worry, Thicko, it's free. Don't pay. The bastards have it all sewn up."

Porky sat and plugged the computer into Bray's four-ganger point. Kylee tapped Bray as Porky sat and took out a shiny disc.

"Remember I said you needed a firm to go online? This is it."

"I haven't paid —"

They guffawed. "You gets a disc, a tutorial, and a number. Free access. Some charge you. The phone people – right swine, them; Dad's in with the local boss – sell you hours a month, then extra time per hour. Fucking robbers."

"They get you either way," Porky growled. He had a terrible cough.

"What is the time for?" Bray asked.

"Don't!" Kylee held up a hand to stay a new Porky explosion. "Leave him be. I'll tell him. See, Bray," she said, "your computer uses the phone lines at so much a tick, okay? Like ringing people up. And a site – like your phone – has a rental. Got it?"

"You going to use it a lot?" Porky demanded, sour.

"When I know what I'm doing."

"You said you teached him." Porky swore crude oaths.

"He's senile." She was confident. "What's it to you anyhow?"

"You're on now," Porky told Bray. "The disc's inside that slot, okay? Who are you?"

"Mr Charleston," Bray said, mystified.

"Silly cunt. Who're you *going* to be?"

"The computer doesn't know you, see?" The lad hacked more coughs. "What it wants is letters so other computers know it."

Bray hadn't thought. Letters?

"Wasting our frigging time." Porky spoke as if Bray was absent. He sniggered. "Leave him and his fucking aerial."

"What do I do?" Bray asked Kylee.

"You're off. You've a fast computer. You can check a zillion chat groups, see? And your e-mail phones apps at local call rates."

He didn't understand, and didn't want to be left alone with the glowing screen.

"Thank you very much for coming. You've been very kind."

Kylee seemed to relent. "I might come tomorrow."

"Shouldn't you be in London? With your mother?"

"Sod her, and fuck London." She paused, spat. "Nobody has aerials, Owd Un."

"Look, please," he said desperately. They were a lifeline, literally. "I'm going to get a brand new shed. Will you come back and fix it up for me? I can pay."

They agreed, gave him a cell phone number to ring, and left through the garden gate. Bray said goodbye. The glowing screen had a series of small figures. He had been shown the mouse by Kylee at Mr Walsingham's college, but it worried him. He needed somebody while he tried his hand. But what if he ruined the entire thing?

He could almost hear Geoff's exasperation: *Buying an expensive machine from two scruffs, Dad? What on earth? And where's the receipt? There's VAT on electronics...*

He sat helplessly before the screen. Lots of blue around. Why blue?

One more thing: How on earth did it turn off? All very well for Kylee to say it was all okay and sail off, but what happened next? He found an on/off switch under the screen's face, but was it safe?

He jumped as the screen suddenly went blank, except for small multicoloured windows seemingly flying through space. Yet he hadn't touched it. Kylee had said nothing about this.

"Heavens, Buzz," he said feebly. "This might be a serious mistake."

The mouse lay on the workbench with its grey cord. Gingerly he moved it, and the screen instantly cleared, the top bar returning with its line of pictures. He felt worn out. A time trick, perhaps? What was the point of that? Kylee had said to leave things on, hadn't she, at that first encounter in the college? So be it.

He called Buster and went inside to go over the instructions. Doubtfully he looked out into the darkness as he brewed up. Buster was due his pint of milky tea.

The shed had a strangely luminescent glow out there between the hawthorns and the blackness of the fence, as if showing some wanderer the way home. He shook himself. Too fanciful.

He got a biscuit and read, read, read.

At eleven o'clock Geoff rang. No significant change. The senior consultant feared Shirley's condition might be a longer haul than at first thought. The dog turned in on his blanket at eleven, sooner if he could get away with it.

Bray went back to his reading, every so often checking that the shed was still glowing out there in the night.

Chapter Twenty

Usually Bray avoided train conversations.

He had suffered down his commuting years, from the woman who showed photographs of her three Charles the Second spaniels that she hoped to "get into films", to the dour man who preached ceaselessly of ancient steam trains. The only way was to hang back and avoid the yackers.

Now, though; times were new.

Computer buffs sat and talked in a cluster, having boarded at Manningtree. They spoke in tongues. Bray had occasionally been caught out, when the train was reduced to four coaches and everybody crammed in willy nilly. Now, though, he made himself sit opposite the grumpiest, youngest computer buff. Uncharacteristically, Bray started to read a newspaper, breathless from apprehension at what he was going to do. Already he had baffled the girl on the newspaper kiosk: "A paper, please."

"Yes sir. Which?"

"Any, thank you."

This was Bray's difficulty. For years he had insulated himself. Emma's departure had made him even more withdrawn. His quest required a fit man prepared to launch out. Establish contact, speak to strangers if that was necessary. It would take time, but he hadn't much.

He went for it, lowering his paper.

"Morning," he said to Grump.

"Morning!" the youngish bloke said, surprised at this novelty.

From the corner of his eye, Bray saw the surprised look on the manuscript woman's face. She knew he was never inclined to speak.

As the whistle sounded and the train pulled out, Grump began a monologue to his friend about pricing. He sat, arms folded. His companion wore a grey suit bulging with gadgets that occasionally bleeped and needed attention.

Bray had worked it out. Nearing London, he could time his intervention just right. Restrict their explanations to twenty minutes, he might follow the sense. Any longer, and he'd be bewildered. He struck as the train rushed through Seven Kings, starting by giving them a rueful smile. They paused.

"How on earth do you keep track?" They glanced at each other, ready to take umbrage. "Computers, isn't it? I need one, but I've given up. Can't understand them."

"Given up?" Grump was aghast. "You *can't*!"

"He's read the wrong things," Calculator said comfortably. "What've you tried?"

"Oh, everything." Bray named the paperback. "I'm even more confused." The manuscript woman was frankly listening, though still pretending to edit her typescript.

"On the net, are you?" Grump demanded. Bray decided he liked the other man better, for all his fearsome electrics.

"I don't know what that means," Bray said ruefully. "I went to Ogden's to buy a computer, Saturday. Came home with a headache."

"Why go there?" they said as one. "You need an independent."

"Independent what?" Bray asked innocently, and they were off.

Some of their eagerness was familiar, from his reading and Kylee's grouchy utterances. Try out even the slickest search "engines", you'd only a 3-1 chance of hitting the right page out of the Web's available billions. They went into asides comparing firms he'd never heard of. Bray asked which they used, how they paid.

Small companies struggled, he learned. If you wanted to become noticed – gloomy news, this, Grump warned – you were charged increasing prices. You had to do a deal with some search engine. It's like, Grump added, sounding really rather pleased about the whole depressing thing, "wanting your postcard noticed in some shop window. You're on a loser."

Bray shook his head and explained he was only a joiner. "I don't want anything commercial, just learn."

By judicious questioning, planned a hundred times, Bray guided their expertise.

"There was a frightening article last week," he explained, to their indignation. He'd memorised four instances in the public library. *"Pupils In Peril On Internet,* teachers going berserk. What if some child —?"

"That's balderdash."

They enlarged on this. Yes, sure, everything from racist propaganda to pornography abounded, but was that the net's fault? Computers were education. The Association of Teachers and Lecturers were barmy sods, calling for Government to act against obscene material. Those articles were loony tunes, restrict something that can't possibly be censored? Bray forced a smile.

"Common sense," Calculator told him. "Those sixth formers reported that Sheffield paedophile ring, didn't they?"

"The nanny state," Grump put in. "Computer programmes block unsuitables anyway."

"They're crap," Calculator countered morosely. "Children write essays on slavery, the Internet innocently goes stat into bondage and perv. Get the point?"

"Government wants every pupil to have their own e-mail." Grump's sour expression relaxed at the thought. "It's good! Children can e-mail world experts. Has to come."

"This 'firewall' concept," Calculator finished, "filters out wrong stuff."

"You can't censor anybody any more."

As the train rattled by Stratford they digressed about Internet access while Bray tried to get them back to his elementary level.

They gave him the summary he needed: Computer expansion was unstoppable. They said, music to Bray's ears, everybody can reach everywhere.

Still talking at Liverpool Street, they were disappointed when he had no time for coffee at Ponti's. He sat alone among crowds in Burger Thing. He felt drained.

They hadn't offered their names, but their enthusiasm was profound and rather endearing. They had served his purpose, and could now be discarded. He didn't want them waiting for him on the platform each morning eager to chat. Nothing malicious; they simply possessed a conviction that the world Out There only needed computers, to move forward singing and joyous.

Bray's plan was the only way.

"May I?" The manuscript woman with a tray holding a

cup and sandwich. "Sorry. It's so crowded."

"Please." He put his drawing away but too slowly and she noticed.

"Good luck with it." And explained. "Your book. Sorry again. Couldn't help noticing. Front cover?"

He felt sheepish. "Not mine," he added, then realised she must have seen him adding to an outline in pencil. "It's, er, my sister's. She's not well. I'm trying to help. Publishing seems hard."

She sighed. "Don't I know it. Do wish her luck. Has she published before? I'm an editor. Cannon Endriss, near St John's Square. Probably not for long, the way things are going."

"No. It's her first try." There seemed nothing else to say. He rose, his coffee untouched. "Didn't realise the time. Excuse me, please."

She said unexpectedly, "Tell her not to be upset if it gets turned down. Keep going."

"Thank you." He stood, hesitant, wanting to ask, then left, knowing he'd missed an opportunity.

The Euston walk-in medical unit was crowded when Bray arrived. A doctor was ready to see him within a few minutes. It was satisfactory.

"Mr Charleston, you are a reasonably fit man for your age. Fifties is nothing."

The doctor perused the file, where Bray glimpsed his long form.

"We found no hint of illness, Mr Charleston."

"Thank you. Do I need to come back?"

"Not unless you want. This clinic isn't National Health, hence the fee." The doctor sounded on the defensive. "You can have free follow-up examinations with your own G.P."

"I particularly didn't want to go there."

"Fine. Just remember the four defences for the ageing man. Smoking, you say you don't."

"Gave a pipe up twenty years ago."

"Then shun secondary smoking risks – that means smoky places. Two: fitness. You may have heard of the body mass ratio?" Before Bray could reply he went on, "Your weight in kilogrammes. Your height in metres. Remember the formula W divided by H^2. It gives your body/mass value, called Quertelet's Index."

Bray didn't say he'd already looked that up. Square the height, divide the weight by it, and pray the result is 25 or just a bit less.

"Your index is ten pounds too heavy. Don't take dietary supplements, and cut down saturated fat. I'm sure you know the drill. Obesity starts at an Index of 30 plus."

The doctor frowned. "Circumference at waist and hips. Your ratio is 1.0 exactly. Get it down to below 0.95. We're now pretty sure that men who carry larger bellies proportionate to their hips have an increased risk of heart disease. Don't go frantic, just be sensible."

Exercise was the next thing.

"Walk an hour each day. Work up a mild sweat – mow the grass, gardening, whatever – twenty minutes every other day. The fourth is, no stress."

Bray thanked him, took the sheaf of pamphlets, paid and left.

He was satisfied. Money and health enough to be going on with, and a computer that could reach across oceans, God knows how. Was it enough?

That night, alone in the house after more sad news about Shirley, he deliberately watched a travel programme about America. He had bought three videos on travel in the USA. He and Buster did a night walk, quicker for better exercise, to Buster's indignation. Then it was midnight.

He watched the videos over and over. At four o'clock in the morning he boxed them up and threw them into the dustbin.

Ready, steady, go.

Chapter Twenty-One

The party was over. His desk covered with shaving foam, fake whiskers adorning his locker. His place at Poppers was marked by a polystyrene headstone with hilarious inscriptions he'd seen a dozen times in similar farewell laugh-ups. He had one last session.

She was in when he arrived. "Stairs get to you, Officer Stazio?"

"Always did, ma'am."

"Your medical went well, right?"

"Olympics next time round."

She placed her chin on her linked hands. Young, too young, active in her work, eager to issue data, get the perps. Once too keen, now after six years she was right-on, work any late hour for results. Marva wasn't pretty, had a stable home life, a kid in junior school. The boys made jokes about her thick legs. She knew all about them, said nothing, all the same refused to wear thick trousers.

"Sam says you're taking stacks, huh?"

"Habit of a lifetime," Jim said, giving her a laugh. She knew his lateness with reports.

"You called on some local names lately, Officer Stazio."

He was always Officer Stazio to her, Sam Tietze was simply Sam. Why *was* that? Too late now.

"Things on my mind." He felt sheepish. "Retirement. Never thought it'd come."

"Here in Data we're used to retirees doing a little end stitching."

"Any clinic come up more times than the rest?"

"Mentions? Nah. The ones who come up most often get investigated fastest, mostest. It hits the fan."

"What about the ones who come up least?"

She looked her surprise, nodding slowly.

"It's a great thought. I did that – both ends of the statistical distribution – last year. Somebody up-state in Walmo County dug into it, came up nada. Want me to go again?"

"Not if it was no use before."

They spoke casually after that, Jim taking his leave and making sure he escaped more goodbyes. He would call in Poppers after meeting with the Union reps, loose ends.

He'd seen the trailer park home he was doomed to inhabit for the rest of his life. River not far away, walking distance to golf, good bars, nice smiley folk, not too many dogs dirtying the universe out there.

And one shelf reserved for past papers, old files. Tomorrow, he'd move out and start the rest of his life. Retirement.

His cup had gone cold.

The shed's new-wood scent was an aroma. Reluctantly he admired the beams, the window structure. Good modern job, and heartlessly efficient. He too would be heartless. This place would be the instrument of his search leading to Davey.

No, he thought, nervously waiting as the screen began to glow, no, wrong word. Not *search*. That was a word applied to, say, discovering where young Maitland had left Bray's old wooden folding rule. Quite beyond Bray's comprehension, for a craftsman's implements were his special creativity. *Seek*, then? You sought out something "lost, stolen or strayed" in the nursery rhyme's words, was it A.A. Milne? No. Altogether too innocent.

Hunt?

Hunt, you were a hunter. Hunt, you kept on until you dropped. A hunter *never* stopped.

He stared at the screen's logos and icons, for a moment baffled until he remembered Kylee's cryptic insolence: "This gadget's a fucking moron. Can't do a frigging thing unless you tell it. If it doesn't do right, then you've tellt it wrong."

Gingerly he moved the mouse, touched the screen's arrow to the logo and saw the screen change. He was hunting.

There was a small screen clock, bottom left, that for some reason told how long he'd been going. Why? Numbers also racked up, seeming to know what they were doing so he ignored them. Several times he had to cancel everything and restart. Foolishly he found himself muttering apologies to the damned thing, the way he did to wood. He knew workshop youngsters laughed at him. They just didn't understand. Wood was a living creature's heart. It wasn't called heartwood for nothing.

He found the rectangular space and diffidently typed in the term he'd never been able to think. He found difficulty placing the arrow – couldn't they have made it bigger? His confidence increasing, he made it get there and the screen rolled.

In an hour he made, for him, stunning progress. It was exactly as Kylee told him, with her usual scorn: "Five minutes on your own, you'll see computers are right fucking idiots, okay?"

Bray was amazed when he made the printer, with its peridot light, start shoving out pages of data, the machine chuntering to itself before disgorging the sheets. He worried at first but guessed that something was merely queueing up. Kylee's other dictum: "Everybody in the effing world logs on, see? So make the other buggers wait. Be boss, see?"

The information concerned missing children.

The computer could detail cases. One or two he even remembered. One however was heartening. A little boy had been abducted. The kidnapper had a respectable job, and raised the stolen boy as his own. Nine – *nine!* – years later, the man had stolen another boy of six. The first lad by then was fifteen. Some dim memory had stirred in the teenager, who had courageously taken the six-year-old to the police station. The kidnapper had been apprehended, and the children were rescued.

Bray almost wept at that. Okay, lesson one for a hunter: you can't recover stolen time. Weep if you must, but tears dim a hunter's sight. Blot your eyes and plough on.

Famous abductions abounded in literature, in history, in statistics. Some enthusiasts wanted the world to log on to the abducted Helen of Troy. Biblical instances crept in from all sides. He began to spot deceptions in titling. You couldn't ever be sure, so had to try more out than you actually needed. The computer clearly remembered which titles he wanted more data on, and signalled them to itself by coloured changes. Had Kylee made it do that?

He made progress. Except that satisfaction was a trick.

So often the same feeling had proved treacherous in his early days at Gilson Mather. His first encounter was with the notorious "upsets" in mahogany as a young apprentice. He had wrought a truly beautiful piece of *Swietenia mahogani* mahogany, only a small discarded chunk but true of the species. The Australian Rosewood or Rose Mahogany, that Bray still called *Dysoxylum*, were all not true mahogany, though bliss to work. Bray had been so proud to handle a real piece of old Cuban. He had laboured hours, until calamity befell, for its interior had been a mass of thundershakes, still known as upsets among woodworkers. From being exquisite, his work instantly became worthless, the fibre torn to shreds during the tree's growth. A beginner, he had marvelled too much. He never made that same mistake again. The hardest thing had been throwing it away.

Thirty years later Bray invented an electronic gadget to detect thundershakes in mahogany. The electrical impedance of wood along a measured length, in line with the xylem and phloem's line of growth, was different in unaffected mahogany. Were the rips in the wood actually caused by thunder? He didn't know or care. Mr Winsarls had patented the device in Bray's name.

He felt the same now, going into this country of screened words, of guesses. Data everywhere, yes, but on a terrain of surmise and doubt.

One remarkable story he came across lifted him. A little girl had been stolen. The parents gave up hope. Years afterwards, as an adult, she had incidentally visited the town of her origin even though she retained no memory. In a baker's shop – a *shop* – she had chatted with another lady. The baker looked at the two faces before him across his counter, and remarked on their remarkable likeness.

This had started a discussion, and the two women realised that they *were* sisters.

In a shop! Years after!

You see, Bray told himself. He had no need of encouragement. He simply wanted evidence of memory. He came across mentions of Little Lord Fauntleroy, who in the eponymous novel accidentally strayed with his gypsy friends cheerily calling that no, this was the way, and so walked home.

Agents on the screen promised to find lost ones. He printed the list. Kylee said he could sort things alphabetically, in seconds. What if he eventually had to send somebody to America, even? Could a computer system be carried? He knew of small discs, but what if American computers didn't work the same? He trusted notebooks more. He'd heard that some writers still stuck to handwriting, and understood why.

Long hours later, he caught himself missing an entry and reluctantly decided to close down. He forgot the routine Kylee had shown him but hoped it would know what to do. The printed sheets he left to sort through in the morning. Buster flopped tiredly along with Bray back to the house for his pint of tea and sleep.

Chapter Twenty-Two

They were astonishingly cooperative. It would be a cash sale, he assured the man.

"Cash, sir? Do you mean certified cheque?"

"Money. The minute the thing is finished."

"You are aware of the cost, sir?"

"Look," Bray said, getting good at lies. "My, er, brother's away in Torremelinos. He's wanted one all his life. I've got the money. You want a deposit?" Bray had no idea where Torremelinos was. He'd heard a lass mention it on the train, a place for holidays.

The new Scandinavian shed was erected the following afternoon, Buster so excited he had to be banned to the Lumleys'. Bray slipped the men a good tip. It had electric light, seven power points, a fan heater. He was astounded at the speed. It was actually delivered in parcels like a child's toy kit. Three hours, and there stood the new wooden cathedral, with four windows, blinds and awnings.

That night it rained heavily. The following evening he carried the computer into its new home. Kylee and her sullen friend Porky arrived an hour late. Porky moved the phone point and Bray was *on line* in an hour.

"Won't the phone people complain?" Bray asked. He had a terror of Bye Laws.

"Is he fucking real?" Porky demanded.

Kylee sat at the console. "Right, Bray. What're we doing?"

"I want this web thing, please."

Porky snickered, his insults a constant litany. Kylee did her complicated nail-varnish painting of the keyboard while Bray read each keyboard letter aloud, Porky smoking under the house porch meanwhile. Then they were off, the girl tapping and laughing. Astonishingly, the computer talked, actually said words as they appeared.

"Takes a fucking whole night," she explained. "Porky learns me marker sentences. I tellt them. It'll take dictation, and read out loud whatever comes up." She was aggrieved, though. "We had to *buy* the talk programme. Bastards. You've to pay us."

"Of course."

"Here, Porky. That frigging git's still on the TALO," she told Porky.

"Fucking nutters."

Kylee asked what Bray wanted his computer site to be called. He told her a name. It was one of Davey's lesser KV characters. Choosing it had cost him sleepless nights.

"Queer fucking name, that. Secret, is it?"

Bray watched over her shoulder as the letters came up and he saw his designation for the first time. It moved him beyond words. He told Kylee to please leave it untouched, so he could get used to starting up unaided. He paid them, and sat down alone in the brand new shed after they'd gone.

* * *

Next day he went to George Corkhill's workshop.

The workshop was busy. Two women, four men, two lads, and incredible noise.

"I expected it to be really quiet."

"No such luck. See those?" Corkhill indicated the presses. "Four thousand pamphlets by noon!"

"Good heavens!" Bray followed him into the office. "Professional."

"Craftsmen are, Bray." George looked at his visitor. "The job?"

"I'm writing it now. Can I drop it by?"

"My house is next door. What's the arrangement?"

"You print me one copy. I'll pay you. If you can date the bill some months ago, fine. But don't get in trouble."

"How soon?"

"Less than a week? There is one thing, Mr Corkhill." Bray had rehearsed, but now hesitated. "Might I ask that you keep all details to yourself, whatever my enterprise turns into?" He was too embarrassed to go on.

The printer smiled. "Never even heard of you, Mr Charleston."

George showed him out among the machines. The workers all nodded and smiled. In Geoff's car Bray felt refreshed, and drove home to the new shed where he logged on without trouble. He wondered if he should buy himself a motor, things going apace now.

Three evenings later he had an unexpected visitor. Mr Walsingham came knocking, in a blazing temper.

"I want to know what's going on between you and my daughter!" he bellowed, elbowing his way into Bray's hallway. "I followed her here, so it's no use denying it!"

Bray was astounded at the man's vehemence. "Kylee's

busy. She's in the shed. I'm just brewing up. Do go through."

"Busy?"

"In the garden. Follow the light."

Bray made tea and carried it to the new shed. Walsingham was standing shouting questions at his daughter, Buster worriedly making small dashes. Kylee was unfazed. She had blanked the computer.

"It's a question of what's right and proper!" Walsingham yelled as Bray put the tray down. "You and this *old man*! I won't allow it!"

"What on earth do you think —?"

Walsingham rounded angrily on him. "This is between my daughter and me! She's been due at her mother's in London for —"

"Fuck London and fuck school," Kylee said calmly. "I've got a job. Two hours a day."

"Where are you staying? Tell me that!"

"At Porky's." She stood, stretched. "Nothing funny. This old geezer's got a job on and knows fuck all. I'm showing him because your crappy college is fuck all use." She almost smiled. "I'm a computer consultant! The only difference between me and you is I got a fucking job."

It took another thirty minutes before Mr Walsingham was even partly mollified. Her implacability won in the end. Bray said nothing, listening as the child – she was nothing more – wore her father down with abusive insistence. They were still arguing when Bray interrupted to ask Kylee if he ought to shut the computer down, save money on the phone line. She was delighted.

"See?" she exclaimed. "He's a fucking moron!"

For reassurance Bray added that his son and daughter were next door most evenings. Mr Walsingham hadn't made the connection between Bray's surname and any dreadful news. Bray suggested that Kylee might come at whatever times Mr Walsingham wished. Kylee heard this with a sardonic glance.

"I think, Kylee, that you should go home after working here," Bray concluded. "Instead of staying with your, ah, friend. Think how agitated your dad must feel."

They settled for vague promises and Kylee left with Walsingham. Bray agreed to notify Mr Walsingham of Kylee's whereabouts if she failed to arrive when expected. The arrangement was, she would be along every other evening.

In the new shed, all that space, he tentatively began, a stack of plain cards beside the console on the detestable plastic.

He penned *Abduction of children,* and switched on.

Chapter Twenty-Three

Four days later Bray finished *The KV Story*. Virtually Davey's own words, the brief tale concerned the cloaked, lop-sided creatures he and Davey had made up, imaginations running riot. He used only three drawings of the KV folk with their angular outlines and skew-wiff headgear. They flew kites among straight-edged clouds. The dozen pages looked absurdly sparse.

He delivered it to George Corkhill's house. The printer's wife was as rotund as George was lanky.

"Don't say it, please, Mr Charleston," she said, smiley, when she took the parcel. "Incongruous, aren't we? The long and the short of it, the old music hall act!"

Her homilies ran out in consternation. She knew. He nodded acknowledgement.

"The script is terrible, Mrs Corkhill. Please apologise."

"He'll be across in a minute." She seemed eager. "Won't you wait?"

"I'd best get on."

On the way home, he ordered a small new car for himself. It looked too squarish for comfort, but as long as it was reliable he didn't care. Geoff was pleased.

The following noon he rang Leonora the publisher. He was endlessly put on hold. Publishing houses seemed impenetrable, the secretaries offhand. Bray wondered if it was his manner. Too diffident in everything, except handling wood.

With twenty minutes still to spare, he sat in St John's Square. These days he eschewed caffs and sandwich slots. Better have wedges of wholegrain bread he prepared in the morning. Apple and a banana, crushed in his tatty old briefcase. Dry bread with jam, salad cream made with grapeseed oil, lettuce, celery, cheese only twice a week and thinly sliced. Five pieces of fruit a day seemed hell of a lot, but easy once he got in the swing. Oranges were best eaten at home because of splash, and orange oils lingered on wood.

Every noon break he walked half an hour, even in rain, carrying a folding brolly, and took to wearing an embarrassing tweedy hat, determined not to catch cold. He couldn't afford interruptions.

Publishers, though? During the afternoon he went to see Mr Winsarls. He had been sizing the owner up. The previous week he'd narrowly avoided getting caught staring appraisingly at Mr Winsarls as he'd gone by.

"Sorry to interrupt, Mr Winsarls. Just a thought?"

"Anything, Mr Charleston."

"About Gilson Mather, Mr Winsarls." Bray noted the other's surprise, and forged on, "The firm is London's oldest, wouldn't you say?"

"It certainly is, of its kind." Winsarls often used silence as an affable prompt, the way his old father had encouraged visiting buyers. "We've often been approached by other firms, for mergers. Every one of which," he quickly added, "I've refused."

"Of course," Bray conceded courteously. "Only, isn't it time we reviewed Gilson Mather's past work? Did a pamphlet, maybe?"

Bray hesitated, the way he'd practised.

"Published sounds so formal, Mr Winsarls," he said reluctantly. "But our many personal buyers must constitute quite a list." He resumed just as the owner made to speak. "A landmark, even, for an anniversary…"

He knew, of course. He had scrolled his way through Companies House lists. After today's conversation he would make a historical summary. It would put his name on record, but so?

"Our tricentenary, Mr Charleston, take a lot of delving. Family vaults!" Mr Winsarls smiled. "My ancient aunties will need placating!"

"Oh, how is Miss Alice?" Bray put in as if reminded. "And Mrs Boniface?"

They discussed the Winsarls. The owner was pleased Bray remembered the ladies' visits.

"You know more about Gilson Mather than the rest of us!"

"Hardly, sir. I was thinking more of our furniture."

Mr Winsarls was taken in. "I ought to have known you'd concentrate on the craft!"

"Well, it is why we're here, sir."

He went to a different publisher's on the way home – address from the phone book – but the editors had already left for the day. They, he'd learned, were the ones who mattered.

That evening he began the sequel to the children's book he'd delivered to George Corkhill.

Drawings were a particular problem. He had come across Arthur Ransome's stern advice to the two ambitious schoolgirls, the teenage Misses Hull and Whitlock, who unbelievably had sent their novel to the eminent children's author. Kindly, Ransome helped them to publish, but said to make their drawings less complicated.

Bray copied more of Davey's drawings over and over. He was meticulous with the originals, replacing them behind the panel in his old shed. Davey's shed, he decided, was the one that mattered, where he and Davey had spent so much time carving and arguing. The new shed had no relevance. Brash, clean, spartan, it was merely the shed of a hunter. A bothie, a place of refuge for a stalking hunter.

He drew, drew again, constructing the famed Balloon Game of Davey's imaginary country. Three times he returned to Davey's shed for information, making sure, Buster accompanying him. Davey's flat pencil was still there on the floor. Bray left it untouched. His computer code word was Davey's word.

Hunting so short a time, he knew enough to ridicule the TV crime films where some daring girl whisked her way into secret American CIA files by guessing a code word. Kylee had said nobody could do it except by accident. She would come and spend time with him. "Forty fags and as many marshmallows as I can eat, okay?" she'd said on the phone. What did that mean? Bray agreed.

He had a faint unease. The feeling was growing that she knew what he was about. Late into the night, Buster on the door mat of Davey's shed, Bray fretworked letters on a cedarwood panel. He planed, filed and sanded. He gave it a coat of yacht varnish. In the morning he stained it russet and nailed it above the inside of the hunt shed door.

Let the world know.

Chapter Twenty-Four

The following week he even began to feel like a hunter.

Everything seemed to come at once. One night he even slept, midnight until six-thirty. A mixture of panic drove him on, all the *time*. He dared not let himself think of what might be happening elsewhere.

Shirley's progress was sadly downhill. Geoffrey now spent most nights at the hospital. Bray went to see her, planning on visiting once a week. The computer was starting to impose demands of its own.

A letter finally came from a publisher, Cannon Endriss (est. 1782) plc. He rang, and a girl said she'd give him a few minutes, her brusqueness putting him in his place. She asked if he had an agent. He told her no. George Corkhill's parcel had come by a motorbike courier.

He stared in astonishment at it. Small, the size of a paperback thriller. The front was stiff almost like real cardboard, covered by a dust jacket, blue and red, embossed with gold lettering.

The title read, "*The Story of KV*". On the front was his crude drawing, two little figures on a hill, crazy kites, square clouds in the distance. *By Sharlene Trayer*. The name had caused him heartburn. It wasn't an anagram of his own name or Geoff's or Shirley's, for safety. He didn't want to warn anybody Out There. Sharlene Trayer, he hoped, was simply impossible. No Sharlene Trayer in the phone book, none anywhere. A woman's name would deceive.

For quite a time he gaped at it and kept opening the pages, inspecting the binding. A real *book*, just like in a library. Inside was the whole thing, the publisher's address given as George's printing firm as arranged. A brief biography of the mythical Sharlene Trayer, born in the USA, living in a location carefully unspecified, this was her first book.

As if that wasn't breathless enough, next day he got from Mr Winsarls lists of notable customers who had bought antique and reproduction furniture from Gilson Mather. Bray told Mr Winsarls he would compile a tick list before the weekend. Mr Winsarls was pleased his leading craftsman was recovering. For the first time Bray felt flustered. Hours in the day, was his problem.

"The trouble is," Bray explained with diffidence to the young lass in the office at Cannon Endriss, "my stepsister Sharlene isn't well."

"You've some children's book, you say." She made it sound offhand.

Lindsay Belmontral was plainly determined to avoid looking like one of those young executive women who went about being gorgeous for a living. She was in charge. While waiting, he'd heard her angry shouts, setting girls scurrying. Blonde, unhappy, her desk piled with manuscripts, chairs stacked with books. Bray counted nearly two dozen women about the offices. One was the manuscript woman off the train. Well, she *had* mentioned this firm. He looked away. Was it tradition, women do books, and men print them?

"Yes." He held his small package. "It's been published. By me. I got a printer to make it for her. But I'm afraid it sold out."

She focussed for the first time.

"It *what*?"

"Sold out. I've only this one left."

She held out her hand. "Let me see."

He made no move. "Do you think I did right?" He fumbled and brought out the folder of invoices for Corkhill's firm. First things first. "Orders kept coming in." He sounded querulous. "I couldn't cope. Sharlene had a breakdown over it. I wonder if I did wrong, encouraging her in the first place."

"Sold *out*?" Her voice spoke of shock, heresy. Bray felt on the right track.

"Her doctor gave me quite a reprimand. By letter, of course. She's in the United States. We've no other family."

"Give it here."

He handed her the book. She squinted along its spine, rubbing the dust wrapper.

"It's not the best product, is it?" she said disparagingly. "Who's Corkhill?"

"The printer. Sharlene sent me the text, I took it to Corkhill."

She leafed through his folders of invoices. "What's NLSO?"

Most of them were fake, fabricated by Bray at home in the dark hours. Some however were recent arrivals from the Kings Cross accommodation address in response to his adverts. He'd left those in their envelopes, showing legitimate dates.

"None Left Sold Out. I put it on to remind me. I've many others." He passed his letter of apology to his mythical buyers. "I said sorry."

She stared at him. He could see why she, of all the young women in the office, had climbed.

"How many?"

"Letters? Forty or so there. But many more." He tried to placate her irritation. "I printed a thousand copies, but they went in a fortnight. I keep having to write and say there's none left. It's getting tiresome."

"They want books," she said like he'd offended God and the kingdom, "and you tell them to get stuffed?"

She shook her head. "I don't believe this. It's fucking absurd." She flicked through Corkhill's invoice, the sheaf of orders.

Bray was nonplussed. What was it these days, when young women swore like troopers? Then the hunter he now was smiled inwardly. He was the phoney one here. Wasn't Ms Lindsay Belmontral, foul language and all, doing her proper work? He was the fraud, lying in his teeth.

"You're a clown," she said. She spoke to him directly, a colonel giving orders. "I've an old editor. She can judge this book's potential. If it's a go, we'll maybe take the book on."

"Take the book on?" he said, blank. Now he knew he'd been deceiving himself.

"Publish it." She lifted her phone and added sarcastically, "To sell. You understand *sell*?"

Lindsay Belmontral was disgusted. She'd wanted youth, and that he no longer had. He was being palmed off on some reject. She caught his eye, gave a grimace at the tardiness of phones. Anxious, he smiled back, feeling his way.

"Lottie?" she cooed, all sweetness. "Lindsay here. Only a possible, but right up your street." And after a pause, "I know, Lottie, but it's definitely a query."

That evening Bray met George Corkhill in the Donkey and Buskin. Squaddies from a local army camp were usually in but a darts match had prised them away. The place was almost deserted.

"I want a thousand books, please, George," Bray told his co-conspirator.

"Real this time?"

Bray recognised the printer's joke but couldn't share the levity. "Can you print something in it saying that it's the second...?"

George seemed able to absorb a pint by some power other than mere suction. Bray watched with admiration as the beer level lowered evenly. His own went in jerks and starts, froth untidy about the rim.

"The Christie trick? Agatha Christie crime novels. Inside the book they gave a printing history. Remember? First printing, it'd say, then a date. Then second, then third, sometimes up to twenty-third printing."

"Proving the demand for it?" Bray guessed.

George laughed, his Adam's apple yo-yoing.

"You fell for it! Each printing was scanty, see? Maybe only a few hundred. Readers thought the whole world was reading it!"

Bray was instantly worried. "I thought I was being original."

"In book sales? Don't make me laugh, Bray." George

became serious. "The only original thing is that you've a reason other than money." He paused. "I meant *we've* a reason."

The world clouded. Bray cleared his throat.

"Thanks, George. Send a proper invoice. Correct ledgers, tax records. Can the book show a different price? The publishers are sending it to some old biddy. If they accept it, I'll tell them you'll do the printing."

"They might not like that, Bray." Bray tried to finish his ale but couldn't. The printer added, "Don't worry. If you have to go along with them I'll understand, and good luck."

Bray already knew that. For the rest of the hour he told George his impressions of the publishing house. Bray actually began to almost enjoy the feeling of progress made despite everything. He also felt a kind of warmth, and recognised it: he trusted George. One ally wasn't much, but it was something.

Chapter Twenty-Five

"It's been a month since we spoke," Pop told Doctor.

"It's almost time to take your boy."

Doctor preferred speaking with the man. No patience, women, with their insulting reluctance to accept a medical process. Purchases had to come like baked beans from a shelf. No such thing as a system leading inexorably to perfection. See them in Miami sales. Herds behaved better.

This man too was impatient. Correction: this multi-millionaire *client* was impatient. "Tell Doctor to get a move on," she must have brayed.

Their insolence was beyond belief. Doctor controlled his contempt. They were supplicants. He was in power here. The boy was his to hand over, when he alone decided.

"Almost?" Pop said. He was frozen in his chair, yet more determination instilled into him by his querulous mate.

"Let me define it for you, Pop," Doctor said. "The boy is showing total acceptance. Moving step by step into total adaptation. He watches television, every programme meticulously, huh-huh-huh, screened for content. He thinks he's switching programmes. He isn't of course. He's orchestrated."

"For how long?"

"I invited you here this morning," Doctor said comfortably, smiling, appeasing, certain of his authority, "to give you a precise date, Pop. Two weeks from today, he's all yours."

"Two weeks!"

Doctor watched Pop wipe his forehead with a folded handkerchief. The multimillionnaire had the insolence to return the linen to his pocket carefully folded. Was it any wonder the oaf remained a serf? Commercial emperor he might be, but his inadequacies were ingrained.

Doctor's smiles comforted the rich buffoon.

"The priceless work I do here at Rehabilitation Par Excellence, Pop, is its own pleasure when delivering a successful transferee." He steepled his fingers. "People," he intoned, now on a roll and talking over Pop's disgusting display of emotion, "are just about every single thing in life."

"Thank you." Pop blew his nose. Even then the cretin folded the handkerchief away. "Doctor, we're eternally grateful."

"Mine is the most valuable undertaking ever accomplished for humanity," Doctor said portentously, knowing it did no harm to remind the wealthy dolts just what they were getting for their miserable dollar. "Take away people," he announced with the trace of melancholy they all went for, "and there's nothing left."

"That's so true."

Doctor agreed. "And you know what? The people out there forget that."

* * *

Bray revised the drawings.

They looked so clumsy in print. He wanted a perfect job, to match up to what he dreamt Davey might recognise. Truth to tell, he'd often been wrong in that. Like this purple thing. Purple trees abounded in Davey's world. Fish were mostly purple. The ubiquitous kites had any amount of purpling. Cars were powered by purple stones. The balloons used for the Great Balloon Finals against Prussia were, paradoxically, anything but purple.

For a week Bray laboured on revisions of the second slim volume. His limitations were an embarrassment, the only consolation he wasn't trying to embellish, merely reproduce. Match Davey's imaginings exactly, and he'd be right. It was the one weapon this lone hunter possessed.

Kylee called.

"This'll cost you eighty fags, Owd Un," she told him, bringing Buster to deliriously noisy life by her sudden arrival. "I got you four more. They'll coon in any time, fags extra."

Coon? "Er, is that good, Kylee?"

He refused to bring beer, she being under age, but she accepted cola. He kept a stock under the bench for her and Porky.

"You wanted a team, right?" She displaced him at the keyboard by simply shoving him with her hip.

"Er, team, Kylee?" He hadn't said anything about a team.

"Off your pulley, are yer?" She worked her way into the logos, cursing. It began to speak. Bray hated the voice, but Kylee needed it. "A fucking dozen. Take any longer, they'll forget."

He guessed, "Electronic mail?"

"Time you got on wiv it, mate."

"I've done it, actually, Kylee."

Modestly he placed a folder beside the console. She looked quizzically.

"You're really a cunt, know that?"

He read it aloud for her. It had seemed too easy, the computer, a summary of Sharlene Trayer's biography.

"What you write it fer?"

"Well, I want it on the, er, advert."

"Then whyn't yer just put it on? It's your fucking address, innit?"

Impatiently she clicked the keys and sat back. The double speakers began to speak stored messages, his words, her voice checking back.

"I was afraid," he admitted.

She swung to gape. "You silly bugger. What would you've done if I hadn't turned up tonight? Sweet fuck all?"

"No!" he cried, on the defensive. "I'd have carved, done some drawings. I've not enough hours in the day."

"You take my fucking breath, straight up." She worked herself up to real anger. "I've two blokes tellt me to fuckin stuff it while you're tarting about. How the fuck d'you think it makes me look?"

He didn't know why she was so angry, or what about. "I'm sorry, Kylee. But what if the computer didn't work for me?"

After all, he was paying her. Surely he was entitled?

"Fucking moron. *You* tell *it*. Not the other way about."

Miserably he stood there while she berated him. "I'm sorry."

"Don't be, mate," she said, unexpectedly bright. "Here they come!"

He stared at the screen in bewilderment. "Here who come?"

"Your team!" She crowed, clapped her hands. "Just watch! Know what?"

"No." It sounded surly, ungracious. He tried again. "What, Kylee?"

"I bet the fuckers've bet who comes in first!" She laughed, fizzed a tin and swilled it back, gulping.

Bray felt daunted. She rattled the keys, exclaiming. Messages arrived, the computer reading the words aloud. Two of them were abusive though the criticism seemed aimed at other mailers. Was this cooning? He didn't ask.

The messages were a torrent, then slowed to an occasional query. Most of them ended, "Rep SSS."

"Answer soon," Kylee told him when he asked. "That first one's a fucking nerk, but he's a laugh. He's a Trumpet Windsock freak, can you imagine?"

He didn't undertand that, either. "Kylee," he observed. "They all read the same, don't they?"

"Don't get on your shitty horse with me, mate. You tellt me what they had to say." She narrowed her eyes, bargaining for better terms. He called it her money squint. "You said you'd pay."

"Fine, yes, okay." He stared at the screen. "Can you print them out?"

And as they watched the typed pages emerge, "I didn't realise they'd all read the same." It was true. Apart from misspellings and odd phraseology, her friends had reproduced his request verbatim. "I know I *wanted* people to ask for more information about my story book, but —"

"So?" She was unfazed, sat swinging her legs. "You've a sackful."

"I wanted them to sound spontaneous."

"When more come in, change what they say. Don't use letter programmes. They're a giveaway in the music charts."

"You mean others do it too?" He was shocked, his fraud shared by others.

"All the fucking time." She returned to the computer. "You don't think thousands vote?"

"Well, yes."

"Know what, Bray?" she said, falling about, "I like you, even if you are a pathetic prat. What you want them to ask, and they'll do it, okay?"

In the next hour he learned that to coon in meant to send a message by way of this e-mail. A message completed was a hand. At the end of the session he felt really depressed. He paid her.

"I'm really grateful, Kylee. Sorry if I irritate."

She thought that was hilarious. "People all over electrics'll soon want news of your KV book. Gimme a frigging rest."

"I'm out of my depth."

"It'll look good. You've set up, sacks coming in. That's what you wanted, innit?"

"Well, yes."

"You've a proper place instead of that rotten old dump." She indicated Davey's hut. "A month, you'll be all round the fucking world." At the door, she saw his illuminated sign, *Hunt Shed*. "What's it say?"

He avoided her eye. "Tell you later."

Buster and he watched her go, Porky sounding his horn in his rickety van. The neighbours would have complained, in different times. Now they said nothing.

"Kylee?" he called as she climbed into the vehicle. "Thanks."

The pickup moved off with a jerk that almost slammed the door on her. He went inside. What she said was true. He had come a distance. He just couldn't judge how far.

Chapter Twenty-Six

Officer Stazio rang at an unusual time. It was not, thank God, the worst news, but sad enough. His retirement papers.

"Are you happy, Officer Stazio?"

The policeman heaved a sigh. "Jim, please. I hate the whole effing notion, God's truth. Here, unemployed means you're nobody."

"What will you do?" Bray avoided the question that mattered.

"Security work, I guess. You know the sort of thing, shine a light in all them nooks, make out reports. I've a sister in Miami, but who wants Miami?"

"Will you be able to keep on with, er…?"

"No, Bray. Finish in the US of A means finish. There's a woman officer here. I'll fix to introduce her."

Bray's pause was too long. "Very well."

So Stazio had been putting off telling him. Bray felt a spurt of anger, even as Jim said his keep-in-touch. Like the closing courtesies on a civil servant's letter. You shuck off the really hopeless tasks onto some retiree. Like a pathetic little book, to some retired editor?

America had some federal system, hadn't it, each state virtually a law unto itself? He rang off after a desultory remark. No progress anywhere, Bray thought in rage.

He went back to shuffling the e-mail enquiries he'd bribed Kylee to arrange. They were now quite a pile. He'd answered a few, those Kylee had picked, and received further queries back. He wondered how long they should go on collecting them. Maybe this publishing lady Lottie Vinson – another has-been – would say.

Calling Buster, he went to give Geoffrey the bad news about Officer Stazio. His son looked unbelievably tired, the long drive from work to see Shirley, then home for fresh linen. Bray used Shirley's washing machine as a routine now. Christine Lumley's Aunt Gladys did the ironing on Mondays.

"I already knew, Dad. I didn't want to tell you, in case it upset you." *As much as it did me,* Geoff meant.

"He promised to keep in touch. It's what folk always say."

"Maybe he will." Geoffrey's optimism had all but disappeared.

He thought a moment, then broached it. "He's sending me a list of addresses, voluntary agencies that sometimes help."

Tears showed in Geoff's eyes. Wearily he stretched. For the first time, Bray really saw Geoff had given up.

"Shirley's going to take a long time, Dad."

"What about you, son? Would some time off help?"

"And do what? No, Dad. Work keeps me on the rails." Geoffrey looked at his father, also as if for the first time. They looked at each other in surprise. "And you, Dad. What about you?" He blotted his face with his sleeve, as he had done when a boy. "You were close to Davey. I blame myself."

"There's no sense in that, son."

"No, Dad. You don't understand. All the things Davey would have liked, wanted to play at. Those lunatic stories he used to concoct." Geoff almost laughed in his own weeping. "Quite barmy. What was it? Some crazy name you made up, all that purple, those odd bloody wooden hats."

Geoffrey was laughing weakly now, a hateful sound of sobbing in the quiet guffaws, the noise of a baby being sick down a mother's shoulder.

"And those carvings. God, but Shirl hated them, the hours daubing on the shed wall, you doing exactly what Davey said. Whatever will you do with them now Davey's gone?" He appraised his father for an instant. "Is that new shed to preserve the old hut, like some shrine?"

"No, son. I need space for this computer lark. I'm compiling Gilson Mather's reproductions, and antiques I've restored, some advert." He lied on, to disarm his distraught son. "Mr Winsarls thinks it will be superb publicity. Foreign sales, I suppose. It could have come at a better time."

They sat in embarrassed silence.

"The psychiatrist says fewer visits until she's out of the wood, Dad."

"Right, son." Bray was relieved.

"I regret sounding off to you and Davey about those carving games, Dad. Me and Shirl were worried he'd get behind at school. It seems absurd now."

"All parents think that, Geoff." His son had accepted his tales. "And you did absolutely right."

They watched a football match, neither caring which side won. When Geoff went to bed Bray returned to the computer shed and finished his sequel to *The KV Story*. If that Lottie Vinson refused it, he would go ahead without her.

He slept for three hours that night, was on the train at seven o'clock, and left a message on Ms Vinson's phone asking for an interview.

To his surprise he was put straight through to Mrs Vinson when he dialled again in the lunch hour. They agreed to meet after five-thirty at Liverpool Street station.

Lottie Vinson was seated just near the yoghurt stall, gazing expectantly at the milling concourse. He hesitated, annoyed with himself. As ever, no suavity. She smiled, the manuscript woman.

"Mr Charleston? Lottie Vinson." She indicated a seat.

"How do you do?" he said formally. "Can I get —?"

She moved things on the table, revealing an extra cup of tea and a cheese roll. "After a day's work. Best I could do."

He made awkward work of gratitude.

"Lindsay told me the details. It must be difficult for you, your step-sister and everything. That's the sister you mentioned in Burger Thing, am I correct? You've been splendid, doing all that for her." She wryly appraised him. "There isn't much family feeling in publishing. Very cut throat, or shouldn't I be saying that?"

She was plainly dressed, fawns and greys. Fading blonde hair, pleasant roundish face and level eyes. He liked her. His trickery embarrassed him.

"Sharlene Trayer," she mused. "Can we change her name?"

"If you like." He ought to have a lie about asking his step-sister first. "We spoke of it," he added lamely. "It was her married name. She lives alone."

"She's ill, Lindsay said. No hope of her coming over?"

"The flight would be too hard."

"I understand." She brought out his book. "I've read it, Mr Charleston. It's really rather...exotic."

"What were you about to say?"

She laughed without embarrassment. "Caught! I meant strange. But the sales! How can you account for those?"

"That's the problem." He deliberately chose to misunderstand. "Folk got shirty when I'd no books left."

"I spoke to Mr Corkhill," she alarmed him by interjecting. "He said he's just begun printing your repeat order."

"Yes." Bray knew he was stammering, going red. Had George played the game? "I couldn't wait on help."

"Help?" She toyed with her spoon. "An odd word, Mr Charleston."

"Help me, I meant. I'm out of my depth, Mrs Vinson. I've got letters from the tax people." He hadn't.

He took the book back, felt a momentary pang at Davey's copied drawing on the dust jacket. "Failure would have been easy. Success is a burden."

She smiled at that. "Look, Mr Charleston. No illusions about where you stand in this. You've been shunted – we actually call it that – to somebody who's past her sell-by. I'm no whizz-girl in her twenties."

"Is this no?"

"I'm recommending we accept." She reached for the book but he withheld it. "What's KV mean?"

"That's coming." He felt himself redden. "I haven't worked it out yet."

"But Sharlene has?"

"Erm," he said, taken aback, his imaginary step-sister here again. "I meant I don't know what Sharlene'll decide."

"I presume it's multiple sclerosis?" Lottie was concerned.

He felt an irrational annoyance. How on earth could he be expected to know what disease a mythical step-sister had? "It's downhill, I'm afraid. She's very brave. She uses a word processor."

"How soon can I see the sequel?"

Leave it to me, he almost blurted out. "I'll phone her tonight."

Lottie said, "I presume she's your younger sister?"

"Yes." Safe to eat, now he'd survived the awkwardness. "I'm famished. This'll save my life."

They spoke of journeys. Mrs Vinson lived along the coast, mercifully not close to his own village. She told him of her husband in Canada, no chance of reconciliation. Two offspring, both overseas.

"It's the old question," she sighed. "When you retire, do you park yourself on your children, a load of trouble, or become a pensioned seasider waiting for letters?" She laughed to make comic incongruity of her plight.

He told her of his work, then caught himself. "I talk too much about joinery."

Guardedly she asked him. He told her he had one married son, and he had an ex-wife he never saw. This too made him redden. He wanted to like this lady.

"Better get onto first names, Mr Charleston," she admonished eventually. "Lottie to you. Bray, isn't it? In publishing, formality suggests something's hidden," she worried him by saying.

"Is it?" His remark brought on her laughter.

"No! Cynicism is publishing's wit. I can see you and I are going to get along! I've never met innocence!"

He felt emboldened. "Is there any hope of, well, getting some advice?"

"I've already said we'll go with it. You're unique,

defining a total sell-out as a problem. We need to rationalise details. This printer might prove dicey."

He gave her the phone number of his computer shed and lied, "I'm in the Dark Ages. No fax, no e-mail, none of that Web thing. Is that all right?"

"Thank heavens for that!"

She caught the coast express. He pretended he'd someone to see. He'd had enough personal chat. He watched her walk down Platform Nine, and felt stupid when she caught him looking. But where was the harm in liking someone? He felt exhausted. So far, he was pulling it off, but far too slow. He had to accelerate.

Chapter Twenty-Seven

"It's real clear over Illinois, Clint," Pop said. "We say it's the greatest state in the Union."

The Chrysler was waiting at the airport. Pop dismissed the uniformed chauffeur, electing to do the driving. Mom smiled and smiled, speaking endlessly on her carry phone. Mom had two phones. Clint asked why she had two phones in her handbag.

Mom and Pop exchanged swift glances.

"In my *purse*, Clint," she responded quickly. "Two cell phones in my *purse*? Well, Mom's a busy lady! You'll soon remember just how busy your Mom is!"

"Who're you phoning?" Clint watched the scenery go by.

"Who am I *calling*?" Mom cooed. "Why, my helper lady in Tain. My secretary."

"Tain?" It sounded strange.

"Our new home, honey. We picked it especially for you. You'll have a bright new start. Won't that be marvellous?"

Pop smoothly changed lanes. "Tain's a great town, Clint. We love it, don't we, Mom?"

"And you'll love it too, honey."

"See, son," Pop explained, smiling, "I've my own corporation. I can handle things right from home!"

"Isn't that great, Clint?" Mom exclaimed. "We can be together as much as we want! Most families aren't so lucky, are they?"

"No, Mom," Clint answered.

He was tired. His eyes closed. He'd liked the palm trees outside the clinic windows. There were birds there, near where tidy people played golf and tennis. The birds were not ducks, but sort of. The palm trees made patterns. He remembered those. The previous week he'd got out of bed and traced the outline of one with a finger on the window pane. The nurse had no crayons. Clint slipped into oblivion.

"You hear that, Pop?" Mom whispered to her husband. Tears shone in her eyes. "You hear him say it, just like that?"

"Music, Clodie, sheer music!"

"He makes us complete, Hyme." She dabbed her eyes. "You expect no trouble relocating to Tain?"

"The usual gripes from those commission fuckers."

"Can they affect us?" Mom was alarmed.

"It's business, Clodie, Chrissakes, not a sewing circle. Jesus, I'd like a smoke."

Mom warned, "Doctor said no smoking – Clint's medication."

She could recite Doctor's rules over and over. Hyme's own doctor allowed him one smoke a day.

"Tain is set up, Clodie. I might have to go back east a coupla times. My office click ware's already installed." Pop was silent as a huge interstate truck overtook. He allowed the vehicle to draw ahead. "I'll kick ass if the move doesn't go smooth."

"Pop," his wife reprimanded sternly, smiling fondly at the sleeping boy. "You'll be giving *our son* bad language habits."

Pop chuckled. "Can't be too careful, huh?"

"No first names even when Clint's asleep, okay? Doctor said!"

"The clinic covered every single detail. Jeez, I paid enough."

"Pop!" his wife cried softly.

"Know what Doctor told me? He has six news clippers, do three hundred newspapers a day! Can you believe that? Every detail, for six months after an abduction." Pop whistled. "Professionalism."

The man glanced in the rear view mirror, adjusted it to see the child's face.

"He's sleeping like a babe, Clodie," he said. "Right on course. It's what we paid for. Just remember that."

"How far are we?"

"Coming into Tain." He chuckled, everything perfect. "Home!"

Any doctor's waiting room depressed him. Nobody was there this time. No anxious fidgety woman, with her hand-washing movements. No pots of Cyclamen along the windowsills. Bray waited.

When the receptionist called him he made an unfortunate entrance, stumbling over the smooth carpet. Dr Newton came to help, but by then he had his papers back into his plastic envelope. She must have noticed the *Scientific American* articles he'd photocopied. He stood, red of face, and was introduced to Dr Bateson.

The man was monosyllabic. They sat like chess rivals. Dr Newton made light comments about a viva voce examination at the Royal Colleges. Bray pretended to understand the experience. Dr Bateson masked his impatience in a smile. All of us pretending away, Bray thought. The man was all but bald, his tie slack as if he was hard at work.

"Shall we get down to it?" he said eventually after pleasantries. "Your young relative's plight. Dyslexia?"

"I should like guidance, please." Bray indicated his plastic file. "I've read extracts but I'm no nearer."

"Ask away, then."

"A young lass helps me – with parent permission, of course – with a computer. I pay her."

"And she's dyslexic?"

"She colours the keyboard with special inks, varnishes. She makes the computer talk, to save having to read or type." He waited, but neither of the doctors spoke. "She gives me lessons."

"Are you improving, Mr Charleston?" Dr Newton asked, smiling.

"I'm terrible. She says I'm stupid. She's quite right, of course."

Better to say nothing about her antisocial behaviour. He wanted her dyslexia cured. The rest could wait on better times.

Dr Newton prompted, "Be frank, Mr Charleston. Dr Bateson has worked with dyslexic children for twenty years."

"She is in difficulties," Bray said. For all he knew doctors might have to report things to Social Services, and that would be the end of Kylee. "I don't want her judged. I don't really have the right. I'm not her father, you see."

"And might you bring her here?"

"No." Bray tried to justify his weak attitude. "I want to

know where I might go wrong talking to her. She's been a godsend, teaching me. I couldn't get to a proper night school."

Dr Newton slipped in a lie, helping. "Mr Charleston has work commitments against the clock."

"I've read medical textbooks, but I don't know their words."

"Very well," Bateson said slowly. "How old is this girl?"

"She says fourteen, but I'm unsure. She gets annoyed if I ask."

Bateson leant back, fingers clasped behind his head. "It used to be said that boys were the main sufferers from dyslexia, but we now know it's in both genders."

"What *is* it, though?"

"The brain operates in sections, Mr Charleston. The front parts govern speech output." He tapped his brow. "There's a patch called Broca's Area near the front, that governs your mouth, lips, tongue – controlling speech as it comes out formed into phonemes others can comprehend. Broca's Area helps to change the act of *seeing* a letter into a related *sound*."

Bray had memorised a diagram on the train in.

"And there's a special lobe of your brain," Bateson went on, observing Bray's alert attention, "near the crown of your head, called the parietal lobe." He tapped his bald skin, leaning forward as if that helped Bray to see the anatomy within. Dr Newton smiled at Bray, don't worry, keep listening. "The Angular Gyrus is there. It arranges what you see – letters, words, patterns printed on a page – so they hook up, so to speak, with various libraries of sounds a child's brain has stored up."

"A child's brain stores sounds?"

"That's it. The Angular Gyrus makes sure that a child's

collections of sounds are hitched to the right visual. That is, the letter evokes the necessary sound. Once that's done, the child is reading."

"It seems simple." Bray was edgy, wanting to ask bluntly then why was Kylee having to use colours and rely on talking machines?

"It isn't," Bateson said with feeling. "There's Wernicke's Area that analyses sounds for the brain. The more parts to the microanatomy, the more things can go wrong and cause dysfunction. We examine blood flowing through a child's brain while he sorts out words and sounds, by functional magnetic resonance imaging. It isn't difficult. There are other tests. We can usually discover dyslexia and the range of the defect by simpler tests that don't require instruments."

"Can a child be cured?"

"Vastly improved. Catch it early. Six years of age is optimal."

Bray felt dismayed. He wasn't so naif that he'd come expecting Kylee to be given a simple tablet, but this was a real disappointment. The doctors exchanged glances.

"Dr Pringle Morgan described it first, in Sussex a century ago," Dr Newton said. "The child was a bright youth of fourteen. Very good at maths, games, verbal skill. Nothing wrong with his sight. Now we try to pick it up at much younger."

"You see, Mr Charleston, *Homo sapiens* is a relative newcomer. We evolved a mere 200,000 years since, when speech began. Writing started less than 10,000 years ago. Reading and articulacy isn't something we come into the world ready equipped with. Parents hack it into our consciousness."

Bray sat thinking, the doctors waiting him out. "What's

best?"

"Support," Bateson said immediately. He had known the question was coming.

"What does that mean?" Bray sounded testy, and apologised before going on, "Sorry. It's a catchphrase from talk shows, isn't it? Where somebody asks questions and an audience whoops."

Bateson smiled. "Giving her something useful to do, use her talents and appreciate what she does."

"Thank you."

They exchanged civilities and Bray left. Not much, but he felt better about what he was doing. Support Kylee. He'd do that, in exchange for her help. She'd regaled him with crude jokes about dyslexia clinics her parents had insisted on when she'd been eleven. It had made her ill. He'd have to do what he could.

Support. Sounded easy, if you said it quick.

Chapter Twenty-Eight

Lottie Vinson – how she hated that name! – wished the woman on TV nothing but chin spots, stubby eyelashes and moles. The woman was thin-lipped anyway, a bad sign. Her talk-show interrogator was a tall lawyer, silver of hair and glib with his limited-intelligence and catchphrases ("When your husband left and your children loathed you, how did you feel?" among today's imbecilities).

The woman said the unforgivable, a ragbag word. "My marriage collapsed."

Nobody, least of all the besuited wart, asked what the hell she meant by "collapsed". Why not? New girls in publishing either learned how to define and so got on, or they didn't and stayed useless typists. She scrutinised the woman's garb, looking for reasons to hate her some more.

Now, Lottie, she admonished herself, cut it out. What's she ever done to you? It's her few seconds of fame, let her be. Despite her better intentions, Lottie found her eyes drawn to the screen, so irritably switched off.

Meeting Bray Charleston had made her edgy.

She watched the estuary, standing at her window. Several boats were out, one of them Bill Iggo's, with whom she'd spent time and lived to regret it. Difficult to shelve Bill, but she'd managed it.

Her husband Stanley was living it up in Powell River, Canada. The divorce, a product of differing careers, had been dismayingly amicable. The children, Ian and Barbara, were frequent visitors to him, neither settled down yet. Maybe that too was the modern thing, roam until those first wrinkle lines appeared and party invitations dried up, then find an afterthought partner, pretend it was young love at last? Decent jobs, both, thank God. They visited her when the mood took. She was shocked, realising she didn't care if they came or not.

How irritating, that a twerp like Lindsay in editorial had the nerve to shunt Bray Charleston to her. Jesus, Lottie thought angrily, I've run the entire office in my time, you pompous whizzkid! They'd forgotten that. Retirement meant goodnight nurse, then who's this ageing face at reunions? That's what they think.

That she'd been slipped this drogue was Lindsay's clue: your only purpose, Lottie, is to handle the doubtfuls. Retirees were for reading scripts from fading agents, and provide polite but chilling rejections. Yet this man's tale sounded vaguely something, with its brief track record. Quite likely, Lindsay was merely making sure she didn't drop a clanger that might cripple her promotion.

If the little project went well, who'd get the praise? Why, good old – no, *young* – Lindsay! If it went calamitously bad, well, had Lottie Vinson *ever* amounted to much? Forget her.

Lottie felt unsettled, troubled. Something wasn't right.

Strange how the quiet cabinet maker – he'd said joiner, she must get the OED – kept coming to mind. And his remote step-sister, Sharlene, who evidently hadn't to be

approached at all costs. And Charleston's determination to
promote his step-sister's stories. Did he have the slightest
idea how many new writers tilted that particular windmill?

Except he seemed embarrassed, feeling his stuttering
way. And more than determined. Was there a word for that
grave look of his, that readiness for endless setbacks? Like,
when she'd explained that manuscript-to-book took a year
maybe, his response had been odd, to say the least.

Anybody else would have nodded eagerly, said fine,
they'd go along with that. Bray Charleston had stayed
silent, then said, "There's another way."

"What?" She'd laughed at the arrogance of the man.
"Tell me!"

"I don't know," he'd replied evenly.

Weird, yet not weird. No word came to mind.
Implacability? Resolve?

Watching Bill Iggo's ketch – two bunks in it, she
remembered, wincing – preparing to tack, she thought of
the impression Bray Charleston had conveyed, with his
embarrassments and his ignorance.

Bray Charleston was in for keeps, she thought. That
was it. For keeps. She'd read of his missing grandson,
Davey was it? Local papers had Bray's picture. Was this
children's book thing by way of compensation and guilt?
Yet guilt, for keeps, must be wrong.

He stayed in her mind.

The lady in the next trailer was called Charmianne.
("That's the spelling, Jim," once they'd said hello.) She
grew pansies and wanted to share plants. She offered to
paint the stones white near his one step. He declined, told
her he was still thinking, like he was planning a shuttle
launch. She understood, but said it like a threat; he wasn't

off the hook yet, no sir. He avoided her.

The trailer park was smart, the investment company choosing pretty well. He'd never been into golf, but went over, listened to the talk, had a beer. Occasionally he ate there, met folk at the leisure centre, getting into the place. He walked. He walked some more. He talked with people who'd got dogs, should he get one for company, finally pleaded allergies and folk said shame but what could you do with allergies? Doctor's fees killed you.

He called Bray, grimaced with chagrin at the phone bill. He had a cold beer immediately after. Strange, but he wanted to ask Bray if it was true they drank their beer warm, did he go bowling and was his bowling on grass he'd heard some guy say in the Army Air Force, and did they bowl to nine pins in them old English pubs, was that right?

Days after his retirement pension finally came through he took down his photocopied file, C for Charleston. The guy was a carpenter, made furniture. Seemed the sort who'd keep coming. He phoned on the dot, kept saying sorry if the time was inconvenient. Jim thought, how long can he keep this up?

The day before he left, Jim had gone to see his replacement in the missing kids section. She was pleased with herself. No, she hadn't checked through the list, give her a moment to settle in. He offered to tell her what he could about the cases. She said sharply she didn't want patronising, meaning piss off out the building.

He'd wished her luck, gave her his trailer-home number. Over and out.

The map he'd brought with him, he didn't want to put up – Charmianne might peer in and wonder what the hell. He kept a police badge, a farewell replica. Originals had to be handed in. He marked the medical clinics on the map, some hundreds, and compiled a key for addresses.

Nine o'clock he felt a whole lot better, decided to walk to the leisure bar for some live company. Tomorrow he'd start an alphabetic list of the people running those clinics. Maybe no use, just keeping going like Bray. Must be catching.

Balance was everything to a hunter, a realisation that took Bray by surprise. Some progress seemed founded on daft premises. Some came at breakneck speed.

Think of it, though. Like Hereward the Wake, mediaeval hero of the English fen country, stealing through the wetlands while wicked Normans scoured the terrain. Some nights, mustn't he have wilted, fagged out, against some damp alder? Perhaps the lulling of distant bells for vespers, cattle lowing homeward – surely, just for one fleeting moment, mustn't the great outlaw have thought, sod it, rest a while, dream of a cottage fireside and a loving woman? Weakness must have fragged Hereward's resolve.

But history *knows* that he didn't. He kept the balance of the hunter. How do we know? Because after a thousand years he's still legendary Hereward *the Wake*, not Hereward the Dozer who took time off and got caught. Hereward remained at liberty.

So it was that, sternly correcting his balance of time, commitment, Bray gave Lottie Vinson the sequel by the Barbican restaurant fountains, astonishing her.

"She's finished it?" Lottie marvelled.

Balance, Bray remembered, his lies even better this time. "Sharlene plans her days."

"I suppose she has to." Lottie looked at the folder. "These drawings! D and A want to re-do them." She saw his puzzlement. "Design and Art do graphics."

"No," Bray said gently. It was unthinkable. He would have to fight this.

"They're worried about tints, densities." Lottie too had the bit between her teeth. She kept going, leafing away, taken aback at the colour. "Can Sharlene do a conference call? Georgina's a brilliant pictorial girl. She says that in nine months it'd be really something."

"Lottie." In a way, rejection would make things easier. Costlier, but he and Mr Corkhill could race ahead. "Sharlene says no delay."

"Can't we ask her?" They strolled along the waterside. Ducks came to pester. "It takes only a second to phone."

Bray stared at the noisy mallards. Maybe publishers were a mistake. Maybe he should have gone on alone, him and Corkhill's printing firm, his phoney orders from non-existent buyers, Kylee's flurry of attention-seeking on the Internet thing. But might he run out of money within reach of Davey?

The mallards also lost balance. One drake, desperate, rushed at Bray's shoe. Bray carefully didn't move, so as not to hurt the foolish creature. Yet wasn't the poor thing also striving for balance? Pestering could become begging, begging turn into demand, a demand into war. Ducks, and Bray, were each in conflict zones.

"Her answer must do, Lottie," he said, realising he hadn't spoken for a long time. "Shall I get some food for these creatures?"

"Talking couldn't do any harm."

Bray was not as prepared as he'd thought. "It would serve no purpose." He started inside the building. A bread roll would do it. Did they eat cheese? "She's determined."

"I understand that, Bray. They can do draft proposals.

She could fax us back directly."

He faced her. "Sorry, Lottie. I've had it all out with her."

She glanced at the folder in her hand. "It might be turned down."

He thought, better to hear it now. "I'm sorry." Sorrier than he'd thought he could ever be. "Sharlene is adamant. Nothing added, nothing cut."

"A tough lady."

He felt rueful, holding the restaurant door for her. "I want it printed and out."

"The ink wet?" She laughed, shaking her head. "Lindsay'll really know I've lost it!"

"I'll feed the ducks, then would you like a bite?" This was as smooth as he could get. "I've got time owing."

She said that would be lovely, and sat by the window to watch him give the importuning drake some bread. When he returned she was well into the second KV tale. She kept wondering about this step-sister, so close at such an impossible distance.

Chapter Twenty-Nine

The child was abnormal, Bray thought, guiltily but with qualification. He looked up terms: autistic, autism, dyslexia, dyslectics. Then borrowed McKeith's *Numbers*, and two computer paperbacks.

"Normality" was in the eye of the beholder. He realised that here he was, mostly self-educated but still a so-say respected craftsman, unable to tackle even elementary computers. This, note, when the whole world used them. And when a strange youngster blithely overcame her atrocious handicap, making the damned things the easiest gadgets imaginable.

Grim for Kylee, poor child, unable to read. Yet she ruled a whole mess of hieroglyphics with her mad keyboard colours. She made the computer speak aloud. She had a phenomenal memory, could make her scanning device absorb anything and hear it read back. She was brighter with her disability than he was without.

Who then was "normal"?

Her black moments disturbed him. She would go mute, stand unmoving then slowly shift, sometimes after twenty minutes. And then repetitive movements would begin.

Tapping, rocking slowly for maybe a full hour before she'd speak, then blurt out a gross incongruity. If he was too baffled to reply, she would erupt with snarled abuse. Astonishingly, Buster tolerated these moods of hers with a casual eye.

On occasion, she revealed a compassion that moved him.

He was examining a sample of Kauri Pine in the shed when she walked in. She asked what it was. He started to explain. She sat to listen.

"It's *Agathis australis*," he explained. "From New Zealand. A sample, hoping we'll place an order. See its lustre? I've always liked it. It has few defects, but it's a devil. Patchy as anything, with its absorption. Good in joinery, but don't let the straight grain deceive. It can warp..."

He noticed she was asleep, lolling on the stool.

Wryly he smiled. She must be worn out, or he was being boring again. He edged round her, sat at the computer, and switched a tutorial on. After an hour she roused, instantly pushed him aside and brought up e-mails as if nothing had happened, nodding as the computer spoke them out.

"Sorry I sent you to sleep."

"I didn' wanter know about your fucking plank," she told him casually. "I felt sorry coz you've nobody to tell about it."

She paused for so long he began to wonder. Then she said, "It's Dad."

"Mr Walsingham? Is he still angry that you come here?"

"Wants me to go to a special school. I've had them up to my tits. It's that probation fucker. Doing the world a favour."

"He must think he's doing the best for you."

"Don't talk like I'm as thick, Owd Un. He wants to get rid."

"Look, Kylee." Her pale eyes were rock hard. "Can I do anything? Get you a job somewhere? There's computer firms. Look how clever you are. Good heavens, you invent things!"

"Whaffor?" She leaned away, vixenish, ready to run.

"Frankly," he admitted, "to keep you here. I need your help. I'll try to find a firm."

And pay them to keep you on, he thought but did not say.

She gazed at him. "Honest?"

"I'd be lost without you, Kylee." Into the silence he said, "You know it's true." He almost thought she'd slipped into one of her trances when she came to.

"That'd be one up their pipe, eh?"

"Try to behave, if I get us an interview."

"If you want," she said offhandedly, turning to the screen.

Next day, he phoned around.

The school they passed was clean. Pop's automobile was smooth. You could hardly feel bumps in the road, like a ship.

"Pop," he asked, so many children playing. "Have I been on a ship?"

"Not yet, son!" Pop grinned at the boy. He liked to drive these educational trips round Tain. "Want to go on one? Ask Mom."

Pop notched the question into his mind. He'd give Doctor a call, ask the significance of that. Clint's queries were down to two or three a day. This familiarisation was all expected, Doctor had explained. Next, a ball game, select a decent diner, show the boy culture.

"Thank you, Pop."

Thanks was the proper response, Clodie decided, listening. One more mention when Hyme spoke to Doctor, that wonderful but expensive expert. Doctor ruled that there was no such thing as a *small* variation. Conformity must be hundred per cent. Doctor had been in child provision for years, every one a winner. No evidence, no police trails.

Doctor's words set the rule: "Those original parents failed the boy, let him get abducted by my finders, right? The parents didn't *lose* the boy. They *abandoned* him. Follow my *rules* and you can't go wrong."

And here Clint was, perfectly adjusted to his Mom and Pop, driving about their new home town.

"Like the ride, son?" Pop asked.

Clint said, "Can we stop at the corner by the shop?"

"By the *store*?" Pop asked, notes for Doctor. "Sure, son."

At Concorde and Vine, Tain's main superstore boasted a CD place. Youths congregated on the sidewalk. It didn't appear very edifying.

"You want anything, son?"

Sound spilled out, some heavy metal. Youngsters moved in desultory synchrony. Two garish displays acclaimed new videos, discs, tracks. Window posters had fanciful cartoons in outlandish colour. Pop thought the scene decadent.

"No, thank you, Pop."

Pop felt an irritation. Chrissakes, Clodie'd got what she wanted. Couldn't she make the boy talk right yet? *Thanks*, not thank you. How much longer? Pop itched to return east, put the block on the sister company, goddam regulations crippling entrepreneurs every fucking where.

The auto moved serenely off.

"We'll take in the school again, Clint, see how you like it, okay?"

"Okay, Pop."

There! Pop thought. That sounded better. Headway!

Chapter Thirty

Things came to a head with Kylee.

Bray tended to think more in sayings. His old Gran came to mind. "Can't," she'd say, "means won't." She had a catalogue of expressions. Occasionally as a child Bray had tried to give them back to her. Each time she'd cap him. "Rome," he told her once, unknowing, aged five, "Rome wasn't built in a day!" He'd heard two nuns say it in the playground. Gran returned, "Who said it was?" which stumped him.

So things "came to a head", first with Kylee who suddenly turned on him one evening while culling e-mail.

"We're flogging some crappy books, is that it?"

"Er, I hope to. They're for children."

"Whaffor?"

"Well, I've had them printed. It seems a waste not to."

"How much?"

This worried Bray. He sat behind her as she "bled" – her term – messages.

"Listen." She'd been out for a smoke in the garden, where Porky was watching some football on a hand television. Porky too smoked odd cigarettes and sometimes seemed hardly able to stand. "Not knowing what you're fucking *doing's* a frigging waste. How much is this costing you?"

He had some idea.

She grinned at him, elfin but wicked. "It's naff, innit?" And translated, "Illegal. Snuff? Drugs?"

"Certainly not!" He continued grandly, "They contain nothing hidden, if that's what you mean."

"Porn?"

He hitched closer, not wanting Porky to hear.

"No. Look. I wrote this children's book. And a second one. I had it printed. I'm trying to sell it. A London publisher's gone quiet on me. I'm hoping your computer net thing —"

"How many we got?"

"A thousand." A real thousand, he thought ruefully.

"Fuck them. I'll do it." She shoved him. "Where d'you want it sold?"

"Where?" He blinked. "American schools, maybe. Little children."

He was astonished at Kylee's alacrity. She talked at the computer, worked from a United States map she got from the computer's innards. Somehow she made that speak, too. In an hour she had an endless list of American schools. She laughed helplessly when he asked her to print it for him. ("Why *print* any fucking thing?") They'd not enough paper anyhow, so shut up. He obeyed, and watched his plan unfold.

She was right. Forget everybody, start selling.

Late that evening, Kylee having left with Porky on some coughing scooter, he phoned George Corkhill to ask how books were actually sold.

"I can ship to a bookseller, Bray. The US customs are

sticky. Small prints like yours we'd ship to a bookseller, bookshops order from him. He pays you monthly."

It was suddenly too fast.

"Want me to arrange it, Bray? I don't want to come at you like a salesman."

"Please." The looming vision of thousands of envelopes, and Customs and Excise forms, faded. The printer seemed so matter-of-fact.

"By tomorrow night?" George paused. "It costs, Bray. Small distributions are notoriously unprofitable."

"Hang that."

They rang off. Geoffrey was standing in the doorway. He'd heard every word.

Did mothers and daughters have these turgid moments, just as fathers and sons? The two of them sat like bookends. They no longer had a fire. Bray thought fires a woman's thing; maybe anciently fires signalled the male?

"I'm lost, Dad." Bray knew not to interrupt. "Shirley's proving unresponsive. Now you're worrying me sick. This thing you're up to. It's not Gilson Mather, is it?"

"One is. And I'm trying to develop something myself."

Geoff looked away. "I came out earlier. That young lout looked drugged. You were telling that slut about selling books in America. Am I in the dark, Dad?"

How often does a father find he's kidding himself?

"Everything is taking me by surprise, Geoff." No acting now. Bray decided on honesty. "I found myself writing a children's tale. A printer says he can make it like a real book." Not complete honesty, but close, the characteristic of sound and trustworthy lies.

"What for?"

"To sell, give away. Who knows? I can't even say it's

sensible." Bray grimaced. "Maybe it's primitive, making amends for God-knows-what. Psychiatrists might say it's an act of reparation." He tried a frank smile. "Spending my pension!"

"Compensation." Geoff spoke dully, notching points of recognition. Bray hoped he'd got away with it. "I do it too, take on something bizarre and not knowing why. I did a scan of Thailand investments. It's not my field. I barely made the last train."

Bray remembered. He'd assumed Geoff was at the hospital.

"The psychiatrist wants us to attend as a family." To his father's sceptical expression Geoff said quickly, "We never have yet. He wants to give us proper guidance."

Expectations of grim tidings? The doctors must simply be going by odds. They were preparing Geoff and Shirley, as they had done bereaved parents before. Jesus, he wondered, how often did this happen?

"Right, son. I'll come."

"One seemed to know a doctor you saw, Dad. Asking about memory."

"Oh, that." He had this lie ready, thank God. "I thought I was losing my mind."

"It might mean we'll move house, Dad, for Shirley's sake."

"Whatever it takes."

For a while they talked quietly of Officer Stazio's retirement, and came to no conclusion. Geoff had stopped ringing Florida, left it to Bray, insulating himself.

There, Bray told himself as Geoff went home next door, it had been surprisingly easy. Geoffrey must still be shellshocked or he'd have spotted the mistakes. He sat before the cold grate. No news from Lottie Vinson about the books. And he'd already finished writing – copying really – Davey's third story. Were they becoming easier, or was he somehow learning to cope with the grief?

The alarming thought was that he might be making new stories and not replicating Davey's own imagination, which would never do. He had to keep faith to the images.

By the time he locked up and took Buster out he'd made up his mind. He would take Kylee on permanently, and simply give the girl her head while he turned the books out one after the other, until his savings ran out.

Next morning at Gilson Mathers he was summoned to Mr Winsarls's office and invited to go to the USA.

Imbalance.

Life, Bray realised when Mr Winsarls spoke about America, could take over. It moved time in patches. Some periods it simply ignored, so that whole days sped by unremarked, then slowed so you wondered why time was frozen.

Mr Winsarls began the oddly convoluted conversation.

"Would you be willing to visit North America, Mr Charleston? Represent the firm?"

"I'm not ready, Mr Winsarls," Bray replied, getting over the astonishment. Shock settled into surprise. It was exactly that episode with Rewa-rewa wood, *Knightia excelsa*, all over again.

He'd been seven years into his articles, when he'd had to work with some of that lustrous New Zealand wood, scarlet-russet, of inordinate weight. A craftsman told him the piece was spare. He'd not checked further, used it for a simple batten and so earned the derision of the firm's three master joiners. Hadn't he bothered to look it up when he felt its turgidity and innate strength as he'd cut?

For the precious antipodean Honeysuckle wood resisted fires, and was of giddy value. He'd known he was encountering something unique, but had ignored the signs in his excitement.

He'd never made the same mistake since.

Now the sense returned. He'd been here before. He almost smiled at the image of New Zealand's lovely Honeysuckle wood and its exquisitely mottled silver grain. He'd learned once from that catastrophe. He must learn from it again, this time in connection with something else far more vital.

"I rather thought the opportunity," Mr Winsarls replied, clearly disappointed, "ahm, of a means of, ahm, perhaps…?"

The English trick, the cause of so much humour among Caribbean folk – of lifting the chin with a concealed sigh to show exasperation – was Mr Winsarls's habit.

"Perhaps in a while, Mr Winsarls."

"Of course, Mr Charleston! We must send somebody. There's only James."

"Is it to do with the history booklet?"

"Sort of. It's rather grown."

"Grown, Mr Winsarls?" Though Bray knew.

"To do a tour, several centres. Talks. At least three American societies."

James Coldren was older than Bray, somewhat arthritic, and now mostly supervised the younger workers. He had joined the firm after service in the Royal Engineers. Highly skilled and with natural aptitude, he lacked Bray's flair. He could not, Bray heard Mr Winsarls say, "put it over with the Yanks."

"But you could, Mr Charleston."

"I need a little more time, sir."

The honorific tended to signal the end of formal conversations.

"How long, exactly?"

Bray hadn't thought it out, but now knew with a terrible certainty that it was a precise duration or none at all.

"Can I say within fifteen months?" Mr Winsarls winced.

"I know, Mr Winsarls. It's when I shall be ready."

"Ready?" the owner picked up sharply.

He quickly made calculations on his desk blotter. Bray himself had made that desk, using *Xylocarpus* wood for its figure. Let botanists argue about *Carapa* names. The beautifully fine rays showed a curious ripple that had made him late home to Emma the day he'd first cut and seen the precious wood's gleam. Ignore the dull russet, one edge showing sombre gum streaking to perfection. He thought it blindingly gorgeous. Wood was sanity, in a world gone mad.

"No later?"

"Definitely not," Bray promised with grave conviction. "The reason is, I rather understated the case. Gilson Mather's work might need quite a book."

"I don't want to press you, Mr Charleston."

Bray managed a smile. He was the one making haste, no one else.

"I shan't complain, sir."

Chapter Thirty-One

Bray's position suddenly soared.

The firm had grown, owing to demand for restored and lookalike antique furniture. The year before, Mr Winsarls had briefly taken on a promotional unit of pushy youngsters from Moorgate ("We're P 'n' E," they kept saying, "Publicity and Evaluation.") to explain the unprecedented increase in orders. They couldn't explain a thing. The surge was put down to fashion, but where did fashions originate, and why?

Now there was another headache: the commemoration book Bray suggested.

Documentation of Gilson Mather's products to be was excavated by the quiet Tracy. Loggo was in awe when lists were put up on a new wall-board. Even the timber delivery blokes congregated to read. Old Harry Diggins, Cockney yard boss, had a high old time bragging exotic tales of Middle Eastern potentates who'd wanted Sheraton, Hepplewhite, Ince, Mayhew, all the great designs. Many reminiscences were true.

"Mr Charleston did that one," Harry Diggins would say, pointing. "Get Tracy to find the drawings. Mr

Charleston sent the designer's sketches back. Christ, the fuss about that!"

Particular woods were remembered, problems with routers, tools spoken of as if they were gifted men of the past. Bray found himself beginning to smile at elevenses. Dick Whitehouse, master joiner in his sixties, matched memory to photos. Loggo and the two sawyers Mick and Pete were full of questions. Mr Winsarls had to restrict tea breaks, too much talk in the busiest season.

No longer did people ask Bray how "things were going at home." Bray was still the same quiet man who sat on the end bench at break times slowly going over the historic files occasionally marking with his HB pencil. It became quite a topic, which of the Wellington chests, what exploits of craftsmanship, Mr Charleston would select. Billie Edgeworth, fervid Manchester United supporter, wanting more of a say. The others laughed, said Billie wanted the place filled with arty girls from the Metropolitan College down the Barbican. He waxed indignant. A festive air developed.

And the list grew. Letters shot round the world, to wherever famed pieces of furniture were traced. Familiar antiques came to light. Correspondents sought provenance trails. Memories were scoured and exotic woods recalled. Loggo started a different display board, soon becoming a nuisance by spreading along two walls, showing famed pieces. His misspellings became a butt of workshop humour.

Tracy now had a young lad called Danny Purchase, who arrived with a potent new computer system, to develop Mr Charleston's proposal. Within a week Danny was a feature of the place. Overseas replies increased exponentially. In no time at all he had indexes, records, addresses, locations, whole maps for the master joiners to goggle at. One marvel was that Danny could somehow turn drawings full circle on the screen, quite as if it stood there in real life. To the owner's exasperation, it became yet another tea-break amusement.

Even Bray went to see. He conversed with Danny Purchase in initials like HTML, and knew without being told what a gopher was.

"That old geezer picks things up fast, dunn he?" Danny said to Tracy. "Is he —?"

Tracy said quickly, "He doesn't talk about it."

In the following weeks the proposed pamphlet became a booklet, then a book, and soon an unwieldy illustrated volume. Bray suggested changing the modem link to save Gilson Mather telephone money.

"Something I heard blokes talking on the train," he apologised. Danny suspected the old man was a smart arse, until he suddenly made several unbelievably clumsy mistakes that Danny instantly rectified with noisy explanations. Mr Charleston smiled, computer technology really beyond him.

"I can't see what's wrong with pen and ink and the ordinary post," he said wistfully. It gave Danny a laugh, and Danny felt secure again.

Lottie Vinson arrived unexpectedly at Bray's home one Friday. He was in his shed after supper and heard the relay doorbell. Buster barked, eager to mock-attack intruders, and together they went to answer.

"The contract's in, Bray!" she exclaimed, delighted. She stood on the doorstep, looking half the age he remembered. "I couldn't wait to tell you. Your phone's always on hold."

He stared, embarrassed. She hesitated. "Is this a bad time?" She held an enormous envelope.

"No. I was just pottering. Do come in."

"Are you sure? I could easily —"

"No, no." He led the way into the living room. "Only, I've rather gone ahead." He shrugged as she seated herself. "I heard nothing from you or Miss Lindsay, so I've done it myself. A rather scatty job…"

"With another publisher?"

"Certainly not! Just me."

"Done what, exactly, Bray?"

"The reprint's on sale, Lottie." Frantically he checked past falsehoods. "Sharlene insisted."

"On *sale*?"

"I've got this bookseller, by post. I've got a computer."

"But didn't we agree, Bray?"

"I'm sorry if I jumped the gun. That's why I wrote to you." She shook her head in puzzlement. "Care of Miss Lindsay."

Lottie's voice became sleet. "Saying…?"

"That I'd go ahead, if I didn't hear soon." Her silence unnerved him. He put in, "Would you like to see?"

"Perhaps I better had."

He took her out into the garden and diffidently admitted her to the computer shed. She stared around. He passed her his two printed books. She sank onto his stool, tilting them for better inspection.

"You really have 'got on', Bray," she said at last. "They're pretty."

"Mr Corkhill's work."

"Another thousand of the second volume, I take it?"

"Well, more than that." Bray felt foolish, flustered, losing track. "I had to ask for three thousand this time, and two thousand more of the first book." He sighed. "You've no idea, Lottie. It's all such trouble. I find it makes one a bit peevish, new orders coming in. See this?"

He showed her messages on the screen.

"It's not hard once you've done it a few times. Make a page – that's a screenful – about the writer. See? Sharlene, her life? I did that. It's called *About The Authoress*. Then a separate screenful about each book."

"What are all those names?"

"Guest book signatures." He felt stupid. "Takes an inordinate amount of time. I've just learned how to update. I'm doing one computer page per book, see?"

"And the sales?"

He sighed. "They're the trouble. Booksellers get frantic. They don't know it's only me."

"I can imagine."

"Mr Corkhill left a message yesterday about another printing, but what can I do? The payments are slow. I'm close to breaking even." He looked at her anxiously. "That's quite good, isn't it?"

He found her watching, and babbled nervously on.

"There's a programme that generates HTML, a godsend…" He petered out. "I don't really have the time to keep nipping round to Aldersgate." He almost started on straight-editor systems as her eyes glazed.

"Sorry, Lottie. You see, I thought you'd given me up."

"Sharlene insisted," she finished for him, and rose. "I'd better go in tomorrow and see what they say."

"Do please tell them I'm sorry."

She gave a curt laugh. It came like a snap. "Not as much as I, Bray."

They remained standing in silence.

A night bird made noises in the garden. Something

screeched. He saw the light come on, saw Geoffrey pass a window, go rummaging in the fridge. Bray had made curry and rice from Sainsbury's packets, and left Geoff his by the microwave. Enough, with bread and butter.

She sighed. "That's it, then, Bray. Is Sharlene pleased?"

"She wants everything done yesterday."

He led the way back to the house. Bray quickly introduced Lottie to Geoff, "My friend from London. My son, Mrs Vinson. Shirley's poorly for the moment, back very soon."

He managed to make sure that the courtesies didn't go on. Afterwards he felt he'd rather bullied her to the front door, but there was Geoff's meal to see to, the book orders to check and the laundry to do. He was dismayed, guessing he'd seen the last of Lottie Vinson. Geoff asked about her disinterestedly. He heard Geoff out about Shirley, then left to cope with the demanding screen. He was so tired. It had been really pleasant having a woman about. Perhaps she'd thought him boastful?

He was shocked to find a series of messages asking when the third book was due. He had given a weak promise a fortnight before saying it was "almost ready", and now some enthusiast in Portland in Oregon – where was Oregon? – wanted dates. Transatlantic e-mail readers wanted a website for a fan club. Was this yet more Kylee?

That night he had a terrible headache. It was all becoming too much. At work the hurried draft of the firm's early history loomed. The following Monday he'd said he would check through it, a huge labour he could hardly face. He was behind in his actual cabinet work. He wondered if he was up to any of this, but was determined to press on, keep going. Hunters did that.

Chapter Thirty-Two

Lottie's visit disturbed him.

Some days he couldn't quite focus, once almost snapped when Kylee burst out at somebody in Louisiana "moaning about these fucking books". He kept control and asked her not to let her invective appear in her computer response.

She glared up at him.

"Why d'you talk like that? You're not like that inside." Sullenly she returned to the screen. "It's that old fucker, the bitch."

"Who?"

"That Lottie cow. You're too fucking old for thinking shagnasty."

He asked Kylee how she knew about Mrs Vinson.

"She's come on here, coupla three times."

"On the computer?" Bray was startled.

"Two-faced old cunt should keep her ugly hooter out of it. She's nothing to do with us."

"What did she say?"

"Wanted to come here." Kylee glared accusingly. "Like party time. I told her to fuck off. I'm going to prog a key *Fuck Off.*"

He couldn't afford more headaches after coming so far. Progress couldn't be an illusion.

"Please, Kylee. Reply with politeness, or…"

"Or what?" she demanded in fury.

"What's up?" Porky grunted at the shed door. It was dark. His cigarettes were more scented than ever. He swayed, coordination almost gone.

"Keep out of it, you!" Kylee was shouting now. "Well?"

Wearily Bray sat, his vision flickering, jagged multicoloured scags invading whatever he looked at. This never used to happen.

"Please don't go, Kylee." She got up and shoved Porky into the garden. The lad fell down, contentedly smoking on. "I don't know the direction. I've just got to keep on. You're my only help."

She didn't return to her stool, stood glaring. Supine Porky chanted some football song into the night air.

"Who's the old bag then?"

"She belongs to London publishers. The books, well, they didn't decide quick enough. So I got Corkhill's." It was almost true.

"We could've wet them."

"Wet?" This was already too much on a bad evening. Bray had Part One of the Gilson Mather draft history indoors, a zillion scraps, sheets, clippings in folders, now swollen to the size of a theology treatise. He hadn't been able to carry more than one section.

"Bribe," Kylee translated. "Give them money to do it for us."

Us. Bray noted the plural with relief.

"They would do it here, Kylee, see how sales went. I couldn't – can't – wait a month, let alone two years. And it's got to be America, nowhere else."

She swung her knees. Buster stirred, hopeful the movement might signal a walk.

"Does the old bitch know? Is she your friend? You shagging her?"

"Of course not." No to all three, he thought, for rectitude's sake.

"We need a website virtual. Want me to knock one up?"

"Yes, please," he said. What was it? And why virtual? He felt worn at an end, but tears weren't a man's prerogative.

"Through that Yank bookseller, or not?"

He had no idea. "I think so, don't you?"

She emitted one of her cackles, old style, all disbelieving hilarity, the promise of coming confusion already in there, and swung back to the console. She reactivated the screen's voice, listening.

"We've only two items, for Christ's sake."

"Three," he said wearily. "I'm on the third book."

"This bookseller doesn't advertise for us."

"I haven't asked her."

"Sod off, while I do it." She seemed kinder, fully restored. "You're a pillock. Nobody sez yes. Proves you're a cret. I reckon the bookshop's cutting us. I'll slice past her a few times, see how bright she is, the rotten cunt!"

"You won't do anything that might prejudice her cooperation?"

"For fuck's sake, get out of my fucking *hair*."

She was already licking her lips, fidgeting, muttering abuse. He said he'd be across in the old shed. Buster stared after him, emerged to look at Porky, then surprisingly returned to Kylee.

As he left he heard the girl mutter, "I'll prejudice her thieving *cooperation*. Who the fuck calls herself LuAnna-Louise?"

He wrote and drew until midnight. He returned to the computer shed, its lights still burning, to find Kylee and Porky gone. A printout was stuck to the dead screen.

Bray

that fancy bitch in st paul don nart in advts so iv sd shed better

or we pull the rug at wk nd n shes nt webbing like us iv told

her update us in her stok list or thats fuckin it Kylee ps pay us

thursday iv dad with that probashen bstrd wed

His money was holding out, but now this.

Illiterate blurb from his only ally. And she in trouble with the probationary court, her divorcing parents, God knows what else. He knew she'd started some fire at a correctional institution, her ruptured family in litigation over it.

He looked round, wanting to simply rest but not daring to. A shed. A computer he still hadn't got the hang of. And drawing pictures from a lost grandchild's fancies in scrapbooks beginning to fade.

Buster sat, chin on his paws, worried.

Bray's eyes needed wiping. In sudden anger he pressed the On and watched the screen come to life. News on glamorous Florida. That, then geography of continental USA. Why not?

They wouldn't have sold Davey in Florida, where memories might be reawakened. New York? Bray was unsure about New York. Too much traffic with London, possibly? California? Possibilities there, so vast were its population movements. Alaska was out, or was it? Hawaii?

He tried to work it out. If I'd stolen a child, where would I hide him? Blank out the child's memory, yes, then take him where to grow up? Somewhere safe from the annual toll of 160,000 gunshot injuries/deaths that the computer said America had these days. Somewhere where schooling was safe, away from tourists. Coincidence had a long arm. And wasn't there that little lad stolen in Greece, sold to Germans a few years back, and recognised after years by a bus conductor on holiday?

The screen's images clicked before his unseeing eyes. He took nothing in, dully going nowhere.

They would have to be rich... He shut down and went in.

A few minutes after midnight the phone rang, scaring him awake.

"Hello?"

"Bray? Lottie." He was still dully working it out when she said gently, "I came, remember? You didn't get my e-mail?"

"Er, we've had hitches." Kylee had admitted she'd scrapped whatever Lottie sent.

"I guessed. I want to help, Bray. Any good?"

"Well, I might have enough help to be going on with, thank you."

A ground war, Lottie versus Kylee, in his shed when he got home? No thank you. And another person to explain to, to serve. It was exactly the dilemma Kylee had seemed to be at first, until she bullied her way in with her computer wizardry. His old Gran used to exclaim, "Lord, save me from mine helpers!" It was the same in the workshop, youngsters coming in for Government financed experience. They all needed continuous help from seniors. Assistance was welcome; assistants were a burden.

"Help finding Davey, I mean."

He stared at the receiver in his hand.

"Are you there, Bray?"

He said nothing. Nobody had said those words before. He had not let them out. He was done for. He told the black phone sorry, and replaced it.

Next morning he boarded the train, in a state of exhaustion. He sat and opened his notebook. Lottie got on and sat opposite.

"Morning," she said.

"Morning." He couldn't think what to say, and sat with his notebook all the way to London. Once, his gaze caught hers. She smiled.

Chapter Thirty-Three

Clint took the arrival of a teacher without anxiety.

Roz Saston came recommended by a leading agency. Highly qualified, she stood up well to Mom and Pop's exhaustive interview, conscious of the fantastic salary. She was ambitious, seeking tenure at the prestigious Gandulfo-Meegeren Foundation, the best anywhere.

"It's a question of Clint's recovery," Mom told her over iced tea.

"Was it very traumatic?"

Mom liked the woman's sympathy, but she wasn't fooled. The teacher was plying for hire, so needed the money. Doctor's guidance: measure your words. Measure, weigh, sift. "The equation equals safety," Doctor repeated, "and the boy is yours for ever." He'd made them write it down, an edict from the infallible expert.

"You've no idea," Mom sighed.

"How long ago was it?"

"Three months since he left hospital. Clint is fine physically. Doctor says he will do well in the right hands."

Mom let the barb settle.

Roz Saston was the third candidate. The first had been

too bossy for her own good. The second, dark to the point of swarthiness, was highly qualified but unable to look Mom in the eye. Something amiss there. You couldn't be too careful. You heard such horrendous tales.

Roz Saston had married young and raised two children. She'd brought snapshots. Her husband was in accounts. Still wed, the offspring in university. Make-up sparse, hair compact, smart skirt, the twinset modest rather than prissy, said she believed in family values. And her references were in order. And yes, she could stay late, given sufficient notice.

Roz Saston gone, Mom phoned the referees for lengthy converse.

"Is she too good to be true?" Hyme asked, getting Clodie's account.

"I'm still checking."

"Use that investigation agency. References can be falsified. It's done in business. Remember that Savings and Loan?"

Clint sat quietly watching baseball on television. His medication was almost withdrawn now. Every day they took him out, the aquarium, sporting events, a school now and again. They'd daringly called on a head teacher while Clint talked with other children. ("Hey, don't you talk pretty!" one little girl exclaimed to Clint, making him go red.) Clint asked if he would go to school.

Mom and Pop promised soon, soon. Doctor had to make sure he was completely better. Clint would have a private teacher at home first.

There was no doubt, Clint was beginning to develop interests. He would watch the fountains in the public gardens for as long as they'd let him, hours at a time. And the stonework carvings at City Hall particularly appealed, depicting machines and agriculture of the Twenties. When they reached home after those outings, the boy seemed tired, and once fell into such a prolonged sleep that Mom phoned Doctor in alarm. Doctor promised to make a domiciliary visit once the new home tutor was into a routine. For extra fees, of course.

The new teacher's duties began the week after. She and Clint got on well. She accepted Mom's list of proscribed topics and words. Mom listened to the teacher's first lessons, recording them exactly as Doctor instructed and posting the tapes off to his clinic. Sentimentally, eyes glistening, Mom made duplicate tapes of her own little boy to play over in years to come.

When, after a fortnight, Clint began to write and draw, Roz Saston was over the moon, and asked Mom's permission to write a monograph about Clint for the local teachers' association. Mom flatly refused, insisting on absolute confidentiality.

Roz was immediately contrite and withdrew the request.

"You're right. I got carried away. It's such a delight to find a child so willing. You have a real talented boy there!"

"Haven't we just!" Mom said fondly.

That night, as Clint slept and Hyme clicked the TV, Mom wept for joy. She had "a real talented boy". It was official, decided by a real educationalist. She told Hyme, but he was going wild at the bastards on CNBC too lazy to give him the stock prices he really needed. She glowed, positively glowed.

Bray knew how fractious he'd been. He worked steadily, missing his breaks. He'd brought an apple, and two banana sandwiches curled at the edges. Women could wrap them so they kept shape, some gift women had. He couldn't. He ate them anyway.

Worse, he made a serious mistake. In front of two students, he absently took up a millwright chisel when working an unusually figured piece of Chi wood from Central America. He realised his mistake even as he made the stroke. The sound of the split resounded through the workshop. He turned, red-faced, to see Billie Edgeworth frozen and Curly and Natalie, two college observers, idly wondering why the older craftsmen were all glancing at each other.

"I'm sorry. Natalie and Curly, please come and see."

Work resumed as he began to point out his ghastly error. He also called Loggo and Suzanne over, the more the merrier.

"Chi wood," he began, showing them his error as they clustered round. "There is a Chinese variant, but this is New World. You notice it seems a shade reddish as you tilt it? Yet it's known as Golden Spoon."

They looked at him. He tried to simulate his usual animation, but the revelations he planned to make to Kylee oppressed him.

Natalie asked, "Are you okay, Mr Charleston?"

"Thank you, yes. I admire woods that are hard and weighty. We call them hearty in the trade. See this has a roey grain, like roe? Makes the wood difficult to bring to a lovely level finish. Chi wood is never huge, which is an extra difficulty."

"Is that it?" Curly asked. "Why the fuss?"

Bray came to. He must have had a blank moment. Harry Diggins lurked nearby, ready with some invented message just in case.

"I was wondering how to explain my mistake." He

looked round at their faces. "I used a millwright chisel instead of a paring tool. It is unforgivable. See the split? Its coarse texture invites catastrophe. My sloppiness has damaged the wood."

"We've got some more." Suzanne pointed to the sleeve stocks. "It's only middling price, yeah?"

"Be that as it may, Suzanne, I still ruined a beautiful length of *Byrsonima crassiflora*. I shall enter it in the book."

He went to tell Mr Winsarls. As he tiredly climbed to the owner's office, he saw James Coldren, a fellow master craftsman, stroll across to inspect the calamity on Bray's workbench. And he heard Curly say to Natalie, copying, "Be that as it may…" A joke.

He confessed his mistake to Mr Winsarls, who dismissed the incident.

"Bray. You're the only master who still keeps a book of errors. Nobody else would as much as notice the flaw."

"I shall stay late and see if I can eliminate it, Mr Winsarls."

The owner watched him thoughtfully all the way down to the workshop floor.

That evening Bray was two hours late reaching home. He got a hero's welcome from Buster, and found that Kylee had left a message saying she'd gone with Porky to the Three Bells pub.

He fed the dog, got his lead and walked to Harrow Road. He found the pair in the public bar and signalled. Dogs were not admitted. They came out to join him.

"Look," he said. "I'm afraid I need help. I'm going to tell you what I plan. I'll put money over the bar for you, Porky, if you'd rather wait inside?"

"Bray means fuck off," Kylee told Porky. "It's summat

secret. Play snooker. Bray, bring some grub out here. I'm fucking starving."

Which was how the ruinous day drew in, Bray sitting with the girl in the garden shelter of the Three Bells while Buster ate a meat and potato pie by their feet.

"Kylee. Can you keep this just between us?"

"Cops, is it? Money?" She cackled her laugh. "Wrong way round innit? You the hood and me frigging holy?"

He drew breath. He dared not be wrong. "Not tell anyone, Porky or anybody else?"

"'Kay."

"My grandson, Davey," he said, braving the words. "He was...taken. Abducted. I hope to find him."

"Nicked? Rotten fuckers. Where?"

"I don't know. Nothing's been any use. Except you."

"Me? How me?" she demanded, belligerent.

"You'll know a way to find him. I think you can do it."

"How?"

He was a long time answering. "Through you, Kylee." Buster finished his pie, looked hopefully up, and sank for a nap. Kylee rubbed the dog's head.

"This book thing? That it?"

He observed her. Kylee usually meant she was disgusted with him for some reason.

"It's all I could think of."

"Any idea who did it?"

"No. So I want you to work out a competition. About the characters in the books and what they do. I've written some questions, with answers."

She nodded. "You shrewd old cunt. What if nobody takes any notice?"

"Maybe somebody will."

They held silence. Buster scratched, heading into a

sleep. Bray was unable to eat the bar sandwiches. Buster might want them. Geoffrey was always on about wrong food for the dog, but what could you do?

"There's some trick in the books," she asked finally. "Davey knows, but nobody else?"

"That's it." He was relieved she'd got it.

"What?"

"It's clues. I only have four. Not even Geoffrey or Shirley knows them. Only Davey can get the answers right. I'll need a statistician."

"Bollocks," Kylee said rudely. "You fucking well won't. They're ignorant cunts. I'll do it. Look." She sipped from his glass, grimaced. "Don't tell anybody the answers, and you've no problem."

"How?" This was his worry. He had the bow, had the arrow, and neither would fit.

"Easy-peasy."

"I don't think you understand, Kylee. When the time comes to set the competition, there might be thousands and thousands of Internet replies, e-mail, whatever. Shoals. And maybe Davey won't even get to see the books anyway. It's a million-to-one chance —"

"It's no problem, you stupid old fart." She finished his glass. "This tastes like pus."

He was past worrying about the girl's drinking age. "I can set four questions. I'll promise a massive prize, so schools will answer. Very valuable. No," he interjected quickly to forestall her, "I don't know what, but it will be rare. If I get that far."

"Look," she said, suddenly angry. "Don't keep giving me this *if I ever* shit, okay? I knowed straight off you wus going for summat and wouldn't give in, so less crap, okay? Pretend with everybody else, but it's fucking pathetic wiv me, yeah?"

"I apologise." He looked away. "I am grateful."

"One thing. No telling anybody the clues. No envelopes in lawyers' offices."

He marvelled, wondering what sort of life the suspicious girl had endured.

"I rather think," he said awkwardly, "we'll need a system of checking answers."

"Test run." She was now bored by his ignorance. "Take me an afternoon. That's not the problem."

"What is?"

"Getting rid of Porky. I'm fed up with the pillock."

Bray exclaimed in alarm. He could see Porky stooping to play a shot at the snooker end of the tap room. What did one say? "Hasn't he been of inordinate help?"

She guffawed, swaying. Buster woke with a start.

She appraised Bray. "You're a weird old bugger, aincher? Like, part of you's clued up, the other bit's not got a fucking light on."

He almost said thanks, as if for a compliment, before catching himself. It might have been an insult.

"Stop pissing yourself wondering if I'll let you down."

"I wasn't," he began nervously, but she cut in.

"You were. No bullshit. That's what you said."

Caught out, he nodded agreement.

"I'll work it out for any number of answers. Try a system out, yeah? You make up four phoney questions for a test run. We'll do random placement. Pi, that squiggle for diameters, works for randomness."

"Does it?" He tried to follow. "Shouldn't it be the less random the better?"

She inspected his glass. "Stick to your fucking planks. Get me another."

He handed her Buster's lead and fetched her a refill. When he returned, she'd eaten his sandwiches and sent him back for more. He brought them. Feed an ally.

Bray found himself telling her of his mistake at work. She was interested in the workshop youngsters, and was amazed they were only going to saw wood for the rest of their lives. She became abusive. He felt relief.

Chapter Thirty-Four

The living room was made ready for the first real teaching session.

Mom confided to Hyme during the night. "What if it's a disaster?"

"Disaster how? With what for Chrissakes?"

Clodie spoke to the air above the bed. "Sleep in the same bed, eat off the same table," her mother had lectured, "and marriage stands a chance. Wise is double shrewd. What a man is, forget."

Well, Clodie tried, but business was always business and sometimes got in the way, sure, but lifestyle and money made up for it. Look at how it brought them Clint, *saved* from uncaring parents. Doctor's word *transferred* was best.

"Clint *remembering*, Hyme!" she gave back.

"He doesn't remember!" Hyme growled, sleep failing because of the Euro.

"Roz Saston might say something!"

"For Christ's sweet sake, what?"

"Anything could set Clint's little mind going!"

Hyme's body rose in the sheets from exasperation.

"He *can't* remember! Jesus, Clodie, how many times?

Didn't Doctor promise, hand on his fucking heart?"

They calmed only when Pop agreed to let Mom postpone the first teaching session until Doctor could be induced to come and oversee.

Doctor, the expert, arrived Tuesday, and was given sumptuous accommodation in Tain's best hotel. The following Thursday he was brought in a limousine to sit listening while Clint and Roz Saston set to work.

Clint knew there were others in the apartment.

Food came from Manuela in the kitchen. The dishes smelled of...he didn't know what they smelled of. Shadows were missing at the bottom of the carpeted stairs because there were so many lights, and there was a thick round railing – wrong to say bannister. It was shiny.

Before TV time after dinner, which was when it started being not bright outside, you hadn't to go downstairs any more because that was when Manuela talked in a language she brought from a long way off. Clint knew he might meet Hessoo there, who was a man with a moustache.

What was wrong with Hessoo?

Clint asked that once, causing Mom to go stiff and rush to the phone and call Pop at work. Clint had been scared for a bit, then it had been all right. Some questions made Mom do that.

Like the time he asked what the little boy was doing out on the grass with a pole near the pond. Clint was staring out of his window, and laughed when the boy almost slipped and fell. Mom had hurried him away and said not to take any notice.

Mom didn't like questions.

That night his tablets changed their colour and Clint was glad because he hated the stinging medicine that looked like oily water. Sometimes he started crying. But now he got pink tablets that were oval in shape, quite like a funny shape he'd forgotten.

There were purple ones he had to swallow, after the Rose Bowl talk-ins started on kids' TV. They talked of numbers and players' names that even Pop didn't know and Pop was a clever man who made a lot of money so they could have a lovely home with Manuela downstairs to cook.

There was a joke.

The joke was the boy who'd fallen over, slid really, with the pole near the pool on the grass below the apartment windows when Clint was watching. He'd only pretended to tumble but really hadn't. He did it to make Clint laugh at the window but Mom didn't know that. Mom didn't understand, not like…

Manuela, funny this, was noisy. Clint knew that because Mom told her off, saying it sharp so Manuela had to shut up but Manuela gave Clint a look that showed she wasn't scared of Mom.

Manuela had a bag made of leather that smelled nice so Clint always wanted to look at it but Manuela wouldn't let him. And the one time – say "once" and Mom got so worried it made her sick – the *one time* Clint said it right out in Manuela's kitchen Manuela put the bag, not satchel, under a kitchen chair.

Manuela's bottom was so fat she bumped into chairs so her frock (except Mom reminded Clint that frock wasn't a word Manuela understood) so her *dress* swung from side to side when she mixed things in bowls fixing dinner.

Manuela was the jokey falling boy's Mummy, Clint knew, but it was secret.

Manuela didn't mind when Clint asked if she was the boy's Mom. She laughed so much she almost crumpled and then told him he was a smart cookie but not to say if he saw the jokey boy because that had been a mistake, okay? And Clint said okay.

Manuela made him say okay again and link little fingers with his other fingers pointed and she said, "You don even know that? My, you got some learnin to do!" Mom came and made him go upstairs because it was time for counting lessons on TV. Clint found some easy but some hard. Mrs Saston was his own teacher and soon he could go back to school with other children liked usual.

Manuela stopped him asking why she never brought the little boy inside while she fixed meals. Manuela's tellings off weren't bad. Clint liked Manuela.

Manuela got scared when he asked was Hessoo the jokey boy's daddy. She made him promise never to say that to Mom, or Manuela would have to go a long way away and never come back again. He promised hard because Manuela was scared.

He made his very best promise. Manuela stared and stared, then went quiet and never said anything for a long time after.

Manuela had been scared, Clint guessed, because he'd said Daddy instead of Pop when asking after Hessoo. Or maybe he'd promised in a wrong way? He said his best promise with his fingers as usual and Manuela's eyes went wide, looking and looking. Then Mom called him and he'd gone upstairs and seen Manuela looking and not smiling.

Manuela let him make patterns in dough when she was baking.

Then Roz Saston came to do teaching and though Clint knew Mom's friend was sitting listening in the next room where Pop sometimes copied numbers from CNN Clint didn't mind.

He wished the jokey boy could be let inside so he could maybe play. Soon he would be going back to school if Mrs Saston was a good teacher like Mom said.

Kylee's smoking was an embarrassment. Bray asked her not to use her small charring cigarettes. She didn't reply for an hour, then erupted.

"Don't pull such a miserable fucking face."

"They can't be healthy." He'd made some fish paste sandwiches. "The scent lingers."

"You'll be telling me they're illegal next."

"Since you mention it," he said drily. She began a tirade before she realised the joke. "Buster hates them."

The golden retriever lay snoring under the porch.

"Tell him to stop smoking."

"Did you manage," Bray caught himself, remembering she couldn't write, and quickly amended, "to work it out? I can't see how we cut down all America to a few places."

She shook her head in disbelief.

"Thicko. Suppose we get a hundred answers, 'kay? We ignore the common answers, 'kay? Cos we only want the weird answers, 'kay? They're, let's say, three out of a hundred."

"Won't there be more than a hundred?"

"Of course there fucking will," she said, stone of face. She blew smoke down her nostrils. Even when Bray had smoked a pipe, he'd not been able to do that. "You're thick, so I'm making it easy. Three per cent, 'kay? That's to Question One. Then three per cent to Question Two. Same for Three and Four, 'kay?"

"Yes." He wrote it in tabular form, four questions, three correct for each.

"Davey gives weird answers, yeah? Nobody else does.

Or else you chosed wrong questions."

"Yes."

"So what's the odds?" She waited. "C'mon!"

"I don't know. I'm —"

"Don't say sorry. I can't fucking stand it. It's three per cent of three per cent over and over, innit?"

Laboriously she repeated it. "Jesus, you're bone. It's 81 in hundred million, innit? So'f we gets forty thousand answers and five per cent weirds, then Question One scores 2,000, yeah?"

Bray felt stricken. "Search two thousand towns?"

She almost hopped with fury. "You don't *have* to. It goes down wiv every answer."

Grumbling, she dictated the working step by step, her feet up on the table.

"See? The answer's less than one, 'kay?" While she smoked another roll-up he went over the calculations. Her smokes burned with inordinate speed. "Got there, have yer? Nought-point-two-five?"

He stared at the arithmetic. It couldn't be so simple, so clear.

"I'll have to search less than one place?"

"You want fucking jam on it. Want a drag?" And when he shook his head said, "Welcome to Planet Earth, Grampa. Davey *has* to be in the last fraction."

"I see." He couldn't, but nearly could. There seemed to be a definite sum with an answer that was Davey.

He could hardly make her out for a sudden blurring of his sight. He went to the standard lamp as if to read in a better light.

"When we're in a right fucking mess," she said, admonishing him like a child, "read them numbers through, yeah? Get your balls back."

"Kylee." He plotted phraseology, not wanting her in another berserk rage. "Can your numbers lie?"

"No," she said evenly. "Only words do that."

Recovering, he said, "Thank you."

She was so certain. "No matter how big, they reduce by the weirdo fraction."

"I'm sorry I've taken so long."

She shrugged. "It's fucking chancy, depends on your questions, yeah? Choose ones only Davey knows, we're in. Choose wrong, the last fraction'll be so fucking big we'll still be hunting him when we're ninety."

"Thank you, Kylee," he said. We, he thought; she said we.

"Time you learnt to fucking count, Thicko. Want a calculator cheap? It'll be clean, not nicked."

"Thank you, no," he said politely. "I shall depend on you."

"Remember your numbers for once, yeah?"

"Yeah." His mimicked pronunciation almost made her smile.

Chapter Thirty-Five

Disturbances at Gilson Mather never bothered Bray much. The firm had its moments of course, but they were beyond control. Destruction in Indonesia, wars halting hardwood shipments, strikes on distant waterfronts, all wore patience down. Worst of all was the slowness of supplies, especially when forest fires seemed pandemic.

These things the young did not understand. They listened but never took them in. Suzanne, reorientating into her new career, couldn't comprehend. She caught half a conversation between himself and Mr Winsarls about having to abandon a pair of serpentine fronted knifecases because of delayed delivery.

"Why don't you order from somewhere else?" she asked.

Bray looked at the floor. Pleasant to see wood shavings about, but this time of day it should have been swept. Mr Winsarls began a convoluted explanation about matching orders to shipping.

"Calamander's not in the book," Suzanne accused Bray.

"Look it up under Coramandel." Embarrassment came too easily, Bray always found. "And under *Diospyros quaesita.* Many joiners mean any sort of variegated ebony, and assume the wrong wood."

Suzanne went to grumble at Harry Diggins about the loss of her corner clamps. Bray mentioned that chain moulding was an error in something so compact as a knife urn.

"It's what's been ordered, Mr Charleston," Mr Winsarls said.

The owner's exasperation had lately been on daily show. He invited Bray to come up to the office and closed the door.

"I'm beginning to think we're understaffed, Mr Charleston," Mr Winsarls began. "Nobody ever seems to finish a job. I'm not," he interposed hastily, "saying the whole workshop floor's gone to pot."

Bray helped. "The anniversary volume, Mr Winsarls?"

"That's it." Winsarls was relieved. "I wonder if we should postpone it."

"I'm sorry to have —"

"No, no, my decision, your advocacy. How long is it, nearly three months? Perfectly proper." Winsarls sighed, tipped back his chair. "I mean, how many London firms with our history haven't had commemorative publications?"

"None, sir. We are the only one without."

"Right! But just look!"

A separate, tiresomely modern, table had been set up in the corner of the owner's office. It was stacked with letters, faxes, papers.

"Sorry, Mr Charleston, but every one of those asks for information, or has historical news about our pieces. There are three messages from one Arkansas lady who has a Loudon style kitchen dresser made by my great-grandfather. Christ Almighty, Bray. She wants a bloody pen pal back in 1833."

"It could be fairly —"

"No." Winsarls seemed broken. Bray carefully showed compassion. He'd known this was coming, and was ready. "A fortnight ago I counted. That stack represents seven hundred items, plus descriptions of four hundred others. That's eleven hundred pieces of restored antiques, or our own repros. Auction houses alone fax us a hundred a month."

Bray's lie was ready. "I'd no idea it would grow like this."

"Danny's all right." Mr Winsarls waved Bray to silence and swung his chair, a sure sign of testiness. "But he hasn't a clue what the hell we're talking about. He misclassifies every damned thing. I'm coming unstitched, and that's a fact. It's not his fault. The lad can't even copy right. The girls are just typists. Not like old Mrs Elton."

"Is Mrs Elton…?" Bray began with seeming hopefulness.

"Afraid not. She's gone to live in Carlisle."

"I rather feel it's my fault, Mr Winsarls. Can we back out?"

"No. We've gone too far, sowed the dragon's teeth." He gave Bray a wry smile. "I'm in the classical dilemma. Stop or go on, either's catastrophe. The problem's reaching the work floor. Just listen." They made a show of listening. Raised voices about the loading bay not being cleared, the outer doors still ajar, and Harry Diggins having to ask Bill Edgeworth and Dick Whitehouse, master joiners no less, to spare him Loggo. "Hear that? There's been such a response. It's mushrooming. In fact, a real bastard."

Mr Winsarls lowered his feet.

"Apologies, Mr Charleston. I'm not quite a ruined man."

It was a poor attempt at humour, but they were back on the rails. Anyone looking in would see a boss quietly talking things over with his head craftsman, nothing amiss.

"The youngsters on part-time day-release never contribute," Bray said. "I think we must exclude them."

"My opinion too," Mr Winsarls said, guardedly waiting for more.

"They're a falsehood, sir, with respect. How many will ever have the knowledge Loggo will acquire? And he's the last near-apprentice we will ever see. New starters like Suzanne are sometimes good, but truculent because they want to skip learning, seeing only status."

"Go on." Mr Winsarls began to look hopeful, knowing his man.

"Gilson Mather is either marsupialised or extinct. The former means we'll survive as a curiosity, slowly continue to get new orders, go on the way we are now. The latter means we must close or get taken over. Extinction will come about by misjudgements," and Bray paused for effect, "of management."

"Meaning what?"

"We must go ahead with the commemorative volume, Mr Winsarls. Develop it, not cut it down, make a real show, a splendid effort, two volumes if need be. Go for gold. We've done what banks, manufacturers, purveyors of brand goods, would give their thumbs for. We've accidentally got the world interested. You say the queries —"

"A deluge, Mr Charleston. We've not had this week's yet. I'll bet that bloody pile's from overseas."

"Then we get somebody experienced who'll know how

to sift the records of a firm like Gilson Mather. Send the two girls back to routine."

"I had rather hoped you would have been that person," Mr Winsarls said wistfully. "You've already got too much on."

"Antiques are becoming priceless. You know that, Mr Winsarls. Now the rest of the world has learned it. It simply means our volumes are overdue!"

Mr Winsarls polished his spectacles, a decision was coming.

"Where do we find such a person?"

"Actually, sir," Bray said, "I've been almost as concerned as yourself lately. An idea came to mind. Nobody's fault, but that bloodwood caused me lost sleep. And the yellow *Limonia* – did you see the *acidissima* last Friday? Nobody seems to realise how small the Indian tree —"

The owner waved him back to the problem.

Bray cleared his throat. "I'm sure the person would cooperate with a good printer, given precise instructions."

"Sounds a godsend. Would you sound the notion out?"

"Yes, Mr Winsarls. Could you give me a day?"

The following week, Lottie Vinson started at Gilson Mather in charge of the historical publication. She was given a free hand.

"She here, that old bitch?"

"Mrs Vinson? No. And remember secret."

They met in the bus shelter outside the town's Odeon cinema. Kylee carried an immense carton of cola and a sack of popcorn. Mercifully she offered him none. It was headachingly sunny. They sat on the cinema steps. She was going in with friends.

"The picture's crap."

He didn't ask. "Did you think about a system?"

"Coded thirty questions. Got to graph up."

"The four specials?"

"No, Dumbo. Them all."

"There might be tens of thousands."

"What's one and one, Thicko? That's my Question One."

"Two," he said, startled, glancing about, hoping nobody could hear.

"So Question One gets forty thousand answers all saying the same thing: two. But we get some nerk who'll say three, and another moron who'll say it's maybe two-point-five, okay?"

"Possibly."

"*You'll* secretly know that the storybook answer you want is eighteen – because one person Out There knows that. Got it?"

"Ye-e-es."

"The correct answer doesn't matter a tinker's fuck. We only want the one weird answer that matches yours, see?

"So how do we weed out the immense mass of correct answers?"

"We don't. The computer does. Me."

Three shabby youngsters were approaching. One waved. Kylee didn't wave back.

"Don't worry."

He left before her friends reached the steps. He felt a million years old. If it was simple to her, why wasn't it to him?

Her confidence touched him. At home he celebrated with a bottle of the same beer from which Davey used to smell the bubbles.

When dawn came, he'd worked out his four questions

and the answers he wanted. Needed. Had to have, from some child – how had Kylee put it? – Out There. He wrote nothing down, left no trace, no evidence. He memorised them, for when the time came. He went to work breathless.

Chapter Thirty-Six

Subterfuge was unnatural to him. Now, though, news was policy because that's where deceits came from. You had to stay sane, so he shunned newspapers and mostly ignored the TV news.

Across the road from Gilson Mather's stood a bingo emporium. Once a cinema, wrestling venue, music hall, it now had a bowling alley where youths played obsessionally on machines that clanged and flashed.

It also had banks of public phones. From a bored girl in a booth he obtained a weight of change, and dialled. It was ten-fifteen. Mr Maddy proved difficult to reach, but Bray stuck it out through layers of doubting receptionists.

"Charleston?" Mr Maddy questioned. "You say I'm expecting your call?"

"Well, no." Bray had notes. In a flurry he abandoned them. "I'm from Gilson Mather. Seven months ago, a Lancashire settle?"

"I'm in your bloody queue," Mr Maddy grumbled. "Aye, I remember. A foreigner got in first."

"Do you still want it, Mr Maddy?"

"Course I do. You're the head maker I spoke to?"

"Charleston, yes." He ran on. "I could do it next. At," he gambled recklessly, "no charge."

Silence. Then, "What's the racket?"

Youths were brawling good-naturedly nearby.

"I'm in a bingo place, Mr Maddy," Bray apologised lamely. "There's some sort of scuffle." He couldn't get started. What did one say when bribing one of the principal collectors?

"There is no catch, Mr Maddy."

"Look. Winsarls shoved me down the list, and charges me a fortune. Now I get it free?" He chuckled. "Spit it out, man. You want something I've got."

"You run a computering firm, Mr Maddy?"

"I *design* computer *systems*. If you want a cheap PC —"

"Certainly not! I pay the proper price." He drew breath and went for it, in for a penny. "I have a young, er, relative who's extremely able. I'd like, please, for her to be employed."

"If she's such a wiz, why isn't she already employed?"

"She has difficulty with words, Mr Maddy. Dyslexic, with some autism."

"Autistic? A rival firm's got two – playing the Benefits Agency, squeeze the government. Too much malarky for my liking."

"No, Mr Maddy." Bray said, almost not lying. "She's developed her own colour scheme and, er, everything. She invents computer bits as she goes along."

"Relative, you say?" Maddy mused. "Very well, I'll see her. How much longer would I have had to wait for my order if I hadn't agreed?"

Shamed, Bray confessed. "I moved your order to priority this morning, Mr Maddy. I didn't want you to think I was trying to bribe you."

The businessman laughed. "Mr Charleston, don't ever go into business. You'd starve."

They made arrangements for an interview.

Roz Saston was pleased by the boy's progress. He spoke oddly. She told her husband, and put it down to being raised in New England.

"Marvellous that she was able to have a child so late, though of course Clint's rising seven."

"Doctors can do anything," her husband Phil said. "It's money."

They discussed Roz's tutorship's fantastic salary.

"He'll probably go to the Gandulfo-Meegeren." Roz became wistful. "Costliest in the state."

"It might help you get tenure if he gets in."

"If?" Roz echoed. "She mentioned funding. Money talks."

The boy was increasingly alert, his acumen brisker by the day, though the first lessons needed repeating, some twice over. He showed a curiously lopsided ability to take on facts and images to an extraordinary degree. Roz concluded that somebody had worked herself to the bone. Or maybe Clint was just made that way?

"It's almost," she told Phil, "as if part of him was asleep."

"Hospitalisation, poor kid. Once he's back among kids he'll be fine."

"Some Florida doctor visits. I leave him tapes and reports. I don't get feedback."

"They're being mighty careful."

"Wouldn't you be, if it was Roberta or Clay?"

They agreed parents never lost that feeling.

* * *

Doctor audited the recordings of Roz's lessons and gave Mom a favourable report. It would necessitate – his term – more two trips to Tain, each a three-day sojourn. Hyme grumbled.

Mom rebuked Pop. "Expertise isn't only dollars, Hyme."

Hyme snorted, because life *was*. He'd winced at Doctor's latest hotel bills. To listen to tapes? "We could mail the tapes, Chrissakes."

"And see them lost, is that what you want?" Mom fumed. It was late, Hyme still clicking maddeningly at the screen waiting for some numbers so they could sleep. "We do as Doctor says."

"Once Clint does this, once Clint does that," Hyme said morosely, eyes on the percentages that plagued him. "It was once Clint gets a tutor. Now it's school."

"That's life. *His* life." She lay facing him. "You're not having regrets?"

"Never. Doctor's taking his time is all."

Mom promised to phone Doctor's clinic the very next day and ask outright when Clint could start school. A difficult thing to ask, but she had to. Once Hyme got his teeth into finance he never let go.

The lessons began to make sense.

Clint was surprised that he could delight Roz by remembering something real well. He liked her, tried hard to please.

Manuela was nice, and Maria who sometimes helped Manuela bang pans in the kitchen though Maria was not much good because she kept asking Manuela what to do and Manuela shouted at her in words Clint didn't know. It wasn't really bad shouting.

Manuela didn't mention the jokey boy, and he was careful not to say anything. He could have asked, except that might make her not nice, like that nurse at the clinic where the trees made patterns from sun shadows on the ceiling.

He made some of the same patterns in dough. Manuela kept the knife away, and you needed a knife – any knife, if you hadn't proper ones – or the patterns got slopey. He never got one right. You needed tools.

He made palm tree shapes but they weren't any good. Maybe you could do it better with bread. Maria made bread that got hard and Manuela threw it out. She never put bird food in a carved wood thing, but left it on the balcony in a pot.

Clint wondered if it was time for his tablet. He was having fewer now. Manuela said he'd soon go to school. Everybody was pleased with him.

Chapter Thirty-Seven

The probation officer, Mr Catchpole, turned out to be a harassed individual carrying sheaves of papers. The office was sparse. Bray thought he could at least have shaved, then forgave the worried man. Who knew how many Kylees he had to help?

They made staccato conversation across the plastic table, the officer keeping an eye on the time.

"You wish to help Kylee Walsingham."

"My son and his wife would assist. I'd bear all the expense."

"Is adoption in mind?"

Bray hadn't spoken to Geoffrey about it. "Well, Kylee—"

"Is a near autistic and dyslexic, and in serious trouble. You heard about the police business?" Bray nodded, but he hadn't.

"You're aware of the circumstances, Mr Catchpole." Bray had been frank about Davey after Catchpole's promised confidentiality. "I want to help some child. Kylee's bright. Her father knows she does computer work for me."

"Mr Charleston, your offer is not unprecedented. A family suffers a bereavement and wants to simulate their lost child."

"In case you doubted my motives, I would pay for her education here or elsewhere, if that's the kind of thing you do. And if her parents would agree."

"I see." Catchpole's wariness dwindled.

"She needn't know where the money comes from. Your department could simply bill me, be the disbursing agency and leave me out of it. Even if she was fostered or something. Only, she deserves better."

"Better from whom?"

"All of us." Bray's resolve strengthened before the other's sharp defensiveness. "I'll make no bones, Mr Catchpole. If I weren't divorced, I'd adopt Kylee and do my best for her. If my son's wife weren't ill, I'd try to persuade them to do the same."

They spoke of possibilities, Bray dismayed at the complexity of things. He left after an hour, his offer declined. They would review it in six months. Kylee had said nothing about any police business. What was it? He decided not to ask.

The final report was compiled to Mom's satisfaction three weeks later. Pop thought it wasn't good enough, that Roz Saston must be dragging her feet, lengthening her highly-paid sessions, spreading her butter.

"We both know why, Clodie," he told his wife darkly.

Mom flared up. "Is money all you think about? It's always dollars."

It was safe to raise their voices. Clint was out walking with Roz Saston by the wide lake that lay this side of the public gardens.

There were sands there, real dunes just like a genuine seashore. Ambulatory rest-revision, Doctor told Mom to regard those walk-talk-no-chalk sessions. Clint enjoyed running to the water and back. He always checked where Roz was, though, because they'd warned him he was to do that. Mom and Pop could see him from their roof garden, which was totally enmeshed for Clint's safety. Roz did lessons in the roof's open air, good for a growing child. You had to think of these things. Mom relished motherhood, her forte.

Now he was better, Clint came back red of face and breathless, eyes shining. Look at him in those moments, nobody would ever believe he'd suffered any accident whatsoever. Completely renewed, completely theirs. Clint was the perfect boy.

Doctor said he was bright. Medication was withdrawn "practically down to homeopathic levels". Doctor promised that Clint's first week in school would be the end of all treatment. Doctor's very words: "No problem!"

Mom thought Pop totally boorish and said so.

"I'm donating a year's salary to that school, Clodie!"

"Tax deductible!" she shot back. They lay on recliners in the morning sun, drinks to hand and Mrs Saston's reports on the striped decker. "You regret it? Well, do you?"

"Tax deductible means it's higher value!" You couldn't beat Pop on tax.

"It's still only money!"

"Money got Clint! What if I'd been broke?"

"Donating to a school's an investment, Hyme." Mom turned to wheedling, knowing she'd made a mistake.

"That's true," Pop said grudgingly. He kept his eyes on Clint below, who was looking at some kid flying a kite. "Maybe I ought to walk with them."

"Oh, Hyme. That would be great. Walking with his pop!"

An oriental kid, some thin guy along. Slants were always thin. Pop wondered if exercise might get the gut down on that artificial money-made beach down there.

Clint was watching the kite, talking to Roz. She better be teaching Clint, not just wasting time. Pop thought, how come I pay, everybody else do F A?

"Sure," he said. "I'll go with them tomorrow."

"I'll get the camera —"

"No cameras, hon. You forgot the rules."

"Just one wouldn't do any harm."

"Clodie," Hyme warned. His wife fell silent. No cameras was Doctor's rule.

Lakeside, Roz let Clint run beside the darker skinned boy. They made a pretty picture, Clint so fair and the other, a year older, dark. The boy let the coloured box sink against the blue sky.

Marvellous, Roz Saston thought, how some cultures – what, Vietnamese? – went for garish colours. Maybe organic dyes in their home countries? Clint was laughing.

"I'm Clint," Clint told him. The other boy was Kim.

Clint stood behind Kim and looked along the cord to the kite.

"Dad made it." Kim quickly wound the string as the breeze fell. "It's got three wraps, see?"

Red, and a brilliant orange. Struts poked from the ends. Dowels? Clint thought he'd ask Roz about dowels. He felt excited at the way Kim made the kite stagger then suddenly soar.

"Do it again!"

Kim's father laughed, called some words Clint didn't

know. Kim made the kite dance, its garish long tail waving like a...like anything, then climb. Clint clapped. A straight line was brilliant.

Roz was real nice. She let Clint stay with Kim some more minutes then called him because it was time to do the lesson about pets and fishes, who belonged to different sets. Clint called so-long to Kim and Kim's daddy and the kite.

Roz and Clint started back. Two boats with white sails were gliding on the blue water, except where the clouds made the lake grey.

"Can we come back tomorrow, Roz?"

"If Mom and Pop say, sure."

"Maybe Kim'll be here. Roz, what's dowel?"

Roz thought a moment. "Isn't it round wood? From the hardware?"

"Did you see Kim's daddy's hat?"

"Sure did. Pretty, all colours. Lots of new Americans keep to their usual clothes. On a born American a pillbox hat would look kinda stupid, but on him it's okay, right?"

"Right," Clint said, looking back.

"Okay, Clint. Pay attention. How do we group different living things?"

"Colour."

"Colour's good, honey. But plants are different in all kinds of ways." They had been over this twice.

Clint was looking back, which worried Roz. She was under firm instructions to make precise reports for Doctor. One vital marker was attention span.

"What are the colours on the kite?"

She wondered about Daltonism. "Red, different blues, yellow, orange, purple. And the side panel's dark green. See it?"

He repeated the colours when he stopped to scuff the sand.

"You got a favourite colour, Clint?"

He stood looking back. "Blue," he said, looking up at her. "Is blue okay?"

Roz was touched. He seemed so anxious. "Sure, honey! It's my favourite too!"

Later, she entered up her summary, careful to include Clint's own phrases, his interest in the boy Kim's kite.

She was surprised but pleased when Clint's father said he would walk with them tomorrow. Increased contact could only improve a child's learning, which meant that soon she would be superfluous and Clint would go to school. She was fond of the boy, but how could he develop if he simply stayed at home?

Chapter Thirty-Eight

The visiting college students hadn't done well choosing woods. He'd let them go on for two mornings, ruining several good pieces. It would be worth it, if they learned.

"Pine," he told them. "Spruce, Western red cedar will be fine too. Douglas fir is reliable. Who chose hemlock?"

Silence. A sour youth in a sweat shirt stirred. Him?

"A poisoner?" a girl said, to laughter. Nigh forty years, and the same jokes.

The workshop was quiet. Craftsmen saw the students as intruders.

"The *Tsuga* genus," Bray continued. "It's beautiful, but splits quick as look. The benefit is its grain, so straight and even. Western Hemlock, of course."

"You marked me down," the girl said irritably. She was comely and knew it, so how dare an old past-it bloke criticise. "Some grain business."

"Afraid so."

"You didn't tell us to pick wood sawn like that."

"Quarter sawn wood, straight and even grain." Bray looked away, embarrassed to contradict her outright. His weakness was the reason Kylee was so abusive. Would he ever improve? "I did sketches in your handout."

She only looked angrier. "You didn't say which pages we needed!"

Bray felt his years. "Read all of it, miss."

"Then why didn't you say so, *mister*?"

"Forgive me," he said without dryness. "Shall we look at your cuts?"

The teaching bench held their eight pieces. He mentioned mistakes he'd made, Spruce catching him out with its knots and unexpected resin pockets, showing them how to auscultate by listening for the ominous buzzing sound when tapped. They seemed uninterested and sulky.

He apologised for going on and said they could go. The scruff picked the hemlock up when Bray said they could take their work.

"Ask if you've any questions," he called lamely.

They couldn't get out fast enough. Bray stood for a moment.

Davey knew how to auscultate wood, though his little fingers weren't yet firm enough to percuss. He used a pebble.

Would Davey remember? Would the students? He felt wasted.

"Memory," Doctor said, "is stigmata. Not Padre Pio's holiness, your common insult."

"I don't understand, Doctor," Nurse Linda Hunger said.

Doctor loved to be reminded that he was *the* expert. She'd heard this talk before, when her special friend Lissette was briefed for a snatch kid who'd eventually gone to a showbiz couple in Maine.

"This is your first domiciliary, Linda?"

"Yes, Doctor. I'm thrilled."

A scrip issue, now the clinic was decently valued, would soon come her way. She'd get her share after this job. A nest egg is a nest egg is money.

"Listen up, Linda."

For an instant, Nurse Linda Hunger judged Doctor as a male, and saw that fussiness might obscure steel beneath. The man, for all his wonderful if illegal work, was a dragon in its cave. Perhaps, she reasoned, he really needed company? What a philosophy his was, removing kids from uncaring parents and, who knew, possible abuse, to a better life. Doctor was brilliant. You couldn't argue with success.

There was the usual staff talk about him. Her friend Marge, another nurse, hinted that Doctor had put the question to her when she'd been on a California domiciliary. Marge wouldn't say if she'd done it with Doctor. Another nurse, Leah, fully fledged, went on home visits with scarcely a nod. Plain as day, right out she told Linda that it was one of Doctor's perks. Where was the harm? Leah said you were either in or you were *out*, girl, and remember where the money came.

Nurse Linda listened. Doctor's voice became muted.

"Have you ever considered what an insult memory is, Linda?"

"No, Doctor." And she hadn't.

"Memory is a series of cruelties instilled into the brain. As babies, we're unaware of calamities out there. Then we start to *see*.

"Events, Linda, are all simply trauma. No such thing as a pleasurable event. Slings, arrows, blows, toxins. You feel pleasure sometimes? No! Pleasure is an interlude between pangs we call experience.

"So with the boy. One of many. Clint has been rescued,

Linda. His parents were incompetent uncaring bastards. Anybody wants proof, look-see what happened: they let my abduction team whisk him away. We saved the boy.

"The last vestiges of Clint's infant memory need expunging. The residues will be there. My therapies and your nursing will eradicate them during your housekeeping duties in their home. Any traces that surface, the boy will never know whether it was a dream, or a TTVW – the Tired TV Watcher – syndrome. He'll never know it might represent reality."

"Thank you, Doctor." Linda committed herself. "I hope I can do you justice."

"I'm sure you will, Linda." Doctor poured a bourbon. "The hotel in Tain is confidential. I've a visit in Houston, be back day after tomorrow." He waited. "Will that suit?"

She hardly paused. Her own man needn't know. "Of course, Doctor."

At the door she looked back but Doctor was already jotting notes and didn't return her goodbye. Hundred per cent, she thought, leaving. That's what Doctor is. Never wrong, fixated on success, dedicated. Where was the harm in a quickie with somebody like that? Which was okay, authority wanting repayment, get a return. Ambition paid if done right. Power appealed.

She wondered if he was married, put the thought out of her mind.

Intensively briefed though Roz Saston was, she thought Clint less animated than she'd hoped during his first visit. She was anxious for him to make a good impression at the Foundation, though his admission would mean the end of her teaching. Aware of this, she brought up the question of Clint's medication.

Mom flared up immediately right there in front of the boy.

"Doctor has laid down Clint's treatment, lady! Not another word, hear me?"

It was ejaculated with such venom that Roz actually recoiled. Manuela had just finished serving the breakfast. Roz stammered apologies, said of course she'd spoken out of turn. Mom saw to Clint's sports attire. Some quirk left Clint cold about football items, baseball catchers' essentials, but Roz knew that accidents could do mighty strange things.

The school she already knew, the head teacher Joan Daley. Of middle age, the deputy Mrs Amarance appeared smart and spoke well at fund-raisers. She and Mom hit it off, Pop's large donation influencing Mrs Amarance's attitude.

They were shown round during the morning break by Mrs Daley herself. She asked no questions, which suggested that Mom's lengthy calls had paid off. Clint was calm to the point of docility.

"Yes, we've taken on a new housekeeper, Mrs Daley," Mom gushed at the school's vaunted exhibition gallery. "To coincide with Clint's return to schooling."

"How thoughtful!" the head exclaimed. "You'll have more free time —"

"To focus on Clint's schoolwork," Mom capped pointedly.

Mrs Amarance opened the double doors. Roz exclaimed at the spaciousness. An expanse of grey carpet emphasised the displayed paintings and collages. A feature was the brilliant illumination. Roz remarked on this clever touch. Joan Daley modestly disclaimed originality.

"We copied the style from museums back east, Mrs Saston. It works!"

"Clint seems taken by it!"

He was standing before a cluster of drawings.

"All art is the children's own work," Mrs Amarance announced. "The stage is angled, notice that? Adaptive usage! Even our swimming pools can be automatically covered by a safe — safety first, right? — retractable flooring!"

"That sounds great."

"Roz, why don't you take Clint to see pictures?" Mrs Daley suggested.

As Roz Saston complied, both teachers asked Mom if she had details of Clint's previous school record.

"Next week," Mom replied brightly. "My husband's going over it."

"Fine," the head teacher said. "We keep continuous records."

Mom passed it off with a laugh, reminding herself to catch Hyme.

Clint proved hard to move on. A long display table held some two dozen small figurines, bowls and vases.

"They have a great pottery class, Clint!" Roz said brightly.

He said, "Some aren't coloured."

"No, well, maybe they will colour them later."

It was heavy going with the boy today. Roz could hardly elicit a response. No resuming lessons later. The boy seemed pooped.

"They might," Clint said, eyes on the figurines.

She drew him to the end of the display where futuristic terracotta creations stood on a polished driftwood swirl. Clint came passively.

"Teachers love imagination!" Roz said. There was something wrong. The day had augured so well, yet Clint was in a dream world. Clint said something she didn't quite catch.

"Really, honey?" she said mechanically.

"We'll see the sports fields," Joan Daley announced, advancing to the french doors. "You'll see just how extensive they are!"

For a further hour they toured the school. Mom approved of the close supervision. The exits from the school were guarded by uniformed patrollers.

Mrs Amarance elaborated on the school's security, casually mentioning the costs but pointing out the inestimable benefits to the school community.

That afternoon Mom allowed Clint and Roz to go walking along the lakeside, Pop with them. Clint was quiet. Little Kim the Vietnamese boy was not there. Roz showed Clint where the new baseball pitch would be, telling him how great it would look against the lakeshore. Clint trudged tiredly along.

Later, a new housekeeper arrived. She was called Mrs Linda. Roz left when it was time for dinner. Manuela rolled her eyes at Clint secretly when Linda said something about hot things on the table. Clint knew Manuela didn't like Linda straight off.

Linda was boss. Sometimes even Mom had to look at Linda to see if you were saying the right things. Maybe Linda was boss over Mom?

Clint knew he'd seen Mrs Linda before, maybe at the clinic where the palm trees made shadows on the wall just before it got dark.

That night at home Roz remembered what it was Clint had told her in the school's exhibition room. He'd said the same again by the lakeside. She'd paid it no mind. Now it struck her as a bit odd.

"The table's bad," Clint had said.

"Really, honey?" she'd answered.

"It rocks," he'd said. Yet nobody had touched the solid display table.

She mentioned it to her husband in bed. They marvelled at a child's mind, how strange that some triviality seemed special to a kid. No doubt about it, though, Clint would start at the Foundation, so it was goodbye. Roz felt quite tearful, but that was a teacher's lot. Kids come, and kids go. The usual things.

Chapter Thirty-Nine

The light was fading in Clint's bedroom.

Linda had gone. Manuela was singing in the kitchen. He liked to hear it. Sometimes it stopped.

Manuela had told him to go upstairs and watch TV. It happened when the moustache man Hessoo was outside in an old truck looking at motors, no, *automobiles*.

Only when he'd started school, when hard winds blew and Mom started saying things about winter, did Clint guess that Manuela wanted him out of her kitchen after a pickup went past that you hadn't to call a motor. It went down the road then came back and Manuela told him pretty smart to go and watch TV.

Clint liked Manuela. He liked the little jokey boy who came every time the truck went slow past the house. It came from the lakeside. Clint knew that because he'd seen it when walking with Roz. He'd asked Roz about it once and she didn't know, but grown-up people told you wrong things on account of you being a kid.

The falling boy hung back as the man got out of the truck, and the little boy always looked up to see if Clint was watching him from the window.

Then the falling boy would wait until his daddy Hessoo went in front and he'd stumble on the sidewalk. It was the same joke. Clint always laughed aloud behind his curtains, no, drapes, and watched them slip in through Manuela's door.

Clint liked the joking game. It was a pretend.

The man had darker skin than Manuela. Eventually Clint knew to call them Mexicans, and heard the word wetbacks. They had to pretend they didn't know Manuela at all, when all the time the darker man was Manuela's daddy and she was the laughing boy's mummy. Just like Pop was Mom and Clint was their kid.

He knew right off that Manuela would say she didn't know the jokey boy. She pretended, so as not to spoil the game. Clint thought it wasn't much of a game, but they thought it was so that was fine. Cool, he said now. It was cool.

The first days at school were only adjustment.

Clint's introductory report was glowing, if weak in some subjects. Mrs Daley's summary sent Mom into raptures.

"It's been a complete success, Hyme! He'll be fifth in the whole class!"

No doubt about it, Pop was fond of the boy. He'd soon go to a school game. Seeing him walk the lakeshore with Clint was a pleasure. Much of it was, Pop knew, his own adjustment to fatherhood. He had to work at it. Worth every cent.

Doctor finally withdrew the medication. No need any longer. Linda Hunger was in there housekeeping, fine by Pop because Mom needed help around the place. They had a gardener, a Tijuana Tourist like people in Tain called immigrant workers. Manuela took on four other temporary women whenever Mom decided to throw a dinner. A firm sent extra help over for Mrs Hunger. Clint accepted his place, his family.

Everything worked.

There was still a hidden cost. Doctor came up from his Florida clinic monthly, and Linda Hunger went to the hotel. Pop picked up the tab, so he knew to the dollar. Enterprise meant after sales services. Pop chuckled at that. He did a little, back east.

Clint was the success, so the future was assured.

After Gilson Mather's workshop, Mr Maddy's firm seemed gigantic. He met them in the foyer.

"I'm only a dogsbody," he said, leading them through a succession of plush offices.

Except, secretaries beamed and showed the man deference. They also exchanged looks as the rough-looking girl and the workman passed by. Mr Maddy's office bore the title General Manager Development.

"Kylee," he said affably. "You're not alone with your reading difficulty. We've got others here the same. Grampa explained."

Kylee said evenly, looking at Bray, who reddened, "Grampa did, did he?"

"I'd like to talk about computers, how far you've got. Is that all right?"

Kylee remained standing and wandered to the window. "I get fed up."

"Oh. Right. We find workers with your, ah, very rewarding."

"Gerron with it."

Maddy laughed, raising his eyebrows at Bray. "You're

certainly direct. Now, systems. What can you do with a computer?"

"Time they got fluid. Conduction's asking for it."

The manager stared at her. "It is?"

"You make them talk like wankers. Fucking waste of space."

Mr Maddy coloured and said coldly, "I developed some of those, miss."

"Costs the earth for fuck all except a load er strife. Some old git sits down, the CD's like a dod, talk-in all week. What good's that?"

Bray listened, uncomprehending.

Mr Maddy eyed her, frowning. "Then what would be better?"

"Folk don't know any different. Any voice, no read. Do it fluid. Bugger crystallines at first, or you blam recursive. There's got ter be a dozen fluids in line crystal, int there?"

"Ah, what kind?"

Kylee turned to Bray. "He's fucking thick." Her expression didn't alter as she added, "Grampa, I'm frigging starving."

Bray rose apologetically. "Sorry, Mr Maddy. Perhaps we'll come on another…"

"Wait a moment. I'd like Kylee to meet one of our university development staff. He has ideas like Kylee's."

Kylee wandered and peered into rooms. Bray caught her up. She ignored hazard notices and sauntered into a laboratory. Maddy took Bray's arm as Kylee watched a technician build a circuit board.

"We'll just let her wander for a few minutes," he said thoughtfully. "I have a feeling she's in her natural environment."

"Are you sure?"

"Autistic geniuses might just run in your family, Mr Charleston."

"She has a heart of gold," Bray said desperately. He felt helpless, wanting to bribe, coerce, anything so Kylee was saved from those unrelenting social people.

"Quite honestly, if she's anything like she seems, I'll take the risk."

The following week Kylee received an offer from Mr Maddy of an associate scholarship in computer development, grade II. Bray worried about the documentation. Kylee replied with abuse, saying she could create any certificates anybody wanted. She finally accepted, "as long as I can keep coming here, 'kay?" Bray smiled and wrote her letter of acceptance, to start at Maddy's firm in Halstead, fifteen miles away.

Chapter Forty

Drizzle needlessly affected the spirits, Bray used to tell people when the subject of weather came up. A bloke on the train complained that Bray must be a Buddhist, talking like that.

When he bought the anniversary cake he felt almost uplifted, though it wasn't much of an anniversary. It was actually more a commemoration. Considering what he'd started with since the horror, he had come a distance. He had *progressed*.

The weeks were edging into months now. Doubt had become obstacles in a season's turning, yet luck occasionally blessed him. Look at Kylee, who still jeered as she took his money. She was now a trusted, well, friend or something similar.

The cake was hard to manage on the crowded train home. Two women asked him what the cake was for – no disguising the cake box of an exalted confectioner's. Shamefacedly, he'd said he was going to surprise a friend.

"She's helped me quite a time," he'd told them when pressed.

They said that was sweet.

"I don't cook much," he'd admitted. "Maybe I'll get something in."

That started them off, scandalous prices, supermarkets up to their dreadful games. They wished him luck as he alighted, quite as if he was off to some romantic coup.

Miraculously he caught a bus in the gloaming, its lights haloed by rain. Luck was with him. It was running late, saved him ten damp minutes. At home the porch light was on, Lottie's signal that she was working in the shed.

He put the box on the kitchen table, shouted through the door and saw her bent over the computer. She heard him and waved. He went upstairs and spruced up more than usual.

Twenty minutes later he lit a candle, and called her.

"What's this, Bray?" She appeared in the doorway.

He felt woefully embarrassed. "The best I could think up, I'm afraid. Sort of five-month anniversary."

"Really? I'm touched."

"Blow it out." A knife, he'd forgotten a knife. "Tonight's going to be in the wrong order. Cake first. It might have to count as a pudding. Then we go out for supper. Winstanley's should be open."

The little ceremony felt a failure after that. Bray became more solemn than he'd intended and Lottie seemed to absorb his mood. They sat. They each had a slice as if putting on a performance. Bray had to force his piece down. It was repellently sweet.

Winstanley's was almost empty, something on television or maybe one of those rainy evenings where folk ached for bed.

"I won't know what to do with the rest of that cake," Bray confessed.

"It was a charming thought."

"We have come far, haven't we?" Put like that, Bray sounded disgracefully weak. "Since Kylee and Porky."

"How is Kylee?"

They ordered. Bray worried about wine.

"She's doing well at Maddy's. Two weeks! That fax drives me mental."

Kylee's e-mails came intermittently, sometimes three a day. Porky was never mentioned now, though other youths occasionally came into her messages as "a laugh" or "a mate".

"Stays with her aunt and uncle in Halstead. I wish she'd phone instead." He tried to smile. "Too old fashioned."

"Does she ever ask how we're – how you're – getting on?"

"No." He put in defensively, "Kylee knows I wouldn't be able to answer."

"You would now, Bray. You haven't heard."

"Heard what?" Lottie wore her I-have-news look.

The time when he trembled at possible news had long since gone. Bray expected it would be something technical from Corkhill's over the next KV volume. Like childhood games you threw a six and climbed a ladder.

"Did George say the setting was all right?"

In *The Triumph of KV* he had introduced a mystery. Brief as the rest. Bray had done a dozen rewrites only to find it finishing up exactly as he'd started.

"George liked it. We're five hours ahead of America."

So? Sometimes Lottie grew coy about the soaring sales figures, or another distributor taking the KV stories on.

"The series has been adopted." She saw his incomprehension and touched his hand. "Their Department of Education has pooled us. KV is acceptable."

He stared blankly at her. The waiter brought their starters.

"It's what you aimed for, Bray."

The candlelight blurred Lottie's features.

"Your tales, Bray. Davey's stories. They were very commendatory. We can add it to our publicity, *Advised reading for children.* You don't understand the tide of responses on our e-mails," she inserted neatly. "Genuine ones now. They add to the shoal of Kylee-generated falsehoods! That American distributor Candice is over the moon. She's doing a release featuring Sharlene!"

"What does it mean?"

"It means an American TV contract is on the cards now."

They sat in silence. Lottie started saying how Candice, their main USA distributor, had sent no fewer than seven exultant e-mails that morning.

"It's tremendous news, Bray. I wondered if you'd heard at work. Playing about," she added with a smile, "while I slogged."

She worked at Gilson Mather two weekdays now, on the firm's history.

"We'll be flooded, Bray. Educationalists are all eager for copy." She looked rather shamefaced. "That's actually Candice's phrase. Do we do it?"

"We do what?"

"Give Candice her head. Let her use the official reco – her term again. Sales should blast off. I really must abandon these Americanisms," Lottie said as they sipped wine. "They're catching. I did a sectional series of e-mails, Bray."

"What are they?"

"Look." Neither began the meal. Their waiter hovered.

"Go on like we are, we'll improve, but *only* in sales."

"Isn't that the point?" His special evening was usurped, things spinning out of control.

"Partly. We must try new things every single day."

"What did you do?" He was beginning to know her.

"I used Gilson Mather," she said bluntly. "I've taken the addresses of the responses to Mr Winsarls's survey, and used those."

"You've *what*?"

"For the KV publicity. It was necessary, Bray." She was defiant. "I've identified over a thousand American buyers of Gilson Mather's restored antiques and reproduction furniture. I've sent details of the KV stories into the elementary schools in their areas, towns, districts. And the next thing."

"Tell me."

"Is everything all right, sir?" their waiter asked anxiously.

"Yes, thank you."

"I've advertised a charity competition for educational purposes. You planned it, right? You and Kylee keep talking the mathematics. Children of Davey's age. It will centre on the TV series. Link-in."

"You…" He passed his hands in front of his eyes. "It's too soon."

"And I've done something else, Bray. I've promised all respondents a Sheraton repro, made by the senior joinery master at Gilson Mather's, for the one connoisseur who can get our KV stories accepted in most local schools. As an aid to anti-illiteracy campaigns."

Bray stared, aghast. "Does Mr Winsarls know this?"

"No."

"Lottie, it's exploiting the firm's trust!"

"I know," she said blithely. "Your idea was a competition based on the books. We just shift it to TV!" She started her meal. "You're missing the point, Bray. Speed!"

He said faintly, "We're running amok, Lottie."

"Bray, darling," she said without contrition, "eat your meal. It's lovely."

"My Garvan piece is going to be the prize. But how to explain the one of the firm's own pieces to Mr Winsarls?"

"It will cost the firm next to nothing! Let Gilson Mather take the credit for helping education."

He saw her earnest expression. She said levelly, "George Corkhill can be trusted. He'll not let anything slip to Mr Winsarls. There is a problem, though."

"There is?"

"The person we never speak of is your step-sister Sharlene. Authoress," she said drily, "of the KV stories. She doesn't really exist, does she?"

It took some time before he managed, "No."

"You made her up."

"Yes."

"Necessary." She nodded, enjoying herself immensely. He couldn't make her out, when he'd thought he knew her quite well. Was she glad Sharlene was a figment? "I can see that. You couldn't do this alone, or the child stealers would spot you and move on. So you invented Sharlene."

"I had to." He was surprised she didn't seem at all offended.

"Of course you had!" Her smile returned. "I guessed a month ago. Face it, Bray. I'm your ally. I'm in with you, however long it takes."

"Like Kylee said?" The girl had been bitter about Lottie.

"Exactly."

"Thank you."

He thought a moment, and added that he'd better let George Corkhill know that Lottie was virtually a partner. She laughed at that, eventually having to dab her eyes, whining about her mascara.

"George has known ever since I came!" she told Bray, still laughing. "It's become a standing joke at the printer's!" Bray failed to see the humour. "I can be Sharlene, Bray, if it comes to it. Except I'm appallingly healthy for my advanced age!"

For a while he felt almost betrayed, the way she had pretended to be taken in. By the end of the evening he had come round. After all, she had only done as he intended. They discussed ways of exploiting the newfound success and the problem of getting round the absence of Sharlene S. Trayer.

Bray was apprehensive about any TV series. Lottie said it would be a hoot.

"Anything on a TV screen about KV is on our side, Bray," she concluded. "Look at it like that."

Chapter Forty-One

The TV offices were ultramodern.

Some aspects of publishing, Lottie thought, gazing round, were truly obnoxious. More so than TV, perhaps. It was the people in the trade as much as anything. Tropical plants, madly naff paintings, scruffy notice boards. Swish receptionists, that Continental indifference showing, and males grumbling into straggling beards, you'd run out of adjectives in a school essay. Today's colours were designer lime and yellows, as horrid as you could get. Blonde, it seemed, was in, and trad skirt suits were back. Hello olde tymers, she thought cattily, here's redundant over-the-hill Lottie Vinson trying to sell eccentric kiddies' tales scribbled by a no-hoper in a shed. Jesus.

"Lottie Vinson?" a nasal girl asked.

Lottie said good morning and got the predictable response.

"Would you wait, please? Mr Heilbron will be with you directly."

Smarting, Lottie sat. As ever, deodorant never quite managed to overcome the tang of Peptic City's bad coffee. She was eventually admitted to where five of the TV junta waited, each exhibiting various degrees of animosity. Lottie's sure instincts for determining pecking order were still there: Heilbron and Moiya Laudrup mattered. The rest were mere number lumber.

Heilbron was a glossily rotund man. Lottie wondered if he'd visited L.A.'s famed Black Tower and was desperately copying Hollywood ethnicity. He wore an unconvincing Van Dyke, surely the butt of office jokes? The Moiya Laudrup woman looked varnished, hair dyed the requisite blonde, teeth a-dazzle. She came round the desk to shake hands, hey, us women against male swinishness.

Her effusive introductions were gilded malevolence. Lottie was clearly a seabed feeder, whose sole purpose was to provide them with profit or get the fuck out. Lottie warned herself to relax, because antagonisms always showed. She went brightly into foils-before-sabres, talked of traffic, this and that.

Lacquered minions, carefully less glamorous than La Laudrup, served coffee then withdrew. A woman launched into a grim account of the difficulties of adapting children's books to the screen. She had false teeth that didn't quite stick. With every word, Lottie's spirits rose. How fortunate, she thought, that I've heard this patter a hundred times before. If the next minion moans about costs, I'm in without a shot fired.

"Thank you, Melie," Mr Heilbron beamed. "Frank?"

A crusty old pinstriped man ahemed his way into a dithery monologue all about pre-production funding ratios. Adaptations were ruinous to any TV company, especially one with a superb production record.

"Downtable stuff." Heilbron gave Lottie a rueful beam, sorry how the meeting is turning out but let's press on. "Freda?"

Freda was a skeletal lady quivering under gorgeous hair. She delivered a saga of trade union setbacks and calamitous markets. Lottie listened with increasing optimism. Moiya would promote Freda, for we ladies infallibly pick out ugly limited-cortex sisters. Quickly she told herself, *Lottie, just remember smiles and quiet confidence.*

"So you see, Lottie, it's a pret-ty sorry outlook!"

For a moment Lottie wondered if Heilbron had marked her card, knew that they were angling to give KV a tryout. This wasn't a conference. It was a haggle.

"Questions," Ms Laudrup put in briskly. "The material?"

"Written by an American lady, seriously infirm," Lottie said. "I'm her sole agent."

A minion stacked KV copies on the table. Nobody glanced there.

"Strange history, don't you think, Lottie?"

"I've seen stranger, Ms Laudrup. There was one writer who —"

"Sure, sure." Heilbron held a hand out. Melie thrust a file into it. Heilbron deigned to peruse the page. "Your graph's bald. Verifiable?"

"All data is available. I won't disclose marketing devices."

"We can't do without those." Frank coughed apologetically. Heilbron and Laudrup laughed in synchrony, programmed.

"If anything did get green-lighted," Moiya said, her smile vanishing so swiftly that even Lottie didn't perceive the change, "the question is adaptation."

"The authoress won't do the TV script. She's too busy."

Heilbron and Laudrup didn't swap looks, but Lottie felt loads lift.

"Conditional or not?"

"Of course. Sharlene's drawn up a list of essentials," Lottie said. The next thing was an outrageous guess. "Fifteen details, and screenwriters have complete discretion." She could have said three or twenty, but what the hell.

"Open discretion suits TV best."

Lottie had never exactly worked the TV end. Open discretion meant they could do whatever they liked to Bray's stories. This team must think Christmas had arrived. Now was the time they realised that Christmas also brought winter.

"No, sorry. I fought Sharlene tooth and nail."

"We could meet with Sharlene…"

Lottie heard him out before refusing. "I have no route round her doctors. Getting the next book out of Sharlene is difficult enough. Any option will be non-renewable, three months."

"It's never less than six!" Heilbron exclaimed, agitated.

"I had to battle for three. Sharlene's definite."

"Soonest being…?"

Lottie smiled. It was time to arm, load, aim. Fire?

"My agent's instinct is to pretend I've a million TV offers. Truth is, I have no more screen appointments." She let it drag a second. "Sharlene will give me hell if I dawdle over contracts. First come gets served."

"Our parent company is American, Lottie. Has textual approval been sought from educational authorities in US of A?"

"Already negotiated," Lottie said smoothly. Inclusion of the KV stories in the Cannon Endriss political lobby was the one concession she had squeezed out of those new enemies, once her old friends. There would be a price, but she was in too far.

"Time scale?"

"No idea," she said, stone-faced. "I already have got approved USA certification."

Moiya Laudrup almost smiled, learning the calibre of her visitor. "We'd like you to hold on until it came through. Otherwise…" She sighed to show a perfectly good deal would be ruined.

"No. That would give you a free pending option." Lottie suppressed the temptation to say that some TV companies might not care whether the stories were approved in America or not. It did matter to Bray and, she admitted with growing frankness, to herself.

They banished the three acolytes after a while, sent for more coffee, and talked until early in the afternoon. Lottie declined lunch.

That evening, she wrote to Officer Stazio.

Dear Officer Stazio,

Forgive this intrusion into your retirement. You may recall that we spoke on the telephone soon after I became acquainted with Mr Charleston.

Might I ask your advice? How much would it cost to hire some reliable investigator, to see if there have been any advances in tracing missing children? I know agencies are only rarely successful, but I do not want to miss any chance of helping Mr Charleston who, incidentally, does not know of this letter.

I enclose International Reply Coupons for return postage. I trust that you are enjoying retirement.

She gave her home address and phone number only. After all, Officer Stazio might only seem sympathetic. She herself had only just earned Bray's grudging trust. Even sending the letter was taking a risk. Stazio knew nothing about Bray's books.

A whole week she deliberated, then Friday evening posted the letter, her hand shaking.

Bray knew that events can arrive already at war with each other, the pandemonium leaving you limp as a rag. It happened on the Saturday he received the latest KV book from George Corkhill – a courier, Buster rushing out barking. Only at eleven o'clock did Bray realise that his friends opposite were in their garden looking at his house. He went to the window and signalled disappointment. Courier or no courier, there was no news.

The new book, *The Rescue of KV*, showed his imperfect drawings on the dust cover, the kites made of purple leaves, the motor car leaf engines looking rummer than ever. But all authentic, exactly as Davey had first drawn them. Bray started reading. Words looked totally different in print. George's note said how pleased he was at the work Bray's series was generating.

The doorbell rang. Bray concealed the little book under a cushion, thinking it was probably Lottie back for some reason. He opened it to Mr Walsingham, standing there with a woman. Bray kept hold of Buster.

"Mr Walsingham!" Bray looked from one to the other. "It isn't bad news?"

Walsingham was rueful. "No, nothing serious. I felt I should call. This is Kitty."

Bray asked them in, wondering.

"We won't stay, Mr Charleston." They sat together on the couch, Bray glimpsing his book as the cushions were disturbed.

"Nothing's wrong, is it? I haven't seen Kylee since Wednesday."

"No, nothing like that." Kitty glanced about the room. Her gaze touched on some flowers Lottie had left as Walsingham went on, "I want to apologise. I must have created a terrible impression. I'm sorry."

"There's no need."

"There is, you see. Kylee's never looked back since you came on the scene."

Bray considered the words. "I don't quite know what to make of that, Mr Walsingham. Kylee's behaviour is exemplary." He smiled awkwardly. "Sorry if that sounds a bit like a probation officer's report..." He petered out at the gaffe.

"She's a new person."

Kitty spoke for the first time. "Our lives were impossible until she started work for you, Mr Charleston." She gave a half-laugh. "She's actually stopped her deranged attacks on us. All right, on *me*."

Walsingham said frankly, "We're going to marry soon. Kylee doesn't mind. And the job you arranged."

"I only put them in touch."

"She lays the law down, as usual," Walsingham added. "She's content."

"It's been a transformation. We have you to thank."

"Not at all, er, Kitty. Kylee's merely growing up."

"It's more than that," Walsingham said. "My daughter's been in trouble as long as I can remember. She's nothing like she was."

"Can I ask what exactly it is she does?"

"Oh, just computer work. She rigged up a shed. Kylee does it all. I'm the most electronically useless cabinet maker on the coast."

Walsingham asked, "Can I offer my own expertise?"

"No, thanks, Mr Walsingham." Bray felt the man's unease. "Kylee is enough. I couldn't have done a thing without her."

"I just hope her language doesn't bother you!" Kitty said.

"Not at all." Too stiff, too reserved. Bray struggled. "Kylee deserves the very best chance in life."

"It's been the making of her."

The couple left after a few minutes, still exchanging reassurances. Bray felt that Kitty was pleased by Lottie's flowers.

He let Buster out into the garden before resuming his reading of *The Rescue of KV*. It was a slight story, brief as ever, involving some giant who stole the colour essential for the kites, was one of the first tales Davey had ever made up. The rescue was nothing more than a timely change in the wind direction, causing the foe's escaping balloon to disintegrate. Bray's eyes filled as he remembered Davey's face glowing with delight as he'd drawn the leaves floated down to the sea. Bray had retold the saga over and over while Davey listened, vigilant in case a word was missed.

Everything was essential in Davey's stories, every word, every phrase. It had to be word perfect, even to the intrusion of a passing duck that tried to swallow a leaf and kept missing.

Two good things, then a tax document requiring information about Bray's business. Payments were due, and accounts had to be rendered within days.

Before the afternoon was out, two more bombshells. Shirley suffered some sort of relapse, and Geoffrey faced redundancy.

Chapter Forty-Two

Late one evening Retired Officer Jim Stazio phoned. "That you, Bray? No news, just making a how're y'doin' call, no reason."

Bray took it. He'd walked Buster and the retriever was now asleep in his pit. That night was months into the search. Bray could think in those terms now without anguish, though counting the days renewed his anger every single time.

He was becoming frightened. So many things happening – sales, the first TV episode in production, Lottie's determination wrestling deals in the American market, a part-time lady in Gloucester taking over local distribution. But the old question remained, was it progress? Kylee had changed Bray's computer for swifter devices, still mouthing off, still abusive, but less furious and more certain than before.

For the past two months he'd driven himself to the point of exhaustion, until George Corkhill, Kylee, Lottie and Geoffrey, not to mention Suzanne and Harry Diggins at work, everybody in fact tried to tell him to take it easy. Only when Loggo had taken hold of a piece of mahogany to steady it while Bray worked did he acknowledge that he was worn out.

He went through preliminary courtesies with Officer Stazio.

"Can I call you back? I'm just —"

Stazio chuckled. "Hey, Bray, I'm retired, not broke! I can still afford a call."

"Sorry." It was Bray's cackhanded attempt to save the other's call charges. "Old age creeps on. Retirement suiting you?"

"Love it. Miss everything, though." Stazio sighed. "I called to ask about you, truth to tell. Still doing that sawing? Feller I bowl with midweek mentioned your firm. Gilson Mather? I said nuthin', just listened up. Has an old sideboard and stuff, right proud of them things."

"My firm's doing some USA promotion."

"I hear it's pretty famous." Stazio paused while Bray wondered. "How's Geoffrey and his lady?"

"Going to live in the Midlands. The doctors thought it might be less difficult. I'm minding their house. It's adjacent. And I get the dog!"

"That liaison officer, whatsername, she keep in touch?"

"I ring her once a fortnight." It was hard to admit the uselessness of Jim's replacement. She always wanted to get him off the line. "Just saying I'm still here."

"More hurt than dirt." Again that pause. "You on your own there, Bray?"

"You mean now? No. A lady helps...with my hobby. Just nonsense." Bray watched his words.

"Does romance blossom?"

He felt embarrassed. Was this the reason Stazio was ringing? "Not really. She's a friend, works part time at my firm."

They spoke of Shirley, Geoffrey's promotion, Bray's possible journey to the USA. They mentioned the possibility of meeting. Stazio rang off, and that was that.

Bray looked at himself in the mirror. He had talked with Shirley's psychiatrist, learned much about bereaved parents' ominous temptation to construct shrines. Their house was virtually as it had been all these months. So was Bray's. It is no shrine, Bray firmly told his reflection. And, in Geoff's house, Davey's room was still untouched, simply waiting. It had merely been temporarily vacated. Status quo, as it were. Shrines are for what's gone for good. Davey hadn't done anything of the kind.

Lottie picked up her bedside receiver and heard the gravelly voice of Officer Stazio.

"I just called Bray. He seems fine."

It was she who had suggested he ring Bray, to convince the retired policeman she was not some ghoul.

"Right. Can I ask now?"

"Look, lady. Don't go hiring some P.I. shyster. I'll help in any way I can. I'm retired."

"I understand, Mr Stazio. All I want is information. It would take months if I tried to sieve it from libraries or wherever. It's to help Bray."

"Maybe you're a reporter?"

"If you harbour doubts, ring off now and I'll look elsewhere. Or you can ask Bray outright."

"All off the record, right?"

"Of course." She hesitated. "Mr Stazio, about the 50,000 missing children —"

"Hold on right there. Numbers get pulled out of the air. Way back in 1983, a US senator said that 50,000 kids were abducted annually in the US of A. The Justice Department worked on it, and corrected the number to just 5,000. The jury's still out. But hey, 90,000 kids under sixteen run away from home in *your* country every year, right?"

She kept him to it. "Is there any way of narrowing a search? There's so much written about porn rings and social agencies I don't know where to turn."

"Police have shit lists, excuse me, but nobody's saying names."

"Then there are definitely known suspects?"

"Sure are."

"Could I acquire such a list, say by hiring someone?"

"You'd be wasting your money. There's plenty of P.I.s willing to accept your bank draft and do sweet nothing. You'd get glossy reports, o'course, keep your hopes up while they reel your dollars in. That's as good as it gets. Bray hinted the same. I told him like I'm telling you."

"Do you know *any* successes, Mr Stazio?"

"For local abducted kids? A possible three, in thirty years of police work, all traced close to home, and all Americans. Runaway children are different. Higher percentage for runaways – they return of their own accord, or some church network finds them. Anti-drug agencies, police tracers, there are systems for runaways."

"Thank you, Mr Stazio. I appreciate your frankness."

They arranged to ring periodically.

She sat watching the dark estuary until dawn came over the shore. She felt she had only reached the point where Bray had actually begun, all that time before.

Except his lone quest had gone a distance. Erratic, certainly. Bumbling and with setbacks, inevitably. Yet he had kept going. Never quite knowing what he was doing, he had ploughed on through the nightmare, and he was still there.

Her heart was close to breaking for him. She ran a hot bath and got ready for the new day. Lots to do.

They took the limo, with a strange driver who kept looking all around and talked into a phone. He had a black hook thing with a blob in front of his mouth, and he kept signalling to another man in the mall. Clint wanted to ask if he'd got kids too but Pop said not to because he was busy.

Thanksgiving was a great holiday. Clint liked it, with people talking about so many Thanksgiving dinners and Mom laughed and said how can we get through all this? Pop was in a great mood and said they'd throw a party and they did, with Manuela and Maria and several of Manuela's friends coming to scream in the kitchen because somebody hadn't delivered stuff.

Clint got to say who was coming to the Thanksgiving party so he said all his friends from school and it was great. Thanksgiving was one day but spread out each side to make a bigger holiday. Everybody was pleased.

They had games. He wanted to invite the Kim the kite boy and his daddy who had a round hat but Pop said no they were just casual people and Mom said that's right honey.

Still they had a great time and Pop said Mom must get real good presents for the kids not tacky stuff from Wealstone and Biggelmod's shop that only sold cheapo Puerto Rican. Mom had special people called caterers. Pop had entertainers come, like clowns and big plastic creatures that made Clint shiver. He went into his room from the garden – yard – shivering and his hands went all cold and shaking for nothing when he was having a great time. Mom told Pop he shouldn't be so and Pop said how the hell was he expected to know. They phoned Doctor.

Pop made it okay. He sent the creatures away and all the kids said are you okay Clint and Clint told them sure and they had a great party and firework colours spread about in the sky. Clint didn't really like them either. Other kids' moms and pops said well they could make you jump so they'd better cool the fireworks.

They played great games and the entertainers were great and two were faces Clint had seen on the new TV cartoon show and the kids got real excited and clapped whooping. Pop said it cost a fortune and Mom said it was worth it just to see Clint's face.

Next day they went to the mall. Clint's friends Carlson and Leeta were there with their folks and Clint shouted and they came over to do shopping with them. They had a great time. The limo driver followed Clint. Pop had a hard time keeping up. Mom didn't like the crowds. Carlson said the black hook thing was a microphone. The limo man was there even when they saw computers that Carlson liked. Leeta said it was kinda boring though she liked the characters on screens all round.

Leeta made everybody laugh because she held her hands on her head like one of the hats the carved people wore in new books she was reading that were on bookstalls now. Leeta was funny, and did the squeaky voices she'd heard on adverts for programmes that were coming on children's TV. Carlson's daddy was a secret in the State capitol and said they were going to be real popular at Christmas and Leeta's mom said oh dear that's another fortune and toys didn't last a single minute. Pop said hey that's the Christmas spirit.

Clint saw the purple scenery on the book fronts and said there'll be a floating balloon come soon. Carlson said bet you a dollar there isn't. Clint said bet you a dollar there is. Leeta hated the purple snow thing and the badgers were the wrong colour anyway. Then the bookstore's screens suddenly showed a floating balloon come right in the picture just like Clint said. The man in the shop laughed and said hey kid can you do that any time or did you just get lucky. Carlson said sure Clint can do it any time and the man said go on then let's see it. Mom and Pop came over and said what's the big attraction. Carlson got mad because the shop man wouldn't believe him. Leeta said come on let's go somewhere else because computers were boring and her daddy was a preacher and said they were Sodom and Gomorrah.

So they went to Zeemer's Coffee Sprawl. Carlson's and Leeta's folks were fun. Clint hadn't even known that Leeta had a baby brother who was seven months but couldn't do much. Carlson said you're lucky I got a big brother and a sister and they stop me doing things.

While they were in Zeemer's Coffee Sprawl one of the big mouse characters came playing mall music and Clint was sick. Mom and Pop said it was time to go and everybody said sure it's kind of airless in these places. Clint and his folks went home with the driving man who kept looking everywhere.

At home Clint was sick a couple more times and Manuela said see I told you too much rich food and Mom got mad at her. They called a new doctor who asked questions that Linda Hunger answered making Mom worse mad. The doctor said Clint got himself overtired with Thanksgiving and all. Clint would be fine.

And that was the end of the Thanksgiving except the next day they went to Carlson's for a barbecue. They played games. Clint kept a lookout but there were no big cartoon characters like that mouse and that dog so it was okay. Mom and Pop said it was a really great Thanksgiving.

That night Clint dreamed of kites and wrong-colour badgers. He wasn't scared any more because in the dream there was an old man who wore a thick apron stiff with paints and it had pouches bulging with rags and brushes. He had thick rag gloves, and filed wood so the surface was ready for the next thing you did to it. He held it up and said see, it was beautiful all the time inside and we've made it show isn't that real cool.

Only he didn't say real cool. He said…

splendid.

He always said *splendid.*

Clint slept well. It was school next day.

Chapter Forty-Three

They watched television, the first KV episode. Buster waited for his evening patrol of Avery Fields, and looking at Lottie as if reminding her to get her things and leave Bray to it.

Lottie said eventually, "It seems different. Don't you think?" They had it on video, to watch repeatedly.

"You mean the music?" Each episode began with an Albinoni *adagio*, one of Bray's favourites. "Davey likes it."

"No. The pace of the episode." Lottie knew him enough by now to say, "What, Bray?"

"TV firms and stations keep merging."

"It's out in USA this week."

Lottie felt nervous. This was the first time she'd even thought of staying over. Nothing sexual, just in the spare bedroom. Geoffrey's and Shirley's adjoining dwelling was vacant. It seemed the natural thing. To herself, maybe, but what about Bray? Who'd said nothing to her. No, leave things as they were.

"We're on edge. So much happening."

It was true. The TV launch had been surprisingly muted. Bray almost expected other commuters to look at him anew, the morning after the KV programme was aired. He felt flat, lost, and couldn't help thinking, is that it? Nobody in the workshop said a thing. How could they when they didn't know? Illogical, of course. Nobody knew, except Lottie and George Corkhill. Not even Geoff. Fine, the printer's people had been excited, and an inch appeared in the *East Anglian Daily Times*, nothing to do with Bray anyway, and that had been that.

To Lottie everything felt exactly right. She was relieved, knowing just what sorts of shambles could sometimes occur. The reviews were favourable. An agency sent newspaper cuttings via Corkhill's. The children's stories about KV's population of odd characters in strange hats were to be broadcast in unknowable TV networks, children's television of course, but that was the idea.

"I'm getting KV talked up in a women's magazine," she said. "I'm manipulating the media." She gave a laugh to distract him from morality.

"More old friends?"

Quickly she inspected him for bitterness and was relieved to find none. The last thing she wanted was Bray to think she was taking over.

"Of course," she said evenly. "It'd happen anyway." She added, "Bray, if I do something that's not right, please tell me."

He ahemed, reluctant to speak. "You've done things I couldn't even contemplate. Like that accountant."

She laughed. "You were so apprehensive. You said, 'A bank? In Burnley?' And sat in silence on the train!"

"And like when…"

"Kylee?"

He always smiled when speaking of the girl. "At first she was like someone from outer space." He gave her a shy glance. "And you talked in parables. I understood nothing. Now look at us. I grumble about networking with the best of them. Two days ago on the train I made a joke about lancing overflow buffers and nicking surfo mail."

"Is the competition worrying you?"

He sobered, so she'd guessed right. "It's all too soon."

"In six weeks, Kylee is teeing it up with two processors. I hired her, meaning Maddy's, to do a software programme for Gilson Mather. And," Lottie couldn't help adding mischievously, "she's included parameters that might help us. Did you know the TV links have been offered sponsors?"

"Sponsors?" Bray exclaimed in alarm. "Advertise?"

"It is rather complicated," she admitted. Time to wash up the supper things and then go home. Six o'clock, the children's programmes ended. "It's vital in the USA, not so vital here. Sponsorship is easy money, which helps. Selling is fierce."

"What do we do?"

She already knew the answer. It was always the same. "Go for maximal exposure, Bray. The contract must guarantee it. It's more lawyers, but so?"

"Geoffrey and Shirley are thinking of trying for another child." Lottie held her silence. "Inevitable really."

"Davey will love it, Bray, you'll see. I'll hurl those dishes through the water and head off."

For a moment she thought Bray was about to make some suggestion, but he only said that he'd clear up. He bussed her on the cheek as usual at the door. Buster stood on the step as Bray waved her off.

She watched Bray in the driving mirror. He was actually scared. Since the first KV book came out there had been no other significant step. Until now, and the consequences were unknowable. The final answer lay somewhere up ahead. Bray was terrified it would be the wrong one.

The pace was accelerating. Articles almost every day about the animators, soon the TV ratings, children's books, and little plastic figures being made by concession people, the transatlantic TV launch. Lottie's concocted biography of the distant Sharlene S Trayer had come out in a mag, only lip service, thank heavens.

She knew the hunt kept him sane. For it, Bray had his own faith. Her hopes were few, yet she'd provided essential expertise he lacked. The determination was Bray's, sure, but she contributed know-how.

And the combination was producing something. Bray wouldn't cut corners, she would. He worried about propriety, she didn't. Bray was honest. Lottie would trample on toes, see if she cared. She was in it with him, and that was that.

Forty minutes later she reached her darkened home and put the car away. She did little for the rest of the evening except have a hot bath and watch a sitcom. She felt too languid to bother with the hall phone's red light. She could get up earlier. It was probably George Corkhill's secretary in a panic over typeface. A vegetable drink, and she went to bed.

"Ah, this is Jim Stazio. Give me a call?"

The voice was gruff yet tinny. Two messages, same words.

Lottie checked the clock. Nine o'clock was what, in America? Crossly she examined her old school atlas for the USA's maddening time zones, and decided to wait until the afternoon before phoning back. In a temper she went straight out and bought a pricey massive atlas. All morning she did her filing.

It came on to rain at noon. She stopped for a skimpy lunch break – lentil soup, cream crackers, tea – and two p.m. got Jim Stazio.

"Thing is, Lottie, I got a sort list. It's kinda long."

"Of suspects?"

"Can't say suspects till they're apprehended, y'foller? Libel being what it is."

Then what was the point? "Is posting out of the question? E-mail, fax?"

"Co-rrect. Where a felon operates from, excuse me saying it, the *product* is sold in another state. Maybe resides in a third state. Know what I'm saying? I've eighteen states."

"And a state could be as big as a couple of European countries."

"You got it."

"Have you edited the list?"

"Y'mean cut it down? Sort of. I got a friend to take out criminals who're been penned or don't figure. Leaves eleven pages."

"Meaning out of reach?"

"Three hundred supposed agencies, a score or so states." He sighed. "Four thousand operatives, maybe."

"Should I come for the list? If it would help us."

"Fly over?" He gave that some thought.

"Tell you what. Reason I called so urgent, I didn't want you wasting Bray's money." She heard the rustle of papers. "Needle in a haystack, trying to list them in order of likely, ahm, Florida activity. Understand me?"

"Very well," she said. "Please don't be offended, but did you incur any expenses?"

"Coupla beers is all." He chuckled. "And I'm drinking anyway."

In the afternoon she savagely pruned the roses in her small garden. So you have a list of criminals in your hand, *knowing* that one had committed the most dreadful crime, and are powerless. Where was the justice in that? You couldn't even read the list over the phone for God's sake. The world was mad.

She over-pruned her favourite hybrid tea, a Queen Elizabeth, so she drove to the library in a temper and failed to find any of the four books she wanted. She was given a parking ticket. Worse, the traffic warden wasn't in sight. She couldn't even have a stand-up row with the moron.

That night she threw caution to the winds and phoned Bray, asking his answer machine outright if she might stay over one day next week, to catch up.

That night she slept badly.

One alternative was to buy a computer system matching Bray's for her own home, which would be ridiculous. Lying awake, she told herself there would then be three – Bray, herself, and Kylee. The irate girl, despite her Halstead venue, was still demonically active interrupting Lottie's e-mail system. Heaven knows who was paying for Kylee's computer time. She surfed with complete abandon. Twice she had lifted e-mails Lottie had not yet handled, making contemptuous comments to Lottie on Bray's screen and insolently mailing "Get on with it, Grannie." Lottie had smiled for Bray's benefit, but seethed.

About four o'clock in the morning she decided she had done the right thing. Then she overslept, arriving late at Gilson Mather's. A terrible headache finished the day. Bray was staying to teach Loggo and Suzanne to make miniature block planes. She travelled home alone wondering what on earth she thought she was up to at her age.

* * *

Clint did well in some grade tests, not in others. His art was so uncertain his scores had to be averaged, unlike other kids. Math was fair, English comprehension good.

"Clint is so wayward," Donna Curme told Mom. "He seems content. He's coping."

"But his grades." Mom wished Pop hadn't had to go back east. He should have been here for this.

"Education isn't numbers," Donna said firmly. She had this out a dozen times every Parents' Evening. "Clint's a great reader, and his team – you know Leeta and Carlson – are up front in several."

"You ought to concentrate on his weak subjects."

Donna sighed inwardly at Mom's accusation. "There's a balance, and he's picking up."

"You marked his science down."

"In technical bits he just goes miles away. I suppose it's his accident."

"Accident?" Mom cried in alarm, then caught herself. "I thought you meant he'd had some fall."

Donna felt emboldened enough to let curiosity show. "Was it very bad?"

"Yes," Mom said abruptly, and closed the interview. She wondered if it was time to suggest that Madam Nosey Bitch Curme's contract should be terminated.

Clint was waiting by the classroom door with Leeta and Carlson and their parents. When Mom left Donna Curme there was talk about the foreign languages beginning the following month. Spanish was a possibility, but Mom knew Pop favoured Russian. They walked down to their cars. Mom now had her own car.

"Mom," Clint asked, laughing at Carlson's antics on the sidewalk. "My accident. Was the first doctor old, with colours on his coat?"

"Why do you ask, honey?" Mom swung the automobile out of the driveway.

"I think he was." Clint turned to see Carlson, who was pretending to kick a soccer ball. "Carlson's good at soccer. Leeta plays too."

"So are you, honey!" Mom said quickly.

"I'm not. I can't slide like Carlson. He's great."

They settled into the journey, got held up at the Hubberson interchange but were home in ten minutes. Clint liked watching the stores go by.

"The old doctor played soccer with me. I said I was no good. He laughed."

"He did?"

"He said I was...great. He said he'd never been any good."

Mom panicked but controlled her anxiety as they went in. She felt she ought to call Doctor and see if it was anything. Doctor hadn't mentioned football.

"That was real kind," she said, staying firm. "It was when you were getting better. I remember him now."

Clint asked, "What was his name?"

"Doctor Kildare," she said desperately. "Wasn't he great?"

Clint dashed to get cookies and orange Manuela always fixed. Mom called after him, be careful racing everywhere like that, then she went to make her calls.

Splendid, Clint thought in the kitchen. The old man in the coloured coat thing said *You are splendid* when he wasn't. And he wasn't called Doctor Kildare. He wasn't Doctor at all and Mom said he was.

Manuela ruffled Clint's hair.

"Dreaming again? Always never here, you! Help me

make pancakes. Special for Mom, special for Pop, and none for you!"

It was Manuela's joke. Clint liked Manuela.

Chapter Forty-Four

The dilemma was impossible to solve. Bray felt alone, which was strange. He and Lottie had begun sleeping together. Actually not sleeping, but making love on his couch during the late evening, after which Lottie would start the yawning drive to home. No great distance, but as traffic worsened and roads began their winter floods she became fractious. Bray found he was testy. Gilson Mather's part-time college students had poor results, and resits meant rescheduling for two simultaneous courses. His work suffered. He had to stay late, and several times Lottie found herself going home alone instead of with Bray.

They came close to falling out. Lottie's resolve wilted. Her doggedness, caught from Bray, weakened. She rehearsed a scenario in which, after making love before his living-room fire, she gently told Bray to find somebody else more in tune with his single-minded obsession.

The anniversary of the loss of Davey once had seemed so far off. Now, it grew imperceptibly on the horizon. Bray was a thinking man. Sooner or later he would make a decision. Why not sooner, with a little prompting from the lady he – surely by now – loved?

Frankly, it was time they settled down together in a shared life. Time was cruel when old age supervened. Happiness wasn't the creation of shrines, rituals without purpose. Joy was to live in peace. There would be memories, some joyous, some pure heartbreak. But she too had had her share of sorrow and sillinesses.

The difference with Bray was that nothing must get in the way of finding his little grandson. Poor Geoffrey's world had crashed. Shirley had disintegrated. For Bray, though, all life was measured against his sombre recruitment. Whatever happened, one question dominated Bray: Does this person, thing, help me or not?

Some of his scheme was successful. KV books were in every bookshop she passed nowadays, thanks to her and that odious brat Kylee. The weird figures were on television, in magazines, and Lottie was sick of the damned things. Comedians mimiced their whispy shrieks and came on wearing strange hats. Even fashion houses made witty statements using skimpy models in purple leaves.

She and Bray were in trouble. She decided, another month then have it out. Time was passing for her as for everybody. She hadn't lost sympathy, certainly not, but there was a limit. She'd given herself unstintingly. Was she heartless to ask him to be realistic? Women were practical, men weren't. She would make Bray face the issue. It would hurt both of them, and God knows Bray would wilt.

A thought sickened her: Bray wouldn't accept an ultimatum. If she laid it on the line – so many Americanisms, the influence of gruff Jim Stazio's laconic chats – Bray would simply sit silent, hear her out, then let her go with one of his regretful nods.

And that would be that.

Yet what other options did she have? It was a new kind of fear, different from those she'd previously experienced.

To his surprise Bray saw George Corkhill in Mr Winsarls's office during midmorning break. Lottie wasn't in today, a particular disappointment. He'd felt something fading lately. Normality surely wasn't too much to expect. He entered, said his greetings.

"We're looking so pleased with ourselves, Mr Charleston," Mr Winsarls greeted him, "because our volumes are out!"

"A good job, Bray," the printer said modestly, unable to keep pride from his voice.

"They look admirable. You've done brilliantly, George."

Several copies of the two-volume history of Gilson Mather lay on the owner's desk. Size, colour, paper, they could not have been more impressive. Bray almost blurted out that they looked really professional. He carefully turned the pages, nodding with approval at particular items. The plates, photographs, his diagrams, every feature was pleasing. He spent too long checking down the list of contributors and owners.

"Lottie will be thrilled, Bray."

"Has she seen them?"

"We sent a boxed set yesterday."

Mr Winsarls said, "I'm planning a celebration. No more postponements, Bray! Requests are coming in!"

"It's splendid, Mr Winsarls. Who'd have imagined?"

Mr Winsarls coughed into his hand, and judged the moment. "The point is, Bray, somebody's got to come."

"Come?"

"With me, to the USA. We spoke of it? I'd better go.

Several antique firms want to participate in lectures. It's free publicity, in a world market. I've got a valuations man. I'm wondering about a historian for background."

Mr Winsarls linked his fingers with a glance George's way.

"The question, Bray, is whether you feel you're ready to come. The alternative," he went swiftly on, "is we take two craftsmen, with a couple from other old London firms."

"Would they come, Mr Winsarls?" the printer asked, wanting to support Bray.

"Like a shot. We'd hire them."

"Is that ideal?" George, still in there batting for Bray.

"Not really. Our firm's principal craftsman is straight in the tradition." Mr Winsarls spun his captain's chair and spoke directly. "You'd be the living representative of three centuries, Bray."

"The rubber chicken circuit!" George tried to lighten the atmosphere.

Mr Winsarls said seriously, "Twenty-three invitations – antique fairs, auction houses, college courses, museums, galleries. Nobody could have foreseen it, Bray."

The second volume was in Bray's hands. He felt its inordinate weight. It was a beautiful summary of the firm's achievements. Several sections had been ponderously dictated by himself, his experience of the most beautiful material on earth.

"When?"

"The sooner the better, I'd say, depending."

Bray thought. The children in the USA had term breaks. He had the dates painstakingly noted. Jim Stazio had provided the information.

His forlorn hope seemed suddenly too slender. Here it was, come at last with its terrible allure. Almost certain failure, yet, deep in that cavernous pit, a lone glimmer of hope. He'd laboured to reach this moment. He looked up.

"I agree, Mr Winsarls. It's time. I'll go."

"Three months?"

"A travelling circus!" George said, smiling.

Mr Winsarls enthused, "You could do it on your own, Mr Charleston."

Politely, Bray told Mr Winsarls that he was looking forward to it, thanked George for the work he'd done, and went back to work holding the railing.

Chapter Forty-Five

"We can never take a real holiday."

"Isn't this a break?"

Lottie's exasperation was showing. They strolled along the Maldon estuary. It was a pretty scene. Children crowded the play pools despite the chill. The narrow lookout spire of Maldon's ancient church was painted a garish mustard, the greensward expansive. Small yachts competed for leeway in the narrow river. Buster was good, never more than yards away.

"Will we be walking here ten years from now?"

"I hope so."

She understood, for Davey was his grandson, not hers. Which didn't lessen the problem; it was just as horrifying. But, she argued with herself, time had gone on. They slept together, and now she sometimes stayed over. Maybe a woman wanted a sense of completeness, whereas a man didn't? Women used different words: commitment, meaningful. Men sank into their minds and kept more within, so maddening. They didn't share the same dependence on words.

What she did know for certain was that she couldn't go

on. Raise the subject, all she got was "I hope so." Time moved, she thought tartly, for her also.

"We never have gone away, have we?"

"I can't," Bray said simply.

She appraised him as a dog chased a stick thrown by two children. Bray smiled, calling Buster not to join in.

"It's the phone, the e-mail, the messages. I'm going over the next TV episodes. They'll have the competition in. Kylee might ring any second."

"Kylee's getting more abusive." Lottie searched for ammunition. "She curses everybody. She's getting worse."

Kylee was now a young tyro, working full time in Mr Maddy's and doing well. Lottie had had occasion to contact her there, and was startled to be told that Kylee couldn't come to the phone. She had last visited Bray a fortnight before. Bray had taken the day off, and they had stayed in the shed most of the day. Lottie felt barred, almost as she was now by Bray's resolve.

"It's her way. She's getting excited about…" The finish, he meant.

"Couldn't we get on without her now?"

He was astonished. "I can't see how."

They sat on the oak benching overlooking the barges. Buster wandered the nearby ditch, occasionally pausing to make sure Bray was still there. Lottie thought how well Bray looked. He wore a long-sleeved Fair Isle pullover she had astounded herself by knitting. His frame had thinned.

"The system's set up. The television stations will not need to screen the competition entrants in USA, because her ladyship Kylee says so." She bit her tongue, quickly amended, "Kylee goes in fits and starts."

"She's never less than a day out of synch, Lottie."

"It's her attitude." The last time Kylee had spoken to

Lottie the girl's scathing comments had quite worn her down. She had rung off in temper.

"It has to be endured," he said quietly. "The benefit, you see."

"*She* benefits, Bray!" Lottie snapped. "You pay her."

"I have a fortune," he replied simply.

He'd established a company and made Geoffrey the beneficiary. Old Mr Haythorn in the bank was having a time of it keeping abreast of the income. It was success, but meant nothing if it didn't find Davey.

"You'll be touring America, Bray."

"That's why I need you, Lottie." The thought was unbearable, but he forced himself. "What if messages came tonight and we ignored it? It might be our only chance."

"Can I ask, Bray?"

She felt resigned, here on the pretty strand with the sailing vessels gliding by, the families at picnics, children splashing in the pools. It seemed to mock her futility.

"I'll be devil's advocate." She turned to him. "You know how I feel. It's only love speaking." Appalled at her temerity, she came right out. "Do you really believe there's any chance, Bray? After all this time?"

He stood, hands in his pockets. Buster came up, tongue lolling, ready to go on.

"I believe, Lottie." He cast about for a twig, threw it with a show of effort. Buster stayed, looking at Bray, recognising a sham.

"When I first learned of it, the horror," he said so quietly Lottie had to lean to hear, "I stood in the garden at night. It was the stars. Me and Davey used to watch them. I realised everybody would give up eventually. Geoffrey, Shirley, the American police. Despair would win."

"I'm sorry —"

"No, let me." He was some time resuming. "I considered how it would be, to take my own life. Strange how rational it can suddenly seem. Then I thought of Davey." He fondled Buster's head against his knee. "And all of an instant it was clear as day. Davey, if he was able to remember back to me, to his shed with his carvings, all our games, Davey would *know* that I would come looking for him. Maybe I'd get it wrong, and search hopeless places. And maybe I'd die, or come up against impossible obstacles. But one thing Davey does believe, is that his Grampa is coming, following, trying to find him."

Bray pointed along the thronged foreshore as if it was a feature she hadn't seen until that moment.

"It's all there is for me. The fullness today, tomorrow, of the future."

"And if your competition doesn't find anything?"

"Then I'll do it again. Make a regular competition, year after year. And anything else I can come up with."

Lottie couldn't keep scorn out. "One crazy scheme after another?"

"I'll grab at any straw."

"And fail time and again?" she heard herself say, thinking even as she spoke, God, no, don't. Her charity had vanished. She felt despicable. "You ought to be making a fail-safe plan."

He froze, Buster wondering why the day had gone wrong.

Lottie thought, I hate that bloody dog, hate it for the totality of its unconditional love. Buster's utter reverence was something she simply couldn't match. They deserved each other, Buster and Bray together. For good. The ultimate Derby and Joan, bonded together in a lunatic quest. She could stay with them, fine, keep her emotional distance. But become involved, you too were doomed, cankered and inert.

She'd had a friend once who had loved a priest well into her sixtieth year. The friend lived forlornly from day to ailing day, her life frittered.

Well, that's not me, Lottie told herself with anger. Become a life-long vestal, tending the flame at some man's shrine? She'd reached the end of her tether. Suddenly she was impatient to be gone from Maldon's foreshore. Tonight, maybe get her best skirt suit on, the powder blue, call up friends and claim, whatever their priorities, this evening was hers. That new raucous club down the coast. She'd had enough, thank you. Life was too short.

"I'm so sorry," Bray was saying, toeing the grass while Buster looked. "In other circumstances, I'd be more..."

"That's it, though, isn't it, Bray?" she said, sadness over her bitterness. "The circumstances. You're never free. I've felt myself changing, becoming a sort of mini-you."

He smiled, for once an open slow winning smile that a stranger could easily have mistaken for humour.

"It has been beautiful, Lottie," he said simply. "Without you I'd have gone under. Kylee too. And George. You've all been superb, friends I never even hoped I'd be lucky enough to have. I don't deserve you. I'll keep going whatever comes. Your knowledge, Kylee's lovely soul, George's understanding. You're all in me now."

"I can't go on, Bray, is what I'm saying."

"I know, love." He gazed at a Norfolk wherry as it glided up river, its sunset sail clapping in the low breeze. "You're with me to the end. I love you."

"But for those circumstances?" She said it bitterly.

"I'm sorry. Yes."

They stood facing a moment, then Lottie turned.

"I'll get the hamper."

Bray was about to apologise but thought better of it and moved with her to their separation.

"Clint's done badly," Lois Marquese told Judy Trabasco in the teachers' common room. "The kid you and Donna Curme were talking about."

"Clint? Impossible!" Judy was annoyed, more for her friend Donna. Trust the art teacher to nit pick. Lois and Donna didn't get on.

The art teacher brought Judy her coffee. "Can't follow a single story line. It's bizarre." She explained the details, adding, "The boy goes off at a tangent."

Judy said sweetly, "You mean he actually invents, hmmm?"

"Plenty of kids are erratic, Judy. There's a weird limit in Clint's mind."

Judy laughed Lois's criticism off. "The assignment was to invent the end to a children's TV story?"

"*Reasoned* conclusions, Judy!"

"You mean Clint's ending was different? Art *is* difference, for God's sake. They're children, mah deah! It happens!"

"His group's out of the competition," Lois Marquese said. "I had to bench them."

Trouble was, Lois knew Donna had a special interest in the boy, and Clint's parents were big funders.

"With his parents contributing to the new sports facility?" Judy countered lamely.

Other teachers were listening now, including the athletics programmer Dale Porrino, a lanky Barbadian transfer via Miami.

He interrupted, "Clint ran the wrong way today."

"Wrong how?" Judy wished Donna would arrive, help her out.

"Softball," Dale said. "Whacked the ball, but kept hold of the bat and ran forward." Dale described it. Everyone present was into the story.

"Was he sick or something?" The best Judy could do.

"No. In fact he was laughing. Did his hit, raced forward. Then suddenly stopped, looked around like puzzled. Stared at the pitcher – y'know, Farlow's kid? – like he expected to see something else. Then ran back and round, too late. The kids went wild."

"He looked okay?"

"Embarrassed. Said he just forgot."

Somebody said, "Never heard of a kid forgetting a baseball pitch."

"Sent him to the med facility." Dale shrugged. "He was fine."

After that, Clint's art was out of the window.

They were in a car pool. That evening Judy told Donna about Lois's remarks. Donna had seen Clint's mistake at the softball game. Children did weird things, where was the problem?

Donna had her own viewpoint and gave it to Judy on the way home. "Lois is hooked on event sequencing. She's totally in-course assessment. Okay, so the kid's a dreamer."

"What kid isn't?" Judy said supportively.

After two days more Dale Porrino ran into Donna Curme outside the cafeteria. She asked if Clint had shown any more behavioural oddities.

"He's academically patchy, give Lois that," Donna admitted. "But he's fine."

"Didn't he have some accident?"

"It's on his record. He seems a normal seven-year-old."

"They all mess around that age."

Dale paused as Donna made to walk on.

"A couple of kids made that same mistake," he said, grinning. "A Trinidadian. And that Nelson kid from Nassau, y'know, Bahamian kid last semester? Ran straight at the pitcher, kept hold of the bat. Like in cricket."

"So it's common?" Donna was relieved, still irritated by Lois Marquese's decision to drop Clint's group. Kids were grouped up to enter the competition. It was innocent, based on a children's TV programme. It was receiving statewide publicity. Success would do the school no harm at all. There was media talk of a fantastic reward for the winning school.

"They played the wrong games when they were just out of the egg."

They parted then, Donna happy now with one more remark with which to counter Lois Marquese's scepticisms.

Chapter Forty-Six

Mom saw Clint's holidays as a threat. Pop didn't. Mom cooled, because the staff hadn't left for the day so she had to be on her guard.

"Hyme, I want Doctor here for the holiday."

"Jeez, Clodie! That man costs!"

"We gone through this!" Mom's voice rose.

"You think there's still a chance that Clint —?"

"You think there's *no* chance?"

There was no answer to that, so Pop made the call. Two days before the school's weekend break Doctor flew in, took the penthouse at Tain Herrome International Airport Hotel, with three "personal family". Pop covered the entire cost. Mom rejoiced. She made Doctor promise to pay Clint daily visits right to the end of the break.

Clint didn't like Doctor.

The man was real important. Mom and Pop said. He had to be nice to Doctor because Doctor saved Clint's life in hospital. What Doctor said was always true.

He was always careful when Doctor came. He listened close, only saying what Doctor would think was right.

School was better than home. Whatever happened in school got back to Mom and Pop. At home Linda Hunger knew everything. It was easier when Doctor came, because Mrs Hunger stayed out and didn't come home to her apartment along the top corridor. Clint knew this because she had a growly motor – auto – that made noises that made him smile.

Pop wasn't as much fun as other kids' dads. Pop didn't run races. The second class cookout Pop stayed away, though he was home. Mom came with other moms.

Christmas was lovely, no, *great*, all those colours. Clint told Miss Curme his class teacher that blue and yellow were better than red and green. She asked him why but he didn't know.

"Can I choose?" Clint liked drawing one particular colour.

"You certainly can!"

The class were creating a long picture called a panorama. Clint's group had to draw a hill and trees covered in snow. Other groups in class had to do a stable, shepherds, animals and Three Wise Men and an angel with wings.

Miss Curme was nice and sometimes pretended she forgot words and sums when really she hadn't, to make the kids think she was dumb. They had fun telling her the answers. She was thin, wore glasses, and had too much hair round her head. Clint wondered what she'd look like in a hat. He liked her.

Planning Christmas displays, Miss Curme put the drawings up on sheets. Two others in Clint's group, Leeta whose daddy was a minister who shouted in a Baptist church and a boy called Carlson whose pop was a secret in the State capitol. Leeta and Carlson were good at cutting, but Clint was better at drawing.

So they did the cutting out and he did the drawings. He asked Miss Curme if he could have more paints and she said fine. That was when she said about choosing colours.

The kids did their piece of the big panorama. Miss Curme said it was a quiet period so she could get on with her marking. Her tongue made a slow wriggle in her mouth, slow as a worm. Some kids called her secret names. Carlson called her Dozy Donna and Leeta said shhh.

Leeta cut out the shapes that Clint drew and Carlson cut out the people Clint drew. He drew on white then coloured them in. Once, Carlson cut across a part he shouldn't have so Clint drew it again and Carlson cut it right this time. Miss Curme said it was okay if that was the shape Clint really wanted but try to save paper next time.

The second afternoon Clint spilled some water. It wet the floor. Miss Curme said never mind and everybody started wiping up the wet. Clint said he was sorry. Leeta said it was an accident so God would forgive it. Carlson blamed the other kids for putting their papers down wrong. Miss Curme said none of that, please, or we'll never finish before school's out for Christmas.

Carlson liked Miss Curme. Carlson said she was cool. Leeta didn't like her. She said she was too new to be any good. Carlson said she got great grades. Leeta said Miss Curme was from Delaware and that meant she was a reject and rejects were crap.

Clint said where's Delaware. Leeta didn't know. Carlson said it was back east so they went and stared at the Map of the Americas, shiny and too high up. They supposed it was on the righthand side, this Delaware.

Miss Curme collected their drawings and made one big picture. Leeta said it would be wrong because her daddy in his Sunday sermons at the Tain Memorial Baptist

Congregational Assembly on Bankstone and Revere said life was always wrong.

Miss Curme said "Really great!" as the last ones were handed in. She stared at Carlson's and Leeta's and Clint's piece, eyes round as anything, and said, "Oh my! Won't you looka here! This is something else, you three!" and they felt real proud because it was the best in the whole panorama.

"Boats, though, right there in the stable?"

A whole row broke out. Some kids said sure they had boats because Saint Somebody walked on water and that meant he was a fisherman like Al's dad who'd won a fishing championship last Fall. Others said no because it was a stable and that's only for horses. Carlson said the manger was probably a boat if you really went into it.

"And these towers and kites? It's very imaginative, but..."

A girl called Perlina who had a horse in a field near Tannerville said Leeta and Carlson and Clint shouldn't get marks because it wasn't fair. Everybody started talking. Some kids said could they do colouring like that. Other kids shouted no, the Christmas Baby had only a white towel like all kids started off with. Carlson and Leeta and Clint shouted back. Others yelled about babies they knew.

Miss Curme stopped the whole argument by making them sit still for a count of a hundred while she figured what order pictures should go on the wall. Somebody lost her wall board glue so she set them counting another hundred.

End-of-term PTA classroom tours were a worrying time. Leeta said Miss Curme didn't want the kids to have any Christmas because she'd been thrown out of Delaware.

Long after she had dismissed the children Donna Curme spent time trying to incorporate the Clint-Leeta-Carlson picture into the Christmas panorama.

Her friend Judy Trabasco, who taught fifth grade, found her friend almost in tears fifteen minutes before the Head Teacher Session.

"Christ sakes, Donna!" she exploded. "Do it in sections, any order. Let the little bastards' parents guess."

"But they're so influential, Judy! It *would* be their group!"

"Then do a link drawing yourself. Here!"

Judy set to with a Magic Marker, filling in.

"It's supposed to be children's work!"

Judy withdrew, inspected the drawings already tacked to the display.

"You know, hon, there really is a hint of talent there. How about calling the odd chunks Christmas Of The Future?"

They settled on this.

In ten minutes they had written out two huge titles, and the panorama was in two lopsided parts. Judy Trabasco said the odd figures, the kites, towers, the strange hats reminded her of something she'd come across in a magazine. But then Judy had hordes of nieces and nephews, the Trabascos breeding famously.

Donna Curme was relieved. Maybe Clint simply extrapolated images that entertained him? He read a lot.

Maybe she could incorporate that observation in his end-of-term report? She said this to Judy, who said she'd be stupid if she didn't.

Chapter Forty-Seven

The celebration was held in the Romeo and Giulietta in Romsey Street, Soho. Several youngsters had a drink then left. To his embarrassment Bray found himself shaking hands with several. Three youths from former cabinet-making courses also dropped in. One had started an antiques business, repairs to Long Acre eighteenth-century antiques a sideline. Bray was quite moved. The lad had journeyed all the way from Bromley. "Making sure the old bugger's gone," one joked, getting a laugh.

Bray was glad when the talk became technical. Alice and her friend Josh were perennial jokers from two years before. They had brought with them a fragment of wood on which they couldn't agree.

As the party grew and the waiters circulated, Bray told them he admired Australian Mountain Ash.

"*Eucalyptus regnans,*" he said, lovingly examining the piece. "Close cousins, they are. This light brown colour would've been almost pink. Looks like oak, doesn't she? Easy wood, never picks up when you plane it. Did you polish this?"

"Me," Alice claimed, staring hard at Josh, who laughed.

Bray squinted along its surface. "Look out a figured piece. It comes up lovely. I used it for veneers, four Regency copies."

Josh shook his head. "How the hell d'you remember?"

Bray looked at him. "Just because wood lies still doesn't mean it's stopped living, Josh."

"Mr Charleston recognises furniture he worked on as an apprentice," Mr Winsarls claimed. "If I could do it, I could sack the lot of you!"

He was sweating heavily in the restaurant lights. His wife was chatting to Lottie and other wives nearby, discussing the menu.

"Only, we want to come back," Alice said suddenly. "Me and Josh."

"I said to wait," Josh cut in under his breath.

Alice said, "Are there vacancies, Mr Charleston?"

She was a stocky girl. Bray remembered her as a vigorous worker, eager but careless. Josh was a promising youth lacking in patience. Bray suspected that they lived together at an antiques shop in Camden Town.

"Perhaps when I come back from the USA," Bray temporised, making a silent appeal to Mr Winsarls.

"How long will you be away, Mr Charleston?"

"He's staying," Suzanne said laughing. "He's got a blonde."

Bill Edgeworth was talking with Dick Whitehouse. He chuckled.

"Then I'm going too. We're not sending young scruffs like you lot!"

There was general laughter. Loggo was already on pints even though the meal hadn't yet begun, with James Coldren, third master joiner.

"Aren't the publishers coming?" Mrs Winsarls asked her husband.

"No," he said. "Lottie's representing them. They're sulking because Lottie did a better job than they ever could."

Lottie edged into the conversation, smoothly dislocating Bray from Alice and Josh. "They were glad to stick me here with you lot."

The meal went off in a melee, how the publishers should allow a third volume. Mr Winsarls worried about the restaurant's arrangements. It was a starter/buffet, wives and friends allowed. Mercifully the talk never faltered. Bray found himself with Lottie as the meal ended. He had wondered if she had been trying to avoid him.

"Not long now, Lottie," he managed to say.

They found themselves in a lacuna of quiet. One or two of the guests were slightly tipsy by then, Gilson Mather supply merchants arguing about coastal ports, nobody sure of the roads. Mr Winsarls was with Bill Edgeworth and the masters' wives, discussing recipes. Everybody was slightly flushed. The restaurant was packed.

Lottie poured Bray a glass of red wine. He carefully did not sip.

"Still working the alcohol out?" she asked wryly. "You've only had one glass." Bray coloured. She'd been watching. "In case your mobile phone rings?"

"Sorry."

"Your endless apologies, Bray." She seemed close to laughing, except it threatened to be something else.

"What will you do now, Lottie?" The place was becoming fairly raucous. "Stay with the firm, I hope?" Bray felt a near-panic. He'd almost said *stay with us*, leading to all sorts of heartache.

"For a while. Until the anniversary escapade is done with."

"You'd better!" Bray made light of it. "That third volume's trends and specials. You're badly needed."

"Then what, Bray?"

Even as she spoke she could have kicked herself. Was anything worse than a petulant woman who couldn't get her own way? He had a dream forcing him to sacrifice his life. Let him get on with it.

"I can't see that far, Lottie." He measured the quantity of wine left in his glass. The old predicament: half empty or half full? "Thanks for doing my itinerary. All those places with odd names, a thousand miles between. Hard to believe."

"I wish you well, Bray. I hope it goes really splendidly."

They could have been diplomats arranging sanctions. Lottie defiantly accepted wine from a pressing waiter. She had no particular reason to keep a clear head, and no crazy dreams either. His crusade was like all crusades, a lost cause. Reality was here, in some noisy Italian restaurant, not in jaunting across a vast nation neither she nor Bray knew. She would last out until Bray left for New York, and then pick some new job. Her old publishers, Cannon Endriss, had lately made cooing noises after the Gilson Mather success, sensing a market in which, she thought with a frisson of malice, they hadn't her experience.

She said evenly, "All you have to do is turn up. Couriers will meet you, hotels are booked. Credit's arranged."

"I'll be bewildered."

"Worried about the public speaking? You'll be fine. Antiques, joinery, they're your subjects, Bray." She smiled determinedly, adding, "James Coldren, Bill, Dick, even the auctioneers, all say you're a natural. This year's been one long success."

Not quite, Bray thought.

It was getting late by the time they left. Mr Winsarls spoke a few words of caution to Harry Diggins about the youngsters and uncharacteristically shook Bray's hand. He'd already done a congratulatory speech, raising ironic cheers. It was as they were saying their goodnights that Bray realised that they had all genuinely forgotten about his loss. To them today was merely another day. Perhaps it was the wine, but fright took over: if nothing came of his search, would he too sink into the same dull apathy where time was the mere now of existence, with no past and countless tomorrows? He thought desperately, I must meet Kylee. Now, tonight if possible.

"You all right, Bray?" Bill asked.

"Just a bit squiffy."

Mrs Edgeworth took Bray's arm. "Night air, Bray. Deep breaths."

They made the garish lighting of Romsey Street.

"Are you going home, Bray?" Lottie asked, suddenly there. "The firm's booked everybody into the Piccadilly."

"Home, Lottie."

She went off with the others, not far to walk. Bray caught a bus in Shaftesbury Avenue. The moment he was seated he checked the messages on his cell phone. None. He dialled Kylee.

She wasn't home, but he spoke haltingly to her recording device.

"Things are coming to a head, Kylee." He made certain no other passenger could overhear. "I think maybe I've talked myself into a stupor, not wanting to face it now it's here. I want you to formulate the scheme now, please. The one we talked of. You did the test run, remember? Can you do it now, and run it for me while I'm away?" He forced out the final words, "In America."

He reached home soon after midnight to find a voice message from her. It was characteristically slurred of speech.

"Wotcher, Bray. I'm with these boring old farts. Tomorrer, 'kay?"

Relieved, Bray got Buster back from Christine and Hal, walked over the fields, and settled him down for the night. Buster kept looking up while Bray wrote under the porch. For once Bray left the porch light on when he went to bed.

Chapter Forty-Eight

Gratitude could be an emotional flux, welding convictions into place. A convert before the city, so to speak. Bray waited for Kylee at the station. An hour after he'd got there, he was still waiting.

So many passengers alighted, football fans joshing two busking girls playing violins. He sat owl-eyed on the platform. Mr Winsarls had said, "Bray. After all these years, why ask if you can have a day off?" And for once the owner had been don't-bother-me testy, even dismissive. Youngsters saw every handout as entitlement. Maybe, Bray wondered uneasily, I'm a born serf. Disgusting.

He had no idea what Kylee did at Mr Maddy's firm. His early worries about Kylee had resurfaced. She had grown away even in so short a time. Bray recognised it in Mr Walsingham's behaviour – he'd phoned Bray twice since his visit – as a sad attempt to encounter his erring daughter. Each time, Bray carefully let Kylee know that her dad had rung in, because she was Bray's ally, and he was on her side.

He still saw her as the soiled girl snarling curses in that echoing laboratory. Her visits to his hunting shed were now infrequent, always unannounced, and marked by print-outs on his calendar. She tended to hurtle in, bully him into tackling some shortcut, tell him off for not checking the e-mail, then play with the dog.

Some of her visits took place when he was at work. Then, late evening, he'd find notes blinking on his computer, with a barrage of loud addenda, and usually some terse Churchillian imperative to phone her, often gone midnight. She cursed him when his cell phone wasn't charged. He thought she was unfair.

"Penny for 'em, Bray."

"Oh, I was just…"

He reddened, caught out, Kylee standing there. To his astonishment she was more than presentable.

"I got wheels." She bullied her way through the platform mob. "What you carry that fucking bag for? Got a tent in it?"

"No," he said earnestly. "It's a book, bottled water, and a brolly —"

She turned to him, laughing, elbowing to make a path.

"I don't wanter fucking know, gettit?"

He was off kilter. Only one minute, and already she had him stuttering.

A motor stood at the kerb, a portly driver opening the door. "Found him."

She flung herself in, beckoned Bray, and was instantly on a cellular phone saying no, where the fuck was Del at eleven o'clock. Bray anxiously tried to tell her the correct time. She pushed to silence.

The journey took half an hour. ("Doze, because you're old!" she ordered rudely.) Old times' sake, Bray thought wryly, and spent the journey looking at the scenery. The buildings managed to appear temporary despite the array of flags and the stencilled lawns.

"They say fucking office, not work." She walked into the front entrance. "Biggest load of shit."

A stylish receptionist invited Bray to sign in, please.

"No," Kylee told him. "This way, mate."

"It's the rule!" the receptionist bleated. "Miss Walsingham —"

"Piss off, Ca-ssand-dra." Kylee didn't even pause, did some magic with a card and they rose in a lift to a corridor floored in thick fawn. "See? Crappy."

She talked a few minutes with a man of about twenty-five at a console in an office. He was dishevelled, muttering, switching screen numbers and sets. Bray found his admiration for Kylee returning. She focused instantly and gave undivided attention. Three other screens glowed on the wall. Bray felt proud. She had her own desk, her name on it and everything. A suited man of Bray's age nodded off in an adjacent office. There was quite a vista from the window, parkland and a distant river. A man and woman walked their dog, as he and Lottie had walked Buster at Maldon.

Kylee pressed a button and a partition moved, settling into a groove with a hiss. Without getting up, Kylee's desk and Bray's chair were isolated.

"They think it's natty," Kylee said contemptuously. "I tellt them it's pathetic. I want to fuck off out of here."

"Leave?" he asked in alarm.

"Stay whaffor?"

"Please think before —"

She burst out laughing. "Fucking dodo. There's your tea." A small pillar rose from the desk bearing a tray with tea, milk, sugar. "Cola makes me piss all day."

He'd forgotten quite the impact she had. Everywhere

looked sterile. Kylee hadn't sat down. He felt an intruder. It must have showed in his face because she flopped to the carpet and hunched her knees.

"Not leave before we finish."

She still had the unnerving knack of speaking words directly into him, as if actual sounds didn't quite matter while her thoughts did. She was right. He was a dodo.

"Who finish?"

"Scared I'll leave you, arncher?"

Careful, he warned himself, and stammered, "Yes. I worry things'll go bad."

"Me getting in trouble."

"No…" He felt his face colour at her sideways look. "Yes."

"Why d'you not talk straight? You're scared some fucking words might get out. You say yes so it'll come out no."

He was distressed. "My conversation's not good."

"Like me." Amused, casual now. "You drove me fucking mad till I saw we're the same. Old Stone next door does sod all except he comes to and invents summert. Usually it's no use, like summat makes your eyes easier. Or a fluid switch that thinks faster. He's old like you. He farts all afternoon."

She went sober, for once not vicious. "Me and Porky did your shed over."

He looked away. She meant burgle. "Yes. I knew."

"We wondered what you got behind them painted panels. We did the whole frigging wall. I felt a right cunt. Bare wood. Porky give me a black eye."

Bray remembered the black eye, but had never asked. "I moved it all. A precaution."

"You guessed we'd do it. See? We're same. You made replica panels."

"It's not that I didn't trust you, Kylee."

"It was." To his alarm tears showed in her eyes, first ever time. "I never seed it before. So I stay on."

He was lost. "Seen what?"

"I'm allers trouble. No good Dad and his tart trying. I'm not a kid. You'd gone out walking Buster. We took the shed wall to bits and found nothing."

"I took Davey's wall away."

"Made a fake wall, shutters and all, you cunning bastard." Tears were dripping off her chin. He didn't know what to do. She wiped her nose on her sleeve. "I'd never seen devotion before. I had to get Del to look it up. Dee-vo-shun."

"You're making me out something I'm not."

"Unconditional love. That's it, innit? Everything else come second. See? I know what it means." She wiped her eyes on her sleeve, rubbed her sleeve on the wall leaving a damp smear.

"Don't talk like this, Kylee."

"Porky's flashlight showed us a blank wall, hearing him cuss me. You'd even copied the scratches, pencil marks. Fucking work of art."

"You didn't —"

"Say anything. Nar. I started helping. I'd never known it existed, this love thing. Your old cow got the push, has she?"

He tried to follow. "Lottie? She feels it's hopeless. She still works at Gilson Mather's."

"She's an iggorant tosser. You never said anyfink." And to his silence, "Catchpole. The probation hearing. Catchpole. How you'd adopt me."

He cleared his throat. How terrible females were, speaking when silence was so safe.

"Well, Geoffrey and Shirley, me being on my own, Mr Catchpole said it wouldn't be proper."

She said bluntly, "Don't fuck about. For Davey?"

Bray knew what she meant, for Davey alone or not. This honesty thing was now with the pair of them. "For all your brightness you seemed just another Davey, and just as far from home. I thought it unfair of everybody."

"Then you sponsored me." She spat, missed the waste basket. "Catchpole's a wanker. You meant it."

"One has to," was the best he could do.

"One has to," she mimicked, falsetto. "Let's get going." She watched him replace his cup and rise. "You don't have to wash up, Bray."

"Oh. Sorry." He sat down.

She swivelled out a laptop. "Palmtop and laptop security's pathetic. Watch screen."

She showed him charts, converting them to graphs and sets, making extrapolations. The sound babbled so fast he couldn't tell the meaning.

"The basis. We run our competition, papers, telly, bookshops, anywhere. We ask a zillion schools – mail direct, anyhow – questions. We do it e-mail, internet, everywhere. I've got Maddy to fund the competition as a project survey. It's only fucking peanuts. Many won't answer. The answers graph out like we ask, what colour is sky, and 99 per cent say blue. One per cent says red, yellow, and some nutters saying red-blue-white stripes. But we secretly know we're looking for the one that says green."

He got it. "Green is rare."

"Call them shed answers, the ones we're looking for. I tell the computer to keep only the shed answers. It'll pick out the nutters or mistakers, plus Davey. Nobody'll know except you."

"Then the other questions."

"The other *three* questions," she corrected.

She gave verbal orders to the computer. It showed a screen of sets. With a word it magnified them to show one final overlap marked *D*. It talked in Kylee's voice.

"I blank all the non-shed answers."

"Er, probability?"

"Forget your head. You got me." She shut her computer down, took out a disc and a battery pack. "Weighs a fucking ton. All I need now's your questions. But."

"But what?"

"Tell me the questions to ask. Not the answers."

"One thing, love. Who sorts out the replies we get? I mean, all those e-mails and letters? One of them can't get lost, because —"

"You learnt fuck all. I'll show you." With a word she had the partitions rolling back. "Have a jam butty, then piss off. I'll knock off and come. I can't stand this frigging place. The Design-and-Décor cunt's office is a shithouse."

She led into the corridor, ignoring the man at the console and the dozing genius, and bawled down the vacant door, "I asked for a fucking air conditioner!" She shook her head as they left. "Talk to the fucking wall. Know what?"

"No." He felt stricken, expecting some terrible last-minute revelation. "What is it, Kylee?"

"Here," she said with contempt, "they're fucking thicker than you. Bone. There's jam butties in the car. Tarra."

And she was gone.

He had to ask a reception girl to let him out of the building.

Chapter Forty-Nine

Snow seemed odd stuff to Clint. It went on and on. Pop kept talking about it.

"Isn't it great, Clint?"

They drove in Pop's big automobile through the falling snow among trees to a big house. There was a party for kids. There was a Santa Claus who had a big beard said "Ho ho ho" and rang a bell and everybody was real happy.

There was a Christmas tree with presents on the branches. It was bigger than usual and coloured lights kept flashing on and off. Clint liked the colours of the flashing lights but best of all he liked the shapes of the presents that were wrapped up in different colours.

They played games, kids running round chairs till the music stopped. The kids were all given lanterns with a flashing light inside. They turned off the room lights so the only light came from the Christmas tree, bigger than ever, and the lanterns. They paraded round the room singing Christmas carols. The kids clapped because they sang really well and Clint really liked it and he sang with the rest.

The kids were each allowed to chose a Christmas carol

to sing and they argued and sang "Deck the Halls with Boughs of Holly" that everybody knew best then they sang "Oh Come All Ye Faithful" like as usual and then Clint went straight on with "See Amid the Winter Snow" but somebody said no not that, something different. Clint thought maybe he'd done wrong so he started up "Adam Lay Y-Bounden" but stopped real soon because nobody else sang. Mom came and hugged him and said no not that either because it was too sad. Then they brought in the Christmas cake and Mrs McCallion who you had to call Angie because she was Zoe's Mom and a Democrat lit the candles. The kids blew the candles out. It was real neat. Clint blew most of the candles out with one puff and Mom said he deserved a special clap for that.

Clint liked the snow. When they turned the lights out for the candle cake, shadows were on the snow like in the hospital room at Doctor's clinic.

The shadow time was the time he felt happiest, when the shadows went across the wall. Like the shadows on the snow in Angie's garden. The shapes were even better than the parcel colours.

He told Mom and Pop when they were driving home. Everybody waved on Zoe's doorstep and called bye bye and come again y'hear. Mom and Pop said what a great Christmas party and what great neighbours.

Mom said the snow was real nice but so cold and she hated winter. Clint said he liked the Father Christmas and the colours and the shape shadows on the snow. Mom said say Santa Claus because it was his real name so Clint said Santa Claus.

He asked could he draw some pictures of the patterns on the garden snow at Zoe's house and Mom said you mean yard Clint don't you and Clint said yes. Mom said sure. Clint got a present from Zoe's Christmas tree, a box of crayons with special paper for drawing on and a wooden board. Clint saw the wooden board wasn't much good because it was four-ply. Somebody hadn't used glasspaper, but he didn't say anything. Any case, Zoe and Angie'd made a great party and Clint had a great time. The shadows made him feel warm even though Mom said brrrr she wanted this cold weather to go away.

Clint liked the crayons. One was purple. Another was nearly purple.

Two days later Pop and Mom took him to see the decorations in the shopping mall and they met some of the kids from the party at Zoe's. Clint kept looking for the right shapes but there was none. He didn't really mind because he'd drawn some with his crayons. Two of them looked just right and were his favourite. He got Mom to give him some kind of sticky and put the drawings up in his room. Mom said they were real pretty. He liked them best because they were like, well, like best.

And guess what Zoe's present was when she unwrapped it. It was a little fluffy dog not a real one but still a little dog that yapped when you put the battery inside. Clint liked it and said to Mom and Pop could he get a real one. They said we'll see. Clint knew they'd call Doctor and he'd say no.

In the shopping mall he looked for a dog but didn't see one. Clint drew one with his crayons. He drew a brown dog with a long tail.

It was a great Christmas.

"Notice something odd with the folio?"

They were on Donna Curme's patio, trying to ignore next door's thunderous lawnmower. Rye, her partner, was indoors working a prosecution file. By the time Donna carried the tray out Judy Trabasco had arranged the papers on the cane table.

"This the TV competition?"

"See anything strange?"

Two sets of children's drawings, eight in each, showed the now familiar little figures complete with weird angular hats. The backgrounds showed rectangular clouds and kites galore and odd stones.

Donna looked over her friend's shoulder. "Say what you see."

"Crappy kids' drawings," Judy said, gauging the other's tense mood. "Am I missing something here?"

"You've arranged them in sequence, Judy. That kite propeller thing, third along? It's the *fourth* in the top row."

She looked again. "Okay, there's one missing in the bottom row."

Donna cupped her elbows.

"Move them along. *Now* do you see?"

"They're the same, allowing for normal variation."

"The top row are the kids' drawings *after* the TV programme."

Judy examined the bottom row of sketches. Crude, the figures lacking in perspective, the usual messes. "So they show the same scenes."

"The top row were drawn *after* the TV show, the bottom row *before*."

Judy guessed, "This Clint kid did the pictures *before* they came on TV?"

"You got it."

The lawnmower mercifully puttered to quietude.

"Right. Easy explanation: Clint's folks have reception TV."

Donna shook her head. "Judy, we all get the same reception in Tain."

"Reviews, then? Clint simply copies magazines. Or from some Internet thing. Kids do it all the time."

"You can't believe that, Judy."

"How did you discover them?"

"The kids tell me. Clint's drawings have become a fun game. They're all in on it, wanting tomorrow's story – from Clint. They told me Clint always knows *tomorrow's* story."

"Clint's got some cranky electronics?"

"No way. He's a dreamer. They crowd round, laughing, make Clint tell."

Judy decided to nip this nonsense in the bud. "Then he's got relatives in Canada, or wherever they get it first. Different time zones."

"But surely —"

"Donna," Judy said firmly. "You're making a problem out of nothing. Chrissakes, they're kids' scribbles. Check with the TV company. Ask them. They'll tell you."

"Clint just guesses right. Spooky."

"Don't give me defiance, girl!" Judy reprimanded with mock severity. "Check it out. Clint's got some distant relative sending him videos."

Donna looked at the drawings. "I think it's strange."

"Don't do anything rash, like going for *dahling* Lois, y'hear? La Marquese has friends in high places. Promise?"

"Promise."

The following Saturday Donna and Rye walked by the park where the kids did training.

While Rye chatted to the junior coaches she saw Clint's parents admiring the team's hitting practice. They were older than she'd have expected, sure, but, she sighed inwardly, wasn't everybody? Suppose Clint were adopted – he fair, they dark, so what? It was their business. They obviously adored the boy.

She found Dale Porrino. It was easy, seguing from hello-there to her question.

"What is it about this game? Hit a ball with a piece of wood and run? Big deal!"

Dale laughed. "It's exciting, you dumb broad!"

She saw Clint fail, applauded anyway, shoving and joshing with the rest. Happy kid, no doubt of it. Dale checked her gaze.

"Clint's fine. Healthiest kid on the block."

"What was it you said, some Jamaican kid and one from the Bahamas?"

"Sure. It's not uncommon. Cricket, see?"

No, she didn't. Amused, Dale explained.

"Kids from cricket countries do it. You want to see that Nassau kid spin the ball! They play it at home. Make good outfielders but start off rotten pitchers."

He interrupted himself to bawl outrage at some kid hesitating in a run. Donna joked that she had to prise Rye away from all this boredom, and left. So the mystery was explained. You run different in cricket. So Clint must have cricket-playing relatives. They were clearly phoning him news of the next TV episodes.

Judy had been right. Any case, dear *dahling* Lois Marquese had reinstated Clint-Leeta-Carlson. No more mystery.

Chapter Fifty

Mom and Pop were concerned about the forthcoming school trip.

Mom said. "It's the possibilities."

"It's an ordinary camp."

They were alone, Clint in school. "Hyme, listen up. At home, we control who he meets. Out there, it could be anybody."

"Out there? Jeech, it's Colnova Falls, chrissakes. Everybody's kids go to Colnova."

"That's the point. Everybody's."

He reached for coffee. His wife removed the percolator. Hyme was on two a day.

"No, you listen up, Clodie. The other kids will talk if we keep Clint away. Will they talk about him if he goes to Colnova Falls? No." He sighed, the coffee out of reach. "If a system works, don't fix it."

"It's so far!"

"It's two hundred miles, Clodie. We'd be there in four hours. Christ," he burst out in exasperation, "we could stay there, except they'd talk worse."

"It'll be just terrible without him."

"Clodie. Use the time. Get decorators in. Make surprise."

"Will there be enough teachers? Camp helpers?"

"They've never had an accident. Mrs Daley said so."

"He's never been out of our sight before."

Hyme could have done without this. He wanted a few clear days, fly east, round trip before Clint's return. He had things to sort. Borkanen in Radial Marketing was a real asshole. He'd snafu Hyme's entire fucking fiscal year. He had to be there, hand on the moron's throat.

"Clodie, talk with the teacher. See what she says." He used the concession to grab the percolator. "I'll agree, whatever."

"Do they have a nurse there? A doctor, in case Clint gets hurt?"

Hyme felt he'd made it. He could book a flight east. Clint would go to Colnova Falls. Clodie would decorate. Truth to tell, Hyme was becoming restless. Marketing was a pig. Sometimes reorganisation worked, sometimes not. Vertrek, scheming Dutch bastard, had brought in two ingrates from Boston in his middle tier. Incompetent socialites were putty in the wrong hands.

High time he made a shock visit, in those doors like a gunfighter, scare the crap out of the lot.

The small pond at the end of the garden was as he and Davey had left it except for the far side, where weeds had overgrown the stones. Buster frolicked, foolishly hoping for an extra walk.

"Remember this, Buzz?" Bray asked. Buster started hunting among the large stones. "No. Stop that."

He sat on one of the wrought iron chairs. This was where he and Davey watched tadpoles, the boy squealing.

Buster trotted away, tail high, hoping for a marauding squirrel.

It was here Bray had dug out a rectangular pit inches larger than the shed's end wall. It had taken him two days. A panel beater had built a huge flat metal case, and delivered it late one Saturday. A precaution, in case they'd become too inquisitive and damaged Davey's KV layout. A wise precaution, in view of Kylee's admission. The case was fashioned of light motor metal. Bray had sprayed it with every combination of preservative.

The shed's original wall panels, complete with Davey's drawings and chalked colours, the entire KV story, were neatly interred. The case lay there, to be brought out for Davey to recognise on his return.

He went next door to sit in Davey's room. He had no way of knowing if Shirley and Geoff had made subtle changes, swapped this round, cleaned that surface.

On the window sill were the wooden pieces he and Davey had cut for the first time, a yellow Papri wood rectangle, Davey's original cut. Saw marks everywhere, the angles awry. He could still hear Davey's "Ooooh, party wood!" as the beautiful garish colour emerged. Students were often tricked, calling it Indian Elm.

The pieces were covered by a thick felt, for sunlight bleached. Was it a memorial? That idea was repellent, for it signified a vacancy, of one doomed never to return. No. Let others weaken.

"You're right."

Kylee startled him. She must have let herself in. She stared round the room, noting the toys, the uneven drawings, small class trophies, photographs stuck to walls.

"I don't often come up," Bray confessed. "I couldn't."

Rage, you see. Then it was rage kept me out."

"You and rage? Ooh er! Scary!" It was her old jeering tone but he knew her now.

"I needed one last reminder."

"Daft bugger. You can draw every inch."

He didn't quite know how to say it, but the journey was already upon him.

"You've been my strength, Kylee. I couldn't have gone on."

"Crap," she said bluntly. "Go over it. I'll be downstairs."

He let her go, adjusted the dust covers on the sills, checked each carving, and followed. She was pouring herself a glass of beer. He worried about that, her age, him alone in the house. It wasn't right.

"No changes, goddit?"

He ignored her crude mimicry of an imagined American accent. She seemed to think it funny, without laughter. "I've asked Lottie to fax you any changes."

"I hate the old bitch. You're too fucking soft. Tell me it all."

This was the reason she had come, to see he had the scheme off pat. She was worse than a monkey mother.

"Lottie keeps check in Gilson Mather." He ticked his fingers. "She tells you my times, addresses, auction houses. She'll send word to Jim Stazio."

"And?" she asked like a teacher.

She'd go berserk if he stumbled. "I confirm, morning and night."

"Using your laptop, goon!" She screamed it, swiping at him. "Thirty minutes every night, eleven o'clock proper time."

"You gave me a timed programme." He fumbled, pulled out a printed sheet.

"Your laptop reminds you, fucking Yank time zones."

"I have it."

"Remember you're a silly old fart, so do what the laptop tells. Don't change a fucking thing. No extra talks. Don't go somewhere not on your list. Say it."

"I stick to the schedule. No extras. I confirm everything with you, eleven o'clock GMT."

"Only phone me on your mobile, 'kay? Phone Gilson Mather any old how because they don't matter. No KV talk on the phone."

"Phone only on the mobile. Everything secret."

She belched, scrutinised the bottle's label. "Gunge, this. Memorise the codes."

"We've been over this."

She leant forward angrily. "There's hundreds of millions of the bastards. Them as stole Davey, so don't get fucking careless. Them codes are old dead lingo called Linear B. Some cunt in Dongle Production did them. Got your dongle?"

Bray showed her the small electronic inserts.

"Your laptop won't work without it. If you lose it, I'll courier you replacement everything." She opened another beer with a grimace. "This is gnat piss. Your codes, one more for the road."

Obediently he recited the dozen encryptions with which they would communicate.

"Last," she said severely. "You missed out last. *Twelve* is fucking *twelve*."

"I know." He'd deliberately omitted the one denoting certainty, end of the hunt, good or bad.

She relented. "I'll let you off this once. You'd better get that far." Her watch pinged. She dropped the bottle, simply opened her hand. It fell to the carpet, its residue trickling out. "Is that fucking wolfhound okay?"

"Buster stays with Christine and Hal's sister until... Hal's own dog Mongo's a maniac. Until I'm back."

Bray did his tickets, passport, cards. He straightened and locked the door.

"You have your keys?"

She admonished him, "Do as I worked out. Come back in one piece."

"Ta." He hesitated, seeing the taxi at the kerb. "Kylee, I don't often say thanks —"

She walked ahead. "Talking's fucking stupid."

She didn't bother to answer. All the way to the station she hardly spoke, except to start on about somebody who made a mistake, but grew irritated when he couldn't see the point of her tale.

"Think on," she said on the platform.

"About what?"

"Stick to the schedule. Do your teeth, 'kay?" And explained, "It's what the pigs say in prisonages."

"I promise." He could never recognise jokes, or tell one.

To his surprise she bussed him. "Give me the okay on time, unless."

She didn't say unless what. There was an awkward moment while he hefted his case into the train. Two young football fans in coloured scarves shouted to Kylee as they passed, "Don't worry, darlin', we'll look after your grandad."

"You fucking better," Kylee shot back to them, her grey eyes never leaving Bray. "He's the only one I got."

Bray turned away, the whistle saving him from having to speak. He raised his hand to Kylee. She made no sign and, hands in pockets, walked with the train as it began to move. Suddenly he wanted to lean out, somehow tell her of his gratitude for having stayed so impossibly loyal. The barmier his scheme, the more resolute she'd become. An abrupt jerk of her head seemed a benediction, filled with understanding. He thought, she knows my feeling, just like Davey could. *Can*.

The train glided away from home, such as home was.

Chapter Fifty-One

Lottie thought the building was like a supermarket, with the same anonymity. She wondered if she was doing the right thing coming to see Kylee. She'd been at Heathrow to see Bray's flight leave. She'd imagined Bray looking back, seated among wassailers as the bar opened and friendships burgeoned. He would of course be startled if anyone spoke, giving his slight nod to avoid talking.

Standing there among the planned *Mahonias* and *Berberis*, the lovely *Ceanothus* in bloom, Lottie found it easy to blame herself. God knows, Bray was doing something brave, if loony. She had wanted to say goodbye, but guessed Kylee might be there.

She asked for Kylee Walsingham. The efficiency, of a company rising in fortune, was certainly convincing. Before she could waver, she was ushered along corridors and into a room where Kylee was sitting on a window-sill eating an orange. Plush, new, and not a computer in sight.

"Hello, Kylee. I came to make my peace."

The room was bare. Lottie realised Kylee had chosen her ground.

"Where's the fucking war?"

Kylee spat a pip expertly against the wall, grunted when it failed to reach. Lottie controlled her anger. She'd expected more than this.

"I only wanted to say that if there's anything I can do."

"That it?"

Lottie's irritation grew. "Look. I know you think I let him down, but you haven't looked at things from my point of view."

"Save yourself some aggie and piss orf."

"What did you say?" Even for Kylee this was outrageous.

A man opened the door, made to carry in a stack of files and swiftly withdrew, hooking the door with his foot.

"Leave Bray alone. You've done damage."

"Damage? What damage?"

"Sodding off, that's what damage." Kylee spat a piece of orange skin at Lottie, making her step aside.

"Would you mind stopping that?"

"Piss orf. You did fuck all."

"How dare you! What do you know at your age?"

"More'n you, you fucking geriatric." Kylee simply dropped the orange peel, wiped her mouth on her sleeve. "Sod off and let him do it."

"I'll have you know that I worked twice as hard as you and your ignorant sidekick ever did! I put in hours, weeks. Who made all the arrangements for his tour, set up the visits, dragged that ancient firm into the light? I did!"

Kylee stretched languidly, thumbs in her belt.

"You fucking crone, come creeping round now he's started off. I wouldn't piss on you if you were on fire."

"I did —"

"No such thing?" Kylee's falsetto made crude mockery. "Isn't that what you do-gooders say? It's for everybody else's good?"

She advanced on Lottie, arms akimbo.

"I've had a fucking life-dose of you let-downers. You turds are in everything for what you can get. You used to come to the correction dump."

"I did nothing of the —"

"You did. Twin fucking sets, phoney pearls, tweed skirts and brogues." Kylee nodded her own agreement. "Smiling like some frigging disease. How maaaahv'llous you were to visit such crappy flea-bitten brats! Making," Kylee spat, "an impression."

"You insolent little bitch!"

"Bray don't need a senile fucking relic."

Lottie shouted, giving way, "How far do you think you would have got without me?"

"Farther. You derelict old bat, you should a been out there helping him instead of here bragging at doing sweet fuck all."

Lottie was almost in tears. "That's unfair! I worked as hard as you, as Bray!"

Kylee snorted. "To make your own number wiv him, that's why."

Lottie turned away in rage. "Trying to talk sense with you is like

...like talking to him!"

"That proves we're right and you're the daft bugger."

"I told him straight out. He's a dreamer. Whittling wood at his age! Has he ever done anything else? No! He's just a big kid."

"Of course he is, you silly cunt! Like me!" Lottie gaped as tears streamed down the girl's face. "That's why he's doing it! He's out there with Davey! He always was! And he's the only one who's been in here with me! It happened to him! What happened to the little lad's happening again to Bray, you ignorant fucking crone!"

Lottie felt like hiding.

"He's Davey," Kylee said quiet now. "He's me. He is lost children, see?"

"I don't understand."

Kylee spoke with withering contempt. "Idiot cow. Do you think Bray would've left *me* to rot, like they all did, if he'd seen me like I was?" Lottie had never seen anyone weep as Kylee wept, tears streaming yet without a change in expression. It might have been rain. "Never in a million fucking years. Everything he's doing to find Davey he'd do for me. He doesn't say so. That's because he can't talk proper like you people can. But he would have. He's the dad I never had."

"Look. I'm sorry. I —"

"Whatever he wants to do, you get in his way I'll rip your fucking eyes out!" The last word was screeched so viciously that Lottie recoiled.

Some woman along a corridor called out, nervously asking if everything was all right.

"You haven't the sense to see you might be wrong." Lottie's last stand.

"Numbers don't lie," Kylee said. "You selfish bitches have words to do that." Hawking, Kylee spat directly into Lottie's face.

"You're mad," Lottie said, stumbling to the door trying to get a hankie out.

Kylee shoved past and out of the door without another word.

That evening Lottie found herself on one of the benches on the Maldon greensward. The crowd was thinning in a watery sun. Boats were returning up the estuary, folk collecting children from the paddling pools. The sky still showed traces of blue. A few families congregated round motors in the car park, searching for bags, anxious not to leave half their stuff before setting out homeward. It was all quiet content.

She saw a young father grab his toddler from near the water's edge as a giant yawl's wake threatened to lap against the bank, the child squealing in outrage at rescue. She could still see Kylee's blank face, the girl's cheeks dripping tears.

Had the girl wept so often that she no longer noticed her own weeping? They were honest, not a device. Lottie wondered if Kylee had it in her to be deceitful. Cunning was beyond the child, for child she still was. Yet such hatred. Lottie felt almost frightened at Kylee's vituperation.

Was it true?

Was she right, that Lottie, naturally wanting a settled relationship with an eligible middle-ager, had merely played investment tactics? And became sulky because Bray had a more compelling priority? Worse, it meant Lottie was beyond feeling a devotion the girl understood with such transparent clarity, and that Kylee was more of a woman than a woman almost three times her age.

Lottie dabbed her eyes. She hadn't Kylee's expertise at weeping with such casual physiology. She fumbled for a tissue. A dog ran at the water's edge, barking at the turning tide. For one silly instant Lottie believed it was Buster, but it was only a small Sheltie bent on mischief. Its family called it away.

She took out her car keys. A vapour trail stood out against the blue as a plane, probably from the Continent, headed inland. She watched until the white streak dissolved.

How fast planes went these days, she thought, faster than any train, than any ship.

New York was having a heat wave. The Manhattan air felt turgid. You breathed soggy air, clogging the throat.

Bray was astonished at the pace, all streets one-way. He was unprepared for rollerbladers, swooping on you so suddenly and with such grace. Iron kerbs in Manhattan, shaved to a thin metal strip at street corners. Why? Massive saloon cars, several windows long. The ineffable politeness of some people, the extraordinary anger of others, and the appalling heat. Buildings were unbelievably diverse, no two alike. A Chase Manhattan Bank that was no more than a smart little detached redbrick house set among skyscrapers, as if in a canyon. The wail of sirens, grids of flashing lights on emergency vehicles.

Surely he must be the only person in New York City not yacking into a cell phone? He was struck by the diversity of human shapes. And the verbosity of traffic notices: *NYC Law: Speed limit 30 unless otherwise posted. No honking except for danger.* A logo would have done for either, or had he missed something? And heavy freight vehicles were not allowed down Park Avenue without some special extra permit. Superfluity was everywhere.

The unbelievably tatty taxi set him down at the hotel. He was relieved to find Lottie's booking system working. A young lady told him he was "pre-registered". He would have felt a pang for Lottie's absence, but regret was disallowed, like heavy freight vehicles in Park Avenue.

The evening was hot and sultry. Sweat thickened his collar, dripped down his nape hair. For a while he simply sat in his room. He put the television on to follow the hours. He'd acquired from Suzanne in the workshop a gift to mark his departure, a gadget converting currencies and telling the time all over the world, temperatures, tides, heaven knew what else. He'd set it on Greenwich Mean Time and checked it every few minutes. One TV channel, too quick for him, tried to show him an episode of KV but he got to the remote button before it could flash up the forthcoming All-America KV Competition.

The TV placed the suffix *et* by numbered hours. Eastern Time? But *ct* defeated him. Central Time, possibly, or was there such a thing? If so, central to what periphery?

That day he spent doing runs of lectures. He went down for a nervy meal in the hotel restaurant, fretted and slept. He woke on the Fourth of July, heard people say the frankly unbelievable "Happy Fourth" to each other. The heat was worse.

He walked to encourage fatigue, returned to his air-conditioned room tired. That evening he watched the celebratory fireworks begin along the East River's four sites of exquisite lights. Davey would love them. The comforting thought came that maybe, just maybe, probably, certainly, Davey was seeing them, beaming.

Two more rehearsals of talks, while he waited. He'd got his laptop computer ready. At the hour he tapped in his message. The e-mail went without a hitch. Instantly a return message came:

u 8 secs late how offen i av 2 tell u ok?

Relief almost undid him. He typed *yes all ok* and got back *comp is go then?*

One-fingered, he typed in *yes we do it & thanks*

And got back *get 2 bed big day 2morn do ur teeth luv*

Reluctantly he put the laptop away feeling lost, and

filled up. A ridiculous sensation, she a chit of a child and so far away.

Kylee had said to milk the firm by inventing false expenses but, heaven's sake, who on earth had the necessary convolutions of brain to keep that up, to no purpose? Lottie had warned him to list travel costs and include everything for proper accounting. Who had such vigilance?

No. He was *here* with his plan, faulty and speculative as it was. Vigilance must be hoarded until his chance came, then everything could be expended in a great rush to his last breath. The child stealers would be eternally vigilant, with resources he couldn't even contemplate. Wasn't that what Jim Stazio said?

He felt forlorn, though reassured. Kylee must have been watching the minutes, his unlikely lifeline. Angrily he reversed the words, for who criticised the ropemaker when his thin twine alone stopped you from falling?

Now to message Gilson Mather and say so far he was fine. Even before Bray left Lottie had a map of the USA and two boxes of coloured pins in the firm's office. He had written to Geoffrey and Shirley and asked after Buster. He checked the laptop's battery and puzzled over the bathroom voltage.

One last time, he took out his itinerary, Lottie's instructions in her handwriting: Sotheby's of New York, taxi to a lecture hall, to an antiques emporium, motors at this or that airport, names of couriers, phone numbers in case. He'd arrived. How near, how far away, there was no way of knowing.

He remembered saying that to Kylee. She gave him a mock backhander.

"No way of knowing *yet*," she had reprimanded. "Say

yet, y'old fucker."

He'd been ashamed at his lapse. She was right. He said it aloud in the room, "Yet."

Next morning he rose at six o'clock and made a start.

Chapter Fifty-Two

The camp at Colnova Falls was seriously oversubscribed. The Tain contingent arrived in a crowd. Three more intakes due the following day. One dormitory was four bunk beds short. The first afternoon was spent in fixing sleeping arrangements. The camp was run by Brighters, all vigorous and sports-orientated, with their own hier-archy.

The children thought it an adventure. Clint felt sorry for the camp Brighters, so gaudy in their orange anoraks, but Carlson, Leeta, and Frondy, a Mexican girl who made up their quartet, didn't and wanted more children to make friends.

"They'll be sued," Carlson prophesied. "We'll be witnesses."

"They can't." Frondy's father was a lawyer. "They sign a paper."

It was brilliant, though. Clint's foursome had First Canoeing, which was daring. They did badly. Carlson blamed their instructor, Camp Brighter Sally, who said they were too reckless. Clint asked Sally how they made the canoes but she didn't answer. Carlson said she didn't know.

Evening meals were staggered on account of the numbers at Colnova Falls, mixing children being Falls policy. Every building was a rustic log cabin, though features of modern living were in evidence from muted air-conditioning to indoor pools.

First dinnertime, Clint's four encountered the Chicago children. They were full of the KV competition on television.

"Know what?" Dwight, one of the latecomers challenged the Tain kids. He was a heavily built nine-year-old who had written to a glamorous Hollywood starlet and expected a letter any day, probably with an invite to star with her in her next movie. "We stand the best chance of winning, see? The prize is an old table worth a million. Older'n the whole US of A!"

"The answers are obvious," Frondy said scornfully. "They've gotta be. That way they get pay-off, half the phone bills."

"We do it e-mail," Dwight explained.

"You win a visit from the KV actors. The winners go on TV."

"There's four questions." Dwight's friend Merv told stories of stealing automobiles in Chicago. The Tain children didn't believe him. "I've a cousin who'll get us the answers up front, easy."

"Clint's best." Leeta was always competitive.

Merv nudged Frondy. "Who'd pay a million for a table?"

On the slope was a small waterfall among trees. The trunks were carved totems, showy with gloss paints. Clint was interested. Carlson sceptical.

He said, "Brighter Sally, they're just made up, right?"

"No." Sally was feeling decidedly unbright as she walked her two groups to their dorms, but maintained her determined smile. "They're genuine Amerindian. Real carvings by local tribes."

"Where are the tribes, then?" Leeta took up the protest.

"They might be hiding," Frondy said. "Indians hide."

"Come on, Clint," Brighter Sally urged. "Keep up."

"Clint likes wood shapes," Carlson explained.

"It's why we'll win the KV competition," Leeta said candidly, swinging her bag until Brighter Sally told her sharply to stop that right now in case she hit somebody. "We're going to do it here when it starts."

"Here?" Brighter Sally yelped. "We haven't the facilities! You mail postcards to the TV station, right?"

"No," the children said with scorn. "Everything's e-mail."

Carlson eyed her. "Ain't you got computers here?"

"Clint!" Sally called with a glassy grin. "Clint! You can look at those totems another time."

Clint stared at the totem. It was huge, right up into the sky. The colours were different than the wood must have expected. You couldn't be sure until you'd carved so the Thing in the wood came out. The wood knew.

He stared at the adze marks.

Only big people used an adze. One day, he would be big enough to stand astride the job o' work and swing a huge adze, blade towards his legs. Miss, and you had to go to the hospital. Only you hadn't to swing. Not even when you went back and forward – *forwards* – sawing holding onto one end of that great double saw that was hardly ever used. Then you swung laughing as the handle pulled you near, then pushed you away. And the man in the paint-stained apron, the apron he called a, what, so stiff with colour that it stood up on its own, to Clint's delight, in a corner where pieces of wood lay in neat heaps among – amongst –

shavings that crackled underfoot.

No, you couldn't use an adze yet. Twelve, the smiling sawing man who wasn't Doctor said, *happen, depending how we get on.* Only you'd to say maybe, not happen. The humming sawing man said happen. He knew everything about wood. The man could make a totem bigger than any totem in the world if he wanted to. Wood knows what it wants to become.

"Clint!" Camp Brighter Sally was calling. "Clint. You can look at those totems another time!"

Clint ran and caught the others up.

"Clint could do better'n those," Leeta said.

"Bet he couldn't." Dwight snatched Leeta's bag.

"Give me my bag!" Leeta screamed.

"Stop that before somebody gets hurt!" Brighter Sally clapped hands for attention as they headed towards the dorms. "Now, kids! Guess what we're doing tomorrow!"

"Sailing!"

"Horses!"

Sally tried to keep the enthusiasm going while she distributed the kids into the dorms, but was busy wondering if the other Brighters had considered computers. Kids had too many raves. Panic buys for some movie robot, premiums, all costing a fortune until the rush was over then onto something else. She had three nieces and two nephews, to her cost.

Falling asleep that night, Clint thought of the smiling man in his apron. Turpentine was a big smell, in a bottle labelled with an orange dot that meant no touching. The apron wasn't called an apron at all.

Brat. The old man belonged to Clint, and didn't say apron. "Where's my brat?" he'd say in his carving place with one window, and Clint would say, "You've got it on!"

and he'd laugh because the sawing man had forgotten it again.

The man kept doing that, forgetting it every evening after supper in the wood place with the story panel on the end wall.

He slipped into oblivion.

He was unprepared for the crowd. The small hall at Devace, Hinds and Meltonish's on Fifth Avenue was packed, people having to stand.

Nervously he listened while James Evanders, vice-president, made a fulsome introduction.

"Ladies and gentlemen. Welcome to a very special presentation. We are honoured by a remarkable speaker, the senior craftsman of Gilson Mather. His firm is the only surviving furniture manufacturing company that can still trace its origins back to the Seventeen Hundreds in London's Long Acre. Our esteemed visitor is *the* acknowledged expert in antique furniture. His recent success is the compilation of the classic two-volume work detailing furniture that, over the centuries, emanated from his own firm and that of its eminent rivals…"

Bray tried not to study the audience as Mr Evanders spoke on. They were alert, friendly, smiling in anticipation. Was he worth all this? They seemed so eager, these Americans, to listen to a bloke talking about wood.

"Furthermore, our speaker has kindly consented to accept questions. Ladies and gentlemen, please welcome Mr Bray Charleston!"

He began hesitantly, but soon warmed. The audience took him at his word, putting questions as soon as he got to specifics about a four-drawer chest of coloured walnut.

"Yes, the piece is one I especially admire." He pointed

clumsily with the marker light. "Many craftsmen of the time – say, 1740, give or take – would have eschewed brass handles of such a size for a quite dainty piece. The drawers are lined by pine, edges slightly raised." He smiled confidingly. "Craftsmen among you will know what I'm about to say: walnut is a whole range of types, not just one. And some *Juglans*, like Nogal, is variegated reddish, even chocolate-brown, as here. I love it. It shows a lustre that even the most incompetent duckegg can't get rid of."

There was some laughter, but he shook his head.

"I mean it. We are the worst enemies of the most exquisite God-given material. We have to accept its trust, because it is a living thing. Work ineptly, and we insult Creation. We have no right to be too lazy to bother."

A ripple of applause brought him back to his subject.

"What I'm getting round to is this: Wise craftsmen would choose this wood for its working properties. It lasts. Soft, yet almost unbelievably light to handle. Its grain is rodlike straight. It works easily, and polishes like a dream." He smiled apologetically. "Sorry. I'm getting carried away."

Some lady raised a hand. "What's that piece worth?"

He inspected the slide image above him quizzically.

"Small is fashionable nowadays. Nicely graduated drawers, though without adornment on the raised edges that some still call 'cockbead'. Bracket feet. Plain, whole heartwood, not elegant veneer. Oh, worth at least a half-dozen world cruises."

"Are you sure?" the lady exclaimed incredulously.

Bray heard himself say, "Well, missus, I was positive a minute ago. Now, it's probably twice as much!"

There was laughter. He noted the time and tried to get on. He was going too slowly. His answers became more summary. He concluded five minutes over time, and accepted the applause. Mr Evanders gave his thanks.

"Ladies and gentlemen, refreshments are provided during the break, after which Mr Charleston will discuss the furniture on display in our gallery. They represent four centuries of craftsmanship from England and America. A DHM catalogue is available…"

The lady who had posed the first question approached Bray. Immediately he started a hesitant apology.

"No. I loved your talk, Mr Charleston!" She squeezed his arm. "And I *loved* that 'missus'. How d'you say it?"

She gave him her card and invited him to talk to her antiques group in Venice, California. She was the first of many. Their enthusiasm was a huge relief. Bray found himself enjoying the crowd. He only noticed the time when somebody pushed her way through with the vice-president to remind him that he was due to speak in New Jersey.

"Thank you," he said. "There should be a motor —"

"It's here," Lottie told him calmly. "You'll just have time to drop in at your hotel." She turned to the smiling people. "Thank you for your kind welcome and interest. I'm afraid Bray has another engagement."

"You're not taking him!"

Lottie handled the protests and pleasantries with quips of her own.

"Your slides and folders are in your case," she told Bray, maintaining her smile. "Sorry, but I really do have to get Mr Charleston away or Gilson Mather will hunt me down…"

They made it to the waiting vehicle and entered the air-conditioned interior.

"I was told off," Lottie said, "and made to see sense."

"Is it all right with the firm?"

Lottie gave a half laugh. "Still worrying over pointless details even now, Bray? We're going to have none of that for ever and ever, d'you hear?"

She turned away, shaking her hair down over her face to consult a list. "We have two hours. You can have a rest and a bite." She leant forward to speak to the driver. Bray watched Manhattan, feeling life was suddenly saner.

Chapter Fifty-Three

Evening was a long time coming. Office people called Kylee impatient, but she'd always been called stupid words, no worth in any of them. Not by Bray, though. Bray never called her anything. Sometimes he'd ask if she really ought to do this, that, because he was thick. A kid. She never minded Bray because when she shot abuse back he just nodded like she'd said something clever, and make like she'd won. Friends were a waste of space. A drink and a fuck, not much else.

She still saw Porky for a quick shag or when she wanted something done, like the discs she'd seen nicked from work by a librarian. Porky'd done the librarian's house over without raising a gallop. Except Porky was in trouble again, and this time there was no juve excuse because he was old enough to get done, nicking stuff off of a pantechnicon transporter down the Blackwall Tunnel.

Lately she'd taken up with a bloke in Systems. Creb was tidy and clever, named from his schoolmates' belief that clever meant he cribbed in exams. He was good at snooker, had a brother in nick from a robbery went peary. He slept half the fucking day in the office, then worked threeish and the moon up before he dragged off to his pit.

First time they did it, she had to show him what to do, glad because that meant she was his first shag. He was astonished at the whole thing. She'd laughed. Creb asked her how she'd "worked it out", barmy fucker. Silicon, fluid feedbacks, recycling Boolean over-shoots, he'd sussed all that when he was three, and getting your clothes off was like brain surgery.

She wondered if Bray'd like him. She took to Creb, though he was true weird for somebody seventeen, washed and wearing a fucking tie like he was twenty-eight even. One thing, he had a fucking sister, might turn out to be a right fucking mare, all talons if her precious brother got himself a tart and learnt what. Vital for Bray that Creb did what he was told.

"Are you well, Kylee?" said this prat in the canteen.

"Not good," she confessed. She'd never had to play a scene. Pretence was beyond her. First time in her life she'd wanted to ask some other bint what the hell. They all seemed to know, simpering to get the edge on some lad. Finally she'd not bothered.

"What is it?" he asked. They always sat apart from the others, into fluid recursives that she guessed, no, *knew*, she would invent.

She told him about a non-family, a poxy shagnasty mother, dud dad, the ruination called childhood. He wanted to go and see the courthouse where she was given a sentence, stupid sod.

"It's my grandad," she invented, wondering if she could get away with a tear or two. Except what if tears actually started? Fuck, she might be good at it and then what? "Difficulties."

What difficulties, though? And how should the story go?

"Difficulties?" Creb asked, so gentle she could have stabbed the silly fucker.

"Er, a public relations thing."

"What public relations thing?"

She burst out, "Don't ask so many fucking loony questions. He wants something doing."

The dopey berk asked, "Can I do anything?"

"Them KV things."

"On kids' telly?"

"That's them. He needs them blammed."

She used to pull faces in the mirror. Sighs didn't work.

"It's complicated." She usually finished his chips, if he'd enough tomato sauce, but didn't this time in case she didn't look sincere. "Can't be done."

"Blammed how?" asked this clean marvel.

"It's in books, telly. He's against the whole KV thing."

"What for?"

"How the fuck —?" She halted, began again. "It's bad for children, their education. He's written to the papers. This week it's starting a USA telly quiz. Four-part, one question every episode. The winner gets an antique worth a gillion."

"I didn't know you had a grampa."

"Well I fucking well have!" she shot at him across the table, and angrily seized his plate. He never finished his meal anyway. "He was good to me."

"You said —"

"Fuck what I said," she groused, scoffing. "He asked me to help. Can't be done."

Creb's eyes went into middle distance, face shining. "Everything can be done, Kylee."

"Yeah, Creb?" Like she hadn't a clue.

"Give me an hour," he said. "How long've we got?"

"The first question goes out soon." She shoved his empty plate back across the Formica and waited. The goon couldn't talk and walk at the same time. They left the canteen together.

"You like your grampa, Kylee?"

She spoke the truth. "I'd do anything. I want to ruin the KV series before the quiz ends."

Creb was into his palmtop before they reached her floor. He was glowing. "Grampa's problems are over!"

About fucking time the penny dropped, Kylee thought. She had to get the message to Bray.

The first three days wore them down. Lottie was phlegmatic.

"I'm used to this," she explained when Bray began to wonder. "I'm practical about people. You're a wood man."

They were outside a vast three-storey Tyrolean edifice that had hosted Bray's sixth presentation, the limo already waiting. White wines, enormous quantities of food, the greensward thronged by people who had attended his talk on "Valuable Cottage and Farmhouse Antiques – Genuine and Fake." Bray was relieved there was time to walk round before they moved on.

"We advertise," the owner cut in, eager to show Bray the terracing overlooking the rolling parkland. "Nobody spends like Blenheem Antiquo Ltd, nobody. This decking was built for our first advertising meet."

"Your country has everything." Bray was unable to keep the envy out of his voice. "So many resources."

Dane Blenheem glanced at him keenly. "You want to visit with us for a period, Bray? We'd work something out with Gilson Mather. Antiques, replicas, set up a trimester course at Vergaine. It has quite a reputation."

"That's kind, Dane. I'm tempted." Their stunning frankness was hard to take.

Dane moved Bray away from an approaching group. Quickly Lottie intercepted the visitors and began a conversation about Bray's contentious views on regional variants. One man, a portly figure in loose-fitting greys, ignored Lottie's manoeuvre and strolled after Bray.

"How long could you spend here, if we could work things out?" Dane persisted. "We'd handle accommodations. You'd not be disappointed."

Bray smiled. "I'm not sure I can take more of this hospitality!"

Dane laughed. "Hey, Bray. Look at the people! Three hundred, half of them buyers! That's tribute enough." His voice sank to a confidential low. "Do you know that we had forty – that's four-oh – written questions before you started your talk?"

Bray caught sight of the stout moustached man with the grey hair and spectacles standing patiently by, casually listening to a cluster of dealers. His eyes did not waver.

"I'm afraid my opinions on your Lancashire dresser and the Isle of Man chair stirred up a hornet's nest, Dane."

"Bray," the art dealer said seriously, "some people think antiques ridiculous. But money stops them laughing every time. Your craftsmanship's what's needed!"

The big elderly man was now a step away. He raised his wine glass in salutation.

"We'll talk some more, Bray," Dane said, displeased at the persistent man.

"Enjoyed your talk," the newcomer said.

Bray said levelly, "Notice I didn't mention the things I know nothing about?"

The man laughed. "That's clever, right enough! Wish I

was sensible. Never could keep my mouth shut, though."

Lottie started to drift towards them through the crowd. Dane asked the man if he was a local dealer.

"Retired now." He smiled. "Came a long way to hear your speaker. Interesting stuff, Mr Charleston."

Dane said eagerly, "If you still deal, I'd be pleased to show you the displays, Mr...?"

"Stazio," the man said affably, shaking Blenheem's hand. "Jim Stazio."

Bray extended his hand. "Pleased you came."

"Have you met?" Dane Blenheem asked.

"Have now!" the ex-policeman said, "and that's for sure."

Chapter Fifty-Four

Creb rushed into Kylee's office exactly at the wrong time. She was sulking, refusing to report on a fluid recursive non-crystalline system she'd guessed up. It was only a series of digital three-element interfaces, hardly worth the bother. The ignorant bastards shouldn't waste her time. The head of marketing kept phoning. She told him to piss off, talking into her spread phone while seated on the window. She'd come to work without one shoe, the secretaries staring like it was her fault if a shoe forgot.

"Look at this!" Creb cried. He knew her foibles. "I've got protests everywhere! Newspapers! I have a group lobbying politicians in the States. Four pressure groups —"

Kylee focussed slowly. He meant the competition. She'd heard Jim Stazio and Lottie Vinson were there now, quite a team while she was stuck here in this dump. Creb was jubilant.

"Told you! I'll have them rioting! National newspapers tomorrow." He was flushed. "Their government's banging the education drum." He went shy. "I've twenty-five addresses. Worked all night. Fifty television outlets replied!"

Kylee leaned back. She felt out of things.

"You know what, Kylee?" Creb said wistfully. "Fraud feels really splendid. I only wish I'd started earlier."

He was eager to share his achievement and spread his papers over her desk.

"Commercialism of childhood! That's first, because the stories are innocent, see? That got them going. Then comparisons: the KV lack of aims. Nobody has jobs in KV. Everything just happens." He struck a pose and intoned, "Is this a proper way to teach children life isn't simply all games? Your grandad's problems are over."

"Who?"

Creb looked at his copies critically. "We ought to set up some PR division of our own. Here, I mean. I'm brilliant at it."

"Grandad'll be grateful, Creb." He collected his sheaf. "You don't think it's too much?"

"Too much?" Creb laughed, pleased. "There really is no such thing as bad publicity. That prize – an antique, I think – is like a red rag to a bull. All you need is the angle." He whispered confidentially, "I made so many phone calls I got confused who I was! I'm enjoying this!"

She thought of Buster, who was only a lousy dog.

"Can I meet him?"

"Who?"

"Your grandad." His smile faded. "Aren't you pleased?" Kylee said. "Piss off. I've summert to do."

"See you later?"

She shrugged.

Jim Stazio's idea of quiet disconcerted Lottie.

"The place is so noisy!"

A Country and Western group was hard at it, bars

competing in talk, babble at the crowded tables. The ex-policeman was pleased.

"This is America, Lottie! We play as hard earning a dollar!"

The place pleased Bray. He'd worried that they would run out of things to say. Jim insisted on ordering while they fenced around impressions of the States. Bray confessed that American hospitality took him aback.

"We mean it, sure," Jim reassured him. "Addresses are for using."

"We're not quite like that. We use bland expressions to conclude conversations. They mean nothing. 'Yes, do keep in touch,' sort of thing."

Lottie smiled. "Well, Jim proved difficult!"

He batted his eyelids in mock shyness. "I'm so sensitive, right?"

"Knowing you were in right from, well…"

"The start," he capped, pleased. "Where's the beef?" and translated to their blank expressions, "What's the plan?"

"We think we've a way to narrow the search." Lottie got Bray's nod to continue. "A friend of Bray's into computers."

"Can we do it all at once?"

"Impossible." Lottie watched the food and drinks arrive. "Dear heaven! We may never move again!"

The ex-policeman was delighted. "You get a decent plate in America. The beer's good." He cocked an eye at Bray. "The plan?"

"I have a young friend, a computer talent."

"That's youth for you," Jim sighed. "And what happens?"

"It's a competition. One reply every week for four weeks. The first comes in the day after next. It's the catchment."

"Catchment?" The American gestured at the food. "Start."

"Sort out, and the replies tell where Davey will be."

Stazio paused, licked his finger. "Why didn't we do this before?"

"It's taken time to set up, Jim."

"Sure, sure." They raised their voices as folk began to sing along. "This is the punch?"

"Maybe," Bray said quickly, alarmed. Optimism seemed as much a threat as despond. "One step each week."

"To a total of four? How do we get the gauntlet?"

"Gauntlet!" Lottie repeated. "That's exactly it! We hear from home."

"This catchment shows places where Davey might be, right?"

Lottie waited for Bray to answer.

"Forty-three thousand, minimum," he managed. The beer was the lightest he'd ever tasted.

"Jesus Aitch," Jim said. "That many?"

"I'm banking on narrowing down."

"How do we weed out the phoneys?"

They dealt with the food in silence. It was serious beef and vegetables, gravy thick enough to float on with a dozen different condiments. "It's the only way that makes any sense."

Lottie noted Bray's hesitation. "I wasn't very supportive, Jim," she admitted. "I had a tantrum, said it was ridiculous." Jim watched her heightened colour. "I've seen sense, of course. We must go for it."

"Right." He resumed his meal. "Your friend back there. She reliable?"

"Utterly," Bray said.

"She's a right cow," Lottie said with innocent sweetness,

giving them all a smile. "But Bray's right."

"Do I get to know which locations are still in the race?"

Bray said, "I couldn't do it without you, Jim. That's the truth."

"The nearer we get, the more essential you'll be."

"Can you really cut the numbers down?"

"We don't," Bray said. "I get a breakdown. Kylee works them out."

"Is it safe?" For the first time since they'd met Jim Stazio seemed uncomfortable. "I mean, perps have informants, track infos. They have resources."

Bray said soberly, "I started out trusting nobody. We are it."

"When will you need me?"

"In a fortnight, Jim. Is that all right?" Bray checked with Lottie. "Until then we'll just have half continental USA, always assuming we've got the right country and get the right answers."

Jim Stazio asked heavily, "One thing. What if the gauntlet doesn't work?"

"If there's no narrowing down?"

"Devil's advocate: The phoneys might hang on in whatever your system says, right? We might never narrow the possibles."

After a pause Bray said, "Then I shall have to think again."

"We could have it down to three or four towns," Lottie said defiantly. "That's a workable number."

"Is there a chance your scheme could alert the perps?"

"A small risk." Bray was unwilling to say more.

"The clues come from the boy?" Jim asked.

"Yes," Lottie answered for Bray, seeing he was having difficulty coping.

"Then here's to us." Jim toasted with his beer. "Great

food, eh? This is a multinational pub, right across the States."

"God save us," Lottie said.

Chapter Fifty-Five

Bray waited until Lottie had gone to bed before he opened the laptop and got through to Kylee.

: ur late

Only a split second, he typed, *Jim S. Very pleasant. I hope I can introduce you both some day. You'll like him.*

: get on wi it the 1st q guz in 2 days

Yes. Have I to write it here?

: less u wont me 2 gess

Here goes then: Question One: What are the kites made of?

: is that it

Yes.

: sure it's never bin telt in storiz

Yes, I'm certain. I re-ran all of the television episodes last night & I've checked the books a million times.

: now wot

Bray pondered, and finally supposed she'd not managed to get the difference between know and now. The question mark always maddened her because she had to speak the word for query yet it wasn't a real letter.

No, he tapped in. *What?*

: i rekon will get > 70,000 anserz owzat for gudnis

I think it's excellent. You have done brilliantly. I'm so appreciative.

: wot

He wondered a short while. Her dyslexia seemed so patchy, and he knew how it distressed her. It moved his heart. So dazzlingly numerate, and so limited otherwise. Yet wasn't normalcy a definition asserted by the majority? He considered, then carefully sent *uv dun brill ta luv*, feeling embarrassed, mutton dressing itself trendy.

: is that cow wi u

Of course not. Kindly mind your manners, miss. Separate rooms, of course.

: gd luk wiv it for uz 2

For we two, not for Lottie, Jim Stazio, or George the printer.

Amen. Good night, God bless.

: do ur teef

Her bitter joke from the remand homes and prisonages. He was about to sign off when another message arrived. He read it, read it again.

: u mekt me cri sayin tha

She'd never messaged anything like that before. Would she know how to tell him if anything was actually awry? He took a chance.

: I'll phone pm tmrw?

OK

: Give colours, please.

A list of shapes and colours followed, tomorrow's codes for her cell phones. He noted them down and waited. Nothing else came. He felt exhausted, had a bath, and slept until the alarm woke him at six-thirty.

Bray took longer than he'd expected winding up his talk *Development of Tea Furniture in England from Queen Anne*. Over ninety people attended, tickets restricted to proven buyers. His lecture was taped, and copies sold during the break. Lottie made sure he was given a few minutes before they resumed for questions. He left her vigorously defending Bray's inability to allow his 35 mm slides to be copied. "Sets will be available in response to written requests," she was intoning brightly as he made the public phone in the anterooms.

He rang Kylee's number, arduously translating his scrawled list of colours into numbers.

"Hello?" No names.

"Wotch, Owd Un. I've got a helper'll do as I sez, yeh."

"Are you certain —?"

"Shut it. The thing is, you'll hear of lawsuits an worse, yeh. I gets everybody worked up to stop the telly and the book things, yeh."

He was horrified. "No, Kylee! We want the opposite —"

"Shut the fuck up. Politicos are on our case. Watch fer it, yeh." She cursed a crude mouthful. "You said it yerssel. We got one chance, yeah?"

"Yes," he answered lamely.

During the next hour he fielded questions on fakes. Luckily Lottie had prepared comparison graphs of simulant furniture, reproductions, forgeries and genuine antiques. The session went off well. He was asked to visit auctioneers in neighbouring Cincinnati.

He promised to do what he could. Buyers would be visiting London in the New Year. He undertook to welcome them at Gilson Mather and do tours of London's museums. Lottie checked addresses. The next venue, West

Chester, was a thriving place that had grown precipitately in the preceding decade.

As usual, the place had been chosen for its buyers, this time of Long Acre Regency-to-Victorian antiques, with the emphasis on Gilson Mather and rival firms. During the drive, Bray narrated the news from Kylee. He made sure the driver didn't hear a word. Lottie was as worried as Bray. Neither showed anxiety.

Doubtfully they agreed. No such thing as bad publicity.

"See the letter?" Mom demanded.

Manuela was enjoying a noisy fight with the garbage man, late again. Pop was about to leave for the airport.

"Clint seems to like it there."

"I'm worried, Hyme. That story business. It's not right."

Pop had work to do in Atlantic City. He'd been telling Clodie that it was impossible to get out of. This was the last thing he needed, her inventing difficulties for Clint. Atlantic City would allow time for a little recreation.

The boy had been there only three days. "They do things, Clodie, activities – *supervised* activities – together. Closely monitored. What's to worry?"

"Clint says they're doing a computer story. Some quiz. It's on the news."

"A school gets a prize if the kids answer a few questions? Where's the harm?" He'd seen the reports, heard the criticisms. "If you ask me, a million dollars' worth of antiques is worth having."

Mom said stubbornly, "They send their answers on computers."

"So?"

"They can trace computers, can't they?"

"Only when they've something to go on." Pop felt her argument eroding his sanity. "How many Americans trace lost uncles, legacies from the old countries? Hundreds of millions. We've been into all this. You ever hear," he challenged, "any of them find anybody?"

"I don't want Clint doing it."

He sighed. She thought computers were extraterrestrials that would take over the universe.

"Where's the risk? Make him the only kid in camp can't play some game? That's like pointing him out. Kids talk. Why this, why that."

He put his arm round her.

"Clodie, Clint's got to be like the rest, not a kid everybody looks at and wonders what, why, how. Doctor's never had one go wrong. Okay?"

They compromised. Pop would travel to Atlantic City, do his work, journey to Boston's embattled office, then return home a day earlier than planned. Meanwhile Mom would keep check on Clint's progress. They had a deal with Clint's Brighter, a girl called Sally. Pop said to get Brighter Sally to phone every evening. She was being paid enough, let her earn it.

Clodie wished Pop didn't have to go. Men trusted computers, women didn't. Mom wanted differences she knew about, not ones so new that nobody could understand.

Chapter Fifty-Six

Sally was a second-level Brighter and subordinate to Ricarda, a bitch queening it over everybody. Ricarda ducked the night roster twice in a week, airily saying that she'd make it up later, which pissed Sally off, new staff coming and going like they did. Sally depended on Colnova Camp for her tuition at Arrington Campus State U.

"This KV game," Sally introduced at the Brighters' Meeting when She-Wolf Ricarda threw it open for questions. "We got enough onlines?"

"We've plenty," Vern said. Tall, casual, he wore logos on every stitch to show he was rich enough to do just that.

"*We're* sure, dear," Ricarda said, snide. She'd spent time with Vern and gamester Coach Toke. Votes counted before they were counted, Sally knew.

"Twenty-three's enough, surely?" Coach Toke put in.

"Only four online." Sally decided on calm. No skin off her nose if the camp defaulted. "The kids checked that re-run episode yesterday."

"They *all* watch TV, Sal." Ricarda knew Sally hated being called Sal. "It's a kid thing." Like Sally was a moron.

"Okay," Sally said, for once not putting up a fight.

Less than a month since, Sally had predicted the sleeping-bags fiasco. She'd been overruled, so now let Admin pick these new bones. Except Ricarda, flinging her glorious raven locks about, kept the minutes of every meeting. Such a responsible position, you see, for the Top Brighter.

"When is it?"

That was Mol, another Second-Level, Arts and Crafts. A Milwaukee girl, she proved invaluable when weather ran riot in the timetable.

"When is what?" Ricarda smiled her smile at Vern, her game of divide and rule.

"This KV programme."

"Tomorrow."

"I think Sally's right." Mol looked round. "My kids want to do it."

"This the same programme the state legislature's complaining about, hmmm?" Ricarda said sweetly. "Commercialisation of childhood? Or have I missed something?"

"Let's play it by ear." Vern loafed elegantly. "It's a detail."

"Sounds about right," Coach Toke said.

They took a vote, sixteen to three in favour of Ricarda. Sally shrugged it off. It was the camp's responsibility, not hers.

That evening she took a call from Clint's mom, who wanted private reports on her beloved Clint. Sally was pleased. One more report would make a difference to her money.

And the kids' interest in the competition would be a one-day wonder, no big deal. It would fizzle out if the weather held. Kids were so predictable.

In consecutive hectic days Bray spoke in Washington, Baltimore, and Philadelphia. The entire country was so vast and fascinating, which came in useful when the audience asked, "What do you think of our city?" He was able to answer, "It's beautiful," knowing that it simply would be so. Buildings were astonishing, the vigour of every town stunning.

"I can't honestly see why the USA bothers with the rest of the world," became his stock phrase. He meant it.

If challenged, he would expound on America's resources, the wonderment of size and spectacle. The good cheer and loquacity of his audiences were remarkable. Nobody seemed shy of asking questions straight off.

"You're seen as a television personality," Lottie said candidly.

They were in a shopping mart. Bray liked to watch people, forever looking, listening. She didn't know if he'd always been this way, or if it was only since Davey. Now was too late to ask.

"Because you're from media. Publishing, writing, creating, whatever. Back home, you're a subset of a subset. Here, media is all one."

He wasn't so sure.

"And," Lottie contended, not wanting to let this one go, "remember the majority have Granny's rocking-chair in their attics, and want you to spot it as a priceless Hepplewhite or Chippendale."

He thought this too cynical and said so.

Lottie had taken over Bray's duty of sending off a daily report to Gilson Mather. She got back Mr Winsarl's encouraging replies. Only occasionally did they receive any comment, usually asking if Bray could fit in another talk. Lottie, conscious of Kylee's edict prohibiting changes, remained firm.

"There's a limit," she told Bray.

Neither mentioned reaching the end of the first week. "Is it churlish to refuse?"

"No, Bray. We mustn't lose sight of our purpose. I did once." She was condemning herself. "At Maldon, remember? I never shall again. We'll be here together when Kylee dissects the results."

"Yes, but —"

"Yes nothing." She grew spirited. "Umpteen more sessions will only hinder us. Kylee ruled no, so no it is. After it's run its course, we can accept more engagements."

Grudgingly Bray conceded. He had it all in a system.

There was his basic slide lecture, on one of his sixteen subjects. Then there was the round, as Lottie termed it, a conducted walk among antiques and reproduction furniture in some auctioneer's gallery. Third was the chat session, where Bray judged the personal possessions of enthusiasts. Fourth was the frankly exhilarating open question-and-answer, where he told anecdotes of antiques and forgeries over the years. The trouble, he openly admitted to Lottie, was that he had his eye on the clock, always thinking of Kylee's next call.

"She sent word, Bray. The answers to the first question are mostly dried up."

"What time was that?"

"While you were speaking, an hour since."

Lottie mentioned her exasperation at Kylee's inability to write clearly. "At first, I wondered how much of it was put on."

"Like life," Bray said more curtly than he intended.

"Wouldn't it be sensible to send Kylee the answer with each question?"

"No. Kylee says anybody can hack in. We'd get thousands of correct answers and ruin the hunt. She says restrict it all to what you'd not want read on a postcard."

"What happens if you —?"

"Get run over by a bus?" He'd thought of that. "Kylee contacts Geoffrey and Shirley. It'll come up on my computer."

"Not me, then?" Lottie demanded truculently.

"You'd opted out when I arranged it. Sorry."

The newspaper stacks showed headlines, one related to the KV series. A State governor condemned the competition, TV companies howling infringements of their artistic freedom. A serious contest was developing. That Kylee, Lottie thought wryly. The publicity angle worked if nothing else.

"Isn't it odd how marvellous everybody's been," Bray said, following the direction of her glance.

No question there, she observed, from one so innocent that he thinks everybody only becomes bad from exposure to crime. Like the Ancients, she believed mankind evil and needed to be educated into morality. Another gender thing? Gender was supposed to become simpler with age.

"You mean Jim?"

Jim Stazio had returned home after a long session with them. He'd reminisced interminably, yet conveyed a sense of vigilance. They had a list of his whereabouts, detailed right down to phone numbers of bars and a social centre he frequented. He carried a cell phone. She had spoken with him twice since, just reporting where Bray had reached.

"He's kept two police friends on alert. I know the odds are against us, Lottie, but I've had a lot of luck. I'm so grateful." He looked away.

She rose too quickly. "I'll get us a sandwich. You gape into space."

It was her joke, his amiable looking about at folk. He stirred his empty cup, waiting for the first signal to come from Kylee.

Chapter Fifty-Seven

"There's 93,752 answers," Creb said, crestfallen.

"I fucking know that." Kylee was unnerved. "What percentage?"

"Point three eight. Vague."

Creb was worried she'd go for him, right here on the balcony overlooking Anchor Quay, directors having tea within earshot and secretaries tittering about bizarre whizzkids.

Leave out adults, youths, the rest; include only children six to eight, it was a fucking sight more per cent. She said that. A secretary tutted.

"Can't you mind your language?" the lady called across, an ingrate conscious of directors nearby.

"Mind yours, you boring old cunt," Kylee shot back.

Offended, the women got up and left, twittering.

"Please don't worry," Creb urged, sweating with anxiety. "I shall tell Mr Maddy's deputy that the lady misunderstood."

"Un fucking believable," Kylee said, "shitting yourself over some ugly cow can't stand talk." Her mind raced. "Gotter get them done, Creb. My programme'll sift the blocks out." She had some answers already coded. "Group the one word answers."

"I don't know the question."

"You don't fucking have to. Scan the answers in, auto access'll do a three-stack. The system'll Venn it up, matter of course."

Creb drummed his fingers. She made him eat his scones. She wondered if blokes all had something wrong, like Bray.

"What?" she asked sharply.

"Your grampa." He apologised abjectly. "He'll be disappointed, won't he? I'll try and make it up."

What the fuck? "My grampa?"

"I tried to get the programme and books banned, like you wanted. I've only made things worse. It's become more popular. You'd predicted fewer than 45,000 answers. We got double."

She listened to the silly cunt.

"I allowed for factors. The trouble is, two-point-nine per cent give multi-word answers."

"I saw you with them schoolies."

Kylee had collared four school-leavers. The firm was thick with them, wanting pre-work experience, a government con to provide unpaid hands. Kylee hated them. They were all proficient in writing, reading, kept asking her why she coloured her keyboard.

"They do fuck all. I give them the job." Seeing they could read and she couldn't. She wasn't for telling him.

"And word breakdown," she prompted.

"Like, 'metal' is one common answer. Is it a subset of *sheet*-metal, hyphenated or not? Paper and *rice*-paper, plastic and polyvinyl."

Listen, say nothing, Creb could go on all day about one subject. A stupid mind but a good memory. Kylee had eavesdropped on the school-leavers as they'd re-checked her programme.

There was really no problem. However many categories of answers, Bray would be able to tell at a glance simply by seeing the sorted answers. Twenty minutes, max.

"How many subsets?"

"Hundred and fifteen," Creb said glumly.

Kylee thought flatly, good. Shake them old typists.

"Paper and its subsets," Creb said earnestly, puzzled at her satisfaction. "Next is cloth. Plastic figures high. I've got the schoolies looking up commercial names, some I've never heard of. Then skins, animal-derived materials like woven hair." He gauged her, wondering whether to voice his doubts or not, and went for it. "It's a strange competition, Kylee. Will the firm get commission?"

"Will they fuck," she said. "It's charity."

"That's really kind," said Creb.

She thought, give me fucking strength.

That evening she had to visit Buster. She'd first to do the log-outs of her fluid determinant trials, but inventions were easy in mathematics. It was people who fucked things up. She'd received some government letters and threw them away unread.

She didn't want to run away again just yet.

Clint, Carlson and Leeta were excited at the rivalry between the Tain groups and those from Indianapolis and Springfield, Illinois. Their camp leaders were Brighter MayLou, who was noisiest so everybody could always find her, and Brighter Wanda, who played a guitar. They seemed better than Sally. Carlson said that was because she was broke but Leeta said it wasn't holy to say that because Jesus was poor and couldn't vote.

They harassed Brighter Sally about the chances of going on the computer. Sally said they'd talk about it. Leeta said that meant no because Sally showed her teeth exactly like the Pharisees did when they killed people. Her daddy preached that. Leeta said it proved Sally was a fuck-up.

They did canoes, the morning the first KV question was coming at five o'clock. The Red teams came in last, which Carlson and Elgin who joined them though he was Blue said was discrimination. Clint said why. Carlson said because we was winning but Leeta said turn the other cheek. Elgin said Brighter Sally was a shit.

So they all had to clap while a giggly group from Dayton, Ohio, got the Champions' Cup and got a plaque for their school.

Carlson said he was going to write to the president about the camp principal Mrs E.F.J. Partridge. Leeta said praying would get the bitch for letting cheating become rife throughout the Land of Canaan. They didn't know what rife meant. Leeta said it was a plague of locusts so they settled for that.

Brighter Sally promised a special treat, a cook-out round campfires, and there'd be a singing prize. Carlson said it was political distraction so they wouldn't write to the president about being cheated out of the Cup by Dayton, Ohio.

They were disconsolate because the singing competition would be won by creeps from Evanston, Chicago. Carlson said Chicago people always bribed judges and cops.

During snackout the Brighters announced that only competition winners could use the computers for the KV competition, which made Clint and Leeta and Carlson and Elgin and his new girlfriends Consuela and Melanaya, both from their school anyway, nearly cry. They went to Brighter Sally who said no, they should have won in the exciting activities they'd enjoyed so much on Activity Day.

That evening Carlson said fuck.

Leeta said Brighter Sally was an ungodly Sadducee and whatever happened to her after night prayers was her own fault. Melanaya and Leeta thought Clint was crying inside and voted to kill Brighter Sally with poison if they could find the right berries.

Carlson said fuck again, and told everybody he would send in anyway. They asked how could he without online computer. Carlson said because his brother in any case was twelve so could do anything he liked. He scared Brighter Sally by telling her he'd forgotten his tablets that the doctor said he had to take every night and he was going to die.

Brighter Sally got really terrified and screeched there wasn't anything in his file but he said he was going giddy. So she let Carlson phone home but it was no good because they listened. It was agreed he'd imagined it about the tablets. He came back miserable and said shit when everybody could hear.

A boy Leeta told about Carlson's daring attempt said he had a cell phone. He had a girlfriend in Minneapolis, seeing he was from St Paul, and phoned her every night. They bargained and he lent it. That way, Carlson got his brother by pretending when his mom answered that he was allowed to ring and say sorry, he'd made the tablets up, because he wanted to hear they were okay and his mom said "Why, Carlson, darling!" and cried. So Carlson asked his brother what Question One in the KV quiz was.

"What are the kites made of?" Carlson repeated, amazed. "Kites?"

"That's it," Carlson's brother said.

Carlson, Clint and the others were out by the logging pool watching the camp Brighters put lights up over Paradise Lane. Leeta said nobody had to hear their plot or it wouldn't count like mortal sins so they went to the jetty where there was nobody.

"He says it's what are the kites made of," Carlson told Clint.

They all looked at Clint. Leeta said it would be string and stuff. Melanaya said paper, everybody knew that. Consuela said it'd be a trick. She'd seen some illegals make kites with bells, real bells. Carlson said that was impossible, because the kite wouldn't fly.

Leeta said there was only one way, that was to take a vote, so they did. Paper came out on top. Then Consuela, who was Elgin's girlfriend together with Melanaya, said that Clint still hadn't had a vote. He was the one who always got it right.

"Say paper, Clint," Leeta said, who thought Melanaya was all mouth and a probable sinner.

"Say cotton, Clint," Consuela urged, who thought Leeta shouldn't queen it just because she was holy.

"Clint?" Carlson demanded, holding onto the cell phone. "Cotton or paper?"

"Leaves," Clint said.

Carlson said the eff word again in everybody's hearing but phoned his brother to e-mail *leaves* and sign it from Class R4 at their school. His brother said okay. Carlson said that was a million bucks in antiques down the pan because kites weren't leaves.

Elgin said you never know, Clint might be right, right? Leeta agreed. The others disagreed on principle. In any case, Carlson said, returning the borrowed cell phone, it was one in the eye for Mrs E.F.J. Partridge and Brighter Sally. Leeta said Brighter Sally would get leprosy because leprosy happened a lot from praying.

Carlson wondered about getting the phone again next day without telling Clint, and telling his brother to cancel leaves and put paper instead, because leaves was a shit answer.

Chapter Fifty-Eight

"Beautiful rivers," Lottie marvelled, trailing her fingers in the water despite Andy's warning. She wondered at Emma, Bray's wife who'd married some builder. What on earth had the woman expected? "So wide, flowing so fast."

They had been offered a rest by Andy. Bray was visiting his firm.

"We asked for you," he bragged, "after New York. While I was doing the NY State auctions."

Andy Haarlsen was a tall, outgoing man of athletic build. He'd taken over his father's firm on his thirtieth birthday.

"Never looked back," he was fond of saying.

To judge by his staff, the triple showrooms, and the regular spot-the-hot on TV, he was in line to become the largest commodity firm in the region. He said so, anyway. Lottie believed him. Bray smiled and said little.

Andy's wife Alee was fixing lunch in the galley. Two other friends were due to board a mile up-river.

Lottie knew what was on Bray's mind. He'd heard from Kylee. He'd let her see them. It was in code so, she thought with a taint of bitterness, it didn't matter whether she read them or not.

"Answers are still coming in," he'd observed as they'd got ready to come sailing. "It's over a hundred thousand."

"How many unpredictables?"

His eyes had wavered. "Some," was all he said.

Does he still not trust me? she wondered. Everything hinged on the few, oddest, answers. They were the specials, that might hold Davey's answer, if and if and if... As Kylee bluntly put it, "*If* to the power of ten." But the rough girl had been grinning as she'd said it.

"We're near the wharf," Andy called. "See Bernie and Margot?"

Bray, almost managing a sincere smile, went to the yacht rail to wave along with Alee and Andy. It was a really pleasant interlude. Bray due to start his *Presidential Purchases from Old London Firms* at six. Seven whole hours for Bray to forget his preoccupation, as if he would.

"They're the surprise I said about," Andy yelled, pointing to the new couple on the jetty. Anglers stirred in dismay. "They're in television!"

Lottie's heart turned over. She saw Bray turn and look. Bernie was fortyish, gangling, wearing an extraordinary Sixties kipper tie. Margot was bulbous in bermudas, all bright colours.

"Oh, TV!" Lottie moved along the rail to be by Bray.

"They're fun!" Alee called, busying herself with a painter as they glided in. "They've got a proposal that will just make Bray's day!"

Will it indeed, Lottie thought. There go Bray's restful hours. The newcomers boarded, handshakes all round, jokes flying, truly delighted to meet the visitors.

Several miles up-river, moored by an eyot, the proposal

was made. They'd had the picnic, been playfully disappointed when Bray eschewed the white wine.

"USA presidential purchases from London," Margot mused. "Tall order, huh?" There were chuckles. "Think I'll wait for the movie!"

"Bray was asked to speak on that specially," Lottie explained quickly.

Bernie grinned, winked at Alee and Andy. Here it came.

"No such thing as a free lunch, Bray! We heard your firm is sponsoring some antiques prize linked with that kiddies' TV show. Is that true?"

Lottie took the response on, defensively folding her skirt about her knees.

"Gilson Mather is one of the firms, yes."

"Look." Bernie edged forward on his chair. Margot retired to smoke a long cigarette by the stern. "How about you do a spot for us at X49Y2? You'd not starve, Bray!"

Everybody chuckled along. Lottie put away her smile after a decent interval.

"Maybe, Bernie. Except Bray's schedule is so crowded. And he's contracted to the BBC for guest appearances and the final tour video."

Bernie was electrified. "They're doing one now? Here?"

Lottie laughed. "Of course not! They'll do a construct. That's if Gilson Mather go with it. Would your TV station want to be involved?"

It passed off with Lottie's skilful promises about Bernie's station receiving priority.

"I'll have pencil dates by next Thursday, Bernie. Can I give you a ring?"

They settled for that. Lottie felt the arrows whistle by. She was concerned by the way she'd handled it, but what could she do? It was then that Bray quietly interrupted.

"Actually, Lottie, what the eye doesn't see..." To her amazement, he went calmly on to suggest that he be interviewed at one of Andy's auction venues. "As a visitor passing through, perhaps?" Bray added. "Nothing technical?"

Bernie was delighted, and phoned arrangements immediately. Lottie tried to catch Bray's eye but he spoke with Bernie about what he'd be expected to say. It was almost bizarre.

They reached Andy's marina in good time.

Clint's next letter disturbed Mom. With Pop in Atlantic City she felt control slipping from her hands. That Sally girl had put a stop to Clint's interest in that computer competition, yet her nagging concern persisted.

The competition was across TV networks. And that meant Florida. Who knew what enemies were still searching for her son, spreading their evil tentacles? She'd been right to ban Clint from the TV game. Computers were a sinister all-pervading illness. Contagion could be fatal.

She concentrated on the news, listened to broadcasts incessantly. Even Manuela noticed. The Mexican guessed that Clint was on her mind, saying how safe Clint would be in that camp.

Mom plaintively read Clint's letter out over the phone to Hyme. Pop said the school was only doing its job.

"It might bring back memories."

"Not on the phone," he warned. "I'm, huh, in conference."

"What if other kids ask Clint to stay over? What do we say?"

"We'll have to think." Pop promised to call in the

morning and talk some more.

"They still bother you, Hyme, when you're on furlough?" the girl asked.

He nodded for her to resume work. He wondered if the boy had become something he never really wanted. Finding Doctor to obtain a kid, then paying for Clint's transfer into the new life had cost, yet it was investment. Expenditure was reasonable when a return was guaranteed.

Now, seeds of doubt were sprouting. Think of it another way: if he'd not invested so carefully in buying the boy, finding the one clinic that gave perfect results, he might be paying some dumb headshrinks a fortune in psychotherapy for Clodie.

He sighed, observing the girl's head bobbing, felt the glow of pleasure, and thought how worthy investment actually was. Investment was divine, done right.

Chapter Fifty-Nine

Bray found it hard speaking with Kylee. He felt he'd been away months.

This Creb seemed her good friend, but might he be a misjudgement? Bray had been lucky – Kylee, Lottie, George, Jim Stazio. He'd have been enriched meeting them any time. He could have asked others – train people, computer wizards, his few acquaintances – and been rejected, becoming defeated. He told Lottie this. She'd only answered that their virtues simply reflected him.

"Does it look bad, Kylee?" he asked, determined to keep talk anonymous against electronic ears of hacker trackers.

"The figures? You berk. I said look at your sum when the first question's in."

"Right." He'd been scared to. "Are you all right?"

"Yih." But she wasn't. He could tell. "It's me age."

God, he thought, some growing problem? She'd freely admitted having sex with hash-smoking Porky. Was it the same with this Creb?

"Age, love?"

"Yih. I'm fifteen now, see." A long pause while he got

the gist. "Today." He heard caterwauling music in the background.

"They've discovered you were only fourteen?"

"Yih. I'm fifteen. The firm's rumbled. Mr Maddy's having fucking kittens. That Catchpole cunt's been here. I'm going back in care."

He was a time trying to speak.

"I'll ring them, Kylee. I'll get my son and his wife to take you off the probation people's hands. You can't go back. I'll send Lottie home to help."

A dozen notions churned in his brain. Somebody at Gilson Mather? No.

"You haven't said about the hunt, yer daft pillock."

He was sweating in a bus station opposite the hotel, the noise indescribable.

"No." Everything was coming at once. "I'd best find Geoffrey, get him to see Mr Catchpole."

"I'm lamming off. Got a pen?"

"Lamming off?" He felt frantic. "*Escaping*?"

"Yih. Till yer done." She barked a laugh. "Never thought you'd put summink else first, silly old bugger."

"Please listen. I'll send —"

"Shurrup. Stick to the plan."

"What will you do? How can we stick to the scheme now?"

Passengers were arriving, a convention with fez hats, back-slapping welcomes.

He thought he heard her snuffling, maybe some suppressed chuckle. "Same as usual. Palmtops, laptops, phone."

"But the answers." The news left him stricken.

"You never lissen. Do usual. The fuckers know nowt."

"Can we really keep it going?"

"Leave orf," she said in disgust. "We're on song, wack. Your dog is a fucking chiseller, eats any fucking thing. A frigging runt."

"You've been to Buster?"

"Same contact times, tarra."

No reminder to do his teeth, no joke ending. For a few moments he stood. She must have a way to divert the responses to her, wherever she'd decided to flit. This Creb was her Fifth Column in Mr Maddy's firm. Where had she acquired costly computers? He hated to think.

And she'd been fourteen, until now. Fifteen. Mr Maddy was having kittens. Well he might. Could a minor, a child, patent an invention? Kylee had devised some liquid-state computer. He remembered her telling him.

Now what?

He returned to the hotel, grimly told Lottie Kylee's news. They talked it over and decided that Geoffrey really should be asked to see what he could do. Lottie wouldn't leave Bray. She couldn't do what Geoffrey could, married after all and already to hand.

An hour later he remembered Kylee's admonition, and found her arithmetic. She was confident she could cope with the answers shoaling in. Otherwise she'd have bluntly given him different orders. She stood by him. He knew that.

He wondered if she'd started to cry at one point. Unlikely.

The paper she meant was the one with her quick mathematics. He called Geoffrey. For a whole thirty minutes they spoke about Kylee. He took two more calls back. It wasn't satisfactory, but Geoff finally agreed to do as Bray asked. Later, Bray and Lottie held hands to watch the recordings she'd made of the latest KV episode.

An hour before midnight, he got the second question to Kylee.

Things seemed to be falling apart, but only if you looked at it without optimism. That night Lottie made sure they slept together for the first time since coming to the New World. She rubbed his nape until he began to doze. Hardly the grand passion, but normality returning.

When Bray emerged onto the TV studio set Lottie almost exclaimed, though mechanically she applauded with the rest. She saw a stranger.

Bray was attired – no other word – in a sombre suit, formal as an undertaker. White shirt, navy tie, hair sleeked down, he could have been an elderly Victorian. He was welcomed by the genial talk-show host, seated himself gravely, and replied directly to each question.

Despite her shock, Lottie realised how accomplished Bray was in his subject. Where the presenter Evan Traur, a garish man with dyed grey hair, seemed to invent an attitude – "Mr Charleston, you are pret-ty hard on our approach to art. Is this fair?" – Bray easily segued into agreement then veered towards appreciation of American enthusiasm. His knowledge was a standby, and he had the knack of bringing every flown topic back to the art of furniture.

"I had a customer," he said without a smile, "related to someone in the Middle East. She required a set of five Chippendale-style English oak settees, double-backed. We made them, she then declined them, on the grounds that they didn't cost enough!"

Amid the audience laughter, Bray went on, "So we advertised them at double the price. The same lady saw the identical settees, and paid for them without demur, saying they were a great improvement! Commerce and art become confused."

Evan Traur let the interview run over time. The studio ran a series of legends on the fade, showing where Bray was speaking in the State.

Lottie met them both afterwards. Bray looked drained. They attended the after-show cocktail party in token thanks before making their escape.

"Would you mind telling me what that was all about?" she demanded in the TV station's coffee house.

"I'm scared, Lottie. Kylee's numbers are there – her ratio thing – but I'm coming unglued."

"You're tired, that's all."

"No, Lottie. It's the size of everything. Look about." He gestured to the plate-glass window, the crowds hurrying to a cinema. "How many people've we met since we arrived? Thousands?"

"So?" She'd never seen him like this. It worried her.

"The country's so huge, the people so hospitable." He faced it. "So I'm building a fail-safe, something I said I'd never do. If the KV plan doesn't work, then I'll come here permanently and continue the search. I'll bring Kylee if necessary."

"Don't lose heart."

"I'm trying not to." He tried his coffee, laid the cup down. "See? Even the bloody coffee's perfect. What if something's triggered in Davey's mind and the stealers spirit him further away? I feel I'm ruining my one plan."

"Isn't this what you planned, though?"

"That's the problem. Look at Kylee. She's in trouble because I got her that job. I ought to have left well alone, let her father cope with her. Now Kylee's on the run, our only contact by electronics she probably stole. And there's you."

"From anyone else this would sound like self-pity."

He tried the scalding coffee again, gave up. "Maybe you'd be less encumbered."

"Don't throw my words back at me!"

"Know what the problem really is?" He became self-conscious. "I never was numerate. Kylee's maths about the competition daunt me. She taught me her numbers, starting at a hundred answers. They became forty thousand, and now it's a hundred thousand with more still coming in. That's only for one question. She's pleased, says we're *on song*."

"Trust her. You always have."

"The new book comes out this week."

"It's already out." She smiled. "George sent it today while you were dressing up like a funeral director."

They spoke of the itinerary: Kansas City, Omaha, Fort Worth and Dallas, back north to Oklahoma City.

"Arranged to coincide with festivals," she admitted. "Next time, maybe I'll think of the travelling before I work out destinations."

"Geoffrey will phone tonight."

"I'll handle it, Bray." She took his hand. "Time you left things to me."

Chapter Sixty

"I heard all about the camp," Mom told Clint gaily. "We were so proud, right, Pop?"

"Sure were!"

"What did you like most, honey?"

"The log slalom!" Clint cried excitedly. He felt real strange at home. "We did canoeing, then waterfalls. And backpacking! I didn't like the hidey games."

"Hidey games?" Mom asked, suddenly glassy-eyed.

"We had to chase each other. One of us had to hide. I got scared."

"Didn't you tell that girl, Brighter Sally?"

"No. They would have said I was chicken. Me and Leeta and Carlson and Consuela and Elgin were a team."

"Did you win?"

But Hyme was paying a fortune and didn't want Mom to forget it. That Sally. He wanted value.

Clint told how he'd learned to ride a pretend bucking bronco, because if you fell off you only fell into a sponge. Mom was relieved. After supper Clint watched some kids' programme on TV. He sat still.

"This is the one where we got into the competition," he

offered during the break. It was only five minutes each half, though Mom was sure he must be tired after the ride home.

"What competition, honey?"

"The game." Clint was animated, spinning round to tell her. "You send off an answer when they ask a question, see? We're great. We won the practice game. Ask anybody!"

"Send off?" Mom froze staring at the television.

"We'll get our pictures taken if we win!"

Mom gazed in horror. So this was it, these angular figures with cloaks, odd hats, the landscape's skies filled with kites and rectangular clouds.

"Pop?" she said faintly. "Come and see." She made eye signals to Pop but he didn't heed.

"They give us a million bucks. We'll be famous."

"Million bucks?" Pop emerged to follow the conversation.

"The competition! KV!" Clint used to feel queer saying the initials, but familiarity had made the strange sensation go away. "You guess answers. If you guess them all you get a million dollars!"

"It's the competition, Pop!" Mom exclaimed with a fixed grin. "Kids enter their names and addresses. Remember?"

"We didn't have enough computers to go round," Clint told them joyously. "Brighter Sally said we couldn't join in it. But Carlson's brother sent the answer."

"Did he now," Mom said faintly.

"He's wicked!"

Mom talked about it a while, let Clint see his programme. The new question would be shown tomorrow. He went to bed after his hot drink.

The CNN news briefly mentioned the KV series. It was coming in for serious criticism from educationalists and moral preachers. Mom listened, repeating almost every word to Pop.

"We must do something, Hyme. It's time we left here, go somewhere else."

"Go where?" Hyme was sick of it. Doctor had guaranteed no comeback.

Mom considered. The school, Clint's friendships. It was a threat far worse than she'd perceived. At first she'd only worried about local newspapers, Clint's photograph, possibly some Little League list.

"Anywhere, Pop. Anywhere else at all."

The next morning they packed. Pop called the head and Clint's class teacher. Clint, he told them, had been summoned for a special clinical evaluation. No, they had no criticism of the school, in fact they were very pleased. They wanted Clint's doctors to see for themselves. They would let the school know how long they would be away.

Clint, Pop said, sent his love.

Geoffrey wasn't able to do any more than reassure Mr Maddy. It went against the grain to pretend that Kylee was a relative, but he'd promised Bray.

"My father takes responsibility very seriously," Geoffrey told the computer manager.

"You understand my position, Mr Charleston," Maddy said earnestly. "I was given false information about the girl's age and status."

"Which is the reason I'm here, to convey my father's undertaking to resolve the issue completely. He accepts responsibility for the girl's behaviour."

"Until he returns?"

"He has appointed a counsellor, Mrs L. Vinson, to assume charge of the girl for the next three weeks."

"Very well." Maddy asked about probation.

Geoffrey repeated his father's firm assertion. "My father has an agreement with them until the end of the year."

He left sweating and uncomfortable, wishing to hell he knew exactly what Bray was doing. He felt he'd pulled it off, bought his dad some time. Thank God Shirley had decided not to come.

In Bray's house, Kylee checked the clocks. The house felt her own. She checked the hunt shed first, then Davey's old shed. No sign of intruders.

She made Creb phone the neighbours and tell them that Kylee would be walking Buster. She liked running the dog over the fields.

She settled into a peaceable existence. It was her first real home. Bray seemed everywhere. She collected his letters and put them on the mantelpiece. She got them the right way up, because the stamps were always in the top right corner. On the second morning a post girl called. Kylee scrawled anything, grabbed the package and slammed the door.

Answers to the second question came pouring through the computer terminal.

Chapter Sixty-One

Jim Stazio met them on their arrival in Portland. He thought Oregon dull. Lottie and Bray found it beautiful. The sweep of the river was grand, the countryside exquisite.

"We got a start yet?" he wanted to know.

Lottie was delighted by the riverside shops. Bray was disappointed in the furnishings, but Lottie countered that he had tunnel vision and went bric-a-brac hunting.

"I want to be doing, Jim," Bray told Stazio. "Kylee's working out the second set of answers. Hundred and fifty thousand, give or take."

Jim was unfazed. "Any idea how many are repeaters?"

"Sending in different answers?"

"Them too. I mean the core."

"Not yet. Kylee's got it." Bray thought it wise not to say anything about Kylee's personal problems. "She'll send it today." If she's not caught, that is.

"Three goes out tomorrow?"

"That's so."

"Ten days is all, then."

Bray felt nauseous of a sudden. Jim nodded his understanding.

"Thing is, Bray, you're at the stage of wanting to postpone. Once, I had a man sprung from the state pen, unjust conviction. He was due out. Know what? Proved innocent, clear as maybe, he didn't want to go."

"He was innocent, yet couldn't face freedom?" Bray pondered.

"Couldn't take the emotion." Jim chuckled, hooked a chair with his boot, putting his heels on the seat. "What seemed a promise when he was behind bars changed into a risk the minute he was freed. Get the point? Maybe you longed to see your elder brother for years, but he's due in today and you jess can't meet that plane. Or say you want your niece to call after some argument, and now she's phoning from Atlanta you can't pick up that phone. It happens."

"It's cowardice, Jim."

"It's human is all. I got a couple of sisters together. Didn't know they were related, lived within eighty miles of each other twenty years. Know what? I brung them into town. They took three days – three whole days – before they got up courage to meet!"

"They were frightened?"

"How the hell'd I know? Wouldn't come out of their hotels. Drove me crazy, called me night and day. Wanting to know what the other sister was like, what she'd be wearing. Christ, I lost twenty pounds."

"It's still cowardice."

"That's why I come, Bray." The obese man wanted brown sugar, waited in silence until the girl brought it over. "I got a couple of friends. We're making a team."

Bray didn't understand. "What sort of team? A police team?"

"Private. Not like your search groups, relatives. Not

that. There's all sorts of bureaux for that kinda thing. More like, well, what's happened with your boy."

"For whom?"

"For people the systems don't want." Jim Stazio raised a hand to ward off criticism. "I know, I know. When your son Geoff and his wife came, I admit I was kind of stupid. I thought them more shit delivered right to my door. And went about saying things like why the hell can't folk keep a fucking hold of their kids and save police a load of mess. Thinking this shouldn't be our problem. I admit it. No excuses."

"The first thing you said was, our problem wasn't unique." Bray judged the other for a moment. "You spoke of the thousands of children who go missing, some senator's exaggerations, remember?"

"I'm not liking this, Bray. I also told you any search would be useless. I used different words, but I meant exactly that." He smiled with some bitterness. "I wasn't much good, huh?"

"Best I've met. I'm relieved you're with us."

Jim wagged a warning finger. "No kindness, pal, or the deal's off. I've explored what I could. I've got an ex-cop, and a computer spinner. We're forming a company when this works out. I'll get two more retirees for weight."

"This?"

"Your hunt, Bray." They weighed each other. "Proper channels work sometimes. Other times they only tell the bereaved to piss off and go manage."

"Will your, er, team be any use, Jim?"

"Honest to God, I don't know. But it'll be more than nothing."

"What…?" Bray began, and couldn't continue.

"What if your hunt fails?" Jim took the point. "Then I'll

learn from that. If it succeeds, it *could* be used for others. Know what I'm saying?"

"You came to tell me that, Jim?"

"Not quite. We want to use your hunt as a prototype. Free of charge. Anything you plan, we'll help with, on the understanding whatever you learn we can use later."

"I owe you at least that, Jim."

"Christ, Bray, you're a bastard. Didn't I tell you no kindness?"

Lottie returned. "You two not falling out, I hope? D'you like my Chinese ginger jar?"

They said it was admirable. Bray hated it. If it pleased her, fine.

Jim left that afternoon. Bray promised to give him the breakdown the instant Kylee finished the last set of replies. After ten more days of lectures, attendances at seven antique auctions in three different states, now there were only the crowded hours of hurrying time.

The new place was called Dallas. Pop extolled its virtues to Clint.

"A city of lakes, son," he said, showing Mom and Clint the Trinity River. "Boats, countryside, you got it all here. One of the richest —"

"Pop," Mom cautioned, beaming at her son. "You'll love it here, Clint."

"Will I?" Clint asked.

"Sure will, son," Pop boomed, taking a detour to show the river bend to best advantage. "And you'll do just great!"

Clint looked out at the city. He was sorry to leave his friends, but Mom said it would only be for a week while Pop did some business. On the plane Mom had let him watch a film about space ships.

They parked and went for ice cream. The house Mom and Pop had taken was near University Park and Highland Park close to the huge lake called White Rock.

"Lake in each of its four corners, Clint!" Pop boomed.

Clint wanted strawberry, which was Carlson's best flavour. Next time he'd ask for chocolate, which Leeta liked. Melanaya changed all the time.

Mom said, "We love it here. Right, Pop?"

"Sure. First came before you were born."

Clint started the ice cream. It felt thicker than the camp ice cream.

"You like the house, the garden, honey?"

"Sure, Mom."

As they'd moved in, he heard a dog barking, and two children calling. He saw a ball rise, fall, rise again with an awkward bounce. Maybe he would like it.

"Do I have to go to school here?"

"Why, no!" Mom exclaimed. "The very idea!"

"We'll be going home soon, son." Pop winked. "Then you get right back to school. You're doing so well."

"Right back!" Mom echoed. She didn't like Clint asking sudden questions. "This is sort of an extra furlough, isn't it, Pop?"

"We're really going to enjoy it!"

Clint watched the Dallas terrain and the lakeside, where two groups of families were clustered round something they'd found in the water. There was laughter. Car doors slammed nearby. A car passed with a picnic basket strapped to its roof. A man and a lady were standing in the distance. He couldn't see them because of the sunshine. The man had a jacket over his arm, almost like hanging down in front. The school janitor wore one of those when he was doing the boiler.

There was a public phone nearby.

"Thanks, Mom," Clint said, finishing the ice cream. "That was real nice."

Chapter Sixty-Two

Geoffrey heard from Mr Maddy that Kylee hadn't reported in. When Bray rang, Geoff told him it was too serious.

"She's a minor, Dad. The police'll become involved. Then what?" Geoff had a right to be distraught.

"Mr Maddy won't want his firm involved —"

"Dad. Listen. After everything that's happened to us, we can't take any more. Shirley's on the brink of recovery, though God knows how much longer it'll take."

"Bear with me, son."

"Let *me* tell *you* what *I* think. This work you're doing with Kylee, whatever it is, is frankly unhealthy. I want you out of it. She must go back to the authorities. They're equipped to handle these things. God Almighty, Dad, she isn't *normal*. Semi-autistics aren't your job."

"I made it all right with her father —"

"It's not all right, Dad!" Geoffrey's voice rose. Bray knew there'd be no dissuading him. "I won't have police knocking at my door, never again! I went to the Tech College on Sheepen Road to see Mr Walsingham. He's given up on the girl. She's nothing but trouble. He said as much!"

"Tell you what, son." Bray thought quickly. When all else failed, settle for the best good lie. "If I hear from her – any time at all – I'll phone Kylee's father. I'll talk her into telling Mr Catchpole where she's staying. That lad, Porky, remember Porky? They reach her through him. You keep in touch with Mr Maddy, Geoff," he added recklessly, hoping that offspring didn't know their parents quite as well as they thought.

"What good will that do?"

"She might call in for something." Almost delirious at the risks he was taking, Bray ploughed on. "I agree. Time for authorities to take over."

"I'm glad you see it my way, Dad. I can't keep up this deception any longer."

"Okay, Geoff. Let me take over. I'll get Lottie to phone you. She's sound as a bell. She'll know what to do."

Lottie, seated opposite on the sofa, rolled her eyes. She was checking the map of the USA.

"It's not been sensible, Dad," his son said, dispirited. Bray's hopes rose. Was he going to get away with it? "I know she must have been a help over Gilson Mather's history. And Lottie is a godsend. But this child's a loose cannon that can sink our family ship, careering about the decks."

Thank you, Geoffrey, for explaining the metaphor in full. Time to break off when a chat got this far.

"Lottie'll handle it. She's just gone to check the next venue after Dallas-Fort Worth. Don't worry."

Geoff sounded relieved. "Ring if I can do anything, Dad."

"Right. Love to Shirley." Bray replaced the receiver, shielding his eyes from Lottie's glare.

"I'll do *what*?" She laid the map aside.

"Everything. I knew you'd make the offer."

He didn't make jokes, so she smiled along. She reminded him of the time. Bray was due at a massive question-answer session. Kylee's second set of answers were all in except for a trickle. The next question was due, with its shoals of guesses.

"Have your shower, Bray. You just have time."

"My name is Stefan," the blonde giant laughed, tapping his chest. "I am guard, right?"

Laura was his wife. They had both worked for the police, and ran a security agency. Pop insisted on back-up, a different couple from a separate team.

"You will be careful?" Mom said for the umpteenth time.

"Sure will, lady," Stefan promised.

To him it seemed crazy. The mother was coming with them to the regatta, so what could go wrong? Stef gave Laura the sign that meant make a show of security so tight it was stupid.

"We'll stay together," Mom insisted.

"Sure will. You coming too, sir?"

"No," Pop said. "I've work to do. Just make sure my boy enjoys the show."

Clint was looking forward to this. Boats would do a kind of parade. Some schools would have boats of their own. Some would have sails. He'd seen pictures.

Pop said they could go, if Mom and Clint took special people to make sure they found the best place to see from. Clint was really glad when the big blond man arrived with his blonde lady and said they'd all stick together in the crowd.

So they went, and it was exciting. Stef told Clint they

did it every year.

"They're not supposed to race," he said. He'd put a string on Clint's wrist like Clint was a baby. "Some schools get kinda carried away."

"And get in trouble!" Laura added. "Last year somebody fell in."

"Keep this in your pocket, Clint."

Stef the guard put a black thing inside Clint's clothes. He did it, like Clint didn't know how. It was yuk, with other kids wondering which school he was from.

"Just a small precaution, honey," Laura said, winking at Mom.

Mom was relieved. She had no idea where the second security couple, a man and a woman, were. Pop had engaged them so they'd be there, earning their money. Electronic tags were excellent where wicked people could linger. People these days did anything for money. Pop and she knew how important it was to protect a child, unlike some parents.

Kids talked to Clint. Stef and Laura stood close. Stef had a walkie, its red light glowing. Laura's eyes never left Clint. She stood against him. Love for her boy filled Mom. Clint, her son, was reality. All else was sham.

The boats began their approach. Cries arose amid laughter as one boat, oars splashing, pulled ahead. Cheers rose, school chants. Other rowing boats also began to race, oars clashing as the crews strove to get ahead. Two boats collided. Spectators yelled advice.

"It's so funny, Mom!"

"Always happens, Clint," Stef said, as amused as the rest.

The instant the parade was over Clint asked could he use the rest room. Laura and Stef said there'd be no worry, they'd be right there.

Stef checked the toilet areas. Laura stood outside the door while Stef went in with Clint. They emerged a few moments later.

"Can I call my friend?" Clint asked Laura. Mom was beyond the foyer crowd. "From school. We're pals. I haven't called him since I left."

"Whyn't you call him from home?"

"Didn't think Mom'd let me."

Laura was amused, making coy guesses. "Is it a *girl* friend?"

"I can get the number. But I need the money."

Stef Kirstgaard laughed. "Go on, let the kid."

Laura gave Clint her call card. "You know how to use this, honey? No wrong numbers, now!"

Clint didn't know why they laughed, like it was some joke.

He found the call box, got Carlson's number. Carlson's mom answered, which was scary, but Clint said he only wanted to say bye. She said wasn't Clint sweet and put Carlson on.

"It's me," Clint said. "We've gone away."

"Yeah. Your mom called my mom."

"I won't be back for a couple of weeks. That means —"

"You can't guess us the answers." Carlson was disgusted. "For the prize."

Mom's head was showing among the people by the foyer entrance. "Get your brother to send it in like you did from camp."

"Right! Give a guess, then."

"I don't know the question," Clint said, desperate.

"It's been on twice," Carlson grumbled, but told him anyway.

Clint closed his eyes and saw sawdust. "Put sawdust."

Carlson said it was a stupid answer and he'd feel a nerd.

Clint said, "Sure as sure."

He said bye and got Laura's card back. They all went for a burger in a nice place where Clint was allowed to eat anything he wanted. He liked Laura and Stef. He didn't like the other two, the ones who stayed silent who kept staring at him. They were police like Laura and Stef, but not as nice.

Maybe Carlson and Leeta and Melanaya and Elgin would win the million bucks. He'd helped them, like they'd asked.

Another morning in paradise.

Bray was only half awake. He could feel Lottie's breathing. They had long since given up the pretence of separation.

He rose. Women got out of bed so neatly. A man unfolded in stages, legs do this, spine does that, then the shove upwards. He clicked the tea on.

The curtains drew back on Phoenix, Arizona. From here his third question would emerge. A few moments' typing, a single tap on a keyboard, and Kylee would transmit it to the TV company. Out it would go with the episode of KV, and the answers would come shoaling in.

Another morning in...

Beautiful, spacious, with acres spacious beyond belief. No wonder America had taken to the motor car.

Today's subject *Frankly, Money!* Embarrassingly jazzy, but he had been asked so often that it had to be done. It was a new presentation, worked out from a prolonged question-and-answer session in Boulder, Colorado.

The city of Phoenix woke in the dawn. His last talk with

Kylee had created more problems than it had solved. She gave a tirade of abuse, when he asked where she was staying. ("You boring old bugger…")

There was a choice for this question, decided during the doze-awake nights he sweated through. The sacred luck, that just might do it, lay in choosing ones Davey might still have embedded in his mind. Bray's wry face reflected in the plate glass. Only now did he realise that it was love that did the hoping, and it was love that would keep on trying.

He knew Kylee's calculations by heart. When first he'd read about computers, he'd been thrilled to learn that George Boole – founder of the abstracts of computer logic – was the uneducated son of a poor Lincolnshire carpenter. He had tried to tell Kylee this, smiling as he recalled her scathing insults.

"Ten horses in a race, yeah? One in ten, yeah? Ten horses in each of four different races, what're the chances of guessing all four winners? One in ten thousand, yeah? Jesus, Bray, you're so fucking thick…"

Now, though, he had it like a poem, but he'd got it. The trickles were still coming. And with each broadcast question came backlogging answers to the previous parts. He'd earned his worst abuse when worrying that she might be overwhelmed.

"You saying I can't work a fucking programme?" she'd yelled. "If I wuz that fucking iggoran I'd give up," and so on.

"Morning, darling," he said to Lottie.

"Morning, love." He indicated the day, the moving cars just joining up in streams. "Question Three comes in today. I used to think I was quite good at maths."

"Numbers is different, you barmy old sod," Lottie

quoted Kylee.

"It takes her less than two minutes to do the breakdown." He looked up at Lottie. "Can that be true?"

"If she says, I'd just agree."

"So much agreement," he mused. "The evidence is in some electronic box, wherever she is. She does it all without a calculator."

"What happens after?" Lottie asked quietly, drawing up a chair.

He appraised her. "To Kylee, you mean?"

"Yes. The poor girl will go back into care, won't she? Davey or not, you can't stave off the authorities."

"I've thought of one," he surprised her by saying.

"What will you do?"

"My best," he said. "My very best. She's done it for me."

Lottie felt a twinge of jealousy, quickly suppressed. They watched the traffic thicken as the lights dowsed, then rose to begin the day.

Chapter Sixty-Three

Bray almost got the shakes during the question-answer session. It wasn't the fault of the audience, who were almost boisterously good-natured. Lottie sat with a bookseller who had an array of *Gilson Mather: Three Centuries of Living Design* with Bray's name prominent.

He saw her head lift. He carried it off, clearing his throat and taking time to pour from the carafe, but for a moment he was lost.

"You've caught me," he apologised to the lady in the ninth row, admitting the evident hesitation.

She had asked about trade association websites in England. It shook him. He had a sudden vision of Kylee in a dank cellar, on the run from authorities, the poor girl labouring for his lunatic dream.

"The reason I'm on the defensive," he resumed "is that people hold serious differences about websites in our creaking old kingdom. Our largest association, LAPADA, offers its members a homepage for a subsidised price. They even host your website. They're all hyperlinked, of course, and your personal dealership name doesn't get lost…"

He blagged it, sweating, making out there was heavy

controversy among dealers when there wasn't much.

"Some claim it should be free." He managed a smile, getting an appreciative laugh by adding, "The same old fantasy, marketing for nothing!"

It went well, but he'd never felt so worn.

The party afterwards, with the inevitable wine and finger buffet, seemed endless. The antiques and reproduction furniture, some from Bray's own hands that he recognised like friends, was cleverly distributed on three floors of elegant rooms.

"What was it?" Lottie asked quietly, the minute she could draw him aside.

Five new auction presenters had taken sites, treating the audience to predictions of forthcoming prices.

"Is there a way to help Kylee?" He explained his sudden deep fear. "She's got nothing, Lottie. The cruellest thing in the world would be to stand idle."

"Bray!" Lottie showed a brittle intensity he'd never seen before. "Got *nothing*? Let me tell you this, Bray Charleston! She's got the best friend she could ever have, and that's *you*. Not me, kind sir, but you. She's got an enterprise right up her antisocial dyslexic autistic street. She is paid, paid *for*, helped and nurtured, by somebody – namely you – who could have just passed by. She is helped, as far as she'll let anybody on earth help. She's been rescued, and it's all your doing."

"I've used her, Lottie."

"Can't you see it's the best thing she could ever have? Nobody wanted, trusted, admired her, liked her. They made her a dissolute freak, just some wild thing. To you she's vital. Get it? And you actually like her, for God's sake! To her it's life."

"I don't understand how you see things."

"I see them as she does." Her smile was painful to maintain, audience members still floating by. "Ridiculous to lose confidence when there's so little time left. Some things just aren't your fault."

"That's the point." He heard a scatter of applause, and acknowledged a signal from the Queen Anne stand.

"Bray." Her eyes filled. "You're frightened, searching for delay. You're scared and trying to cover it up. So am I. So is Kylee. You saw the state Jim Stazio was in. And I'll bet George is having kittens."

"Maybe I should extend it," he suggested in despair. "Create a fifth question? Kylee said that each one narrowed it down – "

"She was sure with four, Bray. Kylee harped on it. Four, not five or ten. You decided Davey knew four answers nobody else would even dream at. The last question's due soon. Don't delay it."

She waved gaily to the auction leader, signing that Bray was coming.

"You've never lost resolve. Lean on me, darling. Like in the song."

The auction-house senior was laughing as Bray arrived.

"I'm harassed, Bray. It's the veneer question!" He made out he was overwhelmed in a riot. Folk were making mock threats. "Something you said, I hope!"

"Look," Bray quickly took over the rostrum. "There's a generalisation that's almost perfectly true, often cited in the antiques trade. It's this: no oak period furniture was ever veneered. Anybody remember the veneer date?"

"Isn't it 1660?" somebody offered.

"That's when veneering entered the process. So it's reasonable to suppose that English-made antiques that pre-date this can't have been veneered."

"But oak furniture kept on coming after that date?"

"Right! And we still make simulants, country furniture in heartwood..."

Lottie stood watching in silence. He couldn't resist touching the furniture, nodding at a surface, once moving a light so its beam was deflected from a veneered cabinet. In his element.

The future seemed ominous. It would spell the end of her and Bray. Never mind the girl, she herself would be cut adrift. Maybe a second edition of the Gilson Mather history, and Bray really might tackle the third volume. She wouldn't be without work.

Bray's scheme meant as much success for her as for George Corkhill and his little – now not so little – workshop. And it was a life-saver for Kylee.

For Bray, though? For him it might be disaster. For herself, a mix of loss and achievement. No such thing as pure success.

She heard a burst of laughter from Bray's crowd. The other display leaders had petered out as the visitors drifted towards Bray. The clock showing that he was due at another venue across the city. She apologised to an auction-house assistant and tapped her wrist. The schedule ruled.

"Countdown?" the woman said, smiling. "Pity. They're enjoying it."

"Yes, great pity."

Geoffrey saw the light in his father's house. He parked, wondering if Dad was back. Hal and Christine's house across the road seemed settled for the night, curtains drawn and the car put away.

He heard a TV. Lottie, maybe, returned after all? He'd

only made the detour on a whim, thinking to reassure Shirley he'd driven a few miles out of his way.

He went in. Buster came bounding and wagged about his legs. Geoffrey stood in astonishment, reflexively patted the dog. The air was peculiarly cloying. Kylee sprawled in the living-room, smoking. She didn't move.

"Kylee?"

No need for anger. After all, she suffered EDS, emotional deformation syndrome. He'd heard these catchphrases.

"Don't you know they're looking for you? Your father, the authorities?"

"Fuck them."

She flicked ash from her crumpled cigarette. He guessed it was some illegal substance. He found himself trying not to inhale. Buster was quite at ease.

"Kylee," he said heavily. "I'll have to contact them."

"'Kay." She kept her eyes on some travel documentary.

"Does Dad know you're here?" He repeated the question but she said nothing.

Without another word he went to the hall phone and called Mr Walsingham.

"She can't stay here," he found himself saying. "It's a matter for the police. Yes, I do appreciate the difficulties. What time is it now, nine o'clock? I have to get back."

It was really too bad of the Lumleys, who ought to have known better than allow this girl access. Unless, Geoffrey thought suspiciously, Dad had also deceived them. Lottie must have been in on it too. He felt dismayed. Ever since Davey, everything was wrong.

"You ought to come and take charge of the girl, Mr Walsingham," he said firmly. "After all, she is your daughter. The probation officer's number is…"

They spoke a few minutes more. Kylee's father would immediately call the emergency duty officer. Twice Geoff had to insist that it was not for him to provide social support for a vagrant child. And no, his neighbours also denied responsibility. He had no time to wait for the police, and what would they do anyway? The child was smoking illegal substances.

He went back into the living-room to explain.

Kylee was gone. Buster was standing by the kitchen door, the garden in darkness. He went outside but there was no sign of her. He searched every room in the house, then called Mr Walsingham and broke the news that Kylee had left.

"I'll ring that emergency officer." Walsingham sounded dejected.

"The thing is," Geoff back-pedalled, "the police already know she's missing, so what good would it do to inform them?"

They decided to delay. Geoff would take Buster to Christine and Hal Lumley. He decided to phone his dad as soon as it was morning in Los Angeles. The whole thing made him feel nauseous. What Bray's madness would do to Shirley he didn't dare think.

He checked the house again, wondering if he should have the locks changed. Heaven alone knew what weird companions the deplorable girl had.

"Come on, Buster."

The leather on Buster's lead was still damp. The girl must have lived quite the lady's life here, even taking Buster over the fields. Did she stop for an ice-cream at the corner shop, as Dad and Davey used to? He shut his mind to it, and closed the house up.

Chapter Sixty-Four

Bray heard her voice with such relief he almost weakened. The public call box stood in the cinema entrance. He cupped the receiver.

"Thank God you're there. Are you all right?"

"Wotcher on about? Got the fourth?"

"Yes." He was at a loss for words but badly needed to know. "What happened? Geoff found you in the house. He's taken Buster. Your father's phoned the probationary services."

"Like, the bastards locked me up when I was a kid so they should keep on doing it? Yeah, right. I was in an out of prisonages like a fucking fiddler's elbow."

"Where are you staying?"

"Think I'd tell you? Give over. Same as I sez first, wack."

"No changes?"

"Send Number Four at the proper time. Don't be late, 'kay?"

"Very well."

A pause. "Ending's hard, innit?"

"No." During the previous night he'd come to a point

of resolve. "We just go on, whatever."

"On yer own, or with that cow Lottie?"

"Anybody who'll help, love. With you."

And it would be so. Americans had a knack of assonance. He'd coined the phrase lifetime-schmifetime, and felt foolish saying it in the bath.

"There's trub, wack. Some little cunts send spreads."

"Who?" he asked blankly. "What are spreads?"

"Every fucking word yer ever heard of, that's what a spread is. I'll murder the little bastards. The answer's a naming word, yeah? They're sending every frigging word in the book. I hope they get bankrupt, little turds."

"Can they be picked out?"

"Course. The little shits. My pal says it's di-plo-ra-bull. He means they're a fucking pest."

"Thank you, love. Tell, erm, your pal thanks also, will you?"

"Will I fuck. Some send multiple addresses, like for more chances."

"What do we do?"

"We treat them like they was separate. I progged it right off."

He was desperate to ask how close was it coming, when the numbers would decline and reach a mere handful, named towns he could go to.

"Are we on, er, course?" was all he could say.

"Yih. Too good, if yer ask me."

Too good? What did that mean? "Thank you, Kylee. I'll send Four off. Night, God bless."

"Tomorrer's the day, wack. Steh cool, yeah?"

"Please look after yourself."

Struggling to speak, he realised he was hearing the dialing tone. She'd gone.

"When can I go back to school?"

Davey had the idea it was wrong to ask, but two weeks had almost gone by. He was supposed to be getting letters about the competition from Carlson and Leeta and Consuela. Mom and Pop let him go in the computer stores, but Mom was scared of them.

His walks were always with Mom and Pop now. Stef and Laura never took him out much. They saw shows, but they were like for grown-ups. He had to ask before he could watch television, which wasn't fair.

And in the new house there was no Manuela and no little falling boy who made Clint laugh. Here was neat but not much to do. Mom and Pop talked about it. They phoned Doctor. He heard them when he was doing the math sent by somebody. And there was an athletics meeting with Laura and Stef the guard, but he had a kid's string on his wrist and that electronic beeper.

He'd rather go without Mom and Pop and just have Stef and Laura because they laughed a bit. Mom and Pop always acted like scared. And Pop always looked round, checking the other two.

They always were, standing looking. Pop must have paid a lot of dough, Clint knew.

There was a swimming championship, Stef said, like a show. He would take Clint with Laura, who used to be a good swimmer. She pulled a face at Stef when he said this, and they laughed. Clint asked if he could go swimming.

"Sure you can, honey. Real soon."

"My own school, Mom?"

"Why on earth would we choose a different place?"

"Are we going to stay here?"

"No. We're going on a special holiday! Will you like that?"

"Where to?"

"That's a secret. We'll go back home and all your friends will be real pleased, won't they, Pop?"

"Next week," Pop promised. "Back to normal."

Chapter Sixty-Five

It was his last lecture.

Bray saw the audience arriving. It seemed disappointingly small. He wondered whether his rueful feeling came from the generosity of these engaging people. Maybe he was secretly changed now, and craved popularity? The same suspicion recurred.

He sat in the anteroom. Lottie was checking on the tape recording unit that would have unedited tapes for sale. Sets of transparency slides were now being shipped by Gilson Mather – Lottie's doing. Boxes were being set out on display.

Am I merely a promoter now, he wondered? The image dismayed him. How seductive the process was. It was as if a latent valency had existed within all these years. Inside each craftsman is an exhibitionist waiting to get out, like that?

Except it was temporary. The fearsome word, temporary, meant it would soon be gone. Like his ex-wife Emma, now junketing on cruise liners with her wealthy husband. He had loved her. He supposed he felt a residual fondness, only a fraction. One of Kylee's disappearing decimals.

Early in marriage, he believed Emma loved him. Then years turned, and belief dwindled into a hope that she might love him. Then, again those gliding years, he came to hope that she didn't quite dislike him. Finally – the here and now of it – he knew that really she had felt nothing but hatred. Scintillating Emma, tied by marital bonds to a dullard who cut wood. The description was hers, as she'd left.

Poor Geoffrey, who'd also assumed permanence. He'd been lucky to find Shirley, luckier still to bless the world with Davey.

The shifting sands of this American tour. He felt as if in a doctor's waiting room, staring at impenetrable diplomas. Everything was determined by chance. It was all out of his hands.

"Bray?" Lottie put her head round the door. "It's time. There's only thirty or so. Can you imagine, all Los Angeles?"

He smiled, more at ease than he'd felt for weeks, and went to listen offstage as the gallery owner made the introduction. It could have been his very first day, when he'd waited so nervously in the wings while he met America.

"Co-author of the history of a great furniture house in London, a man whose working life has been in restoring and even recreating the art of the past, whose brilliant expertise…"

Et temporary cetera, Bray thought sadly. He stepped into the applause, smiling. He had twenty slides to show, talk and questions.

He looked at the faces.

"This is my last talk in your lovely country," he began, against all his plans. He was usually straight into the subject. "I've been quite overwhelmed by your kindness and interest, especially as the USA has such splendid furniture makers of its own."

He spoke, moved, of the so-called "writing table" that was actually a mahogany, ebony and laminated wood inlaid with fruitwood, inlaid with silver and copper, that he had seen in New York.

"It was a simple exquisite example," he told them. "As beautiful and intricate as anything ever made. Yet who here remembers the craftsman – surnamed Green – who in 1907 made that wondrous piece, so plain, so skilled, for the Peter Hall Company of Pasadena? The makers live on in their creations. The works I've seen on my way across America will stay in my mind for ever.

"I will find it hard to express my gratitude when I come to the end, so please accept it now."

He cleared his throat and went straight in to his subject: *Re-creation or Restoration?*

It was a success. For once he accepted the invitation to supper. Twenty joined the organisers in the restaurant. Everyone was keen to get in anecdotes about antiques bought and sold, the risks taken. It was the gentlest evening. Bray occasionally caught Lottie's gaze through the amber glow, and felt something vanishing before his eyes.

Next day would be the test. He would feel stripped bare. All deception, all subterfuge, would be gone. He would have to go back into himself and simply be Bray Charleston, grandfather, standing in some foreign street looking up at addresses, checking places against a crumpled list.

He shook hands repeatedly, and promised to accept invitations if ever, if ever.

The travelling was done, his itinerary over.

"LA is hell, Lottie."

"Morning, Jim. Start as you mean to go on?"

He seated himself opposite. They were the first two in the hotel breakfast room.

"You're secretly proud."

Lottie actually believed Jim Stazio spoke with the bitter pride Americans always used when criticising their country. Was there pollution in Korea, Istanbul? A morning in Los Angeles, you'd really *see* pollution! And so on.

"Take driving, f'instance. Worst on earth!" And he was off into data. "We going to need cars, right?"

"Bray insists on paying, Jim." She determined to have the war over by the time Bray came down. "And some sort of fee." She grasped the nettle. "He's at Kylee's list, doing it half the night."

"Can't accept, Lottie." He glared around for a waitress. "I'd accept some coffee, though." And as one strolled over, "Working this search has kept me going. I was bored. Now look at this fine figure of a man! I got a career!"

Lottie smiled, shaking her head.

"He fears catastrophe, Jim. I watched him days ago at his last engagement. Some buyers asked Bray to accept retainers to appraise their stock. A fortune for a week's work."

"What's your point?" Jim saw Lottie sip her Engish tea with disbelief, and closed his eyes in rapture at the taste of American coffee.

"The horror's back. He's frightened it'll be a re-run of that ghastly moment. This hunt has been his lifeline. Now it's finished. It'll either be a delusion, or will expose horrors as bad as anything before."

"Too terrible to contemplate, right?" Jim waved a fork.

"Three decades a cop, you learn to eat when you can. You go ahead with your lettuce leaves."

He pointed, all aggression. "You civilians forget. *What if the boy's alive and well?* Then it's whoopee time."

"That scares *me*," Lottie admitted. "The child stealers might have armed guards, lawyers. We can't just walk up and say that child's ours, can we?"

Jim noted the possessive, poured sauce on his hash browns.

"You got me. We ever make it here, I got friends."

Bray joined them. He looked drawn, and carried two heavy folders and a sheaf of papers. He ordered, went through the pages in silence.

"That it, Bray?" Jim's eyes pinned the folders. "Coloured rectangles?"

"The girl does it by colours. And her computer works by talking."

"She got answers?"

"Yes." Bray stared at his meal unseeing. "There are eight possibles." He looked up. "She's graded them in order of probability."

"Lemme see."

"They're only colours." Bray passed a sheet. It showed a column of printed squares in different hues. "Top is the favourite. Bottom is least likely."

"Each square is a place, right? Eight? What's this hatching?"

"Degrees of probability. Her translation for me." He rummaged in a pocket. "I've got actual numbers here."

"No good showing me that." Jim's voice was harsh, intent now. "The top one's densest. Means she's sure, right?"

"Yes. I spoke with her in the early hours. The bottom

five are false, she says children spreading every available answer."

"Backing every horse in the race, huh?"

"Leaving just the top one?" Lottie asked.

"Precise. All four questions, answered accurately."

Stazio examined one thick folder. It held only closely-printed addresses.

"Jesus. This is all USA!"

"No, Jim. Two hundred thousand."

The Florida man pushed his plate aside.

"*How* accurate?" He shrugged at Lottie, sensing her bridling. "It's gotta be asked, Lottie. Here, we can talk it over. In some hallway, people shrieking we're abducting some kid, it'll be hell."

Bray winced. "I thought that. The first two questions everybody could get right by repeated guesses. What's this made of, what's that made of. The third? Well, maybe, like the second and third pairs might. But not the last."

"What was it?" Jim stared Lottie down. "We can ask now it's over, right?"

"What was the winning score?" Bray cited. "That was the question. The opponents were Prussia, but what was the score? It's the way I taught Davey to count. We invented a game. It always came out the same score."

"What was it?" Lottie and Jim spoke together.

"Mind if I don't say?" Bray felt awkward. "Kylee said there'll be stragglers."

"On the nail, huh? One place?"

"Exact. It confirms the leader."

Jim replaced the folder. "Eat, Bray. Gimme the address. I'll go call my people."

"No, Jim." Bray was quite pale. "I'm sorry. I can't take chances. Jim, would you mind if Lottie and I go on alone?

I'll call you from there when..."

"You saying you don't trust me?" Jim rose.

"I'm so sorry. It'll only be a day. I'll send airline tickets for you."

Jim stared, his face almost puce in outrage, then abruptly sat.

"Well I'll be fucked – sorry ma'am." He laughed aloud. "Y'know what riles me, Bray? It's what I'd do! Keep it close until the cards go down."

"He won't even tell me, Jim," Lottie said.

Jim waved for a waitress. "You're right, Bray. You sure you don't want coffee instead of that tea stuff? Travelling to do!"

To Tain, Bray thought.

Chapter Sixty-Six

The airport was served by tributary flights from major cities. Bray paid untraceable cash for the second flight. Lottie spent the journey imagining Jim Stazio cramming his bulk into the small seats.

"He'll say, 'You sure about this?' and, 'What the hell we do with the legs?', I'll bet!"

Lottie liked the ex-policeman, Bray knew, but he had no emotion now, nothing left to think with.

At Tain Airport's miniature facility he hired a car for cash. They lodged at a motel.

"I rather felt it when you admitted you didn't trust Jim," Lottie told him. "He's been on our side from the start."

The motel was by a trunk road, lorries and saloon cars swishing by. Bray wanted to see hills beyond the advertising hoardings.

"Jim Stazio has been in our search, Lottie." He turned. "Not quite the same."

"You don't mean —?"

"No. I don't think he's one of them. It's still possible."

She went to him, the suitcases unpacked. "Just accept

help. Jim Stazio is a good man."

"You're right, Lottie." Gently he disengaged. "It's a small chance, but why take it?"

Because of humanity, she could have answered. Later there might be time to go into these differences, she thought. Maybe.

It was two-thirty by the time they reached Tain's shopping mall. Bray acquired tourist maps and town guides. They sat in the bookshop's cafeteria to pore over them. He concentrated on schools.

"You back with me?"

She felt disordered, seeing him peruse the pages in silence. Oblivious, he overturned his drink and hardly noticed while she mopped the table with tissues.

A group of youngsters entered, throwing bags on the tables before wandering into the bookshop. Always so free, and such bravado, that young assumption of infinity. And what was always? She'd learned a great deal being with Bray. Lie with a spouse, osmosis happens during sleep, those hours feeling someone breathing, stirring, assimilating the other's dreams never uttered in the day.

Sometimes during her work at Gilson Mather she caught glimpses of Bray in the workshop, concentrating on examining wood just arrived. His deliberate movements, his pauses to tap the surface, listening, were done with such quiet grace that she was captivated. Once, waiting so they might travel together, he'd been alone, a cone of light above his bench the only illumination. He was standing over some dark timber, rubbing it with his thick leather glove. He stooped and inhaled – she heard the breath – deeply, straightening to hold the aroma as if it was the most heady perfume.

It had been a revelation, a display of what was almost

love. Bray looked up at her, glanced round the cafeteria.

"It's eight blocks from here," he said.

He was shaking, found it hard to lift his replacement drink. She poured him half of hers and gave it for him to drink.

"What now?"

"You do it," he told her. "Go to the school."

Her chest squeezed. "I go to the —?"

"Please. It's vital to identify the class."

Her cheeks prickled at the responsibility. "I can't. What if —?"

"You have to."

She felt her mind cast about wildly for excuses, solid reasons, anything to escape the terrible duty.

"Think how it would be for Davey, if he's really there."

She felt frantic. "If? Bray, we're banking on certainty, aren't we?"

"On Kylee's probability," he corrected. Sweat appeared.

Her mind screamed *Fuck your probability! And you can stuff your precious Kylee's bizarre brain as well.*

"Bray," she said carefully, "I've never seen Davey."

"That doesn't matter."

She'd gone weak. "It doesn't *matter*? Bray, what have we been doing, this effort, these plans?"

"Not for what I want you to do."

"Darling." She reached across and took his hand. "Listen. If Davey's there, to me he'll simply be one face in a sea of faces. If you go, you'll see one. His face will jump out, and be the one."

"Subterfuge, Lottie."

"To pretend what?"

"You be a prospective parent. You're seeking admission for your child, a boy Davey's age. You've come back to

America after some years in Europe. You're, what, divorced or something. Invent."

She said faintly, "Wouldn't it be simpler for us to sit in the motor and look at them in the playground, then let me phone Jim?"

"No. Then it really would be the scene that Jim predicted, a tug-o'-war, shrieks for police to arrest us as child abductors. By the time we'd proved who we are they'd be gone. And they'd be forewarned. This is our one chance."

"I'm what?" she asked. "Go over it, Bray."

He stood. No shaking now, she noticed.

"We go there now?" She touched her hair. "Like this?"

"Please, Lottie. As you are. You've just arrived from Europe."

"Can you give me half an hour to smarten up?"

"Twenty minutes," he said grudgingly.

They were due to leave for Tain. "Clint'll be glad when we're home, Hyme," Clodie said. "Will you be?"

"Sure," Pop answered, already into the financial pages. Marriage was lying with assurance, same as commerce, and same reasons. "It's done the boy good."

"He misses his friends. That competition stuff gave me the creeps."

"I blame that school." Deflect conversation, yet more tactics for a sound marriage.

"I thought you approved."

"I do. School's great, like math and business. But half the goddam kids can't even read. Too busy playing cyber games."

"I'm sorry I panicked, Hyme. It's just that other kids were talking about sending their addresses in. One mom said her daughter e-mailed a snapshot of herself."

She shivered at the thought, such needless risk. She was going through her wedding photographs. Marriage was counting survivors.

Pop'd had four sessions down town, made him a younger man. Business did for him what he did for business. And he'd kept the peace with Clodie.

"It's over now." She showed Hyme a picture of their wedding, smiling. "Remember the way they decorated our wedding limo? I was so embarrassed!"

No woman's ever embarrassed at a wedding, Pop thought.

"Did you let Clint call his friend?"

Three evenings before, Clint had asked could he call Carlson. Mom had demurred. Clint's name would go up for some team, training due soon on the Link Fields.

"No. That Carlson boy might not be right for Clint. Differences are okay when kids are small, but what when they're teenagers?"

"Good thinking." Pop was alarmed by one stock's fall, but gratified by marginal rises in three others.

"I let him call that Leeta instead. Her family's devout."

"Preaching isn't decent work." He regarded her. "We've nothing to worry about. Clint's registered."

Mom beamed. "That's why I've got the albums out, Pop. See?" She showed him a centre page, Clint's new birth certificate mounted on ornate corners. "Your son. Our boy. All legal, an American citizen. His birthday's Libra. I must look it up."

"Doctor really did a job, right? Cost, but signed and sealed."

"Now, Hyme," Mom scolded. "I said that right from the beginning. It's not just money. It's our boy!" Her eyes filled.

Pop let it go. Clint's birth certification – some location in Illinois was on the details – was cast iron. Doctor had used special couriers, the money up front. Now Clint was legally registered, good as the next kid and twice as authentic. Nobody, but nobody, could prove otherwise.

Into the family album it went. It wouldn't matter one bit if people wanted Clint's details. The birth certificate was, Doctor had assured him, as genuine as the President's. Perfect documents were pricey. Buy cheap, you buy dear, his sainted father used to say. Doctor delivered, finish.

"No worry now, Clodie." Let her have her fondness. He'd paid for it.

And there would be definite bonuses to returning to Tain. Mrs Hunger had become Linda to Pop. Okay, she was more than a nurse/friend to Doctor during his goddam medical updates. She was useful, cool and without recriminations. And thank Christ she knew how to set up an arrangement for a fee-paying employer just far enough out of Tain.

One more year and he would settle the mutterings in Boston. Maybe they'd go to California, bring the boy up right.

Chapter Sixty-Seven

The earliest appointment Mrs Joan Daley, head teacher of the Gandulfo-Meegeren Educational Foundation, could give Lottie was ten o'clock the following morning. Lottie hardly slept, rose in the night to sit in the light with a magazine. She was afraid to switch on the television in case it woke people. Bray lay awake. They did not speak.

As they dressed Lottie wanted to know who she was supposed to be. Preparing, she bought a new waisted jacket she suspected might be too young, brown court shoes and a tweed skirt she supposed vaguely Continental. She felt dressed for some awful school play, Ophelia with a bad blouse.

Worst was, Bray refused to drive her to the school. He ordered her a cab. "I don't know who I'm to be!" she wailed.

"You'll do it right, love. Just be a returning American."

"I said I was a Mrs Gunnell." Which was as far as her inventiveness went. "There's no point going there without you. What if —?"

He accompanied her in the taxi, resolutely averting his eyes as she alighted at the Foundation. Lottie stood, her heart thumping, hands clammy. He sat hunched as the taxi drew away. Her lip would soon start trembling. Bray had dumped her here to what, rescue Davey, who would be as American as the rest? All Bray would say as they pecked at breakfast was that he had something to do.

The school emitted the faint hum of an active academy, just enough to convince. A secretary admitted her to the office of Mrs Joan Daley, who greeted her with evident pleasure, making a pitch for her school.

"How good to see you, Mrs Gunnell! Welcome to the Gandulfo-Meegeren. May it be the first of many welcomes."

Lottie seated herself, admiring the plain functional office, the friendly air.

"You have a grandson, Mrs Gunnell," Mrs Daley began. "Getting on for eight, I think you said?"

"Yes, seven and a half." To her own astonishment she slipped easily into unprepared lies. "My husband and I are returning from duty overseas. My husband will be responsible for tuition of our grandson..." Oh, God, she thought in panic, what is the mythical boy called? "Jason. We returned early, to choose a school, help our son and daughter-in-law," she added in a flash of inspiration. Shade the lies slightly, you could get away with murder.

"They're still abroad?" Mrs Daley inquired, down to brass tacks.

"For three months. They're concerned about class sizes."

"We can give you a tour of the school, Mrs Gunnell. We have excellent facilities. Is Jason is interested in sport?"

"Very!" Lottie exclaimed, wondering if she was overdoing it.

"You have a home in Tain, Mrs Gunnell? Or home-hunting?"

"Looking about." Lottie felt a heart-stopping lurch at the head teacher's choice of word. "My husband's with realtors right now!"

"Excellent!"

Mrs Daley ushered Lottie out of the office. "Is Jason an only child – so far, Mrs Gunnell?"

"Yes, but in a year or so maybe plans will work out!"

Lottie saw a glint in the other's eye at the prospect of yet another paying pupil.

"Class sizes optimize at twenty-eight, according to most researchers." Mrs Daley opened doors onto the vacant assembly hall. "The Foundation limits to nineteen, though one class exceeds that by a visiting pupil from Kingston, Jamaica. The teacher-pupil ratio has to be kept below twenty to give each child sufficient attention…"

The hum of voices intensified as they walked the corridors. Lottie thought, this isn't happening. It can't be, not right here, with Davey possibly within arm's reach. She glimpsed small heads in rows, faces turning to look at the passing visitor, teachers demanding concentration. One class seemed in darkness until Lottie heard the drone of a movie voice, some film instruction.

On the corridor walls, displays of drawings attracted her gaze. She smiled.

"How exotic! So many creatures!"

Mrs Daley laughed, not without exasperation.

"If it isn't gremlins, worms, ants, or pterodactyls…"

"Those kites! So many balloons!" Lottie forced amusement.

"There's been public criticism, Mrs Gunnell, about a TV competition for some valuable antique prize. They were all into it. Thank heavens it's over!"

The thought that Bray's missing grandson might have

actually crayoned one of the drawings on show shook Lottie. She looked away.

"A passing phase, don't you agree?"

"I'm pleased they are! Heaven knows what the next fashion will be. It was so different when we were little girls, wasn't it?"

They spoke of how compromised the children of today were by commerce. Lottie became a family woman deploring the tendency to rush the nation's young into technocracy. Mrs Daley approved.

"You're so right, Mrs Gunnell!" she cried.

She beckoned a teacher from a classroom.

"Mrs Gunnell, may I introduce Donna Curme, who teaches the age band of your Jason." Mrs Daley explained her visitor's purpose. "How many do you have, Donna? Eighteen?"

"That's right, eighteen." Miss Curme seemed a calm young woman who never let her gaze stray from her charges. "Two away at the moment. One on holiday, back tomorrow for prize day, the other at some family celebration."

"What lovely photographs!" Lottie allowed herself to seem moved at the mounted prints, classes of children in rows.

Donna Curme gave her a shrewd glance. "They're always popular, but there's the usual difficulty."

"Difficulty?"

"Always somebody at the dentist, trying out for some Little League team. Getting the whole class is quite a nightmare!"

They moved on. Lottie couldn't resist glancing into the classroom as she said goodbye.

The clues might be here, she thought, but to gape would

expose her visit as a sham, and then what? She desperately hoped she'd done what Bray wanted.

Mrs Daley's secretary called a cab. Lottie reached the motel to find that Bray had not yet returned. She showered and slept until he arrived at six, soon after Tain Central Library closed for the day.

Chapter Sixty-Eight

Bray felt foolish. He'd rehearsed his questions on the way but hadn't quite perfected it. The lady at Tain Central Library was helpful in a puzzled sort of way.

Local newspapers were computer indexed, with a one-touch operation. The later months were not yet entered, copies of *Tain Herald* available in stacks.

Schools were listed in gazetteers, with their year books and annual reports properly filed. He fortified himself with a glass of water and got down to it.

Kylee's colour code squarely placed the Gandulfo-Meegeren Foundation in, what did they say nowadays, pole position. It was on page 372 of the 500-plus pages in the folder he'd abstracted from Kylee's open-message columns. He'd had to suspend his laptop's ferociously swift printout and used two reams completing it. Cautious, he avoided marking the school's name. Oddly, two separate e-mail addresses showed for successive answers from the winning class.

Davey was at that school. In there. Bray could hardly breathe.

The child gave his name in all four: *I D Source: Carlson.*

Which meant Carlson must be Davey's new name. There couldn't be any other explanation. A sudden anxiety swept through him. Please, he prayed silently, don't let me have a heart attack, not at this stage. Let me keep going. His rejection of fatty foods, determined walks, evening exercises, the pathetic swims in hotel pools, surely must have done some good.

Readers' desks were set out in a single line down one side of the large Reference Facility. The Local Research Section contained photo- copiers, microfiche and consols.

He went through the annual reports first, scanning quickly, going over faces in school photographs. They were incomplete. None was Davey. Carlson was the surname of two children at one school, not the Gandulfo-Meegeren, and as a first name for a cheery coloured lad there. He perused photographs of prize winners.

No sign.

The newspapers gave negative evidence, helping him to exclude some groups. It seemed sensible to deduct at least two months – or should it be less, in case they'd indoctrinated Davey at speed? He just didn't know. From what Doctor Newton had told him, medicaments could excise memory. There was that chemical, wasn't there? He finally settled for one month, and got down to ploughing through the newspapers, searching for mentions of new boys at the G-M Foundation.

Carlson's surname showed once or twice. Another lad – possibly a brother? – appeared in a swimming championship. Different school, though. Two girls also, all evidently older than Carlson, were class prize winners elsewhere. He found their photographs, proudly wearing award sashes, in a newspaper six months old. The same surname came to light nine times in the Tain phone book.

Painstakingly Bray noted them.

The day wore on. He was tempted to phone the motel and find out how Lottie had managed, instead considered property, wondering if he should search out sales of houses in Tain. Tain was a bustling town. There was no telling how far the town limits extended. United States conurbations varied widely, no correlation between acreage and population density.

No; he shelved real estate agents. If he happened on Davey's face in some school photographs, it would be a simple matter to find the address, maybe concoct some imaginary out-of-state family connection. Jim might be of help there.

The hours ticked by too quickly. No sign of Davey. The reference lady returned from lunch. Bray exhausted the newspapers and made a start on church records. Why so many? Back home, you'd be hard put to find a chapel or cathedral that printed lists of its attenders. In Tain it seemed a positive obsession. He found lists of every persuasion –

"Can I help?"

Startled, Bray looked up. "No, thank you." She was a pleasant tubby woman in thick glasses. "I'm doing well."

"Only, you've not taken a break. Researching a book?"

"Populations," he got out, indicating his heaped desk.

"I knew you'd be an academic. We get quite a few here. Tain has grown so. The aero plant, you see."

They made aeroplanes in Tain? He managed to end the conversation by taking a rest. He took his files with him, went for a sandwich and returned quickly. The library was due to close at six. He panicked, called himself to heel and returned to the newspapers, compiling lists, numbers, teachers, community notables.

One list was of educational benefactors.

A giant aircraft corporation was the principal giver. The rest were recorded by the *Tain Tribune,* which pointed out the splendid way in which Tain supported the town's commitment to learning and health.

He copied the addresses of benefactors. He cross-referenced them against recipient schools, the small University of Tain, secular and religious foundations. There was nothing, no face, nothing to tie in. He deliberated whether to call Kylee and question her scoring methods. She'd rightly ask what the fuck did he know. He could almost hear her voice, scathing in her condemnation, super lexics hadn't the numerical brains of a fucking wart. It was her phrase.

"Don't you fucking gerron at me, you 'cking geriatric," she'd storm. "My numbers are right."

Numbers. He knew what Kylee would do. She'd sit there for a split second, somehow revue all the numbers in her mind. She'd once told him it wasn't seeing, just a feeling in her chest. And she'd then know that two, three, five, or any figures didn't match. She'd also know that they varied by 0.0129 of one per cent, whatever, and be correct. It was a gift, unlike the pedantic learning others used. And, Bray thought, we normals scorned autistics and semi-autistics who were supra-genius level mathematicians and inventors. We even called them deranged. It was only right that Kylee should show a little scorn of her own.

Treacherously, he tried to work out how to check her numbers. How to do that? The only things were the photographs, and Davey wasn't there.

The school's annual reports and year books? He turned to the class photos.

Numbers in class? He counted the faces. Numbers in

class were as given, numbers of smiling faces before him. They matched of course.

Except for Class R4 of the Gandulfo-Meegeren Educational Foundation. It was Carlson's class.

One child was absent.

Shakily he found the year book, thumbed through. A child was missing. The day of the class photograph, a boy was absent.

As would possibly happen, say, if the parents were anxious to prevent a child from being pictured? You'd not want it published. Was it somebody hiding from the light?

Clint H. Rappaporter was left out, had presumably stayed at home.

Tain had four Rappaporte addresses and phone numbers, only one Rappaporter with a terminal *er*.

He could hardly control his pen. The address was an apartment, not a house. He identified it on the town map, and tremblingly wrote the phone number. It matched the residence of a Foundation benefactor. In less than an hour, Bray had found the picture of Mr H.L. Rappaporter beaming at the head teacher of the Foundation as he handed over a cheque. No sign of a child.

He thanked the librarian for her assistance, and drove to the motel.

Lottie was already waiting, anxious to tell him what had transpired at the school. He heard her out.

"Call Jim," he said. "We need him now. It's time."

Chapter Sixty-Nine

"I've two problems," Jim Stazio told them, mostly addressing Lottie. They were by the lakeside.

"I've only one," Lottie said with feeling.

"Which is?" He watched children putting model boats in the water.

"Why don't we call the authorities?" She couldn't help feeling exasperated. "We're so near!"

"And?" He waited. She didn't know what to say. "Then it hits the fan, excuse me. Everything's been tried to steal kids. Crooks, kidnappers, passing themselves off as FBI, IRS, any goddam thing, to spirit kids away. It's big money."

"Yes, but we're genuine!"

"You know that. I know that. And, God knows, Bray knows it. We've had this out, Lottie. What if they scream blue murder and call the police? By the time it's cleaned up, they're in Panama, Columbia."

"Thanks for dealing with my one problem," she said unhappily. "Your two?"

"First problem," Jim said heavily, leaning back on the bench, legs apart, "is how illegal you want to be?"

"Meaning we can simply…?" She couldn't say it.

"Snatch the kid back."

"Bray?" Lottie felt real terror. Until now it had been mere anxiety.

Jim said patiently, "We're in reach. He lives in that very apartment. You've done the whole shebang and got here. We can't just sit watching the water." He waxed eloquent. "Let the perps whisk him off where we can't follow?"

"Jim," Lottie warned their friend.

Two children were pushing a toy sailing boat from the sandy beach, their father crouching, using a stick to keep it from turning back. It made a pretty picture. He could see the penthouse where Clint lived. Lights were on in the long picture windows. Were they there, perhaps looking out?

"It's got to be said, Lottie."

"And your second?"

"When to call in the boys."

"The police?"

"My pals. I've friends still serving officers. They'd be out of their jurisdiction. We could bring in the locals, then the FBI. It's a federal crime. Coupla calls."

"Bring the police." Lottie couldn't resist triumph. "As I said!"

Bray cleared his throat. An ice-cream van pulled in, children making for it. A small group playing softball disintegrated and drifted over.

"Can we be certain Davey's back?" he asked Jim.

"He's going to school tomorrow," Jim said firmly. "I made calls. I was a doctor from Immunisation Records. I sounded great."

"For sure?"

"Certain, Lottie. Nobody brings a kid home first day of

school. The day before, sure."

"Then I think we —"

Bray rose abruptly and walked quickly away past the ice-cream vendor and into the ornamental garden.

"Bray?" Lottie wondered whether to go after him.

"Let him be," Jim told her.

She followed the direction of Jim's gaze. From the apartment building a small family group emerged. They took the lakeside path towards the boat hard where she and Jim were seated. Her heart seemed to swell, almost stifling her. She struggled to look away and failed.

One figure was a portly man in a dark overcoat. The woman was stout, Lottie guessing her age about fifty, definitely greying, smartly dressed, with sensible shoes and accessories. A typical wealthy middle-aged couple out for a stroll.

And a boy. Going on eight?

He carried a model sailing ship with white sails, swooping it about. They came nearer. She distinctly heard him go "Wooosh! Wooosh!" and whistling to simulate a high wind. He saw the ice-cream van. The woman shook her head. The boy ran instead to the edge of the lake and floated his ship.

Two people following the family group at a casual stroll suddenly closed in on the boy. The man was athletic, looking round. His gaze lingered for an instant on Jim Stazio and Lottie before moving on. Lottie realised that Jim was holding her hand, presenting a picture of a fond couple. The woman with the guard stood talking to the boy until he left the waterside and returned to the other couple.

Lottie realised she had nearly thought *returned to his mother*. Rejoined the evil perpetrators, was better.

She and Jim talked intimately until the group had gone by, the blond couple trailing behind. After they'd gone from view she scanned the gardens. Bray was nowhere. He must have observed them come out and gone to earth.

Jim nudged her. "Now we know."

"What?"

"A cavalry charge wouldn't work. They got guards. So they've enough money to hire every lawyer up to the Supreme Court."

"I've seen Davey," was all Lottie could think or say. Her eyes filled. "You see, Jim? It's worked out! He's alive. He's here. He's safe."

"He's fucking theirs," Jim capped sourly. "Where's Bray? We got to move."

Chapter Seventy

The TV station proved sceptical at first, until Lottie's formidable number of tapes of Bray's lectures and his broadcasts finally convinced them that they might have a gem on their hands. She hired a lawyer to accompany her, and gave Mr Pawler instructions to sit quiet, offer nothing, merely record what was said. Jim had hired the old lawyer from Condennahy forty miles away.

"The conditions," Lottie said firmly, "are that my client decides everything."

"No way." the outside broadcast director said. "We know the business. No way your client says what happens. We want a re-shoot, we do it."

"Thank you, then. Goodbye." She rose and made for the door, Mr Pawler following. It was a feint, but a good feint.

Ben Maker, the OBD, scruffy in frayed shorts with tousled hair, watched curiously to see how far she would go, and only relented when she didn't stop.

"Okay, okay." But she was gone.

"I said okay!" He trotted after, catching her in the corridor. Two minions followed, one taking notes. "We can compromise here."

"Wrong, Ben." Lottie didn't slow, kept going at the same pace. "I have three hours to fix it with your rival KZ3-P2. Goodbye."

"Okay! I agree, for Christ's sake!"

"You certain?" She walked out into the full hot sun. "Complete compliance?"

"I agree."

"No tricks?" She let him digest that. He eyed the lawyer. Mr Pawler stayed silent. Lottie recognised the tactic. "You see, Ben, things might occur that you don't, won't, can't know about. I've been around TV long enough to know that you'll ruin everything, including your chance of a national TV award, if you as much as belch. Be a fly on the wall, or get zapped."

"Jesus," he groaned. "What *is* this?"

"It's yes or no, Ben, that's what."

"Okay. I agree."

"Mr Pawler has the contract. Do it now and I'll summarise what I know."

"Contract?" Ben Maker yelped. "To shoot an OB?"

"I misunderstood, Ben. You *said* yes, but you meant no. Bye. Come, Mr Pawler."

"Okay, okay!" Maker stared at Lottie. "You want a job?"

"Total compliance will do, thank you. Sign here, and we'll go ahead."

He obeyed with ill grace, the assistants witnessing, Mr Pawler taking forever confirming identities.

"It's only a goddam competition, Chrissakes."

"Ben," Lottie said sadly, "you are an ignorant man. I hope your camera work is better than your comprehension. Be ready in one hour."

"You haven't said where or when."

"Correct."

"You won't tell us who?"

"No. You make no calls, no Chinese whispers. It's in the contract. You wish to renege?"

"No!" Ben Maker yelped, seeing Mr Pawler checking his recorder. "No! But where's the harm?"

"Ben. I'm your golden godsend. Believe it. Do everything I say, and you'll bless the day I walked in. Do it wrong, you'll be the TV OBD director who had the best chance in the universe and blew it."

"Can't I go set it up?"

She smiled sweetly. "No. I don't trust you."

"Then why'd you —?"

"I've noticed your work." It was a lie, but media functioned on frank deceptions. "You come highly recommended."

"Right, right." He liked that.

"I can see your mental cogs whirring, Ben. You're thinking how many places there are within a three-hour radius. You're trying to work out the location. It's sixty miles away. Be ready." She gave him her look. "Don't even think about it, Ben."

"Who the hell *are* your clients?"

"Strong people. Still yes?"

"You got it."

"I provide transport. Your footage will be yours exclusively. That's my guarantee."

She saw from his sideways glance at his helpers that he understood the implications. She felt real aggression.

"Which means, Ben, that if rival TV camera crews turn up, or gaggles of newspaper reporters, it's you who have betrayed the whole thing. The consequences will be fatal for you and yours. Mr Pawler will stay with you at all times. Understood?"

"Right, right." He nodded slowly, darting a suspicious look back into the foyer. The receptionist's desk was nearly within earshot.

"Two camera units will be required, Ben."

"Jesus, I only got one camera crew!"

"If you can't provide two, the deal's off. It's in the contract. Total silence as events unfold. No calling your pals saying what you're doing."

"Exclusive?" he asked, chewing his straggling whiskers.

"To you personally, Ben. Do your own deals. It is global news." She moved to the waiting car. "My client will have no interest in the film or your scoop."

"Scoop!" He went with her. "Not heard that since I was a kid. Scoop!"

"Remember it, Ben. Remember something else. In this, your interests come a long, long way ninth. My client's interests are paramount."

"You got it."

"Not a word until it's over. That's in blood, capeesh?"

"How many of these have you set up?" Ben Maker asked, curious.

"This is the thirteenth," she lied with more certainty than she felt. "It is the culmination of your entire career."

"Right, right."

He was still repeating it as he stood with Mr Pawler. She drove away.

Bray kept opening his holdall, checking the contents. He wore an old suit, one he'd bought many years previously for a starchy Gilson Mather party. Lottie was with him in the school corridor, hearing the teacher telling the class about something special that was going to happen. They were to come into the main hall, but *only your class* because you were the winners.

"Ms Donna Curme," Lottie whispered. "The head teacher's Mrs Daley."

He nodded, afraid his stammer would return.

"The camera people know what to do. One camera's outside by the guards at the gate. The other will enter the back of the hall as soon as you go in."

"Thank you."

"Jim and two friends are outside." She went on repeating the same information, over and over. "Jim will come in when they hear Mrs Daley."

"Thank you."

"Jim's listening on some gadget in my handbag."

Bray stared round the office as if trying to recall his own school.

"Tell me, Bray?" Lottie feared a last-minute change.

"Everything could have been done so differently." He said it with such sadness she felt heartbroken. "Even now I think of alternatives. Our consul, anything."

"We've been over it a thousand times. Jim too. This is the only way."

"And Davey's…"

Yes, Lottie thought in sudden fury, what could you call them, the people who'd stolen a child, who may have cared, seen to his education, given him a grand lifestyle beyond the means of the real parents? What *did* you call them? And answered herself in rage: You call them evil. They might claim to have the child's interests at heart, but evil is total. No decimal fractions.

"They're criminals, Bray. Let me near them and —"

"Lottie."

She suppressed her anger. God Almighty, she thought; don't start being reasonable, Bray, not at this stage.

She heard Mrs Daley's voice, Donna Curme call to the approaching children to be quiet, please, no pushing, everybody in an orderly fashion…

"They're coming," she said stupidly.

Jim Stazio had been with her this very morning. They had seen Davey handed over to the teacher in the school playground by the security couple. Davey had waved to guards and gone in happily enough.

"I'll be with the camera people, Bray."

Her mouth felt dry. She tried to swallow. Somebody came along the corridor. Donna Curme opened the door, smiling with mild surprise.

"Mrs Gunnell!" she said pleasantly. "How nice to see you again! Has Mr Charleston been telling you about our success?" She beamed at Bray. "The class is ready, Mr Charleston. Will you come through?" She smiled at Lottie. "See you later, perhaps!"

"Yes, of course."

Bray walked with the class teacher. Lottie gave them a moment, then left the office. Quickly she walked round and glided into the hall, almost bumping into the camera crew. The main lights were off, only the stage area illuminated. Some twenty children were settling down on the floor in lines. The window curtains were drawn, one slit of brilliant sunlight slicing the gloaming.

Ben Maker heard the click of the door as she closed it. He raised his eyebrows at Lottie, made a gesture of flicking a palm as if opening a wallet. She recognised the sign for police. He held up three fingers. Three policemen. He'd identified three policemen outside the school in waiting cars. Probably Jim and his friends? She prayed, let it be so.

She smiled as convincingly as she could, and tapped her

watch to indicate that they were on time. Ben was puzzled, shrugged, turned his attention to the head teacher, on his expression is-this-all-it-is. The camera gave a starting breath.

"We have a very important visitor today, class," Mrs Daley began. "Because you have been very, very clever. Can anybody guess what I mean?"

There was a babble of answers. The teachers laughed and gestured for quiet.

"Yes, it was a competition. Some of you, I happen to know, were very interested in a television quiz, weren't you?"

"Silence, class, please!" Donna Curme called. "Mrs Daley is saying something very important!"

Into the whispers the head teacher continued, "I happen to believe that our visitor has some really thrilling news. He has come a long way, and has an important announcement."

"We won the quiz!" a child called.

"Did we win the money?"

"Quiet, please! We all want to make a really good impression, don't we?"

Lottie saw Davey's bright hair moving. He was in the second row, leaning to talk to a little fair girl, then to a dark-haired child on his right.

Bray looked pale in the lights, almost grave in his suit. She noticed his holdall was unbuckled.

Behind her the door creaked. Jim Stazio stepped quietly in, making Ben Maker frown. Lottie gave Ben a reassuring nod, pointed to herself to indicate that the newcomer was hers. The camera hummed gently.

"The parents are on their way," Jim whispered.

She moved aside to give Jim room.

The head teacher said brightly, "Now, children, shall we applaud our visitor?"

Teachers led the applause as Bray stepped forward. He was smiling, his eyes screwed up against the light. He held a coarse old garment daubed with colour.

"Hello," he said quietly. "I've come to tell you that you've won. That means you will get the prize. It is worth a lot of money."

A hubbub rose from the children, some clapping, all talking excitedly. Bray smiled against the light and spoke over them.

"The prize is a very special and old piece of furniture. It was made a long time ago." He looked along the two rows below. "Everybody else tried to win it, but it will come to your school because you are the only ones who got everything right. All four answers. Nobody else in the whole of the United States of America. You were right every time."

"Isn't that marvellous?" Mrs Daley cut determinedly in, wanting the party to go with verve. "Shall we give ourselves a special clap?"

Bray waited for the applause to die.

"There were thousands and thousands of answers," he went on. At the rear of the hall Ben Maker fidgeted and signalled to the sound man, who irritably nodded that he was on the button, got the volume.

"Does anybody remember," Bray asked, his voice dropping still further, "what the first question was? I know it's some time ago." And prompted, "The question was, What are the kites made of? The answer was leaves, wasn't it?"

A few children murmured, looking at each other in spite of Donna Curme's plea for silence.

"The second one you also got right: What are the clouds made of? That answer was sawdust." Bray fumbled in the pouch of the old garment he carried, and brought out a handful of wood shavings.

"Question Three was —!"

"Carlson! Please be quiet!" the teachers called together.

A boy in the second row subsided muttering, but his hand was raised.

"I was extra pleased when you got the third answer right," Bray went on. "It was, What game do they play? Answer: balloons!" He smiled. By now the children were talking excitedly, turning to look at Davey. Carlson was fisting the air, grinning.

"But the really excellent answer was your last one. I think it was Carlson who actually sent it, wasn't it?"

"Us! Us!" Carlson yelled. "We got it!"

"Children! Carlson! No more interruptions or —"

"The answer," Bray continued, raising his voice, "was excellent. The question was really hard: What is the score in the balloon game?"

"Twenty-nineteen!" Carlson and three others cried out, clapping in the chatter.

"So you are the winners. The prize is worth a lot of money to your school. Over a million dollars."

Voices were becoming audible outside in the playground. Two sets of car tyres squealed, but the noise diminished in the children's excited babble. Lottie made placatory gestures to Ben Maker's silent interrogation. Jim Stazio menacingly pointed a finger at the television man to stay put, keep filming, not one word.

Bray held up the stained canvas garment to show the children.

"Would you like to know why I did the competition and gave the prize?"

"Yes," the children chorussed.

"I did it because I knew that only one little boy in the whole world really did know all the answers. Because *he* wrote those television stories. And the books. Before he got lost. He is the only one who knows what KV actually stands for. It stands for…?"

Bray cupped a hand to his ear, smiling as if it was one huge shared joke.

"Clint knows!" Carlson stood, dancing with impatient delight. "Clint knows!"

"It stands for…?" Bray repeated, and saw his grandson turn and say something to the boy next to him.

"Kevvy Vol!" Carlson shrieked.

The little girls next to him stood, jumping with excitement and clapping as Bray said, "Yes! Right again!"

Lottie saw Donna Curme's smile suddenly freeze. The teacher stared at Bray, at Davey, at the camera crew at the back of the hall. She made to say something. The head teacher's smile became a ghastly rictus.

Ben Maker frantically moved his crew forward. Lottie didn't stop him, and walked with them. All coherence was gone now. She saw Bray slip the loop of his work apron over his head and walk down, slowly moving among the children, who now were in utter disorder, standing and clapping and talking together. He stood by Davey.

Davey stood looking up at him, slowly reached out, delving into the pouch of the apron. He brought out a figure, turned it once in his hand, and then beamed up.

"Kevvy!" he said, looking, turning round, holding up the wooden figure to show Carlson and the others. "My Kevvy Vol!"

The two teachers were with them, the head calling for order in the pandemonium, Donna standing there looking from Davey to Bray, her face now pale as death.

Bray knelt down, smiling, and looked into the eyes of his grandson. The hall quietened. Lottie saw Ben Maker's frantic gestures to his cameraman to get it, get it, the only movement in the hall. The children fell silent.

"Hello, Davey," Bray said.

The boy looked down at the wooden figure in his hands, gazed back at Bray, made two attempts to speak and said, "Grampa?"

"Yes, Davey." Bray tried to keep smiling. "See? I came." He took his grandson's hand. "I'll not let go." He swung Davey onto his shoulders.

White-faced, Mrs Daley croaked, "The school is not involved in any way..."

Donna said, distraught, "I'm not quite sure what —"

A secretary entered at a run and whispered urgently to the head teacher, whose hand went to her throat. Donna Curme stayed silent, her eyes on Davey and Bray. She looked once at Lottie, saw resolve there and slumped in resignation.

"Right, children!" Mrs Daley called, glassy-eyed. "It's time to play. Hasn't it been exciting?"

They were shepherded noisily out of the french windows into the playground, Davey on Bray's shoulders holding the wooden carving.

"Where's our dough?" Carlson yelled, going dancing ahead.

"It's a cupboard, stupid," a little bespectacled girl with them said scornfully.

"You're Carlson?" Bray asked. They moved among the children leaving the hall.

"We won, didn't we?"

"It's furniture," Bray explained. "It's still worth a million."

"This is Leeta and Consuela and Elgin." Carlson gave a jerk of his thumb. "My team won, okay?"

"Okay," Bray said.

By the gate a cluster of people argued, a camera crew circling, sound boom aloft.

"It's your mom and pop," Carlson told Davey.

"Not really," Bray said.

He waved to a figure standing motionless in the distance, standing alone at the far end of the sports field, watching. Davey looked against the sun, squinting to see. The figure waved back, one laconic gesture, then stooped.

"Clint!"

Mom was being restrained by Jim Stazio and two others. Pop was arguing vehemently, trying to shove into the playing field but was unable to get past. The television crew circled.

Bray lowered Davey to the ground in a sea of children and crouched down. He pointed.

"Who's that, Davey?"

Davey let go and began to walk towards the distant figure, shielding his eyes against the sun. The children called out, some whistling to the dog, all going along with Davey.

For a moment the dog stood, circled uncertainly, looked back once at the girl who had just released its lead, then stood gazing in Bray's direction. It made a sudden jerk as if to start towards him, then it froze, tongue out, ears pricked. It seemed to watch as if in complete doubt, then began to lope forward to the children.

Davey looked back at Bray, still moving towards the

dog. Bray nodded, smiling, waving him on, walking after as Davey began to run, calling, "Here, Buzzie! Here, Buster!"

The dog hurtled, leaping through the mass of shouting children, dodging and swerving in its headlong dash towards the approaching boy. Bray walked after, smiling, explaining to Leeta and Consuela. Elgin and Carlson and the others ran after Davey whooping and waving.

Davey was almost knocked off his feet as Buster leapt on him. The golden retriever fell, wriggled round in midair and almost smothered him again, leaping and licking Davey's face, surrounded by the children as they gathered shouting to touch the delirious pet.

Bray looked across at the cluster by the gate as he passed. The man Carlson had called Davey's pop was explaining to Jim Stazio and his two guards something about cutting a deal. "See," he was saying, "we got ourselves conned. We've done nothing illegal. I'll give you the addresses right now…"

The woman next to him was weeping. The blond couple were standing by in a state of bafflement.

Jim Stazio nodded to Bray and indicated Buster and Davey in the centre of the hubbub.

"Enough proof now," he called, grinning. "Trust me?"

Bray made no reply. He joined Kylee who was watching Davey kneeling while Buster frantically jumped and barked, the children delirious with excitement.

"See?" she said.

"Thank you, Kylee. You did it."

"QED," she said. "Wish I could spell it."

Police sirens sounded in the distance. He put his arm round her.

"We'll manage without spelling."

He beckoned Lottie. "I'll need help. The authorities

seem to be on their way."

"Phone Geoff and Shirley now, Bray." Lottie said.

"Not me, Lottie." He couldn't take his eyes off Davey, the dog and the children. "I want Kylee to tell them. Let them get used to her. They'll be seeing a lot more of her in the future."

Chapter Seventy-One

Doctor replaced the receiver. Always the true professional, he acknowledged the nurse's signal with a smile.

"I'll be with you in just a moment."

Even now, he took especial pleasure in the timbre of his voice. It had served him so well, from *viva voce* examinations in medical school and interviews with child buyers, to admonitory sessions with members of staff.

He walked the length of the Special Rehabilitation Unit and into his office, ignoring his secretary's bid for his attention. He closed the study door and approached the window. Without disturbing the slats, he looked through the louvered blinds. Sure enough, there they were, as he'd expected after that impertinent phone call. Two distant police cars parked, almost but not quite, out of sight. A third approached as he watched. No sirens, no spinning lights. Was this the best they could do when stealth was called for? His lip curled in disdain.

The office seemed strangely silent, remote sounds from the Unit's incessant activities even more muted, as if before a coming tragedy. Well, it was exactly that, Doctor thought. It had finally come.

Strange how little sadness he felt at this final moment. He'd planned for it, of course, for how could such a formidable brain fail to ignore a consequence, however unlikely? Over the years, his acquisition team had saved sixty-three children from undeserving breeders – at airports, theme parks, beach sites, bus depots. And every one had been an enormous success, each stolen child re-programmed into a new affluent existence with new parents able to afford such a wondrous gift.

It was an achievement of genius, carried out against all the opposing forces society could bring.

Of course, it was totally beneath a professional medical man of his exalted status to prepare a means of escape. That would have implied that he doubted the perfection of his scheme. No, the loss was society's. And, make no mistake, when he was gone society would realise how grievous its loss actually was. It would also spell disaster for every single staff member in the Unit, cleaners to nurses, clerks to the four slick members of his abduction team. All would now end their days incarcerated in unspeakable prison conditions, and the fate of the child abductors in penitentiaries was worse than death. Without me, Doctor thought with a curious contentment, you all go down. Such is the penalty. The treachery of one of your number spells disaster for you all. It was even gratifying.

Idly, he wondered what could possibly have gone wrong with Clint H. Rappaporter, once Davey J. Charleston. Surely there couldn't have been a slip in his planning for the boy? Doctor's scheme had been cast-iron, foolproof. His track record was sufficient testimony, was it not? His care, his methods were the guarantees of successful transference of a child into any purchaser's possession. The phone call had come from Tain.

What could it have been? It was beneath him to ask questions of the buffoon who had phoned.

There couldn't possibly have been anything Out There, from the child's past life, could there? Surely, most certainly, not. Nobody could have followed and hunted the boy down. Nobody. Doctor had planned for every eventuality, every possible chance however remote, in every one of his cases. He was simply incapable of letting a single flaw mar the enterprise. Not even a fluke could have done this.

That media man who had just called was nothing other than a worm. The newscaster's smug assumption that he, Doctor, would be deceived by the apparent request for an interview about "the excellent work your clinic is doing, Doctor…" was nothing less than insulting. A mere reader of TV idiot boards, hoping to pull the wool over the eyes of someone of Doctor's intellect. It simply proved the worthlessness of people nowadays. Calling from Tain, some broadcasting station there, while children shouted a weird chant in the background, two words he'd never heard before. There was only one conclusion: the police, or some element in the media, had learnt of his clinic, and what it did.

Applying his impeccable logic, he realised there could only be one explanation. There was a spy in his camp, a traitor who had betrayed him and this marvellous enterprise. And, in doing so, had destroyed his entire scheme that had done so much good and been so marvellously helpful to deprived couples.

There would be only one way out. With dignity.

Logic called for it. His vast intellect could not demur now the moment had come. To quibble would be to deny his quality. That was for lesser people.

One last check at the window, and he became absolutely certain. Four more police cars were on the approach road from the sea, and non-uniformed officers, as transparent as if they wore flak jackets with POLICE insignia, were ambling with studied casualness across the grass towards his clinic. He was being surrounded.

Doctor's logic was faultless; the clinic's scheme was faultless; therefore he had been betrayed. Because he had been betrayed, the traitor and every single one of the traitor's associates must suffer. The only person they could shield behind was Doctor himself; they would claim the odiously repellent Defence of Superior Orders, maybe even wriggle out and escape. Therefore (consider that predicate structure!) Doctor himself must see to the chastisement of every member of his staff and every person who had been a customer, contributor, or company servant.

Only one way to stop them hiding behind Doctor's coat-tails, and it had to be taken.

One method.

His beautiful operation had ended. The traitor would triumph, smug in his – her? – betrayal. They were probably even now glorying in their vile expectations, of giving evidence before cameras, writing autobiographies to sell as a feature movie, while he, Doctor, stewed in prison for life, quivering in terror while appeal after appeal was decided by lawyers, those brainless carrion.

Conclusion: he must remove the resource with which they wished to nourish their betrayal.

He heard somebody heavy footed in the outer office. The intercom buzzed.

The automatic was cold and heavy in his hand. He was vaguely surprised by its weight, for he had not handled it in years, in fact had quite forgotten how to hold it. Pedantically he tested its mass, guessing two, three pounds? He took it more firmly in his right palm.

"Yes?" he answered.

"There are two police officers to see you, Doctor."

"Ask them to wait a moment, please."

"Yes, Doctor."

There was only this final refutation of such treachery left. Logic, that queen of sciences, determined so. No other course would suffice.

Arranging his ledgers meticulously on his desk, he gazed at the diplomas on his wall. He had had them framed and placed opposite his desk, from where he could see them each time he raised his eyes, unlike most of his former colleagues who insisted on having them hung behind the desk where they would impress patients.

The gun felt cold in his mouth. He remembered the anatomy of the buccal cavity, the innervation of the tongue, and dwelt for a random second on the course of the trigeminal branch of the facial nerve. With a brief feeling of immense satisfaction at such a perfect martyrdom, he pulled the trigger.